brought

marrying policeman Bob Andrews. In 1970 Lyn gave birth to triplets – two sons and a daughter – who kept her busy for the next few years. Once they'd gone to school Lyn began writing, and her first novel was quickly accepted for publication.

Lyn lived for eleven years in Ireland and is now resident on the Isle of Man, but spends as much time as possible back on Merseyside, seeing her children and four grandchildren.

Praise for Lyn Andrews' compelling Merseyside novels:

'A compelling read' *Woman's Own*

'An outstanding storyteller' *Woman's Weekly*

'A vivid portrayal of life' *Best*

'Gutsy . . . A vivid picture of a hard-up hard-working community . . . will keep the pages turning' *Daily Express*

'The Catherine Cookson of Liverpool' *Northern Echo*

By Lyn Andrews

Lyn Andrews

Across a Summer Sea

HEADLINE

First published in 2003 by
HEADLINE BOOK PUBLISHING

First published in paperback in 2004 by
HEADLINE BOOK PUBLISHING

First published in this paperback edition in 2017 by
HEADLINE PUBLISHING GROUP

1

Cataloguing in Publication Data is available from the British Library

ISBN 978 1 4722 5350 7

Offset in Janson by Avon DataSet Ltd, Bidford-on-Avon, Warwickshire

Printed and bound by CPI Group (UK) Ltd, Croydon, CR0 4YY

HEADLINE PUBLISHING GROUP
An Hachette UK Company
Carmelite House
50 Victoria Embankment
London EC4Y 0DZ

www.headline.co.uk
www.hachette.co.uk

My sincere thanks go to Peter and Jim McDonald of Ballycowan for their generosity in sharing with me the information and documents in their keeping on the history of Ballycowan Castle, which is approximately four miles from my own home. Sadly, it has been a ruin for many centuries although on close inspection it is possible to imagine the magnificent house it must have been in 1626 when it was built. I hope that the purists and historians will forgive my poetic licence in bringing it back to life in 1910 for the purposes of this novel. Although built and owned by the Herbert family until its destruction by Oliver Cromwell, all its twentieth-century inhabitants are purely fictional, as are the implications of their involvement in the Easter Rising of 1916.

My grateful thanks also to my friend and neighbour, Michael Guinan, for the additional local information and to himself and Kevin Guinan for taking the time to accompany me in climbing around what is left of the once imposing keep, great hall and main staircase of Ballycowan Castle. Without you both I would no doubt have broken my neck!

Lyn Andrews
Tullamore, 2002

Chapter One

Liverpool, 1910

NELLIE JONES WAS FLUSTERED. The heat in the tiny kitchen had caused beads of perspiration to break out on her forehead and her normally florid complexion was heightened to an almost turkeycock red. Strands of greying hair had escaped from the severe knot to which she had that morning confined it. Her small, stout figure was enveloped in a large, unbleached calico apron, which was already stained and creased.

'Why did she have to pick flaming Christmas, that's what I want to know? Haven't we all got enough to do as it is?'

'I thought you were delighted your Violet is getting married at last? Haven't you been adding Lord knows how many decades of the Rosary to your evening prayers that Sam Flaherty would ask her?' Mary McGann smiled as she deftly transferred the rich mixture she had been stirring

1

into the large square greased tin. 'Well, that's the bunloaf ready for the oven,' she finished.

Nellie sighed. 'Oh, I am delighted. I've been storming heaven with me prayers. It's just that it's such a busy time.'

'Last night I heard her going into raptures over a fancy three-tier iced wedding cake she saw in Skillicorn's Bakery window,' Mary informed the bride-to-be's mother.

Nellie looked annoyed. 'She can go into as many raptures as she wants, she'll make do with the bunloaf and like it. Who does she think her da is? Lord Derby? Iced wedding cakes indeed!'

'Do yer think there's goin' ter be enough ribs 'ere, Nell?' Queenie Phelps interrupted, thoughtfully eyeing the long sheets of meat laid out on the scrubbed table.

'There'll flaming well have to be, Queenie! This do is costing an arm and a leg and Fred says I've to manage on what he's given me. His back's near broke with humping sacks all day long.'

'Yer should be glad 'e's 'ad the work, Nell. There's many fellers turnin' up each day on the docks an' gettin' nothin', not even a few hours. There won't be no slap-up dinner fer those families this Christmas – unless they're lucky enough ter get a Goodfellows parcel,' Queenie reminded her. The charitable society distributed food parcels to the poor at this time of year, which were much coveted.

'I know, Queenie, I know,' Nellie said wearily. 'Put the

kettle on, Mary, luv, I'm parched,' she added, depositing her ample bulk into a battered armchair by the range.

Queenie pulled the bench out from under the table and sat on one end of it. Nellie was indeed fortunate to be able to give Violet any kind of a 'do', she thought enviously. Most of the time she didn't even know where the next meal was coming from, and as for keeping her kids in boots and clothes, well, she'd had to rely on charitable societies herself in the past, including the Liverpool City Police. They, out of their own pockets, provided hard-wearing clothes for poor kids. Of course they were of a horrible stiff corduroy material and were stamped so they couldn't be pawned, but when all was said and done they were clothes. She was fifty-two and had been married for thirty two years; it had been a lifetime of back-breaking work and constant hardship. And it showed. She knew she looked like a worn-out old woman with her grey hair and a deeply lined face.

Mary wiped her hands on her apron and placed the large black kettle on the hob. There had been none of this fuss when she had married Frank McGann nearly ten years ago now. Her mam had been a widow with seven children to provide for. There had been no money for the necessities of life, never mind weddings. It had been a simple affair, but Frank's mam and dad had been there, silently disapproving as always. They had both died the following year in an epidemic of influenza and she had always thought that her early years of marriage would have been difficult had they lived. Still, her aunt Molly and her numerous cousins who all lived in Dublin had come over for the wedding and they had certainly livened things up.

She sighed as she pushed a few strands of auburn hair away from her cheeks; thick and curly, it was the bane of her life. It defied all her attempts to keep it in a neat bun as the other women wore their hair. She was twenty-eight now but had thankfully managed to stay as slim as she had been the day she'd been married. Even after three children. She had pale skin and large green eyes that betrayed her Irish ancestry and was taller than nearly all the women and girls in the neighbourhood.

As she gathered the assorted cups and mugs she glanced around. Nellie's kitchen was neither better nor worse than all those in Newsham Street, off Scotland Road in the heart of the terrible slums of Liverpool. At least they didn't live in one of the courts which riddled the area, she thought thankfully. The unfortunate residents of the courts had even worse conditions to put up with. Very little daylight managed to penetrate them and they were damp and freezing in winter and unbearably stifling in summer. But all the women in the overcrowded, narrow streets waged a constant war on poverty and on the dirt in the decrepit old houses they lived in. Daily they swept and scrubbed inside, and took as much pride in keeping their doorsteps and even the pavement and kerbstones outside their doors scoured and donkey-stoned. The

houses were frequently stoved by the Sanitary Depart-
ment but this seemed to have little effect on the bugs that
infested them; it was impossible to eradicate them completely. Every week Frank burned them off the iron
bedframes, but they still came back.

Nellie had made a big effort for the wedding. Her
kitchen and her front room, which also served as a bedroom, had been given a fresh coat of whitewash. The fender
and the ashpans had been polished to within an inch of
their lives and the range black-leaded with Zebo. There
had even been some talk of a roll of new oilcloth for the
floor, but nothing had come of it. Hetty Price from the
pub had promised to lend Nellie the curtains from her own
front room, she being better off than nearly everyone else
in the street. New curtains were far beyond Nellie's reach.

'Well, I think yer've done 'er proud, Nell. I'se never
seen such a spread in a long time.'

'Thanks, Queenie, luv. You've got to try, like.' Nellie
was indeed thankful that Violet, her eldest and large,
loudmouthed daughter had finally found a husband. She
had almost despaired of ever seeing her wed and Violet's
departure to Athol Street to live with her mother-in-law
would give them a bit more room.

'Mary, cut us all a slice of that Sally Lunn. I don't see
why we can't have a bit of luxury. There's still a list of
things a mile long to be got through.'

'Nellie, I don't think we should start on the wedding

breakfast just yet!' Mary laughed, but she dutifully cut four slices from the currant loaf.

'What time did Maggie say she'd be 'ere?' Queenie asked.

'Any time now. She wanted to get the last lot of washing on the line. Not that there's much drying out today,' Mary replied, casting her eyes to the patch of grey winter sky visible through the small panes of Nellie's kitchen window. 'We usually get finished before this, but with her being on her own this morning . . .' Mary shrugged.

She and Maggie Foley took in washing: she to eke out Frank's meagre wages; Maggie to make ends meet, being a widow with no children. Mary, Frank and their three children lived with Maggie, sharing all the expenses, which helped Maggie out. They would never have been able to afford to rent a whole house just for themselves, and neither could Maggie have afforded the rent on her own. And with only the six of them, at least they weren't as overcrowded as most families were.

'We'll have to take it to the bag wash soon. It's getting too cold to be trying to work in the yard: the water in the washtub was frozen solid this morning. Even now we have to have it draped all over the house to get it dry properly and Frank hates that. He says it's like living in a Chinese laundry.'

'Pity about him! He doesn't mind the hard-earned money it brings in, does he?' Nellie said heatedly. In her opinion Frank McGann had got a jewel of a wife in Mary, considering he was such a mean, miserable man who did nothing but complain, even though he always seemed to get more work than many men did. He was selfish too. He always had good strong boots, thick woollen socks, and an overcoat in winter, while to turn her kids out respectably Mary often went without stockings, and had broken-down shoes and, like nearly every woman in the street, just a shawl to keep out the cold and wet. And he liked a drink. He said a working man should have his bit of comfort and pleasure. She wondered what kind of 'comfort and pleasure' Mary ever got? None. Like the rest of them. She kept that house spick and span and there was always a hot meal of some description on the table when he came home in the evening, whether he'd got work or not. What's more, despite the hardships of her life, Mary always had a smile and a ready laugh.

' 'Ere she is now. Maggie, come in, luv. We're just having a bit of a break, like,' Queenie explained their apparent leisure.

Maggie Foley sank down thankfully at the other end of the bench. 'I'm fair wore out! I'm getting too old for all the pulling and dragging and carting water from the standpipe. And believe me, if I had sheets the state of those I've just pegged out I wouldn't have the nerve to send them out to be washed!'

'If I 'ad any sheets at all I'd think meself lucky!' Queenie sniffed. 'It's a pile of old coats on the donkey's breakfasts more often than not.'

Mary smiled at the local name for the straw-stuffed mattresses that most people used.

'Ta, Mary,' Maggie said, taking the cup of strong tea and sipping it. 'Well, Nellie, where are we up to then?'

'The bunloaf's ready to go to Skillicorn's to be baked. It's dead good of them. God knows how any of us would manage to get stuff cooked at this time of year if they didn't let us use their ovens after they've finished the day's baking. I've the ribs, the pig's cheek and the cooked ham bought.'

''Ow much did that lot cost yer?' Queenie asked.

Mentally Nellie counted it up. 'Two shillings and fivepence.'

Queenie was scandalised. 'Nellie, yer was robbed!'

'There's enough meat there to feed half the street!' her neighbour retorted indignantly. Like all women she had to make every halfpenny count. 'I'll get the vegetables and fruit in Great Homer Street market late tomorrow night, you get the best prices then. And if you three want to chip in, we can get thirty Irish eggs for a penny.'

'I wouldn't mind. Frank likes an egg for his breakfast and they're good for the kids too. I'm hoping to get a chicken for Christmas dinner,' Mary said.

'I'll be lucky ter get a pair of flamin' rabbits ter do all of us, an' then I'll be sendin' Alfie ter sharpen the carvin' knife on the front step so folks'll think we're 'aving *real* meat,' Queenie put in wryly. 'But I can run ter the eggs. 'Ow fresh are they likely ter be? An' 'ow do they manage ter get them over 'ere on the mail boat without 'avin' them smashed ter bits?'

'God knows, but they do,' Maggie replied.

'Hetty said she could get me a dozen bottles of port at cost,' Nellie informed them.

'Oh, aye! What does she call cost?' Queenie demanded.

'Fifteen shillings for a dozen.'

'What did yer say?'

'It was going to "cost" too flaming much! I ask you. Fifteen shillings is more than a feller earns in two weeks!'

'It's all right fer 'er an' Bert ter pay that. 'Ow much profit do they make on a bottle?'

'Plenty, although to hear Bert you'd think he was expecting the bailiffs every day. I told her I'd have three bottles and that will have to do. When it's drunk, it's drunk and that's that!'

'Has Vi got her outfit?' Mary asked, hoping to steer the conversation away from the contentious waters of the price of food and drink.

Nellie cast her eyes towards the ceiling. 'She's had me half demented! She's bought a dress from Sturla's, which she's been paying off, and young Sally Price is lending her her new hat, but she says she can't afford new shoes or a jacket and what will her ma-in-law think of her in her old stuff?'

'She can polish up her shoes and if it's not too cold or wet she can go without a jacket,' Mary suggested.

'She'll catch her death! It's freezing out there and not likely to get much warmer,' Maggie said darkly.

'Well, I've had enough of listening to her complaints. Her da and me are giving her a good "do" and Fred's getting the usual barrel of ale as our wedding present to them.'

Queenie tutted and shook her head. 'Oh, I know it's traditional, Nellie, but wouldn't they be better off with somethin' more . . . *useful*, like?'

Nellie looked at Queenie askance. 'And have everyone talk about us for not providing anything for the fellers to drink? Fred would be mortified!'

'There's too many round 'ere who think too much about their bloody ale!' Queenie muttered, thinking about her own Alfie, who was more than partial to a pint of beer – or anything alcoholic, for that matter. Most of his wages ended up in the pockets of Bert Price, the landlord of the Newsham House, the pub on the corner. No wonder Hetty Price had more money than anyone else. But that wasn't Queenie's only worry.

'Iffen yer think yer've got problems with Vi, it's nothin' ter what I've ter purrup with from our Nora!'

'What's up with her?' Nellie asked.

'She's set 'er cap at 'im next door, that's what.'

'Who? Richie Seddon?' Maggie asked with interest.

'The same feller.'

Mary smiled to herself. She didn't blame Nora Phelps. Richie Seddon was the most eligible bachelor in the street.

He was tall, dark and handsome and still a bachelor – which was the problem. At thirty-two he seemed to have no intention of settling down at all. He'd broken any number of hearts, dashed innumerable hopes and dreams and confounded many devious plans. He was a born womaniser, with a smile and a compliment for every woman over the age of seventeen and a few even younger. He flirted with everyone – herself included – but there was no real harm in him. At least she didn't think so. It was just that young, silly girls constantly threw themselves at him.

'She'll get nowhere with *him*! I don't think the girl's been born yet that will walk him up the aisle,' Nellie said vehemently. Her own daughter Maureen had had hopes of him and she was considered far prettier and cleverer than Nora Phelps. Of course nothing had come of it and Maureen was now walking out with a lad both she and Fred fully approved of.

'Isn't that what I told 'er? "Oh, Mam, yer know *nothing*!" she says. I know this, girl, yer're not the one who'll tie that feller down! If she carries on throwin' 'erself at 'im, I'll 'ave ter get Alfie ter talk some sense inter 'er. 'E might even 'ave ter *knock* some sense inter 'er.'

'Oh, Queenie, Richie's not *that* bad. He just likes flirting and thinking every woman is ready to fall at his feet.'

'I just hope he doesn't think *you* will, girl,' Nellie said seriously.

Mary laughed scornfully. 'Me? An old, worn-out married woman with three kids!'

'You're not old and you're a good-looking girl.'

'Oh, Nellie! You're joking?'

'What she's sayin' is, there's fellers who like "ferbidden fruit" if yer know what I mean, like,' Queenie warned. 'Remember all the fuss there was over that one from Burlington Street? She 'ad four kids.'

'Oh, stop it! Stop tormenting me or I swear I'll go home,' Mary laughed. 'Now let's get back to the serious business.'

'I'll give you a hand tomorrow to clean and set up. We've no washing coming in,' Maggie offered.

'And I'll see to the younger kids. Keep them out from under your feet,' Mary added.

'It's dead good of you all, you've more than enough work and shopping of your own to do. I'll be glad when it's all over and she's taken herself off to Athol Street.'

'She'll 'ave 'er work cut out with that auld rip of a ma of 'is.'

'I don't have any worries about that, Queenie! Our Vi can hold her own. She's a mouth like a parish oven! Iffen I've told her once I've told her a hundred times: "Don't be such a loudmouth! Don't be so flaming *common*! You show me up!" Now, who the hell is that?' Nellie got to her feet with impatience written all over her face, as the sound of the front door knocker echoed down the lobby.

Mary, Queenie and Maggie looked at each other and

raised their eyebrows but upon hearing the voice of the parish priest they all got to their feet.

'Now what does *he* want at this time of morning?' Maggie hissed.

'Mary, it's Father Heggarty, looking for you,' Nellie announced deferentially, ushering in the priest and a shamefaced eight-year-old boy whose stiff Eton collar was turned around back to front and whose face was liberally streaked with grime and chalk.

'Tommy McGann! Just what have you done now?' Mary demanded angrily, glaring at her young son who was supposed to be in school. The state he was in!

'Wasn't I on my way to see Mr Owens at the school when don't I see meladdo and two other beauties got up like eejits, trick-acting on the pavement for the benefit of passengers on the top deck of the number twenty tram! And men who should know better throwing pennies and halfpennies down to them for their antics!'

Filled with anger and humiliation Mary grabbed her son by the arm and administered a quick box around the ears. 'Father, he'll be the death of me! Didn't I send him out this morning all clean and tidy telling him not to dawdle, and look at the cut of him now! You wait until your da hears of this, meladdo, there'll be no Christmas treats for you. It'll be the back of his hand you'll be feeling! And you can give Father Heggarty the money those fools threw at you. It can go into the poor box!'

'I've already confiscated it, Mary,' the priest announced.

'Good! Oh, what am I going to do with you?'

'Father, now you're here, will you have a cup of tea and a slice of Sally Lunn?' Nellie interrupted, feeling sorry for Mary. Hospitality was always offered to the clergy whenever they called, even if it wasn't exactly at the most convenient time and supplies of tea, milk and sugar were short (which was often).

'Ah, that's very good of you, Nellie, but I can see you're all busy and Mr Owens is expecting me this half-hour past.' He fixed young Tommy with a piercing and malevolent gaze. 'And you, me fine bucko, if there's any more of this morning's antics, I'll be calling your name from the pulpit on Christmas morning for the hooligan you're becoming! Well, I'll be off now. God bless you all.'

All four women crossed themselves devoutly and Mary nudged her son to do the same.

'You'll end up on the gallows, Tommy McGann, I swear you will!' Mary cried after Nellie had shown the priest out.

'Yer'll 'ave yer mam in an early grave!' Queenie added. She turned to Mary. 'I bet yer could 'ave done with the few coppers 'e got though. Never mind the poor box. Aren't we all flaming poor ourselves!' she added, sotto voce.

'Mam, I didn't *mean* to do it! Honest I didn't! I *were* going to school and then Georgie Price said it would be a bit of a laugh if we were to try and look a bit like clowns and we might get some money!' Tommy cried, regretful now that he had taken notice of his friend. It had seemed like a good idea at the time.

'I *was* going to school, not I *were*, and it would be Georgie Price's idea not yours! Nothing is ever *your* fault! I mean it, you wait until your da hears!'

'Ah, Mam! I'm sorry, *really* sorry, and anyway, our Katie's as bad!'

Mary rounded on him. 'What's *she* done, for God's sake?'

Tommy kicked with the toe of his boot at the frayed edge of the oilcloth.

'Will you give over doing that, isn't it in a bad enough way already and I can't afford new!' Nellie admonished.

'What's our Katie done?' Mary demanded.

'The rag and bone feller's going around the streets and I saw her and Millie Price sneaking out of the schoolyard. Georgie said his mam said they had loads of stuff for when he next came round, and they'd get all kinds of things in return, maybe even a goldfish in a proper bowl.'

'What's that to do with our Katie? *I've* not got anything to give that feller! All the rags I've got are on my back!'

'I heard her telling Millie that she'd find *something* for when he came next and now he's here and I bet that's where she was sneaking off to!' he finished triumphantly.

'Them kids of Price's are a flaming menace! It's all Hetty's fault, she's too easy-going with them,' Nellie declared.

'Mary, you'd better get home and see what she's up to before she strips those tatty sheets off the line and gives them in!' Maggie sniffed. 'Mind you, they're not worth even a goldfish in a jam jar never mind a flaming bowl,' she finished cuttingly.

Mary glanced at the three women in despair then gave her son a push towards the back door. 'Maybe you're right, Maggie. I'd better go before she gives away every half-decent thing I own. Get on back to school, you.'

Mary hastily threw her shawl around her shoulders and left.

Nellie shook her head. 'There's never a dull moment around here, is there?'

'You'd think their Katie would have more sense. She's supposed to be looking after their Lizzie, the poor little mite.'

'I know what yer mean, Maggie. 'Asn't poor Mary enough on 'er plate with Lizzie, what with 'er bein' deaf an' dumb an' *him* bein' such a miserable sod,' Queenie concurred.

'Well, this isn't getting anything done,' Nellie sighed. 'Weddings and Christmas! I'm wore out with them both. And as for our flaming Violet . . . !' The complaints continued as she removed the dirty dishes to the stone sink in the tiny scullery. Maggie and Queenie looked at each other, grimaced, then both got to their feet, shaking their heads.

Chapter Two

CLUTCHING HER SHAWL TO her, Mary ran the short distance to her own home and let herself in the back way. The kitchen was empty but she wasn't happy to see that Maggie hadn't cleared up. There were buckets of dirty water by the door, a bar of carbolic soap and a scrubbing brush on the draining board and she nearly fell over a large basket on the floor. More for herself to do, she thought irritably. Still, Maggie was sixty. She was getting too old to cope with all the work she had – and she had promised to help Nellie. She must have just run out of time.

Sounds from upstairs came to her ears and with her lips set in a grim line she ran up the stairs and flung open the bedroom door.

'Just what do you think you're doing, miss?' she demanded of her eldest daughter.

Nine-year-old Katie raised scared green eyes to those of

her mother. There was a grey flannel blouse rolled up in her hands. 'Mam! I thought you were—'

'Out! I know you did. Tommy told me you'd be here.'

'How did he know?'

'He saw and heard you and Millie Price talking about the rag-and-bone feller, so don't try to deny it!'

Katie's lip trembled. 'Oh, Mam, I . . . I wanted . . . things. Things like Millie has. She's got *everything*. I've got . . . *nothing*!'

'You've got boots on your feet, a coat on your back and food in your belly, Katie McGann. That's more than a lot of kids round here have. Just you be thankful. You've got nothing indeed. I won't have all this nonsense from you or your brother. Sagging off school, having Father Heggarty shame me, you about to give my only decent blouse to the rag-and-bone man!'

Tears had sprung to Katie's eyes. She really hadn't intended to upset her mam but the thought of maybe getting a paper windmill or some coloured chalks for a few old rags had given her courage and blinded her to the consequences.

'And you're supposed to be looking out for Lizzie. You know it's hard for her and sometimes she gets tormented. She's only six and she's still not used to school.'

'I'm so sorry, Mam!' Katie sniffed, tears falling down her cheeks. She'd forgotten about Lizzie. Poor Lizzie could neither hear nor speak and so life at St Anthony's School was doubly hard for her.

Mary relented a little. 'Oh, don't cry, love. I just wish you'd think a bit more before you do these things.'

'I really am sorry, Mam. You won't tell me da, will you?'

'Come here to me. No, I won't tell him – this time – but our Tommy might. I'm going to have to tell your da about that little hooligan.'

Katie bit her lip. She was afraid of her da. 'What was our Tommy doing?'

'Acting the eejit, as Father Heggarty would say. Him and Georgie Price. Oh, I wish you would stay away from those Price kids, they're nothing but trouble.' She felt it keenly that Katie thought she had nothing compared to Millie, but then Millie Price was spoilt and had far too much of everything in her opinion.

'I will, Mam. I promise.'

Mary smiled. 'It's Christmas in three days and you never know what Father Christmas will leave you, if you behave yourself.'

Katie didn't look convinced. There had been years when there had been nothing in her stocking except an orange. It just didn't seem fair that Millie always had a stocking bursting with toys *and* she got more for her birthday.

'And this year there's Violet's wedding as well. You should see the food Nellie's got. We'll have a great time. Now, back to school. You can tell them you've seen me. Mind you look after your sister – that other little tearaway

19

can look after himself. And next time don't be giving my stuff away! There's years more wear in that blouse.'

Wiping away her tears, Katie handed over the blouse. She'd thought it wasn't fit to be worn.

'Give me a kiss?' Mary demanded of her woebegone young daughter, vowing to find something that could be classed as real rags. She hated Katie to think she was deprived.

When Katie had gone she went swiftly back downstairs. There was so much to do. Well, she'd have a quick tidy up down here, go back and give Nellie an hour or two more, then she'd have to go along Scotland Road and get something for tea. Maggie would need help later on to get the laundry packed up ready for collection. They needed that money desperately if they were going to have any kind of a decent dinner on Christmas Day. She would have Frank's wages this evening. At least she hoped she would have them. There had been times in the past when he'd spent part of her housekeeping money on beer. Oh, he wasn't as bad as Alfie Phelps, it hadn't happened very often, but at times like this it worried her. Surely even Frank must realise that at Christmas she would need the full amount and it would have to stretch a very long way indeed. Then after she'd got tonight's meal over and cleaned up she would have to try to find something decent to wear for this wedding.

She shook her head. There weren't enough hours in the day. The list of chores for tomorrow didn't even bear thinking about. In addition to everything else she had promised to look after Nellie's younger children, she had to get Frank's suit from the pawnshop, give the house a good clean and at the end of it all there would be the late night trip to the market. It would be well turned midnight before she got to bed. Still, she didn't really mind. The crowded market was always colourful and entertaining: there was a lot of laughing and joking between the stall-holders and their customers. It was all part of Christmas. And then there would be Violet's wedding and Christmas Day itself and she was looking forward to that. For months now she had been putting away a halfpenny here and a farthing there and she had the princely sum of one shilling to spend on some cheap toys for the children. Nothing much, penny toys mainly, and a few sweets, but they would be a real treat. Maybe it would stretch to some coloured paper for decorations. That would certainly cheer up the drab-looking kitchen. Oh, Frank would complain about wasting good money on stuff that would end up on the fire, but she didn't care. *She'd* gone without things, not him, and the children's pleasure would be worth it. She was going to try and make this the best Christmas they'd had in a long time.

As she tidied the kitchen she thought about Frank. He was often a difficult man to live with. It hadn't always been like this. She'd been happy in the early days of her marriage. They'd never had much money, not much of anything really, but they'd had each other. Frank had always been on the serious side, always thrifty and hard-working. He derived a lot of satisfaction from that fact, and a lot of pride. It gave you standing in the community, he said, to be looked up to as a hard-working man in full employment. They were traits she had admired in him at first.

But over the years he'd changed. She realised now that it had been a slow, gradual process. He'd become more engrossed in himself and less interested in what she thought, what she wanted or indeed needed. These days they never sat and talked about what their day had been like, or swapped bits of local gossip, or commented on local politics the way they used to. Now, it was as if he didn't consider it a worthwhile effort to exchange even a few points of view with her. As if her opinion on *anything* was of no interest to him. She sighed and wondered, had it been her fault? Where had she gone wrong? Had *she* gone wrong?

Reluctantly she acknowledged that he was becoming more and more selfish, silent and *careful* with his money. She would never admit to herself that he was actually *mean*. He's not, not with himself, a little voice in her head said bluntly. No, she wasn't going to think like that! she told herself firmly. They had far more than many families and thankfully he wasn't like Alfie Phelps. Poor Queenie had to stand at the dock gates and wait for her husband, otherwise he would drink every penny he had earned on the way home. She had never had to suffer humiliation like that. And she really didn't mind her life. Everyone had to work hard and watch the pennies. No one expected life to be a bed of roses. That was something young Violet Jones would have to accept too, once she was married, but at least she would come home to a warm house and a cooked meal after a day in the bag works. Until she had her first baby that was, and she had to give up work.

Her thoughts were disturbed by the faint but audible cry of the rag-and-bone merchant. Hastily she ran back upstairs and rummaged in their very meagre selection of clothes until she found an old jumper of Frank's that she had been meaning to try to darn. Holding it up for inspection, she shook her head. There were far too many holes in it. It would just be held together with darning wool. It might be enough to get something for Katie. Something she could share with her little sister. Once again she found herself reflecting on her family. She did try her best with Lizzie in the very limited amount of time she had to spare. Patiently she had taught her to lip-read certain words and phrases but it had been a painfully slow process and her heart went out to her child as she watched her struggle to understand. She hoped that Lizzie was picking up more words from the other children she played with at school. She knew that Lizzie wasn't really learning much at St Anthony's School but the child seemed to enjoy going and it helped her to know that Lizzie was at least being supervised and looked after. There never seemed to be enough hours in the day as it was without having to worry about where Lizzie was and what she was doing. Poor Lizzie.

It was late afternoon by the time she finally made her way along Scotland Road, her shawl pulled up over her head as a cold sleet had started to fall, and already the daylight was fading. It was always busy along here, she thought as she darted between the horse-drawn carts and newly electrified trams. She'd go to Lunt's and see if there were any loaves left. They wouldn't be classed as fresh at this time of day and might be cheaper. If she could get some bones and scrag end of mutton from one of the butchers she could make a pan of scouse. There were some potatoes and a few carrots at home. In Pegram's she would get a pennyworth of tea and sugar and some lentils and a pound of dripping. That would do for tonight and tomorrow morning. Frank would have to make do with bread and dripping for breakfast, but at least there were all the treats at Violet's wedding feast and hopefully a chicken for Christmas dinner for him to look forward to. Besides, she had only a few coppers left in her purse until she got Frank's wages and the laundry money.

She stared longingly at the rows of turkeys, chickens, geese and legs of pork that hung in rows outside the butchers' shops and at the fruit and vegetables piled high in the greengrocer's. Everywhere looked very festive and bright, she thought as shopkeepers lit their gas lamps. Even the damp and dirty cobbles reflected the light. A brewery dray passed decorated with holly and red ribbons; the bells attached to the gleaming brasswork on the horses' harnesses tinkled musically as the four massive but gentle Clydesdales moved smartly along. Ah, well, there would be plenty of bargains at the market tomorrow night. People said if you couldn't get a bargain in Great Homer Street then you just couldn't get a bargain at all.

She was hurrying home with her head bent against the weather when, as she turned the corner of Newsham Street, she almost collided with a young girl.

'Nora! I didn't see you there. Isn't it a raw evening?'

Nora Phelps grimaced. She was a thin, pale and not very attractive girl of just seventeen. 'It's shockin', Mary. I'm frozen stiff.'

'Why aren't you at home by the fire? You look half starved.'

'I finished work early. Well, I was laid off, iffen yer must know, but only until after Christmas.'

'Oh, I'm sorry.'

'So is me mam. Still, it gives me some time ter get somethin' ter wear fer this posh do of Vi's.'

'I wouldn't exactly call it posh, Nora.'

'If yer listen ter me mam yer'd think it was.'

'Oh, you know how your mam exaggerates, but it should be good. I'm looking forward to it.'

The girl simpered. 'So am I. And I've managed to save up enough for something new.'

Mary remembered Queenie's confidences. 'Ah, I see! You want to impress someone?'

Nora giggled and simpered again and Mary thought how very young she looked, so naive and intense. She smiled to herself. Had she ever been as young and foolish herself, long ago? Very probably.

'It wouldn't be a certain feller that lives next door to you, would it?'

'Oh, me mam can't keep her mouth shut!'

'Well, what are you going to buy?' Mary asked, although she was getting impatient. She should be off home and getting the meal started instead of standing here talking to this silly young slip of a thing, but she didn't want to hurt the girl's feelings.

'I dunno. A new blouse and maybe a bit of ribbon fer me 'air. It won't run ter much more an' it won't be brand new either. I'm goin' ter see what Mrs Carmichael's got.'

Mary nodded. Mrs Carmichael ran a second-hand clothes shop of a slightly better quality than most in the area. Her wares were definitely far better than those sold in Paddy's Market.

'Well, whatever you get will look lovely on you, Nora. I'm afraid anything I've got will look third- and maybe fourth-hand, but no one's going to be looking at an old married woman like me, now are they?'

Nora considered this. 'You're not that old, Mary, and I wish I had hair like yours. It's gorgeous. All thick and curly. Mine's as straight as a die!'

'Believe me, Nora, it's far from gorgeous! It's what my mam, God rest her, used to call "a furze bush". There's too much of it and it has a will of its own. Your hair is lovely, especially when it's tied up with a nice bit of ribbon. Well, I'd better get home and start Frank's tea.'

'Tarrah then. I'll see yer at Nellie's if not before.' Nora turned away, pleased that Mary had complimented her on her hair. Yes, she'd definitely get a length of shiny satin ribbon. That would make Richie notice how 'lovely' her hair was.

Katie and Lizzie were both home when Mary got in. 'Where's Tommy?' she demanded, taking off her shawl and hanging it on a hook on the wall.

'Said he was going to see what Georgie's mam got off the rag-and-bone man.'

Mary sighed. He was staying out of her way. 'Well, look what I got you for an old jumper of your da's that was falling apart.' She opened the mesh-fronted press. 'You've got to share it. Take turns with it.' She held out a green paper windmill on a stick and blew on it gently. 'Look, Lizzie, isn't it pretty?' She held it close to the child's face and smiled at her. The pale little face lit up in a smile of wonder and the child copied her mother's actions, blowing on it gently.

'I'll let her play with it for a while, Mam. I'll help you get the tea,' Katie offered, grateful that her mam had got her something.

'You're a good girl, Katie. Peel those potatoes for me while I get this meat into the pan. We'll have a big plate of scouse with lots of bread to dip in. I'm starving and so will your da be when he gets in. I could do with our Tommy to fetch me a bit of coal from McShane's on the corner. They'll let me have a bit on the slate until tomorrow.'

'Will I go for him, Mam?' Katie asked, eager to tell Millie what her mam had got them.

'Go on, luv, but don't be long. I'm running late as it is.'

The child ran out and Mary smiled briefly at Lizzie who was still enthralled with the new toy. Rolling up her sleeves, Mary emptied the potatoes into a bowl and made a start.

She had finished them and was on to the carrots when Katie returned alone.

'Where is he?'

'I told him to go straight to McShane's and then to come back home with the coal,' Katie replied. She was trying to hide it but Mary could see she was upset.

'What's wrong, luv?'

'They got *two* goldfish and *two* yo-yos and Millie says they're having turkey and plum pudding and mince pies and jelly and even lemonade on Christmas Day and she's got a new dress and shoes for the wedding and . . . everything!'

'Oh, Katie! Come here to me, luv!' Mary left the

vegetables and put her arms around her daughter. Hetty Price was really pulling out all the stops. It wasn't fair. It really wasn't. But why did Hetty have to flaunt it all? She longed to tell the child about the things she planned to buy tomorrow but she couldn't spoil the surprise. To her horror she heard the back-yard door open. Surely to God it wasn't *that* late? Frank must have finished early and here she was with no table set, no meal ready, a pathetic fire in the range and Katie in tears.

'Dry your eyes, luv, here's your da,' she hissed before turning to face her husband. 'Frank, luv, you're very early. I didn't expect you so soon. I'm a bit behind.'

'I can see that. What's wrong with her?' These days there always seemed to be some drama going on when he got home from work. And he was cold, tired and hungry and in no mood for hysterics from the kids. He took off his coat and cap and sat down. Mary did try, he'd give her that. Usually his meal was ready and the place was always fairly tidy, but she seemed to have little time for *him* these days. If it wasn't the kids it was the neighbours and the hardships of their lives, as if their own lives were ones of comfort and plenty.

'Oh, nothing much. Millie Price has been boasting about all the things she's getting and what they're going to eat at Christmas.'

The neighbours again! he thought irritably. Not 'Are you tired, Frank? Has it been a hard day?'

'That woman's a fool where money is concerned,' he said sourly. 'Is there no coal? That's a poor excuse for a fire.' He stretched out his numbed hands to the feeble warmth and then sighed. 'I know it's hard to heat these houses decently in winter, Mary, but can't Tommy have gone out and found a few bits of wood? It's freezing in here.'

'He's gone to McShane's for some coal. He won't be long now and then we'll soon have the place warmed up,' she answered, trying to cheer him up. At least he wasn't blaming her entirely. 'Did you . . . er . . . get paid?' she asked hesitantly.

'I did. What there is of it and only a half-day expected tomorrow.' And he knew she would already have that money earmarked. Didn't she realise that they just weren't in a position to splash out at Christmas?

Mary's heart sank. What was he saying? That he didn't have much to give her? She'd banked on that money. 'Well, never mind, luv, we'll manage on whatever you've got.'

Lizzie had sidled up to his chair and was holding out the windmill, smiling and nodding at him.

'Where did she get this? I thought you had no money? Isn't that what you told me this morning?'

'It didn't cost anything, Frank. I got it from the rag-and-bone merchant in exchange for an old jumper.'

He felt annoyance rising in him. There she went again, not thinking sensibly. Probably some of the other kids, like Bert Price's, had been running out after the rag-and-bone man with armfuls of stuff to exchange for junk like that windmill and Katie had come crying to her that they didn't get anything, and she'd taken notice of the child and given stuff away when they had nothing to spare. 'Not my jumper, I hope!'

'Oh, Frank, it was in a terrible state. Full of holes that I couldn't possibly darn. It was only fit for the rag bag.'

'And you swapped it for *that*? It would have done me for work. It would have been an extra layer to keep out the cold.'

'It was just for . . . well, for a bit of a treat for Katie and Lizzie. They don't get much.'

He lost his temper. 'They get more than I ever got as a kid! You spoil them, Mary! You don't *think*! I won't have it! I work damned hard for all of you and I won't have you giving things away.'

Mary was stung. 'I work hard too, Frank!'

'What have you been doing all day? Jangling?'

Mary pressed her lips together angrily as Tommy, followed by Maggie, appeared in the doorway.

'I found him staggering down the street with this,' Maggie said, dumping the small sack of coal on the floor by the range.

'Thanks, Maggie. Tommy, make yourself useful and build up that fire, your da's cold and tired.'

Maggie sensed the tenseness in the atmosphere and looked pointedly at Mary. 'Nellie said to thank you for all your help today, luv. She said she doesn't know how she'd have managed otherwise.'

Frank shot a glance at his wife. So that's what she'd been doing all day when she should have been at home seeing to her own family. 'This wedding's getting out of all proportion!' he muttered.

Maggie raised her eyes to the ceiling. 'Can I help you with anything, Mary, before I go and see to my own fire and tea and then the washing?'

Mary smiled at her. 'No thanks, Maggie. Everything is nearly done now and Katie will help out. You must be tired too.'

'Aye, it's been a long day for everyone,' Maggie said meaningfully. Frank McGann had a bad-tempered look on his face and he was home early. That wasn't a good sign. 'Kids all all right?' she enquired, glancing at a subdued Tommy.

'Fine,' Mary replied firmly. She had no intention of mentioning Tommy's misdemeanours to Frank now. He would blame her and she was determined there wasn't going to be a row tonight. Maggie had spoken the truth. It had indeed been a long and tiring day and there was still the washing to sort and fold. She prayed no one would call for it early.

It was after eight o'clock when the last load of laundry had been collected and she and Maggie sat at the table dividing the money between them.

'Two and sixpence for a week's back-breaking work!' Maggie said irritably, thinking of the long cold hours spent fetching and heating water, scrubbing, rinsing, mangling and pegging out.

'Every little helps,' Mary reminded her, casting a quick glance at Frank who was reading the *Echo*. All three children were amusing themselves by scribbling notes to Father Christmas on the backs of old cigarette packets that Tommy had found. She wondered just how much Lizzie really understood about Christmas and its traditions, although both she and Katie had tried their best, with great patience, using pictures she'd cut from newspaper advertisements.

'Will you come with me to the market tomorrow night?'

'Maybe,' Maggie mused.

'I might need you to help me carry things—'

Frank looked up. 'How much do you intend to buy? I've told you there's only a half-day tomorrow and we finished early tonight.'

'As much as I can,' Mary answered firmly. 'Maggie will be having her dinner with us, won't you, luv?'

'Like always, Mary.' She shot a look at Frank. 'And like always I'll chip in with the cost of it.' Suddenly she felt angry at the way Frank was treating Mary. 'Here, you take it all. Get yourself something to wear for Vi's wedding. You're a fine-looking girl and it's years since you've had anything decent to wear.'

'Maggie, I couldn't! I couldn't spend it on myself when . . .' Mary looked in the direction of the children.

'You worked hard for it, luv. You more than do your fair share. I insist. Otherwise I . . . I'll give it all to Father Heggarty!'

'Take it, Mary, there's enough given to the clergy at this time of year. They'll not feel the want of it,' Frank interjected. He had little time for religion. Any religion. His views were more in line with the Socialists than the Church.

'I'll take it, Maggie, but not for myself.'

Maggie's anger had evaporated. She felt tired. Very tired. 'Just take it, Mary, that's all I ask.'

Mary turned the coins over in her hand, tears springing to her eyes. It was a long time since anyone had been so generous. Well, she'd make sure there was a slap-up dinner and a small gift for Maggie. Maybe a pair of woollen mittens for her poor swollen, red and chapped hands. She'd appreciate that. She had complained lately that her hands were getting stiff and painful with arthritis.

Maggie rose. 'Well, I'm off to my bed.'

Mary also got to her feet. 'And it's time you three were in bed too. I've a pile of mending to get done and it's going to be a busy day tomorrow.'

Chapter Three

NEXT MORNING WHEN MARY drew the curtains in the kitchen she saw that it had snowed quite heavily during the night. The snow had transformed the tiny dingy yard. The shapes of the washtub and the old mangle could barely be distinguished. However, a weak sun was filtering through the remaining grey clouds. At least that would make it a bit more bearable, she thought.

There wasn't time to stand and admire the scene though: there was the fire to mend; the breakfast – such as it was – to be made; then, when Frank had gone to work, the real work would begin. And she was still so tired. It had been late when she had finally finished all the mending last night and Frank had gone up before her, with barely a muttered 'goodnight'. But she set to, and before long she had cleared the table and Katie had washed the dishes and then had joined Tommy's entreaties to be allowed to go out and play in the snow.

'Take Lizzie with you and be careful. It will be slippery underfoot and the last thing I need today is for one of you to fall and break something!'

'Mam, can I take the tray out of the oven? We'll make a great slide!' Tommy begged.

'No, you can't. You'll make the pavements even worse for people to walk on. It's freezing out there. Here, Lizzie, let me wrap this around you, luv.' She gently drew the child to her and wrapped a long hand-knitted scarf over her head and around her neck, wishing her coat was thicker and that they all had gloves or mittens. 'Now, off you go. Take care and don't go making a nuisance of yourselves! Katie, you and Lizzie go and call on Nellie and tell her I'll keep an eye on her kids too, that's if she's letting them out.'

'They'll be out, Mam. Everyone will be out,' Katie answered, pulling her sister towards the door. Tommy had already disappeared.

'As if we needed this!' Maggie said crossly as she came into the room, jerking her head in the direction of the snow-covered yard.

'Oh, I don't mind. At least it keeps the kids quiet.'

'Until they get cold and wet and start traipsing in and out.'

Mary looked closely at the older woman. 'You're not yourself this morning, Maggie.'

'No, luv, I'm not. I don't feel well. I had a shocking night. I just couldn't get comfortable.'

36

'I'll put the kettle on. Shall I tell Nellie you're not up to giving her a hand? You could even go back to bed. Try and get some rest, you deserve it, Maggie, you work very hard and I'll be busy today.'

Maggie was scandalised. 'Take to my bed at this time in the morning! There's time enough for that when I'm really sick! No, I promised Nellie. I'll be fine after a cup of tea.'

Mary cut her a slice of bread and spread dripping on it, then placed the big brown teapot on the table.

'Let it stand for a minute. I'd better make a list of everything I want to buy today so I don't forget anything.'

'Will you be able to manage the market on your own, Mary? By the time I've got through the day I won't feel much like traipsing up and down Great Homer Street.'

'Of course I will.'

'How much have you got? Don't forget what I said last night about getting yourself something. I meant it.'

'Oh, I'll see. I've got a good bit to spend. Now, there's meat, vegetables, a bit of fruit, a couple of slices of Dundee cake, tea, sugar, a bit of butter, Nellie's getting those eggs, salt fish for breakfast, bread and then I'll get some sweets and a couple of penny toys each for the kids. I might even get some holly and those cheap paper decorations they sell. It's a pity we can't have a Christmas tree, the kids would really love that, but it's beyond my pocket and I owe Sarah McShane for the coal. I'll have to get a couple of bottles of beer for Frank to go with his dinner.'

Maggie pursed her lips. 'There won't be much left to buy yourself something. Can't he do without his ale? He'll have enough at Nellie's tomorrow *and* you can bet your life he'll be in the pub this afternoon when he's finished work.' She was certain that Frank McGann had kept back enough of his wages to go drinking with his mates and even if Violet hadn't been getting married on Christmas Eve there would have been little done in the way of work by most of the men in the street.

'Oh, Maggie, it's Christmas!'

Maggie was about to make a sarcastic comment when the door burst open and Katie appeared, her face flushed. 'Mam! Mam, come quick! Our Tommy and the other lads made a slide and Mrs Jones came out of her door and fell flat on her back!'

'Oh, Jesus, Mary and Holy St Joseph! Is she hurt? I'll swing for that lad yet! I *told* him not to be carrying on like that.'

'It was Georgie Price's fault. He had a shelf from his mam's oven!'

'This time Hetty will have to do something about that little hooligan!' Maggie said grimly as she followed Mary out.

Nellie was on her feet but hanging on to the downspout for dear life.

'Nellie, are you hurt, luv?'

'Just a bit shaken up, Mary! I put me foot outside and down I went!'

Maggie took her arm. 'Come on, let's get you back inside. A cup of good strong tea is what you need.'

Mary rounded on the small group of lads who were all looking a bit sheepish. 'I hope you lot are satisfied! And you, Georgie Price, you'll end up in a reformatory the way you're going on! I'm going to see your da about this. You, Tommy McGann, get inside! That's all the nonsense I'm going to stand from you for today. You can spend your time doing something useful for a change. There's wood to be chopped for a start and then you can go to the dairy!'

The little group dispersed, shooting malevolent glances at a subdued Georgie Price. If their das got to hear of this there'd be nothing in any of their stockings on Christmas morning.

Nellie wasn't in fact injured, and after a cup of tea and some encouragement from Maggie and Queenie (and a couple of other neighbours whose sons had been involved and who all swore retribution in one form or another on their offspring), she pulled herself together. They began the final preparations for Violet's wedding.

By mid-afternoon Mary was exhausted. She had swept and scrubbed the house from top to bottom. She had black-leaded the range, polished the fender and ashpans, scrubbed the table until it was white, taken out the few rag rugs, thrown them over the washing line and given them a good beating and had tidied herself up ready to go to Dalgleish's pawnshop to redeem Frank's good suit.

'Right, I'm off to Uncle's for your da's suit. Behave yourselves and don't get this place mucky!' she instructed, wrapping her shawl around her shoulders.

'When will Da be home, Mam?' Tommy asked cautiously.

'Any time now and don't blame me if he's heard about your antics this morning! *You* can explain it all to him.' Mary was aware that this was possible because of the fact that today it wouldn't only be Queenie down at the dock gates waiting for her husband's wages.

'Da's just come up the yard. Now you're for it!' Katie hissed at her brother.

Mary was relieved. Now he could keep his eye on them. She just never knew what Tommy would get up to when her back was turned: more dreadful mischief, if the past two days were anything to go by.

Then her heart sank. She realised that Frank was drunk.

'I see you've been celebrating!'

He glared at her through bloodshot eyes, hanging on to the mantelshelf for support. 'Can't a man have a drink at Christmas?'

'In case you hadn't noticed, it's the day *before* Christmas Eve!'

'What's for my dinner? I'm starving.'

She was becoming angry. Did he have no idea of the amount of work she had to do? 'I didn't know what time you'd be in. Katie will heat up that bit of scouse that's left but there's no bread to go with it. I've the shopping to do tonight.'

'I suppose you've all had *your* dinner though?' he said nastily.

'No, we haven't! The kids have had a bit of bread and scrape. I've had nothing since breakfast and now I've to go and fetch your good suit and then press it and iron you a clean shirt ready for tomorrow. Give Tommy your boots, he'll give them a good clean. Tommy, shift yourself; Katie, put the kettle on,' she instructed. 'I'll take Lizzie with me,' she added. Frank had little patience with Lizzie at the best of times and now wouldn't be one of them. Quickly she bundled the child into her coat, wrapped the scarf around her and took her hand. She refused to have a row with Frank. Let him sleep it off. He wasn't going to ruin either Violet's wedding or Christmas for them.

Lizzie trotted along happily beside her mother. Hers was a silent little world but she noticed many things with her sharp eyes. Things the others didn't see. Like the way her mam looked at her da. Looks that had changed over the months. Like the way some of the men in the street looked at her mam. (Even she could see that her mam was lovely compared to a lot of the women and girls.) Like the way Katie seemed to creep around her da, as if she was afraid of him. She knew Christmas was coming: she had managed to gather that from all the unusual activity that was going on around her and Katie's pictures and mimes. From past experience she knew it meant more food and maybe even toys, but it also seemed to mean that her mam was angry with Da. Da didn't bother with her much but that didn't upset her. He never had. From the route they were taking she knew she was going to Uncle's, as everyone called Mr Dalgleish. She liked going there. He had all kinds of things to look at and sometimes he gave her an aniseed ball to suck.

There was a small queue of women waiting in the tiny, musty, overcrowded shop. Bundles with tickets attached to them were piled high on the shelves; in the corners were stacked household articles: clocks, vases, ornaments, rugs and even pots and pans. The women were all there for the same reason; they all used the pawnbroker's services on a regular basis. The Sunday suits and other best clothes were brought in on Monday mornings to raise a few shillings that would tide them over through the week, and then redeemed on Saturdays.

Finally it was Mary's turn.

'Frank's suit please, Uncle.' She passed the coins over the counter.

'Ready for the big do tomorrow?' Mr Dalgleish asked good-humouredly.

'Word certainly gets round, doesn't it?'

'Talk of the neighbourhood, Mrs McGann.' He always treated his customers with respect. He knew how hard their lives were and a polite word cost him nothing and meant a great deal to them. They got very few of them in their lives. He leaned over the counter and smiled down at Lizzie. 'Hello, Lizzie,' he mouthed slowly and then produced a paper bag from his pocket and extended it to her.

Lizzie smiled, took an aniseed ball and popped it into her mouth, and then nodded her thanks.

Mary too smiled. 'You're very good to her.'

'Ah, it's nothing. Only a sweetie now and then. Hasn't she a hard little cross to bear.'

'I just wish her da thought the same,' Mary replied with a note of bitterness in her voice. Lizzie couldn't help the way she was yet somehow Frank seemed silently to blame the child for her afflictions. Or maybe he blamed herself. Maybe that's when things had started to become cool between them and she'd never noticed it until now?

'And how is himself?' Mr Dalgleish asked, retrieving her bundle.

'Drunk,' Mary answered before realising what she was saying. 'I mean he's been celebrating a bit,' she added quickly.

'Ah, well, it's only to be expected and you have to admit that he doesn't "celebrate" half as much as some do.' He smiled understandingly. If half the men in this neighbourhood were to lay off the drink he would face a decline in business, he reminded himself. Still, life for them wasn't easy either. Far from it. They probably deserved a bit of pleasure although they could temper it with a bit of responsibility towards their long-suffering wives.

Mary smiled at him. 'You've a great way of looking at things.'

'Ah, you have to be a bit of an optimist in this line of work, Mrs McGann. Otherwise you'd depress yourself into an early grave. Well, enjoy the wedding and the holiday.'

'Thanks, and you have a happy Christmas, too.'

He watched her leave and shook his head. She was a striking young woman. It was such a pity that she would lose her looks and become old before her time, but that's what would happen. It always did.

Mary dawdled home, stopping occasionally to exchange a few words with the other women she met who were all bustling around, busy with their preparations.

Thankfully she realised that Frank had gone upstairs to sleep off the effects of the alcohol, and she hoped he would be in a much better humour when he finally awoke. She sighed heavily and drew the curtains. Darkness was already falling. She pressed Frank's suit and ironed his one good shirt and draped them carefully over the back of a chair. She ran the iron over what passed for Sunday clothes for the kids and then held up her dark blue skirt. She looked at it without much pleasure. It had been second-hand when she'd bought it nearly three years ago; now it was limp-looking and shiny in patches. Well, it would have to do. Maybe she could just afford a blouse or a thin jacket, if she could find anything halfway decent in Paddy's Market. *She* couldn't afford Mrs Carmichael's prices. The skirt might look a bit better for a quick press. Then she would have to try and find something for the kids' tea, though God knew what. Then she had an idea.

'Katie, take this and go and pay Mrs McShane for the coal. Then run up to Maggie Block's and get a pennyworth of thick pea soup. Take that bowl, it will do you all for your tea.'

'What about Da's tea?'

'Don't bother with him. Leave him to sleep. I've to go out to the market, I'll bring him something back. Then after you've all had that it's time for a bath. Tommy, you can bring in the bathtub from the yard. It will take me ages to heat up the water.'

'Ah, Mam, it's too cold to be having a bath,' he protested, having a strong aversion to soap and water and the rough bit of towel his mother used to scrub his neck and ears.

'Don't you start, meladdo! You'll all be clean and tidy for tomorrow. I'm not having you go to church looking like little street arabs!'

They were all in bed, the fire was banked up and both Frank and Maggie were asleep when at half past ten Mary again wrapped her shawl around her and stepped out into the cold, dark streets.

There had been no further falls of snow and the sky was clear. The moon was bright and surrounded by a milky white halo. Already the snow beneath her feet was beginning to freeze. Despite the hour the streets were busy. Many shops were still open and the pubs were packed to overflowing. Rowdy, raucous laughter and singing emanated from their open doors.

She walked quickly along, the two hemp shopping bags over her arm, her spirits rising. This type of shopping she didn't mind at all. They were all what she considered luxuries and the thought of the faces of her children on Christmas morning when they saw their bulging stockings and the brightly decorated kitchen and smelled the wonderful aromas of the food filled her with excitement and pleasure.

The street market was crowded. Stall-keepers shouted their wares and exchanged witty repartee with their customers, many of whom had imbibed a fair bit of Christmas spirit already. She called greetings to the women she knew and some she didn't as she weaved her way between the stalls. At knock-down prices she bought a pair of chickens, potatoes, carrots and sprouts. Apples and oranges. Butter, thick slices of fruit cake, the pieces of salt fish that would have to be soaked overnight to be fried the next morning for breakfast. For a penny she got a big bunch of holly and for another penny some red and green crêpe paper chains to decorate the kitchen. From a stall that sold hand-knitted articles of clothing country women had made in their homes she bought a pair of woollen mittens for Maggie.

Finally she made her way to the large covered market at the top of Banastre Street. Officially it was called St Martin's Market but it was known worldwide as Paddy's Market. Here everything was sold but people came particularly for the second-hand clothes. It was much frequented by the sailors from the ships in the docks and every language in the world could be heard. She frequently said it was a veritable tower of Babel.

She rummaged amongst the stalls and piles of clothes that were in heaps on the floor until she found a blue and green tartan jacket that didn't look too worn. The woman had asked for twopence.

'It's not worth that! Look, there's a rip in the sleeve. I'll give you a penny ha'penny for it.'

'Yer look like a woman what's 'andy with a needle, yer can mend it. Tuppence is me price,' the woman stated firmly. Her quick eyes had taken in Mary's neatly mended shawl.

Mary frowned and then caught sight of a white muslin blouse. It was grubby and it too needed mending. 'Here, I'll give you tuppence halfpenny for the two. This is little better than a rag and it needs a good wash!'

The woman nodded. 'All right, but they're a bargain. A bit of a wash and a dip of starch an' that blouse will make yer look the 'eight of fashion.''

Mary laughed. 'It'll take more than that to make me look like a fashionable woman. Put them in the bag, will you?'

She was tired but happy with her purchases. What a treat it would have been to have caught a tram home. Still, it was a bright night and it wouldn't take long to walk even though she knew her arms and shoulders would be aching with the weight of her shopping by the time she reached Newsham Street.

She had reached the corner of Great Nelson Street and Scotland Road when she heard her name being shouted. She turned around. Richie Seddon was crossing the road, waving to her.

'Hello there, Mary. You're out late. Been snapping up the bargains then?' He looked smart and jaunty, his cap pushed back to reveal his thick, dark wavy hair. His dark eyes were full of laughter.

'I have indeed, Richie. Where've you been? Enjoying yourself?'

'Just for a few pints with me mates.'

'Not with the girls?'

'Ah, Mary, there's no one I've seen who compares to you!'

'Don't you be giving me the soft-soap treatment, Richie! The place is full of pretty girls much younger than me and you can have your pick and you know it.'

'What's age got to do with it?' He grinned. 'Give me one of those bags, they look heavy.'

'Won't that spoil your image? A big strong man like you carrying a shopping bag?'

'Who cares? Give it here.'

She handed him one of the bags. It was typical of him. He *didn't* care what people thought of him. Frank, and for that matter most of the men she knew, wouldn't have been seen dead carrying a shopping bag.

'God, it weighs a ton! We're not dragging home with the weight of these. Come on, here's a tram.' He took her arm and pulled her along.

'Richie, I can't afford the fare! I've spent up.'

'I can and it beats walking.' He pushed her onto the platform ahead of him.

The tram was already crowded and the conductor looked annoyed.

' 'Ere, girl, yer can't gerron with all that 'olly! Yer'll 'ave someone's eye out!'

'I'll stand on the platform,' Mary countered, unwilling now to give up the chance of a ride home.

'Yer can't. It's against the regulations.'

'Then we'll go upstairs,' Richie cried.

'It's full!' the conductor snapped. He was harassed and it was nearing the end of his shift. 'Look, mate, there's 'alf the crew of the *Acadia* up there an' they're all drunk. God knows 'ow I'm goin' ter get them all off!'

'I don't care if there's the entire crew of every Cunard ship up there, we're not getting off!' Richie shouted.

The conductor gave up. 'Oh, gerron then! Stand on the bloody platform if yer like, I'm past carin'! All I want ter do is gerrome ter me bed an' that lot up there can sleep in the bloody depot fer all I care! Give us yer money.'

Richie handed over the coins and Mary laughed as he pulled a face at the back of the conductor who was bawling, 'Gerralong in there! Move along inside! Ma, shove over in that seat, yer're takin' up too much space!' This last was to a buxom Mary Ellen on her way home from selling her fruit in the city centre.

'Don't yer "Ma" me, yer 'ardfaced get! Too much space indeed. Yer look as if a decent meal would kill yer!' came the hostile reply. But she moved her voluminous skirts to one side so Mary could sit down.

'Thanks, I'm worn out,' Mary said pleasantly.

'Aren't we all wore out, girl, an' fellers think *they* 'ave it 'ard! My feller will 'ave been proppin' up the bar of the Throstle's Nest since dinnertime. 'E'll be flamin' paralytic by now an' me poor bloody feet are killin' me! Still, I think I might join 'im!' she finished cheerfully.

'How about it, Mary? Fancy a port and lemon in Mary Kate's to round off the night?' Richie asked, referring to the Britannia pub on the corner of Alexander Pope Street.

'Indeed not! I'd be the talk of the neighbourhood. Out

drinking with a wild bachelor and me with a husband and three kids at home!'

'Yer tell 'im, girl! These young fellers is all the same! Mind yer, 'e's not 'alf bad-lookin'.' Then Mary Ellen grinned. 'Now, iffen I were younger . . .'

'Now, Ma, you'll have me blushing!' Richie laughed, not in the least embarrassed by the amusement they were affording the other passengers.

'Tharral be the day, lad! Well, 'ere's me stop. Tarrah then,' she announced, heaving herself to her feet as the conductor yelled out the stop.

Suddenly Mary cried out. 'Oh, God! There's flames coming up through the floorboards!'

'Fred! Chuck yer tea dregs on them bloody electric leads! They've sparked again an' set fire ter the boards!' the conductor shouted down the tram to the driver. It was a common enough occurrence and usually effectively dealt with in the manner he had instructed, but sometimes it didn't work. Then the whole tram could be lost, if the Fire Brigade didn't get to it in time. That's all he needed! he thought gloomily. Would this night ever end?

When they alighted from the tram Richie again relieved her of her burden and they were laughing and joking when they turned the corner and came face to face with Queenie and Nora.

'I could 'ave done with 'im meself ter cart me own shoppin',' Queenie said, eyeing Richie with suspicion.

'I'm glad I met him first then, *and* he paid the tram fare.'

'And the ride was better than Fred Karno's Circus!' Richie laughed.

Nora looked with disapproval at Mary. An old, married woman carrying on like that! It was disgraceful!

'And I won't tell you how he suggested we finish the night!'

'I can guess!' Queenie snapped.

'Now, Mrs Phelps, it was nothing like that. Just a quick port and lemon in Mary Kate's.'

'Can you imagine it?' Mary rolled her eyes.

Nora's mouth was set in a hard line. He had actually asked *her* to go for a drink with him when he'd been ignoring every effort she had made to get him to ask her out.

'Yer got plenty of stuff I see. Is that a new jacket?' Queenie had spotted the tartan jacket that was rolled up on the top of the bag.

'Yes, and I got a blouse too. Real bargains. In Paddy's Market. The jacket needs a bit of mending and a good press and the blouse wants a bit of work with the needle too, not to mention a wash and a dip in Robin starch, but they'll do for Vi's wedding. I'll have to stay up half the night to get them ready though!'

'You'll look great in them, Mary, I'll bet!' Richie said.

Nora felt her cheeks burn. Oh, it just wasn't fair! Mary would look good in them. And once Mary's hair was all done up, *she'd* look nothing beside her, even with her new pink blouse and bit of pink ribbon for her hair. She wished now she'd chosen another colour. Pink was so . . . so babyish. Her mam hadn't been very impressed either, saying she could have got more for her money and she should have known better than to go to René Carmichael with her outlandish prices.

'Come on, Mam, it's freezing standing here!' she said primly, pulling at Queenie's arm.

'Goodnight. I'll see you both tomorrow,' Mary said, smiling.

'Tarrah, both. Don't you do anything I wouldn't do, Nora!' Richie called after the girl.

Nora gritted her teeth. Chance would be a fine thing, she thought furiously.

Mary stopped outside the house where Richie lived. 'Well, thanks, Richie, for the tram ride and for carrying the shopping. I'd better go, it's really very late.'

'No trouble, Mary. It was a pleasure. Er . . . I think your husband's come looking for you,' he added, catching sight of Frank coming towards them.

Mary turned round. She was disturbed to see that Frank was glaring at Richie. 'I'm just coming. I've been to the market. I'll get you something to eat now.'

'It's about bloody time! Where the hell do you think you've been until this hour? It's well after midnight.'

'I told you. I've been to the market. I left it late because they sell things off cheap,' she explained, determined not to lose her temper.

He snatched the jacket from the bag and shook it in her face. 'What's this? Been buying yourself clothes? Just thinking of yourself and me with not a bite to eat for hours and the fire half out!'

'Here, Frank, there's no need to get upset,' Richie intervened. He had no liking for Frank McGann at the best of times and the man had been drinking today, he could smell it on his breath. Mary deserved better treatment than this.

Frank rounded on him. 'You mind your own bloody business! She's *my* wife and I want to know where she's been and who with.'

'Frank, I've been shopping and on my own. I met Richie when I was coming home and I got that and a blouse from Paddy's Market for a few coppers. It's all torn, look!' She took the jacket from him and showed him the torn sleeve. 'Come on home and I'll make us both something to eat. I'm starving myself.'

Frank hesitated for a second then he wagged a finger in Richie's face. 'I'm watching you! I know what you're like and what you're after!'

Mary was mortified and yet angry. How dare he insinuate that her behaviour had been lacking in propriety?

Richie glared at Frank. He felt like hitting him and he knew he could have floored him easily but he wouldn't humiliate Mary further.

'Goodnight, Mary,' he said coldly and turned away abruptly.

'Goodnight, Richie, and thanks,' Mary said grimly. Without looking at her husband, she turned and walked the remaining yards to her own home. She was seething inside.

Chapter Four

◆─❈─◆

THERE HAD BEEN NO further conversation between them. Cutting his nose off to spite his face, Frank had gone straight to bed without any supper. Mary, with her face set with suppressed anger, had unpacked her shopping and had then started to mend the jacket and blouse.

It had been very late when she had finally gone to bed, leaving the jacket draped over the back of a wooden kitchen chair and the blouse that she had washed and starched in front of the dying fire to dry.

She awoke with a slight headache but resolved that she was going to enjoy the day, come what may.

The kitchen was clean, tidy and warm when Frank and the children got up to a breakfast of fried salt fish, eggs and bread and butter, a rare treat. The food seemed to put Frank in a better humour.

'Well, this is a treat. This is what I call a breakfast,' he said with some satisfaction, attacking the fish. Perhaps she was trying to make up for her behaviour last night, he thought, but he still didn't trust that Richie Seddon. He'd be keeping his eye on him today. However, it certainly was a good breakfast and the bits of rags she'd bought at Paddy's Market looked well on her. He was looking forward to the day. Plenty of food and drink and all free. Oh, he was going to make the most of it all right. He deserved a bit of enjoyment.

By ten o'clock they were ready to go and Mary had to admit they all looked smart, herself included. Maggie still didn't look well though, she thought as the old woman appeared dressed in a black skirt and blouse over which she wore a three-quarter-length coat of black wool that had seen better days but was what she always wore for church. The outfit was completed by an out-of-shape black felt hat.

'Don't you look smart, Mary!'

'Thanks, Maggie. It took me half the night to get this stuff ready but it was worth it.' The blue and green tartan jacket looked very well with her dark blue skirt and the blouse, with its high starched collar that emphasised her long slim neck, made her skin seem almost translucent. She had piled her hair up on top of her head in the fashionable cottage-loaf style. The only thing that marred her satisfaction with her appearance was the fact that as she had no hat and she couldn't appear in church with her head uncovered, she would have to wear her shawl over the new outfit. Still, she would carry it over her arm until they got to church.

'We'd better get along to St Anthony's or we'll be walking with the bride,' Maggie stated, ushering the children towards the door.

The Joneses had no money for carriages so Violet and her father would walk to church as many brides did. None of them minded; it was a chance to show off their wedding finery to the neighbours.

The church was full and Mary noticed that all the women had made a big effort to turn themselves and their families out as decently as they could. She also noticed with annoyance that Hetty Price had far outdone both the bride and her mother in an eye-catching cherry-red costume trimmed with black braid and a matching red and black wide-brimmed hat. Trust her. Why couldn't she have had a bit more sensitivity and kept the obviously new outfit for Christmas Day? Katie was eyeing Millie's new green coat and hat and black buttoned boots with envy.

But Mary forgot her irritation as the notes of the organ thundered out and Violet, resplendent in a pale blue fine wool dress and Sally Price's blue and white hat, trimmed with ribbon and artificial flowers, walked up the aisle on her father's arm, smiling and nodding at all the heads that were turned towards her. She was a big rawboned strap of a girl who had a raucous laugh and a voice you could hear two streets away, or so her mam always said. Mary noted that the bridegroom looked a bit pale and apprehensive. The pallor was probably due to the amount of drink he'd have consumed the night before when he'd gone celebrating his last night as a bachelor.

Her mind went back to her own wedding day, here in this very church. She'd had a new pink and grey paisley print dress and a pink hat, but her poor mam had been dressed in borrowed finery. Frank had looked very smart in a new serge suit with a flower in his top buttonhole. She glanced surreptitiously from beneath her lowered lashes at him. How he'd aged. He looked dour and unsmiling as he stared at the wedding group. She doubted that he was recalling their wedding day, and the memory of that scene last night only reinforced her realisation that he'd changed.

After the ceremony they all went back to Newsham Street. Queenie and Maggie walked alongside Mary and her family.

'Did yer see the get-up of Hetty?'

'Wouldn't you think she'd have had a bit more sense than to go flaunting that new outfit today? Did you see poor Nellie's face when she saw her?' Maggie said with sympathy in her voice for Nellie's hurt feelings.

'I thought Nellie looked very well indeed and I'm going

to tell her so *and* I'm going to make sure Hetty hears me!' Mary said firmly.

'Don't let's dawdle, I'm starvin' and once this lot gets stuck inter the food it'll disappear that quick you'd 'ardly have time to blink! *An'* I want ter keep me eye on our Nora an' that feller,' Queenie urged as everyone crowded into the tiny house.

It was with some difficulty that Nora had managed to manoeuvre herself into a position next to Richie Seddon. She had washed her hair and tied it up with the pink satin ribbon and she'd pressed the new pink ruffled blouse and she had thought she looked very well – until she had caught sight of Mary in church. The jacket might have looked like a rag last night but Mary had worked wonders with both it and the blouse. They made a very smart outfit. She had also performed miracles with her hair. Nora had noticed *that* as soon as they'd come out of church and Mary had taken off her shawl. She didn't look twenty-eight. Today she looked more like eighteen, Nora mused, and the thought didn't please her one little bit.

'Isn't this great, Richie?' she said with what she hoped was a dazzling smile.

'It is. Nellie's certainly gone to town.'

'She's delighted that Violet's married and so am I. It must be great being married,' she said archly, shooting him a smile.

'I bet she won't think so in a few years' time. Look

61

around you, Nora. How many women do you see here who still look absolutely delighted with their husbands?'

This wasn't the way Nora had hoped the conversation would go. 'Oh, that's just the old ones like me mam and Nellie and Hetty.'

'Mary McGann's not old and she looks as if she could kill Frank for the way he's getting stuck into that ale.' Richie hadn't forgotten last night's incident. He also thought Mary looked far lovelier than anyone, including the bride and her sisters.

Nora fought down the sharp retort that sprang to her lips. 'Well, I see she's got a glass of port in her hand,' she said primly. 'I suppose she doesn't want him to make a show of her.'

Richie laughed. 'Most of this lot won't care about things like that in a couple of hours.' Then he became serious. 'But Mary will. I don't know how she sticks him.'

Nora was becoming annoyed. Couldn't he think of anyone other than Mary McGann? 'Well, she'll have to, he's her husband, "for better or for worse", like Father Heggarty said in church. Do you think you could get me another drink, Richie? It's shockin' crowded in the kitchen and I don't want anyone to spill anything over me new blouse.'

Richie had been trying to think of a way to get rid of her so he smiled. 'Of course, Nora, and it's a very pretty blouse.'

Nora looked up at him, smiling. So he *had* noticed. Now all she had to do was keep him interested.

'You just watch yerself with 'im, me girl!' Queenie muttered to her daughter as she passed by with a plate of ribs and cabbage in one hand and a glass in the other.

Nora tutted and raised her eyes to the ceiling. Mam was impossible *and* she'd already had more port than she was used to. Then Nora looked round her and began to smile: her da, bearing his most prized possession – an old and battered banjo – was pushing his way into the room followed by Albert Sparky with his accordion and Jim Hayes with his harmonica. It was time for the dancing to begin. She was determined that somehow she was going to get Richie to dance with her.

After five minutes, however, she was getting impatient. There was no sign of him.

'Do yer want ter dance, Nora?' Eddy Hayes asked her, rather tentatively. He was a spotty youth of sixteen with bad eyesight who had a crush on her.

She glared at him. 'Oh, grow up, Eddy! Who in their right mind would want ter dance with you?' she snapped.

Before the lad had time to remonstrate Richie appeared, guiding a flushed and laughing Mary towards the crowd of tightly packed dancers. Mary had taken her jacket off and the blouse, which Nora now noticed was embroidered all over with tiny white flowers, made her look even more young and pretty. Nora felt sick with jealousy and disappointment. He had just abandoned her! Left her here waiting for him to return with her drink when he'd obviously had no intention of coming back. He'd gone looking for Mary McGann. She turned her head away from the painful sight and saw Frank McGann leaning against the doorpost, a glass in his hand. He looked far from pleased, Nora noted. Well, she'd had enough of this. Mary was a married woman, she had no right to be laughing and joking and dancing with Richie, leading him on when she wasn't free.

'I wonder she's got the nerve to be carrying on like that,' Nora said cuttingly, sniffing disapprovingly.

'Like what?' Frank demanded belligerently. He'd had quite a bit to drink already and he had been enjoying the day until Richie Seddon had started paying too much attention to Mary. And she seemed to be lapping it up. She never laughed and smiled at *him* like that these days.

'Well, like . . . that! And especially after the way he was going on last night when Mam and I met them.'

'Just what do you mean by that, Nora?' Frank demanded. He had no real liking for the girl but he wanted to get to the bottom of this.

'He said he'd asked her to go for a drink with him in the Britannia. They'd been on the tram together *and* he was carrying her shopping.'

Frank's face flushed red with rising anger. So, he'd been right in his suspicions last night. There had been more to it than 'just meeting him on the way home' as Mary had tried to explain it away. Why would he ask her to go for a drink with him if it had all been innocent and above board?

'Did she go?' he demanded.

'No,' Nora answered. 'At least, I don't *think* she did.' She tried to look and sound thoughtful, as though perhaps she doubted Mary's alleged refusal.

'The bitch!' Frank growled. The lying bitch. She *had* gone, that's why she was so late. Well, he'd sort this out here and now.

He was about to elbow his way towards her when Katie rushed in past him and dragged at Mary's arm.

'Mam! Mam! Come out into the yard, our Tommy's sick!'

Mary sighed. She had been enjoying herself. 'Oh, now what's he been up to? I can't take my eyes off that lad for five minutes lately! He'll be the death of me. I'd better go and see to him. Sorry, Richie, it's one of the penalties of being a mother, but I'm sure there are plenty of others just dying to dance with you. There's one for a start.' She looked over at Nora who was still standing by the door with longing plain in her face.

He laughed. 'Oh, God! No thanks, I've only just got rid of her. She's like a limpet.'

'Oh, you're cruel. She's mad about you. Do your good deed for the day and dance with the poor girl.'

'I'm not in the mood for good deeds, Mary.'

'Mam, come *on*!' Katie urged, pulling her mother towards the door.

'It's our Tommy. Apparently he's unwell,' Mary said by way of an explanation as she passed Frank, hardly noticing the look on his face.

Out in Nellie's back yard a small group of boys were looking guiltily at a pale and definitely ill-looking Tommy.

'What's the matter with you?'

'They've eaten *all* the ice cream Mrs Jones bought in Fusco's!' Katie said peevishly yet with a note of triumph in her voice. She was greatly aggrieved at such greediness. It was a long time since she had tasted ice cream and she'd not had the chance of even a mouthful.

'That will do from you, miss! Go inside and find Mrs Price and tell her to come out here this minute. I *know* whose idea this was!' She glared at young Georgie.

'Oh, Mam, I feel shocking!' Tommy wailed and was promptly and violently sick.

'Serve you right! Now the lot of you can get buckets of water and the yard-brush and clean this mess up!'

'Mam, I . . . I can't!' Tommy said, still looking green.

'I didn't make no mess,' Georgie muttered sullenly.

Nellie, followed closely by Hetty, appeared in the yard.

'This shower of greedy little pigs have scoffed all the ice cream, Nellie. I'm sorry but our Tommy's just been sick. I've told them to clean up the yard.' Mary glared at her son and Georgie Price.

'Do you know how much that cost me?' Nellie cried. 'And I was saving it for later on.'

Sweeping up her new red skirt Hetty stepped forward and boxed her son firmly around the ears. 'I've had more than enough of you and your antics these past few days, Georgie! Get home to your da. He won't be very pleased to see you, I can tell you! Christmas Eve and a pub to run on his own and now you acting the fool! I can't get five flaming minutes to enjoy myself. This is the first time I've been out for weeks and you have to ruin it!'

'It's the first time any of us has had something to enjoy for *months*, Hetty!' Mary said irritably.

'Go on, get home! Here, give me that brush,' Hetty demanded.

'You'll ruin your good skirt, Hetty, leave it to me,' Nellie instructed.

'*I'll* do it. You've got guests to see to, Nellie. Then I'm taking my lot home to bed. They've had more than enough excitement for one day!' Mary stated firmly. 'Katie, go and find Lizzie and get your coats.'

'Thanks, Mary, luv. You will be back, won't you?'

'Of course. Now get back inside both of you.'

'You're a real pal, Mary, and I'm sorry about Georgie and all . . . this,' Hetty said, pushing her son towards the yard door.

While Katie went to do her mother's bidding and Tommy sat dejectedly on the upturned washtub, Mary grimly set to and swilled the yard. She had no new red skirt that might get ruined. The only consolation was that Hetty had at least meted out some punishment, which made a change.

She took the children home and saw them into bed, promising there would be treats for all of them in the morning if they went to sleep straight away – even Tommy who she felt had been punished enough. He was abjectly sorry and still looked awful. Nellie should have made sure that bowl of ice cream was well out of their reach, she thought as she ran quickly up the back jigger towards the party. She hoped it would still be in full swing; no doubt it would end up in Hetty's husband's pub when all the drink Nellie and Fred had provided was exhausted, and that wouldn't be long now.

Richie was in the yard, smoking a Woodbine.

'I was just going to come and look for you, Mary. Where've you been? What's been going on? Hetty looks furious.'

Briefly Mary told him. 'Well, now they're safely in bed perhaps I can go back to enjoying myself,' she finished.

'So can I. I missed you.'

She pealed with laughter. 'Oh, Richie! The place is coming down with pretty young girls! And you missed me! You're a terrible flatterer!'

'Mary, you *really* don't know just how beautiful you are, do you? I've been noticing a lot of admiring glances in your direction all day and night.'

She blushed and laughed self-consciously. 'Don't be

ridiculous! We'd better get inside.' She turned away and in her embarrassment tripped over the head of the yard-brush.

Richie caught her before she fell but quickly she recovered her composure.

'Oh, I'm getting so clumsy!'

'So, this is where you are and what you're up to!' Frank's bellowed accusation rang out over the yard.

'Frank! I tripped over! It's not what it seems.'

'Don't be telling me bloody lies, woman! I've got eyes in my head!' He staggered towards them and Mary realised he was very drunk.

'Tommy was sick so I took them all home and put them to bed. I came into the yard and saw Richie, then I tripped up. That's the God's honest truth, Frank. There's nothing going on. I honestly don't know what's the matter with you lately.'

'You expect me to believe that? The pair of you out here on your own and him with his arms around you! You brazen bitch! And I know all about where you were last night when you told me you'd been shopping. Shopping, my bloody arse!'

'Frank, there's no need for language like that and what Mary's telling you is true—'

'Oh, I know you were off drinking in the Britannia last night. Don't you deny it! And that's not all, I'll bet!'

'Who told you that?' Mary demanded. The noise had already drawn a few of the guests outside.

'Does it bloody matter? But it was young Nora Phelps, if you must know.' He was livid. How dare she carry on like this? How dare she make a fool of him in front of the whole street?

'And you believed *her*? She's a stupid, jealous kid,' Richie shouted back angrily.

'Yes, I believe her. Why the hell would she lie?' Frank grabbed Mary roughly by the arm. 'I'll teach you, you bloody hussy!'

Mary screamed. Frank raised his fist but before he could bring it down Richie hit him hard on the side of his head and he stumbled and fell, cursing.

'Frank! Richie! Stop this, both of you!' Mary shrieked.

'I won't stand by and let him belt you for something you haven't done, Mary!' Richie stormed.

Frank was staggering to his feet. 'I'll swing for you, you bloody little upstart! I'll teach you, both of you!' He made a swipe at Mary but Richie hit him again and this time he lay sprawled out on the wet flagstones.

Within seconds a group of men had appeared. A few tried to get Frank to his feet, the rest gripped Richie's arms.

'That's enough, the pair of yez!' Fred Jones shouted.

Mary was near to tears. 'Fred, I don't know what got into Frank. He . . . he tried to hit me! Richie was only defending me. Oh, God! What a mess! I'm sorry, so sorry!'

'All right, girl! He's had a bellyful of ale. He'll be all right when he's sobered up.'

'Oh, I'm mortified!' Mary sobbed. She had never seen Frank like this – she had never known him to be capable of such unreasonable behaviour. And he'd never raised a hand to her before.

Nellie and Queenie joined the men.

'Nellie, I'm sorry. Oh, what a family! First Tommy and now Frank.'

'It's not your fault, luv. He's dead drunk.'

'I know whose bloody fault it is! It's 'im – an' our flaming Nora's got an 'and in it somewhere!' Queenie interrupted. She'd found Nora crying on the stairs and had got a garbled tale out of her.

'You want to keep an eye on her, Mrs Phelps. She's a troublemaker,' Richie warned.

'I know, an' she don't need the likes of youse ter give 'er an 'and!' Queenie shot back.

'What do yer want ter do with 'im, Mary?' Alfie Phelps asked. Having bodily heaved a now unconscious Frank to his feet, he had slung him over his shoulder. He wasn't called 'Big Alfie' for nothing.

'Best thing ter do with 'im, Alfie, is take 'im 'ome an' let 'im sleep it off!' Queenie advised.

Mary nodded. 'I'd be grateful if you could get him home, Alfie, I really would.'

The big man nodded and Fred opened the yard door for him.

Mary turned to Nellie and Queenie. 'I'm so sorry.

I . . . I just don't know what's the matter with him.'

'Neither do I,' Nellie agreed.

'I'd just keep away from this feller in future, Mary. 'E's trouble with a capital T. Always 'as been an' always will be. I've given our Nora a piece of me mind about 'im!' Queenie glared at Richie who pushed past her and went inside the house, slamming the scullery door behind him.

Alfie deposited the prostrate Frank on the bed and then Mary took off his boots and pulled the blanket over him.

'Let 'im sleep it off, luv. 'E'll 'ave an 'ead as big as Birkenhead in the mornin' – an' a few bruises.'

'Thanks again, Alfie. You get back now. Oh, we've ruined everyone's enjoyment.'

He laughed. 'Norra bit of it, luv! Just adds ter the night. Yer'll laugh about it in a couple of weeks an' everyone will remember young Vi's weddin' as the night Richie Seddon laid out Frank McGann.'

'That's what I'm afraid of!' Mary said grimly.

'You all right, girl?'

'Yes, thanks. I've still got plenty of things to do so I'd better get on. I'll probably sleep down here. Go on back before they all go to the pub without you!'

When Alfie had left she sank down by the fire and dropped her head in her hands. Oh, what a night! How humiliating! She pulled herself together. She *did* have a lot of things to do and she was determined this wasn't going to ruin Christmas.

Some of her good humour returned as she put up the decorations and arranged sprigs of holly along the mantelshelf and above the door and window. Then she took the penny toys and the sweets from where she had hidden them, selected three apples and oranges from the dish and filled the three stockings that had been hung over the range. Then she made herself a cup of tea and sat down to admire the room. It *did* look bright and cheerful and festive and she couldn't wait to see the children's reactions when they came down, especially poor little Lizzie's.

Chapter Five

———◆———

NEXT MORNING MARY FORGOT the events of the previous night and her lack of sleep as soon as she saw the wondering expressions on the faces of the children and heard the excited cries of delight from Katie and Tommy. Lizzie's eyes were shining and she held up the little wood and paper dolls for Mary to exclaim over.

'Dolls. Pretty dolls. Father Christmas brought them for you, Lizzie,' Mary mouthed slowly.

Lizzie nodded and stroked Mary's cheek as an added sign that she understood. It was a gesture Mary had taught her and now it brought tears to Mary's eyes; she hugged Lizzie's thin little body to her, wishing for the thousandth time that Lizzie could have been born like her brother and sister. She swallowed hard. 'I told you Father Christmas would come. *And* we're going to have a lovely big dinner. Doesn't the room look great?'

'He must have been here for ages to have put all those

decorations up. Did you see him, Mam?' Katie asked, all agog.

Mary laughed. 'Good heavens no! I was fast asleep too. Now, we'd better get ready for church.'

'What's the matter with me da's face?' Tommy asked as Frank, looking very much the worse for wear, came into the kitchen. One side of his face was swollen and his eye was beginning to close, the flesh around it turning purple and blue.

'Your da slipped and fell in the jigger on the way home from the party,' she whispered. 'Happy Christmas, Frank,' she continued in a louder, cheerful voice, determined not to dampen the festive spirit. 'We're about to get ready for church. Shall I make you a cup of tea and something to eat?' she enquired of her husband, who had sat down in the armchair and had leaned his head back and closed his eyes.

'I'll have the tea and then you get off to church. I'm not going.'

Katie glanced quickly at her father. It was unheard of, not going to Mass on Christmas morning, but, seeing the look on her mother's face and her tightly compressed lips, she made no comment.

Lovely! Mary thought. How was this going to look? How was she going to explain this away to Father Heggarty without telling a pack of lies?

They met Nellie and her family also on their way to church.

'Happy Christmas, Mary, luv! How's *he* this morning?' Nellie asked.

'Looks as though he's had an argument with a horse and cart!' Maggie muttered darkly. Frank McGann's behaviour was getting beyond a joke, in her opinion, not that she would dream of saying anything to Mary.

'Not feeling up to Mass either,' Mary added.

'Oh, there's quite a few like that this mornin',' Nellie said, shooting an irate glance at Fred who looked decidedly hungover and had needed a gallon of tea and some very strong words on her part to make him accompany them.

'I'm really sorry about last night, Nellie.'

'Oh forget it, Mary. It's all done and dusted now. Let's enjoy the day. Our Violet's having her dinner with the new family, thank God. She wanted to come home but I told her, "Violet, this isn't your home now, girl. You're a married woman, your place is with your husband. You can't be running home to me after a few hours!" Girls these days, I ask you!'

Mary smiled. She knew that even if in time Violet discovered she'd made the wrong choice Nellie would send her back with the admonition 'You've made your bed, now you've to lie in it!' However, she sincerely hoped that Violet would be happy – although there was no guarantee of it. She'd thought she was happy, until last night. The thought depressed her so much that she quickly turned her mind to the preparation of the food that awaited her when she returned home.

She was annoyed when, after Mass, Frank had announced that he was going to the pub for 'a hair of the dog', but said nothing. She had set the table, the chickens were in the oven and she and Maggie were preparing the vegetables.

'Don't let this dinner get ruined, Frank. It's not often we have chicken!' Maggie had called after him with false cheerfulness. There were many women who, after scrimping and saving and slaving to put a veritable feast on the table, saw all their efforts ruined when the men stayed too long in the pub and came home incapable of anything. Mary was doing her best to make it a special day and she wanted Frank to do his part.

Thankfully, he had returned home a couple of hours later, fairly sober but in not much better humour. However, despite his sullen manner, the meal had been great and they'd all eaten far too much. Tommy had gone out to play with his mates. Katie and Lizzie were playing quietly with their toys and Frank and Maggie were dozing by the fire as Mary quietly cleared the table. She would leave the dishes in the scullery until later: she didn't want to disturb them. Glancing up, she saw through the tiny window the back-yard door open and Richie Seddon come up the yard.

Her hand flew to her mouth. If he knocked he might

wake Frank and there'd be another scene. Quickly she opened the door and went out.

'Richie, what are you doing here? Hasn't there been enough trouble?'

He looked concerned. 'I just came to see if you were all right, Mary.'

'I'm fine. Things are great, thanks. Now will you go, please? I've the washing up to do.'

'Don't you ever stop working, Mary? You wait on them all hand and foot.'

'Well, you know the saying. "A woman's work is never done." It's true.'

He looked at her closely, noticing the frown lines on her forehead and the dark shadows under her eyes. 'You look far from *fine*. You look tired and upset. I'm sorry, Mary.'

She managed a smile. 'That's all right, Richie. It . . . it wasn't your fault. Now, I really must go and I'm sure you have far more exciting things to do than stand here in the cold talking to me.'

'Like what?'

'Oh, Richie! Just *go*!' she urged, still smiling and giving him a gentle push.

'All right! I'm on my way. Happy Christmas, Mary.'

She relented a little. 'Happy Christmas, Richie, and thanks for calling.'

She watched him close the door and shook her head before turning and going back into the house.

Unknown to her her absence had been noticed. Frank had woken, thirsty, and had gone into the scullery for a drink of water. With narrowed eyes and his mouth set in a grim line he watched the brief conversation. By God! She was determined to carry on humiliating him! Even now they were probably planning their next meeting. Rage surged through him. So great was the force it made him shake. Oh, he'd been drunk last night, but not too drunk to realise what they'd been up to out in Nellie's yard. Probably everyone had known, had been sniggering behind his back. 'That poor, stupid fool Frank McGann being led a fine dance by his wife and her fancy feller and right under his nose.' The memory of her laughing with Richie's arm around her waist brought other images, darker images into his mind to torment him . . . and now they were together again. In his back yard, planning God knew what other things! Well, he'd had enough of this and he wasn't going to belittle himself again by tackling Richie Seddon. No, he'd deal with *her*.

Mary was startled to see him standing in the scullery. 'Frank! I thought you were dozing!'

'And you made the most of it, didn't you? Planning your next meeting with *him*!'

Mary was horrified. 'Frank, I was doing nothing of the kind! How could you even think such a thing? He . . . he came to see if I was all right and I sent him away. I chased him off!'

'And you expect me to believe *that*, after last night? You must think me a bloody fool. You couldn't wait to see him again. "Oh, it's all right, Richie, Frank's asleep and anyway you taught him a lesson last night, he won't bother us again!" ' He mimicked her voice cruelly.

'Frank! Stop it! Stop it, it's not true. None of it is true!' she cried.

'Don't lie to me, Mary. Even young Nora Phelps knows what you and he get up to.'

'Nora knows nothing. There is nothing to know. Frank, please, this is crazy, stupid . . .'

Her words made him squirm with humiliation. 'Oh, so now I'm crazy and stupid? Well, I've had enough of it. I want you out of here in an hour! And you can take the kids with you. I'm not breaking my back to keep a roof over your heads, food on the table and clothes on your backs, let *him* do it! Let him buy you fancy white blouses and tartan jackets. Let him pay to dress you up like a tart!'

Shocked though she was Mary fought back. 'Like a *tart*? Frank, I bought those things in Paddy's Market. They were probably third- or even fourth-hand. I buy nothing for myself. You buy me nothing.'

'I keep you – or I did. Now you can keep yourself. I mean it. Out in an hour.'

She stared at him in shock. What was he saying? 'Frank, you can't mean it? I've done nothing wrong, I swear to God I haven't!'

'You can swear as much as you like. I'm not putting up with you and your carrying on for another day!'

'Frank, for God's sake, it's Christmas Day! You can't do this to us! You'll break the kids' hearts!' Mary was beside herself. 'I won't go! I won't go, Frank! I'm not moving an inch and neither are the kids!'

He turned on her. 'Then I'll bloody well throw you out! I'll pick you up and physically throw you out of the bloody door onto the street!' he yelled.

'You *wouldn't*!'

'Just try me, Mary!'

She was horrified, she could see he meant it. 'And the kids?'

'You should have thought of them before you started whoring around! Get their things together now and get out!'

He turned away and she clutched his arm. 'Frank, please? I swear I've done *nothing*. I swear, *nothing*!'

Angrily he shook off her grip and returned to the kitchen.

Mary followed him, almost in tears. She couldn't believe he was doing this. 'Frank, you've got to listen to me! Please?'

Maggie was awake. 'What's the matter now?' she asked irritably.

Frank turned on her. 'You stay out of it!'

Mary threw out her hands in a gesture of appeal. 'Oh, God! Maggie, he . . . he's throwing us out! He won't listen to me. He believes I've been . . . more than friendly with Richie, but it's not true, Maggie!'

Anger flooded through Maggie. 'Of course it's not flaming well true! You're a fool, Frank McGann! You don't know when you've got a good wife. Look at some of them in this street. Lazy slatterns. The place like a pigsty and no meal on the table and no washing done and them sitting in the side passage of the Newsham House drinking every penny they get. You just be thankful she's not like that.'

'I told you to stay out of it. It's got nothing to do with you!' Frank shouted.

Maggie wasn't intimidated. 'It's got everything to do with me, it's *my* house, in case you'd forgotten!'

'And *I* pay half the rent you can't afford. If you insist and she stays then I go and there'll be no way either of you can afford the rent. You'll both finish up in the Workhouse. But it's not me who's going, it's her! You think about that, old woman. Do you want to end your days no better than a bag of bones in the Workhouse? Because if you take her side I'll make bloody sure that's what will happen! I'm going to the pub and when I get back I don't want to see her or the kids here!'

As the door slammed behind him Mary sank down in the armchair and began to cry. 'Oh, Maggie, what will I do? Where will I go? Why is he being so unreasonable? Why won't he believe me?'

Maggie hastened to comfort her. 'Oh, Mary! God knows what's got into him.' She was thoroughly shocked herself.

Mary was beside herself with worry. 'He means it, Maggie, he does! I've never seen him like this. He's . . . terrifying!'

In her heart Maggie had to agree. It was a terrible, calculating hatred she'd seen in Frank's eyes. 'Try to take no notice,' she soothed.

'Maggie, I *have* to. And I can't put you in danger of losing your home and with it your chance to earn a bit of money.'

'That doesn't matter, Mary. I can't see you all thrown out on the street.'

'I know you mean well but we have to go. You can't afford to keep us and even if he went and I worked, if I could get a proper job, we still couldn't manage. You'd lose everything. You heard him, he'd make sure you ended up destitute. I have to go. I can't let that happen.'

Maggie knew she was right and she raged inwardly at Frank's callousness and vindictiveness but she lived in mortal terror of the Workhouse, as did all the poor, and she had no kith or kin to turn to in her old age. 'Where will you go, luv? What will you do?'

'I don't know, Maggie! I've no money, I spent it all on Christmas.' She broke down, unable to stifle her sobs. It was too much to take in.

Maggie was trying to plan, but all she could think was that it was so unfair. Everyone knew that Mary was a decent, hard-working girl who loved her family. She was sure that the women in the street wouldn't stand by and let her sink into destitution until she was forced to throw herself and her kids on the dubious mercy of the Workhouse. No, they'd all rally round.

She drew herself up determinedly. 'I'm going to talk to Nellie and Queenie and some of the others. You make yourself a cup of tea, luv, I won't be long.'

As soon as she'd gone Katie crept forward and clutched her mother's arm. 'Mam! Mam, what's the matter? Why is Da so mad? Why do we have to go? Why was he shouting at Maggie?'

'I don't know, luv, that's the honest truth.' Mary wiped away the tears on the child's cheeks, knowing that some sort of explanation would have to be given. 'Your da's mad at me. He thinks I've done something wrong, but I haven't! I haven't, Katie! And he's angry with Maggie for taking my side.'

Katie was very frightened. 'Where will we go, Mam?' she said, her voice shaking.

Mary bit her lip. 'I don't know just yet, luv. I'll have to think but don't worry, we'll be all right. I . . . I'll put the kettle on, you'd better go and find Tommy and bring him home.' She beckoned Lizzie towards her and the child came slowly, clutching her new toys, afraid her da would come back and take them away from her. She could tell how angry he was.

'Lizzie, Da is very cross with me. Just me,' Mary explained slowly and deliberately. Oh, how hard it was to explain anything to Lizzie, but she had to try. She could only hope that Lizzie would understand. 'We have to leave – go away. Katie will help you. Go with Katie, good girl.' She stroked the child's cheek but Lizzie made no attempt to return the gesture. Mary bit her lip. Oh, dear God, she wished she had a better way of communicating with Lizzie. 'Katie, luv, you try, please? Help her to get her things together, even if she can't understand why right now. I'll try again . . . later,' she added, distractedly.

Lizzie didn't understand, but she had sensed the atmosphere and had looked closely at the faces of her parents and sister before her da had gone out and her mam had begun to cry. She knew something was *very* wrong.

Mary hugged her and then gave her a gentle push in the direction of the door. Then she wiped her own eyes on her apron and stood up. She felt dazed and disorientated, outraged and appalled but she had to keep her spirits up in front of the children.

Maggie had hurried from house to house, explaining what had happened, and four other women joined her as she returned to Nellie's kitchen.

'I've told them,' she announced triumphantly.

'It's a bloody disgrace, that's what it is!' Nellie fulminated. 'And Fred agrees with me. I've sent him down to Bert Price's pub to try to talk some sense into Frank.'

Maggie was doubtful. 'I don't think that will do much good, Nellie. You should have seen the look on his face.'

'An' Alfie says it doesn't do ter go interferin' between a man an' his wife. It ain't right,' Queenie added.

'Oh, a lorra 'elp yer're goin' ter be!' Bella Spriggs interrupted scathingly.

'I were only repeatin' what 'e said. Keep yer 'air on, Bella, it don't mean I agree with 'im,' Queenie shot back.

'What *are* we going to do to help her? She's helped us out many a time, one way or another,' Eileen Quinn from number sixteen reminded them.

'If Fred can't talk sense into him then I suggest we all pitch in and help. If we take her and the kids for, say, a week each, until she gets herself sorted, that won't be too much bother.' Nellie looked around for approval.

'And you know Mary, she'll be only too willing to work her fingers to the bone for you all to repay you,' Maggie added.

'God knows where I'll put 'em. There's twelve of us in our 'ouse already,' Bella commented.

'And there's eight of *us*,' Nellie reminded her.

'We'll manage. We'll just 'ave ter,' Queenie said firmly.

Maggie rose. 'Right, I'll get back and tell her.'

Nellie also got to her feet. 'I'll come with you. She can come to me first. I'll leave word with the kids to tell Fred where I am in case there's any . . . news.'

When they returned Mary was sitting at the table, a cup of tea in front of her, untouched. Katie, Lizzie and Tommy were sitting close together on the old sofa looking frightened and bewildered, each clutching a small bundle containing their meagre possessions.

'Right, it's all settled. Myself, Queenie, Bella, Mabel and Eileen Quinn are all going to take you and the kids in for a week about, until you get yourself settled, like,' Nellie announced. 'And you're coming with me first.'

'Oh, Nellie! You're all so *good*!' Mary cried.

'You've done enough to help us all out over the years, Mary. Now, luv, let's get your things together.' She lowered her voice. 'He's a bloody fool, believing you'd do something like *that*! Fred's gone to see if he can talk some sense into him.'

'Oh, Nellie, I hope he can. I just can't understand him. He's so . . . unreasonable these days. Has he changed or is it me?'

'It's him, luv. You'll never change. You're a good wife and mother and always will be.'

'All I can hope is that he'll come to see that,' Mary said brokenly.

'I'm going to have a few words with that Richie Seddon, too! He's not without blame in all this,' Nellie said darkly.

'No, leave it, Nellie, please? I don't want to give Frank any more reason for suspicion and if he sees or hears that Richie has been to see me, wherever I am, then he'll never change his mind and have us back.'

'If you insist, luv, but I wish that lad would settle down and stop causing trouble.' She shot a warning glance at Queenie. Their Nora had played her part in all this, too.

Fred called in fifteen minutes later, shaking his head to his wife's queries. There was no talking to Frank McGann these days. He was adamant that Mary was being unfaithful and that he'd had enough of being made a laughing stock. 'The stupid, blind sod!' had been Fred's final words before he'd left.

They had packed up what belonged to Mary and some food and were preparing to leave when Frank returned.

Nellie drew herself up. 'Don't you start, we're just leaving,' she said grimly. 'And in my opinion you're the biggest bloody fool in the entire city! She's a good girl and you must be mad to think she'd have anything to do with the likes of Richie Seddon.'

'I'm not interested in your opinions and I won't have *his* name mentioned in this house!' Frank snapped.

'Suit yourself, but you're the loser in all this. Do you think people around here are going to think well of you?' she asked, raising her eyebrows, but Frank said nothing. 'If you do, you've another think coming!' she finished, shepherding the three frightened children towards the door.

Mary tried a last, desperate appeal. 'Frank, she's right! Please, for the last time, won't you believe me?'

He turned away and walked from the room.

'Leave him, Mary. Let's hope he comes to his senses in a couple of weeks,' Maggie said sadly. She was going to miss Mary terribly. Nor did she relish the thought of living here with him on her own. Well, she'd keep herself to herself and she certainly wasn't going to be waiting on him. Let him find out what it was like to come home to a cold kitchen, no meal and no clean clothes. It would serve him right.

Chapter Six

———◆———

MARY LOOKED DESPAIRINGLY AT the pool of milk that was spreading across the newly scrubbed floor. Oh, this was just the last straw! Things were going from bad to worse. It was impossible for sixteen people to live comfortably in one tiny house. Bella had made them more than welcome but her ways were not Mary's and these last few days the atmosphere had become more than a little strained. Bella seemed to exercise little or no discipline over her brood of children, which made it hard for Mary to control her own three, although Lizzie was not much of a problem. All three were confused by the constant moving and the change in routines, which worried Mary – though not as much as the uncertainty over their future.

She got to her feet and picked up the floorcloth. Now she'd have to do it all again.

'Is that the milk fer the tea?' Bella enquired, dumping her shopping down on the table.

'It is – or it was. And I've just scrubbed the floor,' Mary replied sharply.

'Whose fault was it?' Bella demanded.

'Jinny's. She left the top off the can and then she caught it with the corner of the coal bucket she was carting out into the yard.'

'God, she's a great clumsy lump!'

Mary sighed wearily. 'Don't go on at her, Bella. It was an accident, she didn't mean to do it.'

Bella went into the scullery, opened the back door and bawled for Jinny to come back inside.

Reluctantly the child sidled into the kitchen.

'Get yerself back down to the dairy an' get another pint. Me tongue's hangin' out fer a cuppa.'

'Ah, Mam! I've just been!' Jinny protested.

'And yer've just spilt the flamin' lot all over the floor. Now get and don't dawdle.'

'I'll put the kettle on,' Mary said, gathering up the cleaning stuff.

'Sit down, luv, yer're wore out. Yer never stop.'

Mary sat down on a stool beside the range. She couldn't go on like this. 'Oh, Bella, you've all been so kind but this isn't working, I'm going to have to do *something*.'

'I know we're a bit squashed, like, but . . .' Bella shrugged.

Mary nodded. What could she say? The neighbours had kept their promise. She'd spent a week with Nellie, then Queenie, Eileen, Mabel and now Bella, and been willingly accepted into their homes, but she'd never felt so adrift, so *lost*. It was terrible not having a single thing she could call her own and the constant noise and overcrowding was now unbearable.

'I'm going to go and ask Frank if he will . . . reconsider.'

'An' iffen 'e won't?' Bella asked.

'Then I'll have to make some plans. We can't all go on like this.'

The older woman nodded. Four extra bodies put a huge strain on a house like this, to say nothing of the extra mouths to feed. 'Maggie says 'is temper is shockin' since yer left an' yer know she won't do nothin' fer 'im. He 'as ter get 'is own meals an' 'e 'as ter get that woman from round the corner ter do 'is washin' and ironin'.'

Mary knew all this; she saw Maggie regularly. Maggie had refused point blank when Frank had asked her to do his laundry even though he had said he would pay her.

'Your money I can do without. Find some other fool to do it!' had been her reply.

'I'll go tonight, after tea.' She stood up. 'Let's get all this stuff put away, then we'll have a cup of tea and I'll think about what I'm going to say to him.'

'Right, luv, I'll get the mugs,' Bella said firmly.

She'd thought about it all day and had rehearsed it all in her mind. Now as she walked towards her old home she prayed with all her heart that he'd listen to her and relent.

She went round the back way: she wasn't going to risk knocking on the front door and have him refuse her entry. The scullery was a mess, she thought, glancing around. It didn't look as if it had been cleaned since she'd left. Quietly she opened the kitchen door and breathed a sigh of relief. Maggie wasn't there. Frank was sitting at the table reading the newspaper. The room looked untidy and not very clean. She thought of the hours she used to spend scrubbing and polishing, keeping it as neat and tidy as she possibly could. The range looked dull and ashes were scattered all over the hearth. Above it the mantelshelf was cluttered and dusty.

'Frank, I . . . I've come to see . . .' Her words died as he turned around and she saw the expression on his face. His eyes were cold and hard.

'Get out! I told you I want nothing more to do with you!'

'Won't you just listen to me?' she begged.

'Listen to more lies, you mean!'

'NO! Frank, I've never lied to you, surely you must realise that? Frank, please? Everyone has been so good but it's no use. I can't live like this with no home of my own, constantly on the move, pushed from pillar to post. I want my things around me, to work to my own routine, to keep my own place clean and tidy and cook decent meals.'

'You should have thought of that before.'

'Frank, it's been five weeks and I've not said one word to Richie Seddon. I've not even seen him. The children miss you. It's so hard for them, they don't understand why they can't come home. Why I have to keep dragging them around to stay with the neighbours. Please, please let us come back? Look at the state of the place. And it can't be doing you any good to come home from a hard day's work to no fire and no hot meal, and to have to send your washing out.'

'I'm managing fine without you,' he answered sullenly.

'You're not! Frank, it doesn't have to be this way,' she pleaded.

'Yes, it does. I'm not having people pointing at me or laughing at me behind my back about my wife carrying on.'

'Frank, I'm not "carrying on"!'

He lost his temper. It infuriated him to live the way he did but he had his pride. 'Maybe not at the minute but how long will it be before some other feller comes along?'

Mary was outraged. 'Oh, how can you say such a thing? How can you even think like that? I have never looked at another man in all the years since I married you! That nonsense with Richie was just that – nonsense. No one believes there was anything in it except a bit of flattery. No one is talking about you or laughing at you. Frank, you *have* to believe that!'

'I don't have to believe anything! Get out, Mary! Go on,

95

get back to Nellie or Queenie or whoever you're sponging off now!'

She could see it was no use. He was adamant. Sadly, she turned away, shaking her head, her eyes full of tears. Now what was she going to do?

She didn't want to go back to Bella's overcrowded kitchen and admit defeat, she *had* to sort out some kind of future for them all. To do that she needed to think. She walked up the street and onto Scotland Road and began to walk in the direction of town. It was bitterly cold and she clutched her shawl tightly to her, her head bent against the icy wind. What could she do? Should she try and get work, and then find somewhere to live even if it was just one room? But any job she could get wouldn't pay for rent and coal and food and clothes. She wasn't trained for anything. Oh, what had gone so wrong? How had things changed so much from that day ten years ago when she'd stood beside Frank in St Anthony's and made her vows? Vows she'd never broken.

She walked on deep in thought until the laughing words of her aunt Molly came suddenly to mind. Words that had been spoken on her wedding day.

'If you get sick of him, Mary, you can always come over to me!' They'd been spoken in jest but now, as she remembered them, an idea began to take shape. She caught sight of herself in a shop window. She looked thin and sort of wild-looking but was it any wonder? No, she couldn't go on living like this. She'd make a fresh start. She'd take the children and go to Molly. It might bring Frank to his senses, but even if it didn't and she had to make a new life for herself it would be better than struggling in this limbo. She straightened her shoulders. It *had* to be better than this.

'Come in ter the fire, girl, yer're half frozen!' Bella said when she eventually arrived back. 'Where've yer been? I was gettin' worried. What did 'e say?'

Mary sat down by the range and held her cold hands out to the warmth of the flames. 'He wouldn't listen. The place is a mess, he's not looking after himself but . . .' She shrugged.

'Then I wouldn't waste me pity on 'im!'

'I'm not. I . . . I've decided to go away,' she announced firmly.

Bella was startled but her attention was diverted to a row that was in progress between her two eldest daughters. 'Will the pair of yez give it a rest! Me 'ead's burstin' with the row out of yez, now pack it in!' she yelled at them.

Mary smiled tiredly. If a reason needed to be given for her decision Bella's bickering girls had just provided it.

'Go where, luv?' Bella proceeded.

'I've an aunty in Dublin. My mam's youngest sister, Molly. I'll write and ask her if she'll have us. It might be a bit crowded. I know Molly is a widow and that her two lads have gone to America and Theresa is married and has moved out, but I think Rita is still at home. She's a bit younger than me and she is married and has kids but I don't know how many. But I'm sure we'll manage,' she finished firmly.

Bella shook her head. She too had relatives in Dublin and from what she'd heard things were almost as bad over there as they were in Liverpool. Worse, in fact: wasn't that why half the population took the emigrant ship?

'Mary, I think I'd better go for the others. This is something that needs talking about. Discussing, like,' she said, concerned.

Mary sighed. 'Well, I suppose they'll have to know anyway.'

'Get yerself a cup of tea, I won't be long.' Bella turned to her family. 'And youse lot can get yerselves off ter bed, now! Me and Mary and the others want a bit of peace an' quiet. You, 'Arry, get yerself off ter the pub,' she instructed her long-suffering husband. He needed no second telling and snatched up his cap and muffler and was out of the door in a flash.

Nellie was first to arrive. 'What's all this Bella's been telling me?'

Mary poured her a mug of tea. 'Sit down; wait until the others arrive. There's no point me telling the same tale five times over.'

Nellie took the tea and sat deep in thought until Bella arrived back with Queenie, Mabel, Eileen and Maggie.

'Go on, tell them what yer told me,' Bella instructed.

Mary told them how her trip to see Frank had proved fruitless. She reiterated her gratitude for everything they had done for her but said she had decided to make a fresh start.

'But are you sure Molly will have you?' Nellie asked.

'She always said she would.'

'But from what I hear things is bad in Dublin. There's not much work and there's shockin' slums, as bad as here.'

'What if I tell him you're leaving Liverpool? It might bring him to his senses,' Maggie suggested. She could understand Mary's desire to go away but she thought it was a drastic decision to make so soon.

Mary sighed. 'You can tell him but I don't think it will make any difference.'

'What will yer do fer money, luv?' Queenie asked. 'Fer yer fares, like?'

Mary twisted the thin gold band on the third finger of her left hand. Frank didn't want her any more, so what did it matter? 'I'll sell my wedding ring. I wish I had some other bits of jewellery to sell, but I haven't.'

The women looked at each other sadly, realising that she really did mean what she said.

'We'll 'ave a birrof a whip-round, try ter get a few coppers ter help yer, luv.'

'You're all so kind. I've already taken far too much from you and you can't afford it.'

'Well, we can't let you go traipsin' over there with not a

99

penny to bless yourself with. I'll have a word with Hetty Price, she's got more money than flaming sense!' Nellie said firmly. She was sorry Mary was leaving but she could understand her reasons. She too had her pride and it was humiliating for her to be living off her neighbours when her husband was lording it with just himself and Maggie in that house.

'I'll write to Molly in the morning and then . . . then I'll start to get things together. I'll have to find work over there; I don't care what it is as long as it brings in some money. At least I'll know the kids will be looked after when I'm out.'

Nellie nodded and they started to talk about the conditions they'd heard about in Dublin while they finished their tea. Soon after the other women had left, Harry returned from the pub with the news that Frank McGann had had an argument with Bert Price and had been barred. 'God, but 'is temper's vile these days!' had been Harry's final comment. Mary had just stared silently into the fire. How could she have ended up in this plight? She prayed Molly would keep her word.

She wrote the letter next morning and posted it. On her way home she called in to Mr Dalgleish.

'Morning, Mrs McGann. I thought you must be in the money, you haven't been in with Frank's suit for a good while.'

'You must be the only one in the entire neighbourhood who doesn't know what's happened.'

He looked serious. He had in fact heard rumours. 'So it's true?'

'I'm afraid so, but it . . . it wasn't my fault.'

'Of course it wasn't your fault. The man's a fool!' He meant what he said. Of all the women in the area Mary McGann was the least likely to be unfaithful to her husband.

'He won't listen to anyone, so I've decided to make a fresh start. I'm taking the children to my aunt in Dublin. That's why I've come.'

'Mary, that's a bit drastic!'

'I know, but I feel I can't stay here any longer. What will you give me for this?' She slipped her wedding ring off and placed it on the counter. 'I don't want to pledge it. I want to sell it.'

He nodded slowly. She meant it, otherwise she would never have contemplated selling her ring. Things had to be very bad before the women actually *sold* their rings. He turned it over in his hand. It wasn't a very expensive ring but he would give her more than its actual value.

'I can give you two guineas. Let's look on it as a loan. I'll keep it; if you decide to come back and you can pay me, then you can have it back.'

'It's not worth two guineas, you know it's not!' she protested.

'I know it's worth more than that to you, Mary. Take the money, you'll need it.'

Tears sprang to her eyes as she took the two gold coins. 'Thank you, Mr Dalgleish. Someday I promise I'll repay you, even if you've sold the ring.'

'I won't, Mary. You're a good girl and you deserve better than him. Good luck to you and take care of those children.'

'I will and God bless you for the kind, generous man you are.'

He smiled wryly. 'That's an opinion some wouldn't share, but thank you.'

When she arrived home she found Nellie and Bella counting coins at the kitchen table.

'Did yer post it then?' Bella asked.

'I did and on the way back I called into Uncle's.'

'Bella and me went round the neighbours and we've got ten shillings for you,' Nellie announced.

'It were only three and sixpence but Hetty made up the rest.'

'Oh, everyone is so generous. Mr Dalgleish gave me two guineas for my ring. Two guineas! Can you believe it? And he says he'll keep it for me.'

'It's the first time I ever 'eard of that auld skinflint payin' over the odds,' Bella said cuttingly.

'He's got a soft spot for Mary, always has had,' Nellie stated.

'So, that's two pounds and twelve shillin's altergether. 'Ow much will yer fares be?' Bella asked.

'I don't know. I'll have to find out then I can budget. If they're not too expensive I should have enough to tide us over until I get work.'

'When will yer tell the kids?' Nellie asked.

'When I hear from Aunty Molly. I . . . I'll have to send them up to see Frank to say goodbye. He deserves that much.'

' 'E deserves nothing!' Bella said grimly and Nellie nodded her agreement.

Molly's reply duly arrived and it put Mary's mind at ease. They would all be very welcome if Mary was sure the life she'd known in Liverpool was really over, weren't they all family after all? Only Rita and her family lived with her now, there would be plenty of room and she was certain Mary would find work. It was a pity that no one could meet them off the mail boat but they were all just so busy, but she would be sure of a very warm welcome just the same and anyone would tell her the way to the Coombe.

Mary was apprehensive about telling the children and decided to try to make it sound like a kind of adventure. She hoped they wouldn't be too upset about leaving Frank but ever since they'd been forced to leave none of them had even mentioned going to see their father.

'I've got a surprise for you,' she said brightly as she sat them down at the kitchen table.

'What kind of a surprise?' Katie asked cautiously. Life was very topsy-turvy these days and she didn't like it at all.

'We're going to Ireland, to Dublin, to stay with my aunty Molly. Won't it be great?'

'Is it a holiday?' Tommy asked enthusiastically. He thought it did sound great. These days life was always full of some excitement, even if it was a bit hectic.

'Well, sort of.'

'Is me da coming?' Katie asked.

Mary shook her head. 'No, luv, he . . . he can't. He has to stay here and work.'

'Can't he work there?' Katie persisted.

'Not really. His job is here.'

'Will we be going on a boat?' Tommy asked. He'd been down to the Pier Head and seen the ships and it had all looked thrilling.

'Yes, we will and you'll go to school there and make new friends and see all your cousins.'

Katie looked doubtful. She had become really confused these last weeks as they moved from house to house, from family to family; she wasn't sure she wanted to meet all these new cousins or Mam's aunty Molly.

'Oh, it will be fun! You'll love it, I promise,' Mary enthused.

'What about Lizzie? Will she go to school too?' Katie asked, glancing at her little sister who was watching them all intently.

Mary gathered her little daughter to her. 'Not at first. I'll let her settle in; it will take her a bit longer.' She stroked the child's hair gently. 'We're going on a holiday, Lizzie,' she said slowly. 'On a big boat. Mam will tell you about it all later. Promise.' Oh, poor Lizzie. How was she going to try to make the child understand these further changes in her life?

'Will we go and say tarrah to me da?' Tommy asked.

'Of course you will.'

Accepting the situation with his usual happy-go-lucky air, Tommy jumped up. 'Can I go and tell me mates?'

Mary smiled with relief. The children had taken the news better than she had dared hope. 'Go on, but don't be long.'

Chapter Seven

~~~~~~~~

I N THE DAYS THAT followed Mary had little time to dwell on her decision or have regrets. She went down to the offices of the British and Irish Steamship Company and found out the price of the fare to Dublin. In all it would cost her fourteen shillings, which would leave her with one pound and eighteen shillings for their keep until she found work. She wished it were more but it couldn't be helped.

She had washed and ironed the few clothes they had; she had had Tommy's boots mended and delivered a stern warning that there was to be no kicking the toes out of them as she had no money to have them repaired again: he would just have to make do and suffer wet and cold feet. She had managed to get Lizzie a warmer coat from Paddy's Market for a few pence and Maggie had produced a pair of woollen mittens for each of them as a going-away present.

'I'll miss all of you,' she'd said, wiping away a tear. The house was too quiet by far these days, she'd added, wishing for the thousandth time that Frank McGann would see what a fool he was being. She was also finding it much harder dealing with the laundry alone too.

Mary knew Frank was aware that they were leaving but he hadn't relented. She'd known in her heart that he wouldn't. She didn't expect him to come to see them off, either.

'Well, it's his loss!' Nellie stated grimly as they prepared to accompany Mary and her family down to the Landing Stage barely a week later. 'Did he say anything to them? Give them a couple of coppers?' she asked Mary in a whisper after the children had returned from saying their farewells to their father.

'No. Just, "Behave yourselves." I can't understand him, he seems to have no feelings at all for them.'

'Well, pride comes before a fall, I always say. He'll get his come-uppance one day, you wait and see. Now, are we all ready? We're to meet in Hetty's parlour. She's coming as well.'

Mary smiled. 'It will be quite a send-off.'

'We'll all miss you, luv,' Nellie said sadly, echoing Maggie's distress.

The Landing Stage was always busy; the ships of the B & I line and the Isle of Man Steam Packet Company were amongst many that embarked and disembarked their passengers there. It was a cold, dark and windy night as they pushed their way through the crowds towards the gangway.

'I 'ope yer won't all be seasick. It can be shockin' rough once yer get out inter the bay, so 'Arry says,' Bella remarked grimly.

'Oh, trust you, Bella!' Hetty Price said sharply. 'Mary, take no notice. Get yourself a seat and then try and sleep. It's the best way. If you can't afford a cabin, that is.'

'Hetty, I can only just afford the steerage fare! But we'll be fine,' Mary laughed, determined not to be put off. She also wanted to dispel the look of consternation that had come over Katie's face.

'Will yer aunty be there ter meet yer, luv?' Queenie asked.

'I don't think so. She said they'd all be too busy.'

'But yer *do* know where she lives?'

'Of course. And I've a tongue in my head.'

'Well, you'd better get aboard if you want to get a seat. It looks as if it's going to be a bit of a crush,' Hetty advised, taking in the crowd around the gangway.

Mary hugged them all in turn and then gathered her children to her. 'Katie, keep tight hold of Lizzie's hand and hang on to me. Tommy, you make sure you don't lose that bundle and stay right behind me.'

'Take care, Mary. Remember you promised to write each week and if things don't go to plan you know you can always come back. There'll always be a home for you here,' Nellie said, giving her a last hug.

There were tears in Mary's eyes when she reached the bottom of the gangway, gave in their tickets and turned to wave a last goodbye. They had all been such good friends and she prayed she would find similar generosity and kindness on the other side of the Irish Sea.

Hetty had been right, she thought as she looked around the packed saloon. There were wooden benches set in double rows bolted to the floor but certainly not enough for every passenger to find a seat. People were already settling down on the floor between the aisles. She noticed a space on one of the benches set against the bulkhead on the starboard side of the saloon and, pushing the children ahead of her, made her way towards it.

'How many of you are there, girl?' a large woman dressed in a tightly buttoned black coat and with a headscarf knotted under her chin asked kindly.

'Four, but Lizzie can sit on my knee. Is there room, do you think? I don't fancy a night on the floor.'

'If I can get this lazy madam to move up there will be.' The woman dug her elbow into the side of a thin, disagreeable-looking girl who sat beside her. 'Shift up, Breda, there's kids here!' she instructed.

Thankfully Mary sat down with Katie beside her and Tommy perched on the edge of the bench. She lifted Lizzie onto her knee and the child nestled into her, already sleepy.

'She's not a bit happy, you see. She doesn't want to go home. She's been staying with me but her mam's sick, so she's needed,' the woman confided in a low voice, jerking her head in the direction of the sullen-faced girl.

'Oh, I'm sorry,' Mary replied.

'It's me sister and I'm going to help. Well, she's got ten kids and him out of work.'

'I see. Do you know if there's any work for women?'

'I can't say as I do, luv. Is that why you're going?'

'Sort of. My aunty's going to let us stay with her but I'll have to work.'

'No husband then?'

Mary shook her head. 'I'm a widow,' she lied, unwilling to explain her circumstances to a total stranger.

'I'm sorry to hear that, luv, but a fine-looking girl like you shouldn't be on her own for long. And you've only got three kids, not a whole tribe. Some fellers wouldn't take on a widow with a crowd of kids.'

'Oh, I'm not looking for another husband!'

The woman grinned. 'You might find one just the same. Now, I'm going to try to get some sleep – that's if that lot at the bar would make less noise. I'll be glad when they've run out of ale!'

Mary nodded her agreement. There were obviously plenty on board who were not short of money judging by the noise and amount of beer that was being consumed. She settled herself as comfortably as she could and instructed Katie and Tommy to try to sleep. She closed her eyes, wondering just what faced her when they finally arrived in the morning.

There hadn't been much sleep. In fact it had been a terrible journey. Once out of the protection of the land the ship had been tossed around like a cork and many people, including both Katie and Lizzie, had been sick. She and Tommy had not succumbed but she was very thankful when in the miserable grey light of the winter dawn they finally sailed into the Liffey. The air smelled of salt and dampness and the odours of the factories and sheds that lined the North Wall but she didn't mind. After the stink of the saloon it was heaven, she thought. Her gaze wandered over the city and the misty outline of the Dublin Mountains that ringed it. She hadn't realised that the open countryside was so near. Maybe they could take a trip out one day. They'd all enjoy that.

Katie and Lizzie, both pale and tired and confused, clung tightly to her skirts while she and Tommy struggled with the bundles. At first glance Dublin didn't look very different to Liverpool, not quite as big or as grand but of course she wasn't in the heart of the city yet.

'How do I get to the Coombe?' she asked one of the deck hands.

'You walk down the Quays, past the Custom House, down the Ormond Quay to the Four Courts. Then cross the Liffey into Winetavern Street, go straight up Nicholas Street and Patrick Street to the Cathedral and then turn right. That's the Coombe.'

Mary thanked him and followed the crowds along the dock road. It seemed to be quite a way and she wished she could have afforded the tram fare but she cheered herself up with the thought that even though there had been no one to meet them there was bound to be a warm welcome when they finally arrived.

They had trudged along for what seemed like miles, admiring the grand buildings that flanked the Quays and the shops and the stalls of street vendors. Mary also noticed that there were a lot of beggars and poor people and a lot of obviously unemployed men on the streets, but it didn't seem to be any worse than Liverpool. They had stopped to rest a few times and outside the Four Courts she had been moved on by a burly member of the Dublin City Police Force.

'Sir, I'm not a beggar! I've just arrived from Liverpool. I'm trying to find Weavers Street in the Coombe. Is it far, please?' she'd asked.

He'd taken pity on her. 'Ah, it's not far now. Go straight across the bridge, up that road and turn right at the top and you'll be there. Is it visiting, you are?'

She'd smiled for the first time that day. 'Yes, and I was beginning to wonder if it was worth it.'

'Sure, they'll have the kettle on ready for you. It's a desperate journey that at this time of year.'

She'd thanked him and trudged on in the direction he'd pointed out.

Beyond the huge, ornate St Patrick's Cathedral the houses she passed didn't look very inviting. This was obviously a poor part of the city. She could see that once they'd been very grand dwellings but decades of neglect had rendered them little better than slums. Doors were standing wide open despite the cold weather. Their paint was peeling; the steps leading up to them were worn and cracked. The once beautiful glass fanlights above them were broken, dirty and fly-speckled. The long hallways beyond were dark and dirty and smelled fetid. The big sash windows were warped and rotten, many with broken panes stuffed with rags or newspapers. Rubbish was strewn across the filthy cobbles and women, their shawls pulled tightly to them and with barefoot children clinging to their skirts, stood in groups gossiping. It wasn't much better than Newsham Street and she thought of her words to the policeman. What had she done?

Weavers Street was not much better. It had clearly once been a fine street bounded by tall Georgian houses with a tiny park at its centre. Now the park and its railings were gone; just a patch of scrubby grass remained and seemed to be a rubbish dump of sorts where mangy dogs and cats foraged amongst the ashes and debris.

'Is this it, Mam?' Katie asked, looking around with trepidation.

'Yes. Well, at least there's no more walking. Now, which one is number fourteen?' She tried to sound far more cheerful than she felt. There were no numbers on any of the old houses so she asked an old woman who was sitting on the steps of the nearest house.

'Is it Molly Brennan you're after looking for?' she enquired.

'Yes. She's my aunt.'

'Ah, then you must be Mary McGann and all the way from Liverpool.'

'I am.'

'I'm Biddy Malone and it's here she lives. The two pair front she has. That door there.'

Mary thanked her and knocked, wondering just what a 'two pair front' was.

The door was opened by a short, stout, grey-haired woman in her sixties.

'Aunty Molly? It's Mary.'

'Ah, God, aren't ye the spit of your poor mam, God rest her! Come on in with ye, Mary, and the childer too.'

Mary was smothered in a suffocating hug and for the first time since she had left Liverpool she relaxed. At least she was welcome.

'Was it a desperate journey altogether?' Molly asked, shooing the tired, bewildered children into the room ahead of her.

'I suppose it was but never mind, we're here now.'

'Thanks be to God! Now, I've the kettle on. There's only meself here at the minute. Rita and Davy are at work and the kids are at school. The others don't live with me now, thanks be to God, it was a terrible crush,' she announced as she bustled about wetting the tea.

Mary was thankful that they didn't seem too over-crowded. 'Do you just have this room?' she asked, glancing around. It was a very big room with a high ceiling, a big window and a large and very ornate fireplace that had seen better days and was totally unsuited to the purpose of cooking. There seemed to be no range or oven.

'No, there's the other room. Rita and Davy and the kids have that. I sleep in here.'

Mary wondered where she and the children would sleep but she decided not to press the matter yet.

'Now, sit yourselves down and have this tea, then we'll sort everything out.'

Mary was very thankful of both the seat and the tea. She had had nothing to eat or drink since the night before.

'Mam, I'm starving!' Tommy protested.

'Ah, God luv him. Wait now while I cut ye some soda bread. It's all I have in the house at the minute. When ye're ready, Mary, I'll take ye to the shops,' Molly said cheerfully, sawing at a large, flat, round cake of bread.

'That will be great. I do have some money, I'm not asking you to keep us, but I will need to find work. What does Rita do?'

'Isn't she the fortunate one. She's working for Bolands Flour Mills. Sure, she comes home covered in it from head to toe but that's no hardship, and Davy's in work too at the minute. On the docks, thanks be to God. Aren't I the fortunate woman to have them both with work?'

Mary smiled her agreement. Things didn't look too bad at all.

After they'd all had a rest Molly showed them where they could keep their few things and the straw-stuffed mattresses on which they would sleep, which were kept under the large iron-framed bed in the other room. Mary was a little anxious that they would be sleeping in the same room as Molly but said nothing. It was good of Molly to take them all in.

On the way to O'Keefe's, the little huckster's shop on the corner, Mary was introduced to the neighbours, who all welcomed her warmly if a little curiously. They were clearly wondering just why a young woman with three children would leave a husband behind her in a fine place like Liverpool. Molly had not enlightened them.

Mrs O'Keefe was a thin, dark-haired, gossipy woman whose dark eyes missed nothing.

'And is this the niece from Liverpool, Molly?'

'It is so, Annie.'

'And isn't she a fine-looking girl too.'

Mary smiled. 'It's very good of Aunty Molly to put us up.'

'It is so, a living saint she is.'

'Ah, Annie, give over with that!'

'Well, there's not many who would take you in after you being thrown out and all.'

Mary bit back the words that sprang to her lips, the colour rising in her cheeks.

'Now ye know the circumstances, Annie. Aren't ye the only one about here who does and didn't I tell you in confidence,' Molly said with a note of censure in her voice.

'You did too, Molly, and I'm not a woman to betray confidences. There's no understanding some men, Mary. I mean no offence.'

'Then there's none taken,' Mary replied sharply, turning her attention to the shopping for which she paid as swiftly as she could.

That afternoon she had taken Katie and Tommy to the schools they would attend and then they'd explored the neighbouring streets to get to know their way around. When they returned, they found Molly starting to prepare the tea and the room full of children.

'This lot belong to Rita and Davy and there's a couple of their friends as well. That's Maura, she's the eldest, then Bernie, then Niall, then Brendan, and then little Kathleen, and the one trick-acting under the table is Noreen. She'd have the heart across ye with her antics! Say hello to Katie and Tommy and give little Lizzie a bit of a wave, sure the poor little thing can't speak or hear, God have mercy on her. They're your cousins and so is Mary.'

Mary smiled and kissed the girls and it wasn't long before she noticed that Tommy and Brendan seemed to have struck up a friendship. She was pleased to see that little Kathleen was sitting beside Lizzie and holding her hand. It made her feel so relieved that the children seemed to be getting on with their cousins.

Molly chased some of them out to play while she and Mary set the table and prepared the meal. At six o'clock Rita arrived home and, as her mother had predicted, she was covered in a layer of flour. She was a tall, good-looking girl with dark hair and eyes and Mary took an instant liking to her.

'You're very welcome here, Mary. Mam told me about himself and the way of going on he has. It's a living disgrace is what I say.'

'Thanks, Rita. It . . . it hasn't been easy.'

'Sit down and I'll wet the tea,' Molly instructed.

'Wait a while, Mam, until I take off this auld overall. Sure to God that flour gets everywhere. Davy should be home soon now and starving too,' she laughed. 'Youse lot sit round the table now and don't be snatching and grabbing. Don't I have the divil's own job putting manners on them. Is it the same with you, Mary?'

'It's not easy, especially with meladdo there,' Mary agreed, fixing Tommy with a glare.

'Well, they'll all settle in soon,' Molly predicted cheerfully.

Davy arrived ten minutes later. He was a burly young man with thick auburn hair and a mass of freckles. He greeted Molly, Rita and his children in a tired and rather sullen manner, or so Mary thought.

'And this is Mary. I told you about her, remember?' Rita said encouragingly.

'You're welcome, Mary,' he said but rather ungraciously. However, he shook her hand before sitting down and pulling off his work boots.

Molly and Rita exchanged glances, glances that Mary caught, and for the first time that day she felt as though she were not really welcome. At least, not by Davy Rafferty.

Chapter Eight

❦

'ARE YOU HAPPY HERE, Mary?' Rita asked as they walked to work on a cold February morning. Although it was still early and dark, the streets were busy and the cobbles rang with the sound of workmen's boots, carts' wheels and horses' hooves. In the dim light of the gas streetlamps the mist from the river hung in thin damp ribbon-like strands.

'I suppose I am. You've all been good to us and I have work, what more can I ask?'

They had settled in with Molly and her family very well. Mary had taken over some of the chores from her aunt and as she was by nature tidy the place didn't seem too cluttered or crowded. Rita had 'spoken for her' to her foreman and after a couple of weeks Mary had been given a job in the flour mill with her cousin. They worked in the bagging room, where the refined flour came down huge metal chutes and into big wooden trays. Here, a small army of girls and women scooped it up with small, wooden-handled shovels and transferred it into large paper bags and small sacks for distribution to shops all over the city. Rita often said it was a mercy they didn't have to fill the big sacks that went to the bakeries, that really *was* back-breaking work.

'You never speak about himself back there. Do you miss him at all?' Rita asked.

Mary thought hard. Did she miss Frank? If she were really truthful she had to admit that there were times when she hardly thought about him, and yet there were other times when she *did*. She wondered if he was all right, if he was coping, looking after himself, missing the children, but, strangely, never if he was missing her. Now she realised that she never missed his touch or their conversations, particularly as they had dwindled over the last months. At the end he'd hardly spoken to her from one day to the next.

'No, I don't think I do. I sometimes wonder if he's managing or missing the children.'

'Then you don't still love him?'

Mary shrugged.

'Sure, I think I'd die if Davy just cast me aside. No offence intended, Mary. You know I wouldn't want to be upsetting you.'

Mary nodded. 'I know and you're lucky, Rita,' she answered, then fell silent. Rita *was* lucky. She idolised her husband and they seemed to get on well together although from a few remarks Molly had made she gathered that her aunt didn't share the high opinion that Rita had of Davy Rafferty. He was a strange man, she mused: sometimes jovial and amiable, at other times taciturn and even snappy. She never knew how to take him and even when he was laughing and joking – usually after he had drink taken – she got the feeling that he didn't like her or trust her. Once or twice she had caught him watching her speculatively and it had disturbed her. Why, she just couldn't quite put her finger on.

They'd been with Molly for three weeks now and she had got to know the neighbours and grown used to their ways and sayings. In the main they were good, hard-working, God-fearing people. Oh, there were the usual drunks, gamblers and idlers she supposed you found in any neighbourhood, and they all fought poverty, dirt and disease on a daily basis, but she was used to that. The children had all settled well even though Lizzie didn't go to school. Mary had insisted that the child was better off at home with herself and she had to admit that Lizzie seemed happy enough.

Tommy and Brendan had become firm friends and were usually partners in any devilment or mischief that was going on. Sometimes she thought that he was growing into a desperate hooligan without his father's strict hand but there was nothing she could do about that. Whenever she bemoaned the fact all she heard from Molly was, 'Ah, the world's a hard place, Mary, and they're only chisslers for a few years!' to which Rita usually replied, 'And one of these days we'll be after having the polis on the doorstep over them, Mam, the pair of eejits that they are! You mark my words.'

Mary smiled to herself. Despite her dark warnings Rita was quite happy to leave her children's welfare in the hands of their granny while she worked and frequently went out with Davy, especially at the weekends. Nor did Molly complain about the amount of money that was spent on the outings as usually on Sundays, if the weather was dry, the couple took their children and Mary's three for a walk on St Stephen's Green or in the Phoenix Park. Occasionally Mary accompanied them but usually she stayed at home with Molly and took advantage of the peace and quiet.

As they neared the flour mill on the banks of the Liffey they were joined by other girls and women, some calling out greetings and complaints about the rawness of the morning. A group joined them and the topic of conversation turned to the annual night out at Flattery's Oyster and Porter Bar.

'Ye *are* coming with us, Mary?' Sarah Jane O'Brien demanded.

'I don't know if I can afford it,' Mary answered doubtfully. She had never gone on such an outing in her life before and it took all her wages to feed and clothe them and give Molly a few shillings for the roof over their heads.

Sarah Jane wasn't going to give up easily, though. 'It's only once a year!'

'But you've all had a year to save up!' Mary laughed.

'Ah, go on, Mary. It'll do you good to get out and enjoy yourself for once. I'll give you a few shillings,' Rita offered.

'Rita, I couldn't but it's very good of you,' Mary protested.

'I can afford it, Mary. Didn't you just say we've all been saving up. I'll share with you.'

Mary smiled at her cousin. She really was a generous girl.

'There now, ye've no excuse. We'll have a grand night,' Sarah Jane said triumphantly.

'Ye never know, I might catch meself a decent feller,' Kath Noonan laughed, winking at Mary.

'And pigs might fly, Kath!' Sarah Jane retorted. Kath had the knack of picking the most useless and unsuitable men in the city.

'That one has her poor mam heart-scalded!' Rita muttered to Mary. 'She never seems to learn.'

'Some never do,' Mary whispered back.

'Mary, you're a fine-looking girl, you shouldn't have any trouble getting yourself an eejit of a feller to give you a good time,' Sarah Jane laughed.

'I'm not looking for a feller, eejit or otherwise, thank you!' Mary retorted good-naturedly. The women she worked with knew she was married but had been told that

Frank had deserted her. It saved face and innumerable questions.

They all trooped into the bagging room where every-thing was covered in white dust. It got up your nose, into your eyes and hair and dried the back of the throat so much that after an hour or two talking was almost painful. Mary concentrated on the forthcoming evening and won-dered what she had to wear that was halfway decent. Maybe on the way home Rita would accompany her to one of the street markets, although she didn't have much money to spare. That was nothing new, she thought with resignation.

She had confided her thoughts to her cousin during their dinner break and they had been met with approval but at the end of the day she was sorry she had mentioned it. She was tired. Her arms and back were aching, her eyes felt gritty and there was a slight throbbing over her left eye.

'Some fresh air will sort all that out and the chat will lighten your spirits,' Rita stated firmly, dismissing her complaints. Rita enjoyed shopping.

The air, though far from fresh, did help and by the time they reached Henry Street, where they intended to do some food shopping first, Mary felt better. They wandered past the stalls heaped with vegetables from the country districts and Rita stopped and fingered some cabbages.

'They're not very big. How much are you wanting for them?' she asked.

'Two fer the price of one! The bargain of the day, ma'am, at a penny an' I had nothing to do with the rearin' of them. Blame that on the feller I had them off this morning when ye were still snug in your bed an' I was out in the wet an' the slime!' the stall-holder replied.

'Did you hear that, Mary? When we were in our beds! Weren't we up before the dawn ourselves!' Rita replied with spirit.

'That's as may be, ma'am, a penny is me price.'

'I'll take them even though they're no more than babbies.'

'There's no pleasing some folk! Aren't I after giving them away at that price and won't they be gracin' your bacon this very night, ma'am.'

'Crubeens it is tonight,' Rita shot back.

'Begod! Crubeens an' it's only Thursday! There's wealth for ye!'

Mary laughed. It was almost like being back in Great Homer Street Market.

Further down there were two or three women selling second-hand clothes and both girls rummaged through the piles.

'Here, Mary, this will suit you very well,' Rita called, holding up a brown tweed skirt. 'She's asking sixpence for it but it's good thick tweed and plenty of wear in it yet.'

'From the county of Donegal, too, ma'am, and a bargain,' the woman added.

Mary looked doubtful. It was good quality and hardly worn but it was a bit dear.

Seeing the hesitation and not wanting to lose a sale at the end of a none-too-successful day the woman rummaged around and found a brown cord three-quarter-length jacket. 'Now ye have a costume that's fit for the Quality and for the bargain price of one and six! Doesn't it look grand with the fine head of hair ye have, ma'am?' As further persuasion the jacket was held against Mary's hair.

'It *does* suit you, Mary, and it's great quality,' Rita urged.

'I can't afford to buy it *and* have a night out,' Mary hissed, feeling embarrassed.

'Mary, haven't I already said I'd treat you? Here, we'll take it.' Rita delved into her purse and handed the coins over before Mary could stop her.

'God bless ye for the generous woman ye are!' The stall-holder beamed at them both and handed over the folded clothes.

'Oh, Rita! You're too good!' Mary cried, hugging her.

'Don't you deserve a bit of a treat? You work so hard and you never go out.'

'But you haven't bought yourself anything!' Mary protested.

'Ah, haven't I the good coat Davy bought me at Christmas and the red wool skirt I bought myself at the same time and my good white blouse? Now we'd better get home or Mam'll think we've deserted her and be giving out that she's the crubeens boiled and no cabbage to go with them.'

When they arrived home it was to a scene of chaos. All the children seemed to be fighting or arguing except for Tommy and Brendan who were inexplicably sitting on Molly's knees. Davy was in and was sitting by the fire engrossed in a newspaper, looking far from happy, and there was no sign of any meal being prepared at all.

'In the name of all the saints, what ails you, Mam?' Rita cried.

'What's wrong with those two?' Mary demanded.

'Haven't the pair of them had the heart across me! Haven't I been up at the Mater hospital with them for hours!' Molly replied, glaring at her son-in-law.

'And I a man coming in from his work to bedlam and no food on the table!' Davy retorted, glaring back.

Obviously there had been a row, Mary surmised.

'At the Mater? What for?' Rita asked, looking concerned.

'After school didn't they go off to see the cattle being driven to the meat factory by Cork Street Fever Hospital? When the poor beasts are so terrified that they stampede down those narrow streets like the gathering swine and with the corner boys all roarin' and chasin' them.'

'Brendan, haven't I told you a hundred times to stay away from there on Thursdays? You know it's the day the cattle are driven to the slaughter and don't they know it too. Aren't they mad with fear and terror!' Rita cried.

Mary rushed across to her son who was looking pale and had bandages on his arm and leg. On Thursdays the cattle brought from the outlying farms were driven through the streets at a frightening pace by the drovers armed with sticks and no one was really safe as the poor, sweating, stumbling animals crashed about.

'What happened, Tommy? Are you badly hurt?'

'Mam, it was all so quick! We were standing on the corner by the Disinfectant Yard of the Fever Hospital and suddenly a group of them came at us! They were all frothing at the mouth and roaring! We tried to run into one of the shops but they were too quick and then I slipped and fell and one trampled me!'

'Oh, Jesus, Mary and Joseph! You could have been killed!' Mary cried, her face paling at the thought.

'It's only the mercy of God and His Holy Mother that they weren't. Just cuts and bruises, the pair of them,' Molly declared.

'I should be takin' me belt to the pair of ye!' Davy growled.

Rita gathered her son to her. 'Thanks be to God your granny was here to see to you! Well, let that be a lesson to you. And what have you been told about going near that Fever Hospital? You'll catch something nasty and then they'll take you in and no one will be able to come and see you in case we all get it! Oh, you'll be the death of me yet!'

'Well, do you think that now a man could get some peace and a bit of something to eat?' Davy shouted, losing his temper entirely.

'And is that all ye care about, your belly?' Molly shouted back. She had had such a fright when Tommy had limped in and told her that he and Brendan had been 'trampled', she was barely recovered herself.

'Davy, will you sit down and read your paper. We'll have the meal on the table in a few minutes,' Rita tried to pacify him, feeling guilty that they had lingered at the market buying clothes.

'There'll be no meal on the table this hour is what I'm thinking! I might as well go to the pub!' he replied, storming out.

'Oh, Rita, I'm sorry! We shouldn't have gone looking for clothes. If we hadn't then we would have been home,' Mary cried guiltily.

'Ah, take no notice of that feller. Wasn't he only looking for an excuse to go drinking. I could see the puss on him the moment he came in,' Molly said derisively.

'Mam, do you blame him? The place like a lunatic asylum, no tea and no sign of me either! Isn't that enough to drive a man to drink?'

Mary thought it was time to intervene. 'Right, all of you children in the other room! You too, Brendan and Tommy. And no noise out of you. Molly, put the kettle on while I make a start on this cabbage and put the pig's feet in to boil. That's the last time I go gallivanting after work!' she declared firmly, catching up the big iron cooking pot and the cabbages, which had been hastily dumped on the table and forgotten amidst the uproar.

Chapter Nine

'Y E LOOK VERY WELL, Mary. Those colours suit ye,' Molly said admiringly.

Mary smiled and looked at herself in the mirror. Her aunt was right, the dark brown cord jacket was set off by the high-necked white blouse she'd bought in Paddy's Market. She'd swept her hair up and the narrow-brimmed brown and beige hat she'd borrowed for the occasion was perched at a jaunty angle. She had put on a little weight and it somehow made her look younger than twenty-eight.

'And red certainly suits Rita,' she commented, smiling approvingly at her cousin who wore a red skirt, a white blouse and a smart red coat trimmed with black braid.

'Don't you be after having too much drink taken,' Davy instructed his wife a little sharply.

'Would you just listen to him that came falling in the door last Friday!' Rita laughed good-naturedly.

'Get off the pair of ye and enjoy yourselves,' Molly urged, steering them both towards the door.

'I've never tasted either oysters or porter,' Mary confided as they walked to meet the others.

'Then you'd better go easy with the porter or it will go straight to your head. They do say oysters are an acquired taste, but I like them well enough.'

'Do they only sell porter?' Mary asked, thinking that she'd really prefer a port and lemonade or even a glass of Madeira wine.

'No, they sell all kinds of drinks.' Rita laughed. 'You can tell you don't drink much.'

'There was never the money or the occasion, except for weddings and funerals.'

'Well, you mind what I said and watch the porter.'

'I will indeed!' Mary promised.

They met up with the others on the corner of Anne Street and there were exclamations of delight and admiration for the outfits they'd all managed to conjure up – mainly by begging and borrowing from sisters, cousins and neighbours.

The Oyster Bar was a dark, low-ceilinged, smallish place further up Anne Street and was already crowded.

'Sarah Jane, go and see if you can find us some room at that table over in the corner while Mary and me go and find a barmaid,' Rita instructed.

Sarah Jane and the others pushed and elbowed their

way through the throng, while Rita informed the barmaid: 'There's six of us for oysters and five for porter.' Then she turned to Mary. 'What will you have?'

'Do you have any Madeira wine?' Mary asked a little hesitantly.

'Ma'am, this isn't the Imperial Hotel!' the woman replied with heavy sarcasm.

'Then maybe port wine?' Mary thought it best not to ask for lemonade as well.

'A large or a small glass?'

'Large,' Rita said before Mary could reply. 'We're at the table in the corner.'

The men who had been occupying the table had moved after much light-hearted bantering with the girls and soon the drinks and the oysters were brought. Mary looked at the plate of greyish-green shells with apprehension. 'How are you supposed to eat them? She's brought no knives or spoons.'

They all fell about laughing at her inexperience until Rita explained that you just tipped them down your throat, directly from the shell.

'Go on, Mary, they won't poison you!' Maura Grennan urged.

Mary lifted a shell gingerly to her lips.

'Tip back your head!' Sarah Jane instructed.

Mary did so and swallowed hard. It tasted salty and rather bland. It was a very strange experience.

'Well?' Maura enquired.

'Not bad,' Mary said cautiously.

Rita laughed and raised her eyes to the smoke-stained ceiling.

After three more drinks Mary felt decidedly light-headed but was enjoying herself. They were a lively group and there was much laughter and as the evening wore on the singing and the dancing began. It was mainly traditional dancing that Mary couldn't do, but she was dragged to her feet for a couple of rather stilted and confined reels which left her breathless and flushed. When yet another glass of port appeared she protested but the irrepressible Sarah Jane just laughed and waved aside her protests.

Before she had time to take even a sip she was hauled to her feet by a tall and good-looking young stevedore.

'Oh, please, I can't catch my breath!' she cried.

'And sure a fine-looking girl like you can't be sitting on your own!' he laughed.

'I'm not on my own.'

'Well, I don't see anyone else sitting with you. Come on and take a turn around the floor with me.'

'It's a bit crushed.'

' 'Tis nothing! I've seen fifty people on their feet in here many a night.'

She could say nothing else and so, smiling up at him, she let him guide her towards the dancers.

'You're not from Dublin, are you?' he shouted over the din.

'No. Liverpool.'

'I was in Liverpool once myself, a grand place it is.'

'It is indeed.'

'So, why did you leave it?'

'My husband . . . died, so I came to live with my aunt.' She could have bitten her tongue. Now he would think she was available. 'But I have my children to care for,' she added hastily.

'How many have you?'

'Seven,' she lied.

'Begod! Did you wear the poor feller out?'

She hid a smile but at least the ploy had worked. At the end of the dance he led her back to the table. She had no wish to pick up any man. She had enough problems already.

'I thought you were getting along famously with your man over there,' Maura said curiously. 'What did you say to him that made him take fright?'

'I told him I had seven children and no husband.'

Rita pealed with laughter. 'Holy God! Mary, aren't you a gas!'

'I remembered a woman telling me that there's not many men who would take on a woman with a gang of kids and anyway, apart from not wanting to get mixed up with men, I'm not free to do so.'

Rita nodded. She supposed Mary was taking the sensible attitude.

'Ah, well, it's only a bit of fun anyway.' She laughed again. 'Now, Maura, have you enough drink taken to give us a song?'

'Try and shut her up! You know what she's like after a few glasses of porter!' Sarah Jane replied, rolling her eyes expressively.

When they finally left the Oyster Bar it was late and as the fresh air hit her Mary swayed. 'Oh, Rita, I think I've had one glass of port too many!'

'Mary McGann, I believe you're drunk!' Rita cried, a little unsteady herself.

'You'll have a head the size of a bull in the morning!' Maura giggled.

'Oh, I hope not! I've got to take Tommy back to the hospital,' Mary groaned. Her head was beginning to spin and she clung to Rita's arm. Why had she been so stupid as to drink so much when she wasn't used to it?

She barely remembered the journey home. Once safely in the door, with much shushing and stifled giggling, Rita helped her to undress and lie down on the mattress, which made her feel even worse. The whole room began to revolve sickeningly when she closed her eyes.

She struggled to sit up, afraid to lie flat in case the awful nausea swamped her again. Rita had gone to bed and Molly was snoring gently. The three children were curled up sound asleep. Oh, God! Maybe a cup of water would help, she thought, trying to get to her feet.

'Mary, what ails you?'

Davy's voice seemed to come from far away but she realised that he was helping her to get up. She must have wakened him.

'I . . . I don't feel very well. I think I had too much port wine.'

'And you not used to the drink. Come on, a bit of fresh air will do you good.'

He had his arm around her waist and she leaned heavily against him as he led her towards the door.

'Davy, wait! I . . . I can't go out into the street like this, in my nightdress!'

'Here, put this old shawl of Molly's on.' He dragged the garment from its hook and put it around her shoulders. 'It looks better on you than it does on her.'

Mary began to feel uneasy. Bad as she felt she didn't want to be alone with him in the dark and empty hall-way. 'Davy, I think that just a drink of water will help,' she protested feebly. She had never felt so ill in her entire life.

'Later, after the fresh air. Believe me, I know about these things.'

His grip had tightened and she began to feel afraid. Yet if she cried out, made a fuss, she would wake them all and how would it look? She had no desire to upset either her aunt or Rita, they had both been so good to her.

Once in the hall she tried to draw away from him. 'Davy, I'm fine!'

'Sure, you're far from that, Mary.' He pushed a strand of hair from her face. 'But even though you're jarred you're a good-looking woman. I thought that from the first time I set eyes on you.'

'Please, Davy! You know I'm married!'

'And isn't he an eejit to have let you go? If you were my wife I wouldn't be so stupid. You must miss him – well, miss being in bed with him. Do you miss it, Mary?'

She could feel his breath on her face and she tried to draw back. 'No! No, I . . . I don't miss him, not in *that* way!' she cried.

'Ah, don't be codding me! You're a young, healthy woman with only three kids, there's plenty of life in you yet. And with a *proper* man . . .'

She pushed him away. 'Stop it! I've never done anything to encourage you! Think about Rita and your children. I could *never* hurt Rita!' She prayed he wouldn't do anything that would make her have to fight him. She hadn't the strength; she felt too ill.

To her great relief he turned abruptly away. 'Do you know what you are, Mary McGann? You're a prick-teaser! Ever since you came here you've been flaunting yourself. Don't think I haven't noticed it even if that auld one in there hasn't!'

'I've done no such thing! How can you say such . . . such crude and unjust things about me?' she cried, her cheeks burning at his vulgar insinuations.

'Go to hell! I hope you're as sick as a pig in the morning! Just you stay away from me in the future!' he snarled and stormed back inside.

Mary clutched the broken banister rail for support. She felt terrible. She had sensed only that he didn't like her, but all the time he had been watching her, waiting for an opportunity . . . Now, she realised, she had made an enemy. She dragged herself back into the room and poured herself a mug of water from the big enamel jug on the top of the dresser. At least he'd get his wish, she felt as 'sick as a pig' already.

She awoke next morning with her head pounding and her mouth dry and foul-tasting. She raised herself on one elbow and groaned.

'I can see ye all had a good time!' Molly held out a mug.

'Oh, I'm never going to touch port wine ever again. What is it?' she moaned.

'A "hair of the dog". Drink it down in one gulp and ye'll be as right as rain!'

Mary took the mug but baulked at the smell of the whiskey. 'Oh, Aunt Molly, I . . . I can't face it! I can't face *anything*!'

'Get it down you, girl, it's the only thing!' Molly urged.

Taking a deep breath Mary drained the mug and then began to cough and splutter.

'Mam, are you sick?' Katie asked worriedly.

'She'll be grand in a few minutes. Now, off with ye and Noreen to Kennedy's bake shop and don't let them palm ye off with the catskin! I'll have no cinders from the oven in the crust of *my* bread! And no trick-acting on the way back or ye'll have the bread destroyed altogether.'

Mary lay down again while Molly chattered on nineteen to the dozen about the amount of work there was to be done that day, which was the busiest of the entire week.

She closed her eyes and remembered what had happened with Davy. She was certain she had never given him any encouragement. Oh, if only she hadn't drunk so much, she would have been safely in bed and asleep before he'd even come in. He'd been drinking too, she'd smelled it on his breath. What should she do now? She couldn't go back to Liverpool, that was certain. And she had nowhere else to go. Nowhere. She was surrounded by family yet she had never felt more alone. Wearily she acknowledged she would just have to stay here and try to keep out of his way.

Chapter Ten

MOLLY'S 'CURE' HAD WORKED but Mary continued to worry about her situation all day. A couple of the other women had covered for her at work so she could take Tommy to the Mater hospital. While she sat waiting for him to be checked over, she had been utterly preoccupied, and it was no better later as she helped Molly and Rita with the chores: her mind had not been fully on the tasks, which had prompted her aunt to ask, 'Mary, what ails ye?'

'Nothing. Oh, I suppose it's thinking about all the work we've to do,' she'd replied.

That evening Rita and Davy went out and she was thankful. Davy hadn't spoken a word to her all day but she'd caught the venomous looks he'd shot at her and had prayed that the other women hadn't noticed. It made her feel very uncomfortable.

'I'll be taking to my bed early tonight,' Molly announced

after they had finished tidying up and had got the children settled.

'So will I, I still haven't got over last night,' Mary replied. 'But first I must write to Nellie, it's almost two weeks since her last letter arrived and she'll think I've forgotten all about them.'

'Sure, she'll think no such thing! Won't she have enough on her plate? It seems to be nothing but work and expense on Saturdays or maybe it's just old and crabby I'm getting.'

Mary smiled at her. 'You're certainly not crabby. Don't you have enough to put up with with all of us living on top of you when you should be having some peace and quiet?'

'Ah, what would I do with peace and quiet? I'd be lonely. I'd miss ye all,' Molly admitted with a wry smile.

Mary got the writing materials and sat at the table by the window. She would tell Nellie that she was well and happy and so were the children. It wasn't strictly the truth, of course. She *was* well but not happy, Davy had seen to that. She chewed the end of the pen thoughtfully. Was it in fact possible to go back to Liverpool? Should she try again to talk some sense into Frank? Would he relent? After all, she *had* been true to her word. She *had* left. She looked around the room. It was warm and cheerful and peaceful and she was fond of Molly, Rita and her young cousins. She enjoyed working and having her own money. Oh, if only

Davy hadn't got the wrong idea about her. No, she really didn't want to go back to Liverpool and Frank, nor did she want to leave here, but what was she to do?

She finally made up her mind after pondering the situation for a long while – so long that Molly asked her did she intend to write that letter at all or was she just trying to devour the only pen they possessed? She'd made up her mind to talk to Davy, have it out with him and clear the air so life here would be comfortable. She knew however it would be no use doing so when he and Rita finally came home tonight. If his past record was anything to go by he would be half drunk and she had no intention of trying to talk sense into him when he was in that state. No, she would have to find an opportunity tomorrow.

That opportunity presented itself when next morning after Mass Molly declared that, as it was a fine day, she and Rita would take the children up to St Stephen's Green, then do some window shopping in Grafton Street. Window shopping was all they could afford with the prices they charged in the shops along *that* street, she added. Full of relief mixed with trepidation, Mary declined the invitation to join them, saying reluctantly that she had a mound of mending to do.

When they'd gone she put on the kettle and put two mugs on the table. Davy was ignoring her, studiously reading his newspaper. Well, it was now or never, she thought, taking a deep breath.

'Davy, put down that paper and have this tea. I want to talk to you,' she announced firmly.

'What about? I've nothing to say to you,' he said sullenly, rattling the paper to show his annoyance.

'But I've plenty to say to you. Put down that paper.' Unconsciously she placed her hands on her hips and the gesture startled him. He'd never seen her look so forceful.

'So, say your piece,' he snapped.

'You know how fond I am of Molly and Rita and all the children and I don't want to have to leave here. Davy, I've never given you any encouragement. Never deliberately "flaunted myself". My marriage to Frank might not have worked out, but that wasn't my fault and I take the vows I made on my wedding day very seriously, including "forsaking all others".'

'Well, you certainly don't give that impression!' he interrupted angrily. He wasn't having her giving out to him like this. Who did she think she was?

'Davy, what have I done? What have I said to make you think like that?' she demanded.

'Oh, don't you play the innocent, Mary!'

'I'm not! I honestly don't know. Tell me?'

He looked down at his boots. 'If you don't know, sure I'm not after telling you.'

'Oh, you're impossible! I've never thought of you like . . . like that. To me you're Rita's husband and that's all. I'm not looking for anything else from you except . . . friendship.'

'Friendship! Ah, that's a laugh! Aren't you always giving me the eye, pushing past me, making sure you touch me. I *know* what you're at, Mary, and it's not *friendship*!'

She could see it was useless. 'Well, I don't care what you *think*, Davy, I *know* I don't do any of those things. If we're going to continue to live under the same roof we'd better come to some agreement. I won't have Molly or Rita upset and I don't want a repeat of the other night's performance.'

He stood up, his face red and angry. '*You* don't want a repeat performance as you call it! *You* won't have Rita or the auld one upset! You come here, running away from your husband on some half-baked excuse, which sounds to me as though you were up to your tricks over there, and—'

Mary lost her temper. 'Running away from my husband! My *tricks*! How dare you, Davy! You know nothing at all of what went on!'

'I know enough,' he shouted.

She tried again. 'Shouting is getting us nowhere. If . . . if I've ever given you the wrong impression then I'm sorry, what else can I say? I never meant to. Can't we put it all behind us, forget all the things that have been said and done and start again? I just want to go on living here in peace. Please, Davy?'

He stared at her. She was a beautiful woman and try though he might he knew he wanted her and wouldn't rest until he had her. No matter how prim and proper she acted, just being in the same room as her drove him mad. It wasn't that he didn't love Rita, he did, but Mary was like a drug to his senses and he couldn't get her out of his mind. He didn't know why she had this effect on him, she just did, and there was nothing he could do about it. There was only one solution. She had to leave.

'It won't work, Mary. I . . . I can't help how I feel.'

Mary was taken aback. All the anger seemed to have left him.

'Davy, please?' she tried again.

'Mary, don't you know how beautiful you are? Don't you know the effect you have on a man?' he pleaded.

She shook her head. 'No! No, I'm *not* beautiful!'

He could stand it no longer. Quickly he crossed the room and took her in his arms, his desire for her so strong, so overwhelming, he threw all caution to the winds.

'Mary, you're the most beautiful woman I've ever seen!'

Horrified, she started to struggle. 'No! No! You can't do this, Davy!'

'Mary, I want you! I've wanted you from the minute I saw you!'

He was strong and he was crushing her but she continued to struggle. Then his lips were pressing against hers, cutting off her protests and her very breath. She had to do something to stop him, she couldn't let this happen, she *wouldn't* let it happen! With all the strength she could muster she brought her knee up and caught him hard in the groin.

'You bitch!' he groaned, doubling up in pain and staggering away from her. 'You teasing, tormenting little whore!'

She was fighting for her breath. 'Davy, I . . . had to! Don't you understand I couldn't . . . let you . . .'

Tears of agony stung his eyes. No one had ever done this to him before, not even a feller in a street fight! He was beside himself with rage and humiliation. God, how he hated her!

Mary bit her lip. What should she do? Try to help him? Try to ease him into a chair or just leave him?

Pride gave him strength and he at last managed to straighten up and cling to the back of a chair. 'Get out, you bitch! You're not staying here a minute longer! You're a whore, a common tart even though you act the innocent. It's all part of your act. The deserted wife, butter wouldn't melt in your mouth! Like hell! Get out or I'll tell the auld one just what kind of a baggage you really are and don't think Rita will believe you either! She'll believe *me*!'

Mary paled and began to shake. Oh, God! Now what was she to do? There was no doubting him. He *would* tell Molly and Rita. In that moment she began to hate Frank. This was all his fault. He had driven her away and into this mess. She raised a shaking hand to her face. *Was* she beautiful? Richie had said the same thing. She'd never believed she was. At best she'd only ever thought she was attractive and if she was . . . well, it was a curse if this was the outcome. But what was she to *do*?

With Davy still glaring at her, she snatched her shawl from its peg on the wall, wrapped it around herself and ran from the room. She tumbled out of the front door into the street, her mind racing in panic. Was she destined to wander the streets of Dublin, of the world? Would she never find peace and security for herself and her children?

She kept away from the main roads, she didn't want to meet anyone she knew, especially not Molly, Rita and the children returning from their outing. Without really noticing where she was going she crossed the bridge at the bottom of Winetavern Street and wandered along the Quays towards the docks, silent on this Sunday afternoon, the cranes pointing their arms towards the duck-egg-blue sky. Did she have no choice but to return to Liverpool now? But what awaited her there? Frank still hostile and unforgiving? A life of being shunted from neighbour to neighbour? Being spoken of with pity at her failure? No, not that. She couldn't face it. But she had very little money: she now wished she hadn't spent so much on the new clothes or the night out that had brought this whole disaster to a head. And what about the children? They had only just got used to living here and now she would have to uproot them yet again. They wouldn't understand, no matter how hard she tried to explain. But explain what? And there was the matter of explaining to Molly. Her head began to ache and she felt cold, so very cold.

When she finally reached the North Wall she stopped and sank down on a low stone capstan. The wind coming in from the estuary was cold and damp and she knew that soon darkness would begin to fall. It was a long walk back and she had still come to no decision. Perhaps if she could get a hot drink she would feel better, less numb and disorientated. She got up and looked around. A little further along there was a watchman's hut; she would ask if there was a bit of a café anywhere that might be open.

The old watchman looked at her with watery eyes and indicated that she come closer.

'Come ye here to the brazier, girl, and warm yourself. 'Tis a raw day.'

'Thank you,' she murmured, holding out her cold hands to the flames.

'What has ye wandering down here at all?'

'I . . . I was out walking. I needed to think.'

'Have ye no home to go to?'

'I have, but . . . Is there anywhere near where I can get a cup of tea? It's a long walk back.'

'There's Ma Murphy's beyond a piece. She does stay open late, she'll give ye a cup of tea.'

'Thank you.'

'You're no Dub with that accent on ye,' he commented.

She managed a smile. 'No, I'm from Liverpool and I think I might have to go back there.'

'I was in it once meself, years ago now, and a desperate place it is. The cholera was ragin' and I was on me way to America. I had the fare saved and wasn't I robbed of it by a cut-throat blackguard who told me he'd get me a fine cheap place to lay me head while I was waitin' on a ship?'

'I'm sorry to hear that. We're not all like that.'

'So it's back here I ended. If I were ye I'd not go back there.'

'I might take your advice. Thanks for the warm, I'll be off now to Ma Murphy's.' She nodded and walked away in the direction he'd indicated. Maybe his advice was good. Maybe she'd feel better after a hot drink.

A sharp shower of rain made her duck into the doorway of a closed newsagent's shop and as she pressed herself into the recess she looked idly into the side window where there were some notices pinned up. She read of items for sale, workmen for hire and then her attention was caught by a neatly printed card.

Housekeeper required. Must be hard-working, reliable, honest and very discreet. Experience essential. Salary to be arranged. Accommodation provided to the right applicant. Contact Mr Richard O'Neill, Ballycowan Castle, Tullamore, King's County.

A housekeeper. She would be capable of that. Accommodation provided. Ballycowan Castle sounded very grand

and where exactly was King's County? Obviously it was in the country but how far was it from Dublin? Hope began to creep over her. Such a position would solve all her problems, but would she be the 'right applicant'? And what if she didn't get it? Well, what had she to lose? If all else failed then she would have to go back to Liverpool but at least she could try. Surely Molly wouldn't object to that? The position of housekeeper was a far better one than factory hand. She read the notice again, memorising each word, then, pulling her shawl more closely around her, she stepped out into the rain. She'd forgo the tea. She'd go straight back and tell Molly that tomorrow morning she was going to seek a new position. She'd leave the children with Molly until she knew just what the future held.

Chapter Eleven

M OLLY WAS SURPRISED AND relieved to see her.

'Mary, where have ye been and would ye look at the state of ye! Aren't ye soaked to the skin!'

'I know. But it wasn't raining when I went out and I walked further than I intended to. I needed time to think.' She glanced quickly at Davy who was once more sitting in the chair reading his newspaper. He didn't look up and she breathed a little easier.

'Get those wet things off now or you'll catch pneumonia. Here, I've just wet the tea and I'll put a drop of whiskey in it to ward off the cold,' Rita said.

'Thanks, but I think I've had enough of spirits. Just the tea will do. I'll get changed and then . . . well, I've something to tell you.'

The two women looked at each other mystified as Mary went to get changed. Molly took her sodden shawl and draped it over a chair which she set before the fire.

'Do you have to have the place looking like a laundry?' Davy snapped irritably.

'And how else am I to get things dry?' Molly snapped back. He was in a bad humour, no doubt about it, *and* he'd been drinking.

Rita raised her eyes to the ceiling but said nothing.

When Mary was changed and had taken the mug of tea and sat down Molly looked at her with curiosity.

'Well, and what is it ye've to tell me?'

'I'm going to apply for a job. A different job.'

'Are ye not happy with the one ye have?'

'Oh, it's been great but this one sounds so much better. The only thing is it's not in Dublin.'

'Where is it then?' Rita asked.

'Tullamore. That's King's County.'

'Begod, isn't that a desperate way away from here!' Molly was clearly taken aback.

'Exactly how far away is it?'

'Way down the country, in the midlands. Sure, in the name of God why do you want to move that far away?'

'I told you it's a much better job. It's as a housekeeper at a place called Ballycowan Castle.'

'A *castle*! Holy Mother of God, what for do ye want a job in a place like that? Isn't it a bit too grand for the likes of us?' Molly exclaimed.

'What do you know about housekeeping in a castle?' Rita demanded. 'Won't they have a rake of servants already?'

'Probably, but I can try for it. I've kept my own house, it's probably just the same only, well, a bit bigger.'

'A *bit* bigger!' Davy scoffed. She was mad if she thought she'd get a job like that! But perhaps it was all lies? Just the excuse to leave?

'I don't know how big it is. It might not be very big at all. It might just be a large house.'

'And pigs might fly!' Davy muttered, returning to his paper.

'Where did ye see this job? Was it advertised or did someone tell ye about it?' Molly demanded.

'I saw it advertised in a shop window.'

'Fine sort of a castle it must be to be advertising in a shop window. Why wouldn't they advertise in a newspaper? I never heard of the gentry doing the like of that.'

'I don't know but I intend to find out. I'll go tomorrow morning. Can I get a train?'

'I would think ye could get a train from Kingsbridge Station but ye'd better ask. Are ye sure it's the right thing, Mary? Ye never said ye were unhappy here.' Molly sounded aggrieved, and Mary hastened to reassure her.

'Oh, I'm not! Truly I'm not. It's just that I'd like a better job and it would be nice for the children to live in the country. Plenty of room to run around and play, fresh air and fresh food. You'd like to live in the country, wouldn't you, Katie?'

Katie didn't reply, she just stared at her mother. She had

her cousins and all their friends to play with here and she didn't want to have to move again.

'Of course I won't be taking you until I know I've got it and it's all settled,' Mary said confidently, more confidently than she felt.

Molly shook her head. 'Don't ye be getting up your hopes now. It might turn out to be a wild goose chase.'

'I know, but I feel as though I've got to try.'

'Do you have the train fare? I'll lend you something if you need it,' Rita offered, although she was disappointed that Mary had made this decision without even discussing it with her.

'I might need a couple of shillings, Rita, thanks.'

'Well, I'll go and see Mr Brannigan upstairs. He has a brother who works on the railways, he might be of some help,' Molly offered.

Mary thanked her and began to help Rita to set the table and prepare the meal. Oh, she hoped her aunt and cousin did not mind too much. They were still being so generous, and Mary felt that she was throwing it back in their faces. But she had no choice; nor could she ever explain it to them.

They learned that Mary could get the Galway train at Kingsbridge Station, which stopped at Tullamore, but it was a long journey and she would need to set off early. There was also no guarantee that she would get there and back in one day. Molly, in yet another display of generosity, agreed to lend her enough money for lodgings for the night should she need them.

It was dark and cold and very windy when she left early next morning. She wore her best clothes and the borrowed hat and had packed a few things in a small grip bag in case she needed them. Molly had cut her some sandwiches and a couple of slices of barmbrack to 'keep her going' on the long journey.

She walked part of the way to the station and managed to get a ride on a cart for the rest of it. She was very thankful for she would have been worn out before she'd even started, she thought as she made her way into the cavernous station's dimly lit and rather gloomy interior.

She purchased her ticket and learned from the ticketmaster that the journey would take approximately four hours, providing there were no 'unforeseen circumstances' to delay them. That meant it would be late morning before she even got to Tullamore and then she had no idea of how far Ballycowan Castle was from the town or how she would get there.

'You may be in luck. There may well be an outside car that goes there,' the man answered her query helpfully.

She made her way to the platform and found a seat in a third-class carriage, which was already occupied by two women, dressed in the less fashionable clothes of country women. They smiled and introduced themselves so readily that Mary felt sure the journey would not be without some diversion. At least she could go and see what the place was like. She hoped she would be successful, and if not . . . well, she wouldn't think about that until she had to.

She learned a great deal on the journey from the two women and from two farmers who had joined them in the carriage as they all shared the food they had brought with them. Ballycowan Castle was about three miles from the small town of Tullamore and although there was no outside car she had been assured that she would get a lift from someone if she started to walk the road out there. She also learned that it was not a 'grand' house in the sense that it could boast a 'rake' of servants; she also gathered from the tone of their voices and their knowing glances that Mr Richard O'Neill was neither very wealthy nor well liked, although they would not be drawn any further on the subject. If she needed lodgings she could find them in any one of the taverns in town: most could provide a decent bed and a good breakfast for a shilling or two.

She thanked them all and wished them well as she parted company with them outside the small station. She walked up the hill and then turned right. This was the quickest way, they had assured her, out past Charleville Castle and estate. It was cold but at least it was bright, she thought, looking around at the hedgerows and the bare branches of the trees that flanked the road. She hoped it wouldn't be too long before someone stopped and offered her a lift.

She had almost reached the huge stone gates of Charleville Castle, which could just be glimpsed between the trees to her right, when a cart pulled to a halt beside her.

'Where are ye off to, girl?' a middle-aged farmer asked, leaning over the side of the cart while the horse snatched at coarse tufts of grass at the roadside.

'Ballycowan Castle and I'd be very grateful of a ride, no matter how short.'

'I'm going as far as Mucklagh. It's only a small piece after that.'

'Thank you.' She smiled and took his hand to pull herself up.

'What has ye out there? I've not seen ye before.'

'I've come from Dublin on the train this morning. I'm hoping to get work there. As a housekeeper.'

He looked at her speculatively but didn't comment; he just nodded and flapped the reins and the horse reluctantly abandoned its foraging and moved off.

Since he continued to be silent (which she found surprising), she concentrated on admiring the scenery. Even though it was winter it looked pretty. Hedgerows still bounded the road which was getting increasingly narrow. Rolling green and brown fields ran for as far as the eye could see and away in the distance she could see the dark outline of a range of mountains. They passed farmhouses and cottages and a few large houses, reached by long driveways. Yes, it would be ideal for the children, she thought, away from the dirt and smoke and crowded streets of Dublin. It was so quiet and peaceful here, the only sounds the clopping of the horses' hooves and the raucous cries of the rooks circling high above the treetops.

'Well, I'll let ye down here. I'm after taking the next turning,' her driver announced, pulling on the reins and bringing the cart to a standstill.

'Thank you. It was very kind of you to bring me so far,' she said, preparing to climb down.

'Keep walking down that laneway until you get to the canal. It's the twenty-ninth lock. Walk down the towpath and ye can't miss it. A great pile of rocks it is with five great chimneys, although it took a bit of a battering from Cromwell and his cannon balls a couple of hundred years ago.'

'Thank you again. I'm very grateful.' She waved as he drew away and then turned and began to walk down the narrow lane where the hedgerows were so tall that it was impossible to see the fields beyond.

She began to feel a little apprehensive. Could she convince this Mr O'Neill that she was capable of running the household? Just how big a place was it? How many other servants were there?

After ten minutes she rounded a bend in the lane and the narrow humpbacked bridge over the Grand Canal came into view. There were two cottages clustered on its banks, one of which she realised must belong to the lock-keeper. She wondered whether she should knock and ask if she had the right place but decided against it. The narrow towpath was flanked by fields on the right-hand side and the waters of the canal on the left. A little further along was what looked like a small farmhouse and then she stopped and stared. Rising high into the sky from the banks of towering fir trees were the sandstone walls of Ballycowan Castle, its five tall chimneys making it look even more imposing. It *was* a castle, if not a very big one. Its upper storey was crenellated, its walls looked to be at least two feet thick and there appeared to be five floors. Small leaded panes were set into the stone mullioned windows. The glass sparkled in the weak winter sunlight.

Oh, it *was* a grand place. How on earth would she cope? 'Well, standing here just gaping is no use,' she told herself firmly and began to make her way along the towpath.

The closer she drew the bigger it looked and she felt her heart sink. There was a cottage at the large stone gateway and a black and white collie came out to investigate the stranger.

Mary bent and patted it and then looked towards the cottage. She supposed she'd better knock here first. Maybe it was some sort of gatehouse.

In answer to her knock the door was opened by a young woman with a tangle of dark hair and large brown eyes. A plaid shawl was draped around her shoulders and she eyed Mary with some hostility.

'I'm looking for a Mr Richard O'Neill?' Mary enquired.

'And who are ye?' the girl asked suspiciously, taking in Mary's fashionable outfit and then looking down to her own bare and grubby feet.

'Mrs Mary McGann. I've come from Dublin about the position.' Mary wasn't impressed by the girl's sullen manner.

'Have ye so? Then it's Himself ye'll be looking for.'

'I've already told you that. Does he employ you?'

'Bridie, who's at the door?' a thin, quarrelsome voice enquired from within.

'A woman from Dublin to see Himself, Da,' the girl shouted back.

'I'll thank you to direct me,' Mary said coldly. She hadn't come all this way to be kept on the doorstep of a cabin by a barefoot slip of a girl.

'Go up to the door yonder and ring the bell, but ye'll have a bit of a wait, mind. Mrs O'Shea packed her bags and left three weeks ago. He'll answer the door himself, if he's a mind to,' she added offhandedly.

Mary didn't even thank her as she turned away. If that was the calibre of the servants he employed she had little to worry about.

She picked her way across the yard between half-frozen puddles and piles of dung. What a mess! she thought to

herself. What kind of a man was he to allow such filth
outside his front door? Shooing a small flock of foraging
hens from under her feet she climbed the broken steps up
to the massive oak door set in its arched stone lintel and
pulled hard on the rusted iron rod that set a loud bell
ringing in the hall beyond. She looked upwards. There was
a stone plaque high above the doorway with a coat-of-arms
above, which stated that the house was built by Sir Jasper
Herbert, Knight, and his wife Dame Mary Finglass in the
year 1626. Underneath the plaque were the words 'By God
of Might I hold my Right'.

So it was very old, but some of her nervousness had
dissipated, owing to her initial evaluation of the way this
decidedly ungracious Mr O'Neill appeared to live.

Eventually she heard the sound of footsteps and the
door was opened.

'Mr O'Neill? Mr Richard O'Neill?' she asked.

'Yes. Who are you?'

He wasn't what she had expected. He was quite young,
in his thirties she surmised, and handsome in a dark and
rather saturnine way. He was tall, six foot she judged, and
well made – not fat nor heavy but muscular. His dark brown
hair was thick and wavy and sprinkled with grey and his
eyes were the most piercing shade of blue she had ever
seen. He wore cord trousers and waistcoat over a plain
white collarless shirt.

'I'm Mrs Mary McGann. I've come from Dublin in

answer to your advertisement for a housekeeper,' she replied primly.

To her surprise he smiled and his whole face changed. 'Have you indeed. Then come inside, Mrs McGann.'

She followed him into the dim high-ceilinged hall. The floor was flagged but she noticed that there were numerous expensive-looking rugs on the floor – in need of a clean and chewed at the edges, but still expensive. She caught a glimpse of large, heavy-framed portraits on the walls and a huge sweeping stone staircase that rose on the right-hand side. The only daylight came from a small barred window by the door.

'Please do go in. You will have to excuse the mess. I've been without a housekeeper for a while.'

'So the young girl at the gatehouse informed me,' she replied, entering a large rectangular room, which had a stone fireplace, a low stone vaulted ceiling and a mullioned window that looked out over the boundary wall. It was comfortably furnished but everything looked worn and dusty and neglected.

'Please, do sit down. You must be tired.'

She sat gingerly on the edge of a large, deeply buttoned green leather chesterfield.

'Mrs McGann? I assume you are a widow? You are very young, if I may presume to say so.'

Mary decided that honesty was the best policy. 'No, Mr O'Neill. I am not a widow. My husband and I did not get on. We decided it would be the best policy to . . . separate. He lives in Liverpool.'

He raised an eyebrow and looked slightly bemused. She was a very attractive young woman. Not expensively dressed but fashionable. He was curious. 'Indeed? Have you any children?'

'I have three. Two daughters and one son. They are with relatives in Dublin.'

'Are they young?' he asked, thinking they couldn't be very old. She was only in her mid-twenties, he guessed.

'Lizzie is the youngest, she's six. They are no trouble.'

'And have you any experience?'

She was determined not to appear timid. 'I have the experience of running my own home, which I did exceedingly well, if I do say so myself, and on a limited . . . er . . . budget.'

'You have no experience of large households?'

'Oh, indeed yes. I have lived in households of twelve people and more,' she replied, thinking of her time with Nellie and Bella and the others.

His mouth lifted at the corners. 'That's not quite what I meant.'

She was a little disconcerted and decided that the best form of defence was attack.

'How many servants do you employ, Mr O'Neill?'

He leaned forward in his chair. 'Only three, Mrs McGann, but this is a big house.'

'I can see that and, if you will excuse me, from the little I've seen it's in desperate need of a good housekeeper.' She wondered if she'd gone too far as she saw his brows rush together in a frown but she pressed on. 'I work hard, Mr O'Neill. I've worked hard all my life and I've never had much in the way of material things. I don't expect to be paid a fortune. A fair wage and accommodation for myself and my children. I am quiet, thrifty, honest and a good Catholic. There will be no – how should I put this? – unseemly behaviour. I will be fair if strict with the staff you already have. As I have said, I work hard and I expect others to do the same.'

He leaned back in his chair and stared at her. He liked her honesty but would she suit? Well, all the others hadn't, although they were more qualified for the role. He shrugged. He had nothing to lose.

'Very well, Mrs McGann, I'm prepared to give you a trial. Shall we say a month?'

Mary was so startled that at first she couldn't reply. Then she shook herself. He was actually saying he would employ her! She'd got the job! She relaxed a little, a smile crossing her face. 'Thank you, sir. I'm sure you won't regret it.'

'I hope I won't. Now, shall I show you the rest of the house and we can discuss your salary?'

'Thank you and could I please see the . . . er . . . accommodation?'

'Of course. It's at the back of the house, on the ground floor.' He rose.

As she followed suit, she decided to satisfy her curiosity about something.

'May I ask you a question, sir?'

'Please do.'

'Why did you advertise the job in a small newsagent's shop in Dublin?'

'I wanted no one from these parts.'

'But surely if you had advertised in a Dublin paper you would have been certain to have found someone more . . . experienced than myself?'

'Maybe I didn't want someone more "experienced" than yourself. You *are* discreet, Mrs McGann? It's absolutely essential.'

'Of course.'

'Then I think that is all I need to know and all you need to know. Please follow me.'

She was still puzzled as she followed him out of the room but she pushed her doubt to the back of her mind. She'd got the job and she was determined to make the best of it. At least she would be away from Davy, and that had to be better for herself and the children.

Chapter Twelve

MARY HAD NEVER SEEN so big a house in her entire life. It had taken half an hour to inspect the rooms. All those on the ground floor had stone vaulted ceilings, rather like a church, she thought, except they were much lower. There were five of them. The kitchen itself was almost as big as her whole house in Newsham Street had been and you could have prepared enough food for an army there. It was presided over by Mrs Moran, the cook, a small rotund woman of unfathomable age whose grey hair was snatched back into a bun and covered with a small white cap. Mary had liked her on sight.

'When you've finished doing the tour of inspection, come back here and have a cup of tea. You must be in need of it,' were her parting words as Richard O'Neill ushered Mary out.

The accommodation provided consisted of three rooms: a small sitting room and two bedrooms. All were adequately furnished but she made a mental note to scrub everything out and air the beds before she brought the children here.

'Of course, most of the rooms are not in use, nor will be,' her employer informed her as they moved from a formal dining room into yet another 'reception' room, with two large windows that overlooked fields.

'I presume that's why there are only three servants,' she replied.

'You presume correctly.'

'The house is very old and it does look like a castle,' she commented.

'Most of it was built by the Herberts, although parts of it are older. Dating from the fifteen hundreds, I believe. It is half fortification, half dwelling house. It's been improved over the years, made more of a house than a castle. Now, if you'll follow me I'll show you the upper floors.'

The staircase was totally devoid of any covering and their footsteps echoed loudly around the hall and first landing. She peered upwards at the high, dark, timbered ceiling and shivered. It was cold and smelled damp and musty. The house must be almost impossible to keep warm, she thought.

Here there were six large rooms all with huge stone fireplaces and deeply recessed wide windows. Three were bedrooms, one a dining room and the other two reception rooms. From the upper hall a doorway led into an enormous hall with a high timber ceiling, a fireplace you could stand upright in and two very large windows.

'The older part of the house,' he commented.

The stairs to the upper floors were carved out of the thick stone outer wall and up there there were more bedrooms.

'Are they never used?' Mary asked, thinking of the terrible overcrowded slums of Dublin and Liverpool.

'No. Never. My own room is on the third floor. The rooms up there are inclined to be smaller, more manageable to heat.'

'And are there rooms above them?' She wondered just how many rooms there were in all.

'A few. Storerooms mainly. The battlements are up there and they are in parts dangerous, so there is no need for you ever to venture further than the third storey. Also there is some structural damage, inflicted during the seventeenth century.'

'By Cromwell, so I was told.'

He smiled wryly. 'There is no love wasted on that particular statesman in this country, Mrs McGann. Nor is there a castle or country house that doesn't bear the scars of his campaigns in Ireland, as I'm sure you will learn.'

It was a very interesting house, she thought as she followed him back down the staircase, but a very neglected one. Yet he must have money.

When they were once more in the hall he turned to her. 'So, do you think you will be able to manage it all?'

'Yes, although it will take some hard work to get it into a decent state. Apart from Mrs Moran, who do you employ?'

'Seamus, known to all as Sonny. He lives in the gate-house. He's a general handyman.'

'I met someone who I think is his daughter.'

'Bridie. She occasionally helps out here.'

'Indeed. At first I think I'll need some extra help with the heavy work. Are there any other girls or women nearby who would be willing and able to help?'

'There are plenty but I'll have none of them. I'll speak to Bridie,' he replied curtly and she wondered why he suddenly seemed so hostile. She'd have a hard time getting any work out of that Bridie if her instincts were right about the girl.

'So, when would you like to start?' he asked.

'At the end of the week. Friday, if it suits you. Then the following week I'll arrange for my children to be brought down.'

He nodded. 'I'm not a hard man to get along with, Mrs McGann. I have no extravagant tastes. There are seldom any visitors to be catered for. I keep myself to myself and I expect you to do the same. I will have no gossiping.'

'The children will have to attend school and I presume there is a church nearby?'

'There is a church at Kilbride a few miles down the canal line and a small school at Ballinamere, about a quarter of a mile away, but I must warn you that I will not have the women and children of the Parish entertained here.'

She nodded. It was as if he wanted to shut himself off from all social contact with his neighbours. He was undoubtedly a strange man, but at least she had a job and a home. What more could she ask? It would be more of a walk to church than it had been to St Anthony's and a longer one to school for the children, but beggars couldn't be choosers, she told herself.

'The salary is four guineas a month,' he added.

She swallowed hard. It seemed a small fortune to her, considering the fact that no mention had been made of anything being deducted for their board and lodgings. 'That's very generous, sir. I'm sure I'll be quite happy here and I can promise that I will work extremely hard to make sure you are well served and comfortable.'

He extended his hand. 'Then I will expect you on Friday next, Mrs McGann. Good day to you. Mrs Moran will provide you with refreshments before you leave.'

His handshake was firm and warm and she smiled. 'Good day to you, sir, and thank you.'

Her heels clattered on the stone floor of the passageway and she frowned. Obviously he was a man set in his ways and she was sure he wouldn't want to be disturbed by the noise of the children's feet as they ran along these passageways, but she would sort that out later on.

'Come on in, child, I've the tea wet,' Mrs Moran called as she knocked on the kitchen door.

'Thank you, a cup of tea will go down a treat.' She smiled, sitting down at the large scrubbed table while the cook laid out cups and saucers, a jug of milk and a plate of freshly made soda bread spread with thick yellow butter. 'It seems hours since I had anything to eat or drink, it's very kind of you.'

'So, he's offered you the job and you've accepted?'

Mary nodded. 'I'll be perfectly honest, I've never done anything like this before. I ran my own house very well, but it was tiny compared to this. I just hope I can manage.'

'Sure there's nothing to it. There's only Himself and myself here. Sonny has Bridie to see to him in the gate-house, not that she does much!' She sniffed.

'I gathered that. I called and she answered the door. I found her a bit . . . offhand.'

'She's a lazy strap! Her mammy died ten years ago and all the rest of them are off in America.'

'I'm starting on Friday. I'll send for my children the following week. I have three. Katie is nine, Tommy is eight and Lizzie is six. The poor little mite is deaf and dumb. She was born that way.'

'Ah, the good Lord have mercy on her!' Mrs Moran said sympathetically.

'They're no trouble. Well, Tommy can be a bit of a hooligan at times, that's why I want to get him away from Dublin. Only last week didn't he get trampled by the cattle being driven to slaughter? Thank God he wasn't badly hurt but he'd been warned and warned to stay away from them.'

'That's lads for you. Well, he can help Sonny around the place, there's always plenty to do and he can learn to fish in the river. Himself is partial to a nice trout.'

Mary smiled as she sipped her tea. This was all a far cry from both Newsham Street and the house in the Coombe.

'Mr O'Neill must be a wealthy man to own all this. Did he inherit it?' she enquired.

Mrs Moran looked a little startled. 'He did not! He doesn't own it.'

'He doesn't? I thought . . . Does he just manage it then?'

'You could call it that, I suppose. He's the agent. It belongs to the Honourable Augustus Coates.'

'Why does he not live here?'

'He prefers his house and estates in England, always has. I can never recall any of the Coateses ever living here. They just take the rents. Absentee landlords is what they are, like all their class!'

She made them sound like criminals, Mary thought. 'Is that so bad?'

'It is. Oh, you'll learn soon enough about them and their agents, but Mr O'Neill is not the worst, believe me, though there's many around here would tell you different.'

'He's not liked then? Is that why he keeps himself to himself? He has asked me to do the same.'

'He's not the most popular but he has his reasons. If you've any sense or intention of keeping this position you'll do as he bids.'

'He said he won't have the women and children of the Parish coming here.'

'Nor will he and I don't blame him for that. Gossips and gapers and begrudgers the lot of them!'

Mrs Moran appeared to be getting heated so Mary decided to change the subject. 'Will everything be provided? I mean cleaning stuff, bedding, things like that?'

'It will. I'll send Sonny with the cart to Tullamore to stock up and I'll have Bridie look out the sheets and blankets and air them. I see to the food, the buying, preparing and cooking. We have a kitchen garden and there're hens and geese and ducks. Sonny keeps some pigs and sheep and a few cows, and there're some beef cattle as well. It's a great help to have the canal so close; all kinds of cargoes go up and down to Dublin and we can usually bargain for goods with the canal agents, which saves expensive trips up to Dublin. Now, Mrs McGann, are you back up to Dublin this day?'

'It's Mary and yes I'm hoping to get back but it will be very late.'

'Then I'll have Sonny drive you back into town; we can't have you walking the roads with darkness falling so early. You'd lose your way and miss your train, so you would. Besides, it's not fitting. If you send word what train you will be on on Friday he can meet you then too.'

'I'd be glad of that. I'll have my belongings with me – not that there're many of them.'

Mrs Moran rose a little stiffly. 'You sit there and rest while I fetch him. I think you'll do very well, Mary. I like you and that's more than can be said for the procession of women we've had through here.'

Mary smiled. 'Thank you. I like you too, Mrs Moran, you've made me very welcome.'

She'd found Sonny very talkative and curious about her and her background and they chatted away happily as the horse and trap moved at a smart pace along the country roads towards the station. She'd been pleased to realise that the reedy voice she'd heard on her arrival belied his friendly nature.

'I'll be here waiting on you, Mary, on Friday. Have a safe journey and God be with you!' had been his departing words.

She'd waved and watched him turn the trap in the station yard before she'd settled herself in the waiting room. She had half an hour before the train was due, so the station master informed her, advising her to warm herself by the turf fire he kept burning these winter days for the comfort of the passengers.

She'd been the only occupant of the carriage and after a while she'd fallen asleep, tired out by the events of the day. She awoke as the train, with clouds of hissing steam and a grinding of brakes, drew into Kingsbridge Station. She was cold and stiff as she gathered up her bag and alighted onto the platform. It was a long walk home and she decided she could now afford the luxury of a tram ride. According to the station clock it was ten past ten and it had been a very long day.

'I didn't expect ye back at all today, Mary,' Molly cried when she at last walked into the room.

'How did you get on? Did you get it? Is it a huge house?' Rita asked, full of curiosity.

Mary took off her hat and coat. 'I got it, I start on Friday and it is a big house but very run down and in need of a good clean. It's right out in the country, beside the Tullamore River and the Grand Canal, and Mr O'Neill is the agent – whatever that is. Apart from me, there's just Mrs Moran, the cook, and Sonny, he's the handyman, and a girl called Bridie who'll help with the heavy work until I get it spick and span. We're to have three rooms, would you believe? A sitting room and two bedrooms and you should see the size of the kitchen!'

'Well, don't ye seem to have fallen on your feet there.

How much is he to pay ye?' Molly asked. She was still a little upset that Mary would be leaving.

'Four guineas a month. Isn't that a fortune?'

'Sure, it's only twenty-one shillings a week and ye'll be breaking your back for it. And what about your keep?'

'It was never mentioned that it would be deducted from my wages so I presume that it's all found. For the first time in my life I'll be able to save some money, have a bit of security for myself and the children.'

'Will they take to it do ye think, Mary?' Molly was a little concerned for her young great-nieces and -nephew. This would be a great change for them.

'I think they will. They'll go to school and there's plenty for Tommy to do to keep him out of trouble. He can learn to fish for one thing. There's trout in the river.'

'Begod, trout no less for the dinner table!' Molly was impressed. It seemed Mary was making the right decision.

'Well, I'm worn out and I've plenty to do tomorrow, so I'm off to bed,' Mary announced.

'I'm sorry to see you go, Mary, and I'll miss you but you've done well for yourself and I won't begrudge you that,' Rita said generously.

Mary smiled at her cousin. 'Thanks, Rita. I'll miss you, too. We've had some good times together.'

'Particularly the last night out!' Rita laughed.

Mary thought of that night and suddenly realised that Davy was not in. 'Where's Davy?'

'Gone to a meeting about the stevedores and their paying out in the pubs. There'll be trouble over that before long, I tell you. Trouble with the unions,' Rita replied.

'And that lad will be in the thick of it and could well end up with no job at all, Rita, ye mark my words!' Molly said cuttingly.

'Ah, Mam, will you give over about that!' Rita said irritably.

Mary didn't comment. It looked as if she was well out of Dublin, she thought, if there was going to be trouble and strikes.

Chapter Thirteen

S HE HAD BEEN ASLEEP when Davy had come in but he was up and dressed next morning when she awoke.

'I hear you got the job and that you'll be leaving on Friday,' he said curtly.

'I did and I will. No doubt you will be happy now,' she answered, glancing in the direction of Molly and the children who were still sleeping.

'I will so. It's good riddance but the likes of you always fall on your feet. A grand roof over your head and four guineas a month in your pocket and nothing to spend it on down there in the bogs! And here's the likes of me breaking my back for a pittance and I have to stand the stevedore a pint to get that! But by God that's not going to go on much longer, not if I've anything to do with it.'

'I heard there will be trouble.'

'Aye, there'll be that all right.'

'Davy, shouldn't you be thinking of Rita and the

children? How will you all manage if you're locked out? I've seen it happen in Liverpool.'

'Why should you care? You'll be away from here. But I expect you'll be able to play the Lady Bountiful and take Rita and the kids in if things get too bad here,' he mocked.

She shook her head. 'No, I won't be able to do that. Mr O'Neill made it very clear to me that he'll have no strangers descending on him.'

'And who is this great *Mr* O'Neill? Nothing more than an absentee landlord's agent! Bloodsuckers draining the country of its wealth. Not caring if we live or die as long as they get their rents so they can live the life of Riley over there in their big houses in England. He's nothing more than a traitor and a turncoat! *Mr* O'Neill, me arse! One day we'll be free of all of them. We'll send them packing back across the water where they belong. Ireland will be for the Irish! We'll make our own decisions, we'll run our own lives and country. We'll keep the money here for ourselves. We won't be breaking our backs to have it taken from us to finance their lifestyles and their wars. We'll spend it on *ourselves* – for a change!'

She was shocked by his outburst. She'd never known such deep resentment and hatred was harboured by him, or by anyone Irish. 'And I suppose that includes me?'

'It does. You're English. You don't belong here and you're like all the rest of them. Greedy, grasping, conniving—'

'I'm not! And I'm family. Molly is my own mother's sister!'

'I'm not interested, Mary! I'll be glad when you're gone to live with your Mr O'Neill! You deserve each other.'

She was about to reply when Molly stirred and sat up. 'Is that the time already and me still in me bed?'

'I'm off,' Davy growled and slammed out.

'What ails him this morning?' Molly grumbled. 'I declare he gets more humoursome by the day and now he's woken the childer.'

'Well, it's time they were up. I've plenty to do today and I want to talk to them before they go to school. I'll try to explain to Lizzie later on, when I've a bit more time to spend with her. Will I call Rita?'

'You will so. I'll put on the kettle.'

Katie and Tommy had listened in silence when Mary had told them about the new life that awaited them, but Katie was still confused.

'I just don't see *why* we have to go?' she complained to Tommy as they trudged to school with their cousins.

'Because she's going to earn great money and we'll all live in a huge big house with hundreds of rooms and a river and a canal outside the door. I can learn to fish and do jobs and all kinds of interesting things.' Tommy as usual was enthusiastic about anything that seemed new and exciting.

'And what can Lizzie and me do?'

'Help Mam. Go to school, make new friends. And there're all the fields and woods and other places to play in. Don't be such a misery, Katie. It'll be great!'

'It doesn't sound great. I like it here. There's plenty to do and see here.'

'Don't you want to be rich? Mam says we'll be able to have all the things we've never had before.'

'Like what? Toys? Nice dresses?'

'I suppose so. We might even get bicycles.' It was Tommy's dream to have a bicycle of his own. He'd whiz along the roads at a great speed. It would be fun and a lot easier and quicker than having to walk everywhere. 'Mam says they've a pony and trap and a horse and cart for the heavy things!' That in his eyes set them apart from everyone he knew.

'I'd sooner stay here and be rich and be able to go to school on the tram and have nice dresses and dolls.'

'You're so stupid, Katie! We *won't* be rich if we stay here! No one's going to give Mam all that money for working in the flour mill. She's to be a housekeeper and that's a very big and important job.'

'Will we be able to come and see you in this grand house and play with all your toys and ride your bicycle?' Brendan asked. It all sounded like a great stroke of luck to him, his cousin Mary landing this job in the country.

'I suppose so, though you'd better not mention the bicycle to Mam just yet,' Tommy replied cautiously, kicking a stone along the gutter heedless of the damage to the toes of his boots.

Katie still looked unconvinced and little Lizzie was of course utterly confused, although both Mary and her sister had tried so hard to explain what was going to happen. However, Katie had accepted it a little more by the time Friday came after a week of preparations. Mary had borrowed the money from Molly, Rita and even Davy to rig herself and the children out with what she considered 'suitable' clothes for life in the country. It would all be paid back when she received her first month's salary. She had also bought herself some heavy unbleached calico working aprons, and two white cotton aprons with frilled edges and two frilled white cotton caps to be worn when she wasn't doing heavy housework. Mrs Maguire from next door had been in service when young and had advised her that that was the correct form of dress for a housekeeper. That and a black fine wool dress with a belt from which to hang all the keys she would be expected to carry with her at all times. Mrs Maguire had gone on to explain the duties of a housekeeper, which Mary had found very helpful if a little daunting.

'But it's not really a very grand household. There's no butler or menservants or kitchen maids or parlour maids. Just Cook, me, a handyman and a girl to help out a bit at times,' she'd demurred apprehensively.

'But 'tis still a good thing to *know* about such things,

Mary. He'll think more highly of you and respect you for it,' the woman had replied and Mary had left still wondering about the correct way to serve afternoon tea and lay a dinner table.

Only Molly went to see her off on Friday. Both Rita and Davy were at work and the children were at school. She had said her goodbyes to them earlier that morning and had promised that she would be at the station to meet them when Molly put them on the train in the care of the guard the following Friday.

'Ye will write and tell me how ye're getting on, Mary?' Molly urged, still worried how her niece would cope with such a drastic change of lifestyle.

'Of course I will and don't worry about the money, I'll send everything I owe as soon as I get paid.'

'Don't I know that, ye're a good girl and I'll miss ye. Now ye'd best get on the train or ye'll not get a seat. Sure, I never realised so many people travelled the country.'

Mary hugged her and hoisted her two carpet bags, which contained all her possessions and many of the children's, into the carriage.

During the journey she went over things in her mind. First she would unpack. Then she would get changed, find young Bridie and set her to work, give her own rooms a good clean and make up the bed. Then she would lay the table in the small dining room and serve Mr O'Neill his dinner. After that she would help Mrs Moran clear up the kitchen, set the table for breakfast and make a list of the rooms to be cleaned in order of priority. She'd have to make sure that Bridie was under no illusions about what work she was expected to do. She'd also have a word with Sonny about the state of the yard. She had no intention of scrubbing out the hall and beating and cleaning the rugs only to have it all undone by the muck and mud that would be traipsed in on everyone's feet. A week of sheer relentless hard work by herself and Bridie should have the house in a state fit for a gentleman to live in. After that it wouldn't be too hard to keep it spick and span. In what spare time she had she would mend curtains and linen. She intended to make the most of the opportunity that had been given her really to come up in the world and provide a secure and comfortable life for her children, despite Frank's rejection of them.

True to his word Sonny was waiting at the station with the trap. He greeted her warmly and flung her two bags in effortlessly; she realised that he wasn't nearly as old or frail as he looked.

'What have you in them at all?' he enquired, helping her up.

'Everything I own. I've come to stay,' she replied determinedly.

'That's what the one before last said but I hope you do. I've taken to you, Mary, and so has Julia. Mrs Moran,' he corrected himself, noticing her raised eyebrows.

Their progress was noted with some interest from the houses and cottages they passed after they turned off the main road.

'Ah, they're all wondering about you and how long you'll stay,' Sonny commented as he saluted the neighbours.

'Why *does* no one stay? What's the matter with Mr O'Neill?'

'He's not the easiest to get along with and they don't like being so isolated. He doesn't like company. In fact he forbids it. And then there're his political views . . .'

'Well, I'm not in the least bit interested in politics. Life's hard enough without worrying about things like that and I certainly won't have time to be chatting and gossiping and entertaining. There's far too much to do. That house is in a terrible state of neglect. Would you ask Bridie to come and see me, please? Say at two o'clock?'

'Hasn't she gone into Tullamore.'

'And who told her she could go off into town today? She knew I was arriving.'

'Himself sent her.'

'I see. Well, as soon as she gets back ask her to come and see me. We have a lot of work to get through before my children arrive next week.'

'I hope she'll be able for it. She's only used to looking after myself.'

'Oh, she'll be able for it. I'll make certain of that. She's young and healthy, isn't she?'

'She is that but you have to mind the way you ask her to do things. She's inclined to be humoursome.'

'Really?' Mary replied, thinking that she'd soon change that. She was standing no nonsense from a moody young girl like that and she would have no insolence either.

There was tea, soda bread, home-cured ham and chutney waiting for her when she finally arrived.

'Oh, this is very kind of you, Mrs Moran, to have gone to so much trouble.'

''Tis nothing, Mary. Didn't I have to put a meal on the table for Mr O'Neill? Sonny, sit yourself down and have a bite with us. Did you put all those things in the outhouse like I asked?'

'I did so and there's enough soap and bleach and scrubbing brushes and the like to clean every house in the Parish. I nearly cleaned Jack Hickey out of all his stock.'

'I'll need it all,' Mary said, smiling. 'You won't recognise this place when I've finished with it.'

'That'll make a change,' Mrs Moran commented drily as she poured the tea.

She'd unpacked, changed into her working clothes and given her sitting room and one of the bedrooms a good clean before Bridie appeared at the door.

'You're back then,' Mary said, wiping her hands on her apron.

The girl looked at her sullenly and then her gaze went over the freshly cleaned room. She didn't answer.

Mary noticed that she looked tidier and cleaner than she'd been the first time she'd seen her, and she wore stockings and boots.

'Come in and sit down while I go over this list of things I want you to do to help me. This house is in a shocking state, it's not fit for a decent man to live in. We've both got a great deal of hard work ahead of us, Bridie.' Seeing the expression on the girl's face she continued, 'I don't expect you to do it all. I'll work just as hard. I'm not above getting down on my knees and scrubbing or dragging carpets and rugs out and beating them.'

'Well, 'tis more than the others would do,' the girl replied. Mary seemed fair but just how much hard work did she expect her to do? No smooth-talking English-woman was going to get round her *that* easily. All the others had treated her like a skivvy and maybe Mary wasn't all that different, despite what she said.

'There is no task that I will ask you to do that I will not do myself. I'm strict but I hope I'm fair and if we're to get along well together I expect you to pull your weight. Do you understand?'

'Yes, ma'am,' came the muttered reply.

'I don't expect you to neglect your father and once the place is clean I will only need your help a few days a week. I presume Mr O'Neill pays you?'

'He does so, ma'am, and we live rent free.'

'Then he is a good employer. Now, this won't take long and then we'll both make a start in the main house.'

By the time Mrs Moran came to inform them that she was about to start dinner they had the small dining room fairly clean. The floor had been scrubbed, the rugs beaten, the furniture polished, the windows cleaned and the few items of silver glowed in the light of the oil lamps. Sonny had come in and lit the fire in the hearth and filled the turf basket.

'Doesn't it look grand already,' he'd commented with admiration.

'Give me a few minutes to get washed and changed and I'll set the table, Mrs Moran, then I'll be out to help you,' Mary said cheerfully. 'Bridie, I think you've done enough for one day. Will you come in at eight o'clock in the morning? We'll have a full day ahead of us.'

Bridie wiped her hands on her apron. 'I will, ma'am,' she replied grudgingly. She had to admit the place did look better, and Mary had certainly pulled her weight. But did she intend to keep this up or was it just to show a bit of willing? Well, she'd see what tomorrow would bring.

An hour later Mary in her black dress covered with the white frilled apron and with the cap over her neatly dressed hair, carried the tray into the dining room.

'Good evening, sir,' she greeted her employer cheerfully.

Richard O'Neill automatically stood up. His mind had been on other matters. He'd been reflecting on the meeting he'd had that afternoon with Peter Casey, a local man, which had left him with a great deal to think about and some important decisions to make.

He knew she had arrived and when he'd walked into the room, despite his preoccupations, he'd been aware of the changes she'd made. But he was surprised by her appearance. She looked as if she'd been in service in a big house all her life. He'd never expected her to look like this.

'Good evening, Mrs McGann. You look very well. Have you settled in?'

'Thank you, sir. I have indeed. If you will be seated I'll serve the soup, unless you would prefer to serve yourself?'

'Usually I do but tonight you may serve.'

She did so expertly although inwardly she was very nervous.

'I thought you said you had no experience, Mrs McGann?'

'I haven't but I learn very quickly.' She set a small dish of bread rolls on the table and moved the claret jug to within his reach. 'If you would ring when you've finished, sir, I'll clear your dishes. Mrs Moran said to inform you that it's roast mutton with parsnips and carrots and potatoes.'

'Thank you, Mrs McGann.' He watched her as she left the room. Had he at last found someone who would suit him? He hoped so. He was sick and tired of living in a badly run house, but he knew he was not easy to work for. He wondered how she would cope with the strict code of work and isolation he insisted upon. Mrs Moran, Sonny and young Bridie knew him well and he trusted them. But could he trust her? Only time would tell.

She was a very beautiful young woman, he mused, and he wondered just why she and her husband had failed to get on to such an extent that she had left Liverpool and travelled so far with her family. Still, it was no concern of his. As long as she did her job, asked no questions, did not mix with the local people and kept her children under control it didn't matter about her background or her personal life.

Chapter Fourteen

F OR THE NEXT WEEK Mary worked non-stop. She missed the children terribly: they'd never been parted before, not even for a night. But the heavy housework took her mind off her worries about them. Despite the bitter cold, she was up before six o'clock on her first morning and had the fire in the kitchen range burning brightly and the kettle boiling before Mrs Moran appeared.

'Aren't you the early riser, Mary, and isn't it grand to come into a warm and tidy kitchen. It makes a change, I can tell you. I'm not as young as I used to be and the damp in this place would chill you to the bones,' she said.

By twenty past eight there was still no sign of Bridie and Mary was about to go and look for her when the girl sidled into the kitchen.

'Bridie, I particularly asked you to be here by eight o'clock so we could make an early start.'

'Me da wanted his breakfast,' Bridie muttered.

Mary sighed. 'Then why didn't you tell me that yesterday? Of course you had to see to him first.'

The girl shrugged and darted a look at Mrs Moran.

Mary decided not to press the matter too hard this morning. 'Well, tomorrow morning we'll make it half past eight. Does that suit?'

Bridie nodded reluctantly.

After they had all had their breakfast and Mary had washed up, she put Bridie to help Mrs Moran while she set the table for Mr O'Neill and duly served his breakfast. Then she changed and set to work on the hall. She was on her hands and knees scrubbing the flags, after having thrown all the rugs into a heap on the doorstep, when Sonny came in with the turf baskets.

She sat back on her heels and glared at him. 'Sonny, do you think you could bring those in the back way and not be traipsing the muck and mud of the yard in on my clean floor? And you're leaving a trail of turf dust behind you.'

He set down the baskets. 'Sure, I always bring them in this way, it's quicker.'

'Well, from now on bring them in the back way. It's no wonder those expensive rugs are destroyed altogether and while I think on it, do you think you could do something to clean up that yard? It's not fitting for a gentleman to have the entrance to his home like a stableyard and a not very clean one at that.'

He looked at her with astonishment. 'Himself has never complained about it before!'

'Then he should have. It's a disgrace.'

'Begod, Mrs McGann, you have some strange ways of going on.'

She smiled at him. 'I know. We're strange people in Liverpool. If it's any consolation, I won't be allowing my children to use the front door either.'

'And will I tell Bridie to come in the back way, too?'

'I'd be grateful if you would and she'll see the sense in it if she's to get down on her knees and scrub this floor once a week.'

After that everyone, except Richard O'Neill, used the back door and the yard had been tidied up considerably.

Bridie arrived on time the following morning and Mary greeted her pleasantly. Between them they gave every room a thorough clean: dragging furniture into the centre of the room; taking down pictures and curtains; cleaning and polishing oil lamps, fenders, ashpans and fire-irons. Windows were cleaned, rugs taken out and given a good beating, bedding washed or aired. Because Mary did indeed work as hard as Bridie herself and wasn't overly domineering or demanding the girl began to feel a grudging respect for the older woman. Maybe things wouldn't be too bad at all. For the first time in many months fires were lit in every room that had a fireplace.

'Himself won't like it. It's a desperate waste of turf,' Sonny complained.

'I'm not saying light them all every day, that *would* be a waste. Just now and then to keep a bit of heat in the place and some of the damp at bay. It's as cold as charity in those upstairs rooms. Surely he can't complain about *that*?' she replied.

Of an evening, although she was bone weary, she sat in the kitchen with Mrs Moran and occasionally Sonny and Bridie, and attacked the mound of mending and darning. Some of the curtains and bedspreads, although originally of good quality, were so old and had been so neglected that they were almost beyond repair but she refrained from saying anything for fear she would be accused of even more extravagance.

Apart from mealtimes she saw very little of her employer. She was aware of him going in and out of the front door and occasionally heard him calling to Sonny in the yard, and once or twice she heard the sound of his horse's hooves as he departed from the house, returning later in the evening.

By Thursday she was exhausted, but buoyed up at the thought of seeing the children the next day. She was surprised that evening when, as she cleared away the dinner dishes, her employer signalled her to sit down.

She sat tentatively on the edge of an upright chair that was set beside the fire.

'You are indeed a hard worker, Mrs McGann. I don't miss much of what goes on here and your efforts have not gone unnoticed. The whole place is far cleaner and more . . . cheerful than it has been for a long time, although I have to say I would urge caution in lighting fires in some of those rooms on the upper storeys.'

'I thought it necessary, sir. To try to air the place,' she replied deferentially.

'I'm not complaining about the amount of turf, despite what Sonny might say, it's the chimneys. Some of them are in desperate need of sweeping not to say some repair, and could easily catch fire.'

'I'm sorry, sir. I had no idea. If you could let me know which ones are actually dangerous I'll avoid lighting the occasional fire. I'll make arrangements for the others to be swept.'

He nodded. 'I'd be obliged if you could let me know when the sweep is expected and I'll be away from home. The mess is unbelievable.'

'I will indeed, sir.' She looked down at her hands, wondering when he would dismiss her. She had the children's beds to make up and still more mending to do.

He regarded her thoughtfully over the rim of his claret glass. She looked tired and no wonder, she must have worn herself out entirely, the amount of work she seemed to have got through. Mrs Moran had sung her praises highly and informed him that she had even managed to get a hard day's work out of Bridie. Most astonishing of all had been the sight of Sonny cleaning the front yard. He had been highly amused to be told that these days only he himself was allowed to use the front door or Mary McGann would have all their guts for garters!

'Your children are arriving tomorrow?'

'They are, sir, and I assure you they will be no trouble. You will neither see nor hear them. They will be allowed only in our rooms and the kitchen.'

'Indeed? Will they not need somewhere to play?'

'There is the back yard and there are plenty of fields and woods around the place. Katie will help me with some of the lighter chores and Tommy can learn to be of use to Sonny. I thought he could perhaps fish in the river.'

'Of course. And the other one?' he enquired, remembering she had three but not quite sure if it was a boy or a girl.

'Lizzie has some difficulties. I should have mentioned that she was born both deaf and dumb, although she has spirit and Katie is good with her.'

A look of pity crossed his face. 'Poor child.'

Mary was surprised by his gentler tone of voice. 'She is happy enough, sir. I have always done my best for her – for all of them.'

He leaned forward across the table. 'Unless of course you have traits of character of which I am as yet unaware, I am thinking that your husband must be a very foolish man.'

Mary blushed and picked an imaginary thread from her

apron. '*I* think he is. I did nothing wrong in any way. I always worked hard. I was thrifty. He was well looked after.'

'He has work?'

'Yes. Most of the time. He works on the docks. Liverpool is a very busy port.'

'I am aware of that.' He decided he could not question her more closely but he believed her. Her honesty was transparent. 'Thank you, Mrs McGann. If there is ever anything you need to discuss with me, please don't hesitate to do so. You have everything you need?'

Thankful that she was at last able to go, Mary rose. 'I do, thank you, and everyone has been very kind and helpful.'

'Good. Then you may go.'

She inclined her head and picked up the tray. To her surprise he rose and opened the door for her.

'Thank you, sir, and goodnight.'

As she walked down the passageway towards the kitchen she wondered again why he had found it so difficult to keep a housekeeper. He seemed both polite and thoughtful.

When the dishes had been done, she banked up the fire before going to make up the beds for the children. Afterwards, she returned and picked up yet another pair of worn and frayed curtains from the pile in the corner. But before she could thread her needle, Mrs Moran placed two glasses and a bottle of sherry on the table.

'Put down those destroyed old bits of hangings. Haven't you done enough already? You'll lose the sight from your eyes at this rate. Take a glass with me, it will do you good.'

'Are you sure it's all right? Mr O'Neill won't mind? I'm not a great one for the drink.'

'Neither am I. Just a glass now and then and what Himself doesn't know won't harm him.'

'It's not *his* drink is it?' Mary asked, a little alarmed.

'It is not! Sonny brings me a bottle now and then from town, though I don't think Himself would care about the odd bottle going astray.'

Mary took the proffered glass and sipped the sweet drink. 'Mrs Moran, can I ask you something?'

'What is it?'

'I know that Mr O'Neill doesn't like us mixing with anyone but apart from that – and his being humoursome, which I haven't found him to be – why will no one stay?'

The older woman looked thoughtfully at her glass, deciding how much to tell Mary about Richard O'Neill.

'He isn't *that* bad,' Mary prompted.

'He is not but it's his position.'

'That of agent, you mean?'

'Yes. This country has had a troublesome past, Mary. There have been rebellions against the English Crown and the absentee landlords. There are plenty of folk still alive who remember the Great Hunger when the potato failed. Very few Irishmen own their land, all have to pay rent and need to sell their crops and cattle to pay that rent, which leaves them little to live on. When the blight came and the potato failed the landlords still demanded their rents. Those who couldn't pay were evicted, thrown out on the roads to starve or emigrate if they were lucky.'

'I know. Thousands of them came to Liverpool.'

'And thousands died there too, so I heard. The landlords still demand their rents today and the agents – like Richard O'Neill – are the ones who collect them. There are many around here who hate him for taking what they consider should be theirs. They work hard to scrape a pittance from the land and are bitter that they must hand it over to a man who lives in a grand house and wants for nothing. Who does no manual work himself. Someone who takes their last pennies and gives them to a landlord who hasn't set foot in the place for years and who cares nothing for those who live and work on his estate.'

Mary nodded her understanding. It didn't seem fair but that was the way things worked back home as well. The rich owned everything, the poor worked just as hard as the Irish and if there was no work then they starved too.

'That's why he won't have us mixing with the local people,' Mrs Moran added.

'But you and Sonny and Bridie are local? Why do you stay?'

'Because some of us can see past the title of Agent. He isn't a bad man. There's far more to him than meets the eye. He is compassionate, he *does* care about things and people and, despite what some people say, he is a man who loves his country. He'd not see anyone evicted if they couldn't pay the rent. Mind you, his father did all right.'

'His father worked here?'

'He did until he died, ten years ago. It's usually an inherited position and Richard inherited the hatred too. He . . . he hasn't had an easy life, Mary, especially not with . . .' She fell silent. She'd said enough. Mary had only been here a week, Mrs Moran didn't know if she could trust her new colleague enough to tell her the rest of Richard O'Neill's problems. Burdens, more like. Burdens that were whispered about and distorted and used to vilify him.

Mary gazed into the fire. What had the cook been going to tell her? She had clearly changed her mind about it. 'So, you've known him for a long time?'

'I have so.'

'Has he no family? No brothers or sisters?'

'None. His mother died when he was very young and the old feller never remarried. Mr O'Neill was packed off to Dublin to school as soon as he was old enough and then to the university. Trinity College.'

Mary was very surprised. 'University! He must be very clever.'

'Oh, he's that all right. He was after studying to be a doctor but amongst other things the old feller wanted him to come back here. He was ailing then, though few knew it.'

'That must have been hard for Mr O'Neill.'

'It was. Oh, there were some fierce rows, I can tell you, but he settled – eventually. Well, now I'm off to my bed and if you've any sense you'll be after going to yours too. I told Sonny to be ready at the back door for eleven o'clock to take you into Tullamore to meet the train. Won't the little ones be delighted to see you? They must have missed their mammy and it's a desperate journey to be taking on their own.'

'Molly was putting them in the charge of the guard but I'm sure they'll be glad to see me. And I've missed them too. Oh, I do hope they'll settle well here.'

'Ah, they will. Don't you be worrying over it now.'

Mary smiled at her. 'I won't. And I'm for my bed too. I have to be up early. There's chores to do before I can go off to the station!'

Chapter Fifteen

S HE WAS WAITING ANXIOUSLY on the platform next morning when the train at last pulled in and the guard helped three slightly bewildered and tired children from the carriage.

'There ye are, ma'am, safe and sound.' The man smiled. 'And I've not heard a sound out of them. No trouble at all.'

'Thank you so much,' Mary replied, rushing to them and gathering them in her arms. 'Oh, I've missed you all so much! I really have! I've been counting the days. Are you tired?'

'I'm starving, Mam. Is it far?' Tommy said, looking around.

'No. Sonny's waiting in the yard with the trap and when we get home Mrs Moran will have something for you to eat. Tommy, you bring the bags. Lizzie, hold my hand.' She held out her hand to the child who held it tightly. The whole journey had been a bit frightening for her and she didn't really understand why they had left Molly's, even though Katie had tried to explain. Nor did Katie's unease, which she had sensed, help to reassure her. She had, however, taken some comfort from Tommy's air of excitement. He'd never been on a train before, with or without his mam, and viewed it as a great adventure, although he was a bit apprehensive about this huge house he was going to live in and this Mr O'Neill who, Mam had said in the letter she'd sent to Molly, was very important.

'Give those bags to me, lad, and climb up. Don't stand at the pony's rump, child, he's inclined to be skittish,' Sonny added to Katie who hastily moved to her mother's side.

'You can see *everything* from up here, Mam! It's great!' Tommy cried as they pulled out of the station yard.

'I told you it would be, didn't I?' Mary laughed but felt a little concerned at Katie's whey face and Lizzie's scared expression. None of them was used to a trap.

Mrs Moran was waiting for them at the kitchen door. She exclaimed and fussed over them, sitting them down at the big table and watching with approval as they devoured the meal she put down before them.

'That's what I like to see, Mary, healthy appetites.'

'They're always hungry, especially Tommy. He'd eat you out of house and home.'

'Sure, he's a growing lad. Plenty of good wholesome food will put some flesh on all their bones. The country is a good place to rear up children, much better than dirty, crowded, noisy cities. You have certainly put manners on them, Mary.'

'I try but sometimes they forget. Now, when you've finished I'll take you and show you our rooms and the yard where you can play.'

'And the river, Mam, don't forget the river,' Tommy said with his mouth full.

'What was that you said about manners, Mrs Moran? He seems to have forgotten them already,' Mary said, frowning at her son.

Katie felt much better when she'd seen the rooms Mam said were to be theirs. She and Lizzie were to share a big bedroom with Mam and Tommy was to have the smaller room, which was much better than sleeping on Molly's floor, and the sitting room was warm and cosy and had some nice things in it. She helped Mam unpack the rest of their belongings while Lizzie sat on the bed and Tommy stared out of the window, trying to catch a glimpse of the river which seemed to hold a deep fascination for him.

After that they toured the yard, then crossed the small stile and walked along the grassy bank of the narrow but fast-flowing river. Both Katie and Lizzie held tightly to Mary's hands but Tommy ran on ahead. Next they climbed the bank up onto the towpath where the canal ran over the river on the Hubbard Aqueduct. The children exclaimed in wonder when they learned it had been built in 1803. Mary lifted Lizzie up and sat her on the wall and they all turned and looked at the walls of the castle which seemed to tower over everything.

'It's *huge*! How many rooms does it have, Mam? I've never seen anything so big, it's nearly as big as St George's Hall,' Tommy cried in awe.

Mary laughed. 'Don't exaggerate! It's not nearly as big as St George's Hall! But there are a great many rooms – as I know full well, having had to give them all a good clean.'

'It's a bit big for just Mr O'Neill and us,' he said.

'It is, but you'll get used to it. You'll only use our rooms and the kitchen. Mr O'Neill doesn't want to be disturbed by you three running all over the place. Tomorrow afternoon as a special treat we'll all go into Tullamore. I've not seen much of the town myself yet but there's bound to be shops and churches.'

'Will we have to go there to Mass, Mam?' Katie asked.

'No. There's a church at Kilbride and a school at Ballinamere. I'll go see the priest on Sunday about you starting school. I haven't had time yet.'

'So we won't have to go on Monday?' Katie asked, relieved.

'No. Probably Tuesday or Wednesday. It'll give you a bit of time to settle in. Now, we'd better get back. It will be getting dark soon and I've work to do.'

To Mary's great surprise, when she served Richard O'Neill's dinner that night, he asked whether the children had arrived safely.

'They have, sir, and if it's all right with you I have promised to take them into town tomorrow afternoon. I've not been there myself yet. Just to the station and back.'

'Get Sonny to take you and mind you stay with him,' he replied with a warning note in his voice.

Remembering Mrs Moran's words the previous night she nodded.

'And, Mrs McGann, after dinner I would like to meet your children. Will you bring them here to me?'

'Yes. Yes, of course, sir, if you're sure . . .' she answered uncertainly. She hadn't expected this.

'Get yourselves changed and have a bit of a wash. Katie, brush Lizzie's hair. I don't know what she's been doing with it, I'm sure. Mr O'Neill wants to meet you after he's had his meal,' she informed them, casting a mystified look and shrugging her shoulders at Mrs Moran's enquiring glance. 'Put on your Sunday clothes.'

'Do you wear that frock and that fancy apron all the time, Mam?' Katie asked, unused to seeing her mother in her uniform.

'No, only for serving meals. I told you, Mr O'Neill is an important man in these parts. Now off you go and no nonsense out of you, Tommy.'

She inspected them all before she ushered them along the passageway to the dining room. Then she knocked and waited to be called in.

All three children stood close together, in awe of what seemed to them very grand surroundings. Nervously, they eyed the rather formidable-looking man who had risen from the table and stood looking down at them.

Mary pushed Tommy forward. 'This is Thomas – Tommy. Say "How do you do, sir!" ' she hissed to him.

The lad stepped forward and extended his hand.

'I'm pleased to meet you, lad. How old are you?'

'Eight, sir.'

'And this is Katherine, Katie, she's nine.' Mary urged her daughter forward and the child was greeted as formally as her brother had been.

'And this is Elizabeth, Lizzie, she's six. I explained about her, sir.' To her astonishment he bent down and squatted on his haunches in front of the little girl, who refused to let go of Mary's hand.

'Hello, Lizzie. I hope you'll be happy here,' he said very slowly, taking the child's free hand in his own. He was rewarded with a shy smile.

'She likes you, sir. She seldom smiles at anyone, let alone strangers, and she's had to get used to so many strangers lately,' Mary informed him.

He stood up, after patting Lizzie gently on the head. 'They are fine children, Mrs McGann. A credit to you.'

'Thank you, sir. As I've promised, they'll be no trouble. I'm hoping they will start school early next week.'

'Even the little one? Do you not think it would be wise to let her settle in more first?'

'Lizzie enjoyed going to school in Liverpool, although I have to admit I felt it better that she stayed at home with me when we were in Dublin.'

'Did she learn anything when she went to school?'

'Very little but she enjoyed the company and I hope she will here too.'

'I'm sure she will eventually but can't I persuade you to keep her home for a little while?'

Mary was at a loss what to say. She had never expected him to show such interest or concern. 'Well, perhaps,' she answered at last.

He turned to Tommy. 'You will have to learn to drive the trap, lad, and the cart, and make yourself useful to Sonny.'

The boy's eyes lit up. 'Can I really learn to drive, sir?' No adult had ever shown such trust or confidence in him before.

'Indeed you can. You'll not be much help around here otherwise.'

'And can I learn how to fish?'

'I consider it a necessity for someone of your age.'

'Oh, *thanks*, sir!' Tommy gushed effusively.

'Well, I think that's enough excitement for one day. Say goodnight to Mr O'Neill now,' Mary urged. Any more of this and she'd not be able to do anything at all with her now decidedly exuberant son.

Katie and Tommy chorused their farewells and Lizzie gave him another shy smile before Mary thankfully ushered them towards the door.

'Goodnight, sir.'

'Goodnight, Mary.'

It was only when she was halfway down the passageway to the kitchen she realised that for the first time he had called her 'Mary' and not 'Mrs McGann'. He was a strange man all right, she thought, but she felt pleased. Had he accepted her? Did it mean that after her month's trial she would be kept on? She hoped so. Somehow his use of her Christian name made her feel at home, a sensation she hadn't experienced at Molly's nor anywhere else since that terrible night when Frank had thrown them all out.

The next day it was dull and overcast but the sky had a strange luminous cast to it.

'We're in for snow, I'm thinking,' Sonny announced, coming into the kitchen with Tommy dogging his footsteps.

'Oh, do you really think so?' Mary asked, thinking about their proposed trip.

'It's gone a touch warmer and that's always a sure sign.'

'Will we still be able to go into town?'

'If we don't leave it too late. I can cope with the snow but not darkness and snow together.'

'Right then, I'd better get a move on.'

'Sonny's showed me how to hitch up the trap,' Tommy said with some pride.

'He'll be able to do it *and* drive in no time at all. He's taken to it like a duck to the water, so he has,' Sonny enthused.

Mary was pleased. 'Good. At least he's making himself useful.'

They all wrapped themselves up against the cold but Mary looked anxiously at the sky as they drove the three miles into town. Sonny brought the trap to a halt in the little square in the middle of town and helped them down.

'Now, all of you stay close to me. Don't be wandering off or stopping to talk to people.'

'Why can't we talk to anyone?' Tommy asked.

'Because they'll only be asking questions, that's why. Sure, before you know it they'll have your life story and it'll be blathered to the whole of the county.'

'Do as Sonny tells you and don't dawdle,' Mary instructed, taking Lizzie's hand.

They had toured the main streets and looked at the shops and Mary had bought them some toffee to eat on the way home. She'd also purchased some more sewing thread and darning wool, a couple of papers of pins and a packet of needles, and some black braid which she intended to use to trim the skirt she'd bought in Dublin for best. The woman in the drapery shop had been openly curious and had remarked that she'd not seen her in town before. Mary had replied that she was the new housekeeper at Ballycowan Castle and that she was from Liverpool before she'd intercepted a warning look from Sonny. She'd also noticed the curious, even hostile looks cast in their direction as they'd walked along.

'Best be heading back,' Sonny said at length, casting a glance skywards. They made their way swiftly back to the square.

Just before they reached Charleville Castle it began to snow and Sonny hastened the pony into a trot. 'Thanks be to God it's not far or we'd all be soaked to the skin,' he muttered.

For safety's sake Mary lit the lamps that were attached to the side of the trap and prayed it wouldn't develop into a blizzard before they got home.

When they were a mile away from Ballycowan the visibility deteriorated. Large white flakes were falling heavily, obliterating everything, and she had pulled the collars of the children's coats up high and urged them to pull their scarves over their hats.

'Will you be all right, Sonny? You can hardly see the road,' she asked quietly.

'Don't you worry, Mary, the pony would know its way even if it were blindfolded.'

'What's that? I thought I saw something ahead.' She tried to peer through the curtain of white that enveloped them.

'And I thought I was after hearing the sound of hooves.'

'Is it another cart or trap? Will they see us in time to stop?' She was a little afraid now.

'HELLO! HELLO OUT THERE!' Sonny shouted.

'SONNY? SONNY, IS THAT YOURSELF?' came the answering shouted question.

'It's Himself! Now what's wrong that he's come out to look for us?'

Mary was relieved and yet anxious. She hoped there was nothing wrong back at the house.

Richard O'Neill was swathed in a heavy greatcoat and a wide-brimmed hat was pulled down over his forehead. He reined in his horse as Sonny brought the pony to a standstill.

'I thought you'd have had more sense than to be going into town on a day like this,' he said.

'It wasn't snowing when we left. Sure it didn't start until we were at the gates of Charleville and I wasn't to know it would be so heavy.'

'It's all my fault, sir. I really should have put it off to another day,' Mary volunteered. 'But I'd promised the children,' she added, by way of an excuse.

He didn't reply.

'So what's up now that you've come riding out to meet us?' Sonny asked.

'Nothing. I was worried about Mary and the children and you getting lost.'

'Getting lost, is it? When did I ever get lost?' Sonny was aggrieved.

'You could have wandered off the road and into a ditch.'

Sonny shook his head and tutted in annoyance. 'A ditch indeed!' he muttered under his breath.

'It was very good of you to be so concerned about us, sir,' Mary said sincerely.

'Right then, let's get home before we all freeze,' he said, urging his horse forward into the already darkening laneway. Sonny jerked the reins for the pony to follow.

Mrs Moran was waiting at the kitchen door and it was with relief that Mary got down and helped Tommy and Katie alight while Richard O'Neill lifted Lizzie down.

'Thanks be to God! Aren't you all soaked! Come on in, I've the kettle on.'

Mary turned to Tommy. 'Go out and help Sonny and Mr O'Neill with the horses, then come straight back. It was very good of Mr O'Neill to come and look for us,' she added, seeing the disgruntled look appear on her son's face. She urged him towards the door.

'He went out to look for you?' Mrs Moran said, surprised.

'He did. He was afraid we would end up in a ditch,' Mary replied, stripping off Lizzie's wet things.

Mrs Moran raised her eyebrows but said nothing. She'd never known him do anything like that before. But then no one like Mary McGann had ever worked here before.

Chapter Sixteen

———◆◆◆◆———

THE SNOW CONTINUED TO fall for two days, making it impossible for any of them to travel anywhere. The children were the only ones who enjoyed it, making frequent forays into the yard to build snowmen and pelt each other with snowballs, then returning to the kitchen cold, wet but with rosy cheeks. Even little Lizzie seemed to be enjoying herself.

Unknown and unseen by them Richard O'Neill stood watching their latest snow fight from his bedroom window, a smile tinged with sadness and regret hovering around his mouth. He hoped they would stay. He hoped Mary would turn out to be everything he desired in a housekeeper. He would hate having to dismiss her but would his rules eventually force her to take herself and her children back to Dublin or even Liverpool? Was he already thinking too much about her?

He turned away and sat down in the chair near the

fireplace. Moodily, he threw a few more lumps of turf on the fire. This wasn't the life he'd planned for himself, but everything had conspired against him and the plans he'd made. His father; his education. The taste of a different life in Dublin and the sense of freedom he'd experienced while there, away from the mistrust and hatred here. And not least his own weakness in becoming involved with the beautiful Isabelle Power. Now to all intents and purposes he was a lonely outcast, but that wasn't how he saw himself. He had a small group of friends in the community, though very few people knew that. It was essential to them all that that fact wasn't widely known. He had contacts in other places: in other counties and Dublin and a good bit of his time was spent maintaining those contacts. Many people in the area thought he did very little except collect rents and it served his purpose for them to hold that opinion, but his days were full, his time and his mind were fully occupied. He had the good of all his fellow countrymen firmly at heart, although hardly anyone knew it or would ever believe it. That suited him very well – for now.

He stood up and began to pace restlessly. Despite the weather he had to go out. Peter Casey was bringing a visitor from Cork and he was meeting them just outside Ferbane. No doubt they would be late, but he *had* to go. Besides, he was sick of this gloomy pile of old stones that passed for a house. It was a house that had seen nothing but war, rebellion, famine, death and misery. It could never be called

a home in the real meaning of that word, which encom-
passed safety, security, hope and love. There was no love in
it. No, that wasn't true. There was Mary's obviously
heartfelt love for her children.

It wasn't until the following week that Tommy and Katie
went to school at Ballinamere, further down the canal line,
and Sonny went into town for supplies. Gradually the snow
melted and was followed by what seemed to Mary weeks of
steady rain. She had quickly established a daily routine of
work for herself, helped by Bridie who came in three
mornings a week. The house looked better and was warmer
and more cheerful. The children seemed settled and
content and she herself felt happier than she had in a long
while. The month had passed more quickly than she would
have thought possible and she waited for the summons
from her employer to inform her of whether or not they
were to stay.

It came on the last Friday of March in the middle of the
morning.

'Himself wants to see you, Mary, in the small drawing
room. I was after filling up the turf basket when he said for
me to tell you,' Sonny announced on returning to the
kitchen.

'Will you go back and tell him I'll be along directly I've
changed my dress?' she asked, casting an anxious look at
Mrs Moran, who smiled encouragingly.

In her neat black dress, white cap and apron she knocked on the door of the small drawing room and entered.

'You asked to see me, sir?' She couldn't keep the slight tremor of nervousness out of her voice.

'I did, Mary. Please sit down.'

But Mary was too agitated to do so.

'Is it about my . . . suitability, sir?' she blurted out, standing rather stiffly by the door.

He turned away from her and glanced out of the window. The rain was cascading down the panes from a broken eaves shute and the yard looked sodden and miserable.

'It is. Are you happy here? Have you and the children settled?'

'Oh, yes, sir! *I'm* more than happy and the children are well. Tommy is delighted with himself, Katie likes her teacher and Lizzie has become rather a pet with both Mrs Moran and Bridie. I'm hoping to send her to school very soon. She's better mixing with other children.'

He turned to face her. 'Is she really? It must be hard for her, she won't be able to learn in the same way as the others.'

'No, she can't learn the same way. I've always tried my best with her but I've neither the time nor the skill to make much progress. Katie says Miss Collins has great patience, however.'

'Well, it's your decision. She's your child,' he answered rather curtly.

Mary felt a little apprehensive at his tone but tried not to show it.

'You have improved this house greatly, Mary, and you are everything you promised you were. You suit me very well so if you are agreeable I think we can say the position is yours for as long as you want it, which I hope will be many years.'

Her face lit up. 'Oh, thank you, sir! I'm so pleased. I don't think I'll ever want to leave. What else is there for me?'

'It can be rather dull and quiet here.'

'That's fine by me. I've had more than enough of living in overcrowded houses and cities. I never want to live in one again.'

He smiled. 'Good. Here are your wages.' He handed her an envelope. 'Is there anything you need?'

'There's nothing, thank you, sir. We're very comfortable. Should I bring some tea, as it's such a miserable morning?'

'No, thank you, Mary. Despite the weather I have to go out, the rents are due. It's not a duty I relish, especially at this time of year.'

'I understand, sir,' she said quietly.

He looked at her intently. 'Do you? Do you *really*, Mary?'

She met his gaze squarely and with sympathy. 'Yes. Mrs Moran explained it to me.'

'But you don't approve?'

'Whether I approve is not important, sir.'

He nodded slowly. She was right.

'Will that be all, sir?'

'It will,' he replied, turning once more back towards the window to indicate the interview was over.

Mary let herself quietly out. There were times when she didn't understand him at all. The way his mood changed from minute to minute was highly disconcerting.

He was glad he'd made the decision. She'd suited very well indeed but he was aware of a disturbing feeling deep inside himself. He didn't want her to stay *just* because she had brought order and comfort to this house. He was growing fond of her. He'd begun to look forward to mealtimes because she served those meals. He often heard her singing softly to herself as she went about her work and once he had surprised her when he'd returned to his room and found her making his bed. That had disturbed him, to see her in his room, the pillow he laid his head on in her hands. The next night she had haunted his dreams. He had never met a woman like her before. Of course she wasn't of his class or religion but she had a gentleness of manner, a quiet confidence that many of the so-called 'ladies' of his own rank lacked. And what had his class and religion ever done for him except cause him misery? He pulled himself up sharply. 'Stop this, you fool!' he admonished himself. She was a married woman with three children and she was his housekeeper – nothing more!

After Lizzie had been at school a week Miss Collins came to see Mary. She was a pleasant woman in her late twenties. Mary ushered her into the kitchen politely.

'Mrs McGann, I felt I had to come and speak to you about Lizzie.'

'Is she any trouble? What has she been up to?' Mary asked with concern.

'No, she's no trouble at all. The thing is, Mrs McGann, I don't feel as though Lizzie will benefit from being in school. I don't mean she's not a bright child, she is, it's just that I don't feel . . . qualified, shall we say, to teach her. It's a very small country school and there is only myself and I feel she is, well, left out.'

Mary nodded slowly. 'I know. I sometimes have trouble myself. Katie is better with her than I am. It's very difficult.'

The young woman looked sympathetic. 'It must be, Mrs McGann, and you a stranger in these parts.'

Mary nodded again. 'So, you think it would be better if I kept her here, at home?'

'I do. I'm so sorry.'

'Don't worry about it. Your duty is to your other pupils. I wouldn't want any of them to suffer because of Lizzie and, as you said yourself, we're strangers in these parts. Thank you, Miss Collins, for taking the time and the trouble to come and see me personally. You must be very busy.'

'Thank *you*, Mrs McGann, for being so understanding.'

Mary showed her out, feeling a little aggrieved. She had always spent as much time as possible with Lizzie, helped her as best she could. Well, now that she had sorted out the household she would spend more time with Lizzie. She would educate Lizzie herself. She'd find a way. Lizzie'd have enough problems when she grew up without being incapable of reading or even signing her name. No, she wasn't having that.

She was preoccupied as she served her employer his lunch and it did not go unnoticed.

'Is there something the matter, Mary?' he asked.

'No, not really, sir,' she replied, thinking she should pay more attention to what she was doing.

'You look troubled?' he pressed. 'Can't you tell me about it?'

She sighed. 'It's Lizzie.'

'What's the matter with her?'

'Oh, nothing really. It's just that I had the teacher here to see me about her.'

'What for?' he demanded sharply. Had the woman come to complain?

'She, Miss Collins, feels Lizzie would be better at home. I think she's taking up too much of Miss Collins's time, time she should spend with her other pupils. I don't want any complaints about the children of *strangers* affecting the chances of the rest of the class.'

'Is that what she said?' he demanded, annoyed.

'In so many words.'

He leaned back in his chair. 'I'm sorry, Mary, that you should be tarred with the same brush as myself, so to speak.'

'But you're not a stranger, sir.'

'I might as well be, though I have to say it's of my own choosing. What will you do?'

'I'll keep her here at home and try and teach her myself as best I can.'

He smiled. She had called this place home. 'If you'll allow me, and if Lizzie won't get upset, *I* will teach her.'

'*You* will, sir?' Mary couldn't have been more astonished.

'I wanted to be a doctor, Mary. I feel the plight of people . . . children like Lizzie, very keenly, and there are new ways of thinking, new methods of helping the deaf. Will you let me try? I will send to Dublin for books, papers to assist me. I have heard of a system by which she might be able to understand me. I think it's been more fully developed now.'

Mary was very interested in this revelation. 'She can lip-read, to an extent, but she finds it hard to follow a conversation and sometimes I wonder just how much she does understand. I've always wanted to help her more but I don't know *how* to.' She paused, choosing her words carefully, a little nervous as to how he would react. 'This . . .

system. Could . . . could I learn it? Could you teach me too?'

He smiled. 'I don't see why not. When I've found out more and mastered it myself. It might be a little difficult.'

'I don't mind that. I'm determined to help her. I'm determined she won't grow up wholly uneducated.'

'I'm sorry, Mary. I didn't mean to insult you. I just meant, let me try it out first.'

'I'm not insulted, sir. I just want what's best for Lizzie. And thank you. It's very kind of you to take such an interest.'

' 'Tis little enough, Mary,' he replied, dismissing her. He knew how it felt to live in a world where you were crippled in one way or another. Lizzie's disability was physical, his was emotional, but if he could ease the child's burden in any way, he would.

Mrs Moran made no comment when Mary told her of the conversation but she looked doubtful and concerned. Just what was Himself up to? She'd never known him to behave like this before. Were his concern and his attempts to teach the child just a means to an end?

The books and papers duly arrived from Dublin and there were occasions when he travelled up to the capital to learn more, 'at first hand' as he put it. It was the beginning of the strange relationship between the rather shy handicapped child and the taciturn social outcast. Gradually Lizzie became more and more relaxed in his presence and, Mary noticed, he seemed to have infinite patience with her. Each morning for an hour and a half and again in the afternoon he and the child were closeted in the small dining room while he attempted to teach her to fathom the meaning of words and to write. But, Mary had to admit, Lizzie seemed to enjoy the time. After four weeks he asked Mary to sit in with them.

'It will seem very strange to you at first, Mary, but have patience and watch carefully. It's really quite simple.'

Mary sat down and watched him curve his fingers into a half-circle and Lizzie immediately copied him. Then he wrote down a letter of the alphabet on a piece of paper and Lizzie copied that.

'You see, Mary, each movement represents a letter or word. Lizzie is very bright, she's picking it up very quickly.'

Mary nodded slowly.

He made a number of hand movements that Lizzie copied.

'She's saying, "How are you, Mother?",' he said gently.

Mary looked at the sparkling, intelligent eyes of her child and tears welled up. Lizzie was 'talking' to her! For the first time in her little life the child could in a way 'speak'!

'Will you . . . will you show me how to answer her?' Mary's voice was a little choked.

He was touched by her show of emotion. She must have

felt the child's disability very deeply. More deeply than he had realised. 'Of course I will and I think that perhaps from now on, whenever you have some spare time, you should sit in with us.'

'Oh, I will, sir! Thank you! It's . . . it's just so wonderful to see her little face light up like that!'

When in late spring Lizzie appeared at the end of her morning 'lesson' and proudly placed a piece of paper down on the table for her mother to read, Mary's eyes misted with tears as she read the spidery and childish script. It was the first full piece Lizzie had ever written.

Elizabeth McGann. Age 6. Ballycowan Castle, Tullamore, King's County, Ireland.

'Well now, would you look at that! I would never have believed it,' Mrs Moran said in some awe.

'Neither would I. He's done wonders for her. He's a strange man.'

'Oh, he's that all right,' Mrs Moran had said sagely but with a note in her voice that Mary couldn't understand.

Next day it was bright and fine and as she went to peg out the washing she noticed that there were primroses and daffodils poking their heads from beneath the banks of trees that marked the castle's perimeter. When she had finished her work this afternoon, maybe she'd walk down the canal line and meet Katie and Tommy from school. She'd take Lizzie with her. The sun felt warm on her back and she looked forward to summer out here in the country.

It would be so different to the humid, stinking streets of Liverpool.

However, when she was ready to leave Lizzie proved difficult, refusing to leave the pies she was baking with Mrs Moran's help.

'Ah, leave her. Isn't she happy enough here with me? Bridie will take her to see the new lambs later on. You get yourself off,' the cook instructed.

'Well, if you're sure?'

'Of course I'm sure. A walk in the fresh air will do you good. Go on with you now.'

Mary took her jacket from its peg and left. It *was* good just to walk. It was a beautiful day and all around her were the signs of new life. Birds darted from the canal bank to the trees and hedgerows, their beaks full of wisps of straw and grass to build their nests. The trees were beginning to sprout fresh green buds and everywhere there were clumps of wild spring flowers.

The countryside looked beautiful, she thought as she walked slowly along the towpath, waving to the men on the barges that were plying their way down towards the Shannon. She *was* happy here, and so were the children. She didn't mind the lack of company. She always replied politely to the people who greeted her as she left the little church with her children, but she never made any attempt to engage them in conversation. Both Tommy and Katie had friends at school but they never asked them to come and play, seeming content with their own company and that of Sonny and Bridie, herself and Mrs Moran. When she went into town it was in the company of Sonny and she did her shopping with the minimum of fuss and conversation. She wrote regularly to Nellie and to Molly, keeping them informed of her good fortune and her good spirits. She learned that there was indeed trouble in Dublin between the unions and workers and that at home in Liverpool there had been dock strikes and lockouts and that Frank had made himself even more disliked by siding with the employers. He was still living alone and becoming more and more silent and unfriendly by the month, according to Nellie. No, she didn't wish herself back in either Dublin or Liverpool.

Her train of thought was interrupted by the sound of rather tuneless singing and, looking up, she noticed a man coming towards her, rather unsteadily. She couldn't recall seeing him before and hoped he wouldn't want to stop and talk. As he drew nearer she could see that he was quite plainly drunk.

'Good afternoon to you, ma'am! Isn't it a grand day altogether?' he called, catching sight of her.

She sighed. Well, it cost nothing to be polite. 'It is indeed.'

He peered at her with bloodshot eyes. She reckoned he was about fifty. He was dressed in what she assumed was his Sunday suit.

'As grand a day as you could get for a funeral,' he said, attempting to appear sober.

'A funeral?'

'Ah, poor Mrs Shanahan was laid to rest this morning.'

And quite obviously he'd been taking a drop of the hard stuff in consolation with the relatives of the deceased Mrs Shanahan, she thought.

'May God have mercy on her soul,' Mary said devoutly. He was so close now that she could smell the drink on his breath.

'Amen to that, ma'am. And where might you be living? Sure, I haven't seen you before, have I?'

'I don't think so.'

'Well, I'm pleased to make your acquaintance.' He swayed a little, then continued formally, 'And whom might I be addressing?'

She was amused. 'Mrs Mary McGann. And you are?'

'Dinny Casey from Mucklagh. Where do you live?'

'Back there at Ballycowan Castle. I'm Mr O'Neill's housekeeper. I'm originally from Liverpool,' she added before any comment was made on her accent.

'Ah, so it's yourself. I've heard about you.'

She smiled. 'All good, I hope.'

His demeanour changed. 'Why should it be?'

'Why should it not? I'm a respectable woman doing a respectable job,' she answered sharply.

'No *respectable* woman would work for the likes of *him*!'

She was growing angry. 'Then good day to you. I refuse to stand here and be insulted or hear Mr O'Neill insulted either.' She made to move past him but he grabbed her arm. Crying out, she tried to shake off his grip.

'Insult *him*! Sure, there's not words enough in the language to insult *him* with!'

'Take your hands off me!' she said icily. She refused to let him see she was afraid of him.

'You know nothing of him and his way of going on.'

'I know that he is a gentleman who has shown nothing but consideration and concern for myself and my children and *he* isn't drunk at three o'clock in the afternoon and assaulting and insulting respectable women on the King's highway!'

His face contorted with rage. 'The *King's* highway is it now? And may God blast him to hell! The last one was a drunkard, a glutton and an adulterer and will this one be any better? When did they ever give a tinker's curse for the likes of us? But *our* day is coming, I can tell you! And I don't need the drink to tell you what kind of a *gentleman* Richard O'Neill is. He's one who keeps his poor mad wife locked up in that castle, thinking no one knows about her. You ask him about her. That's why no *respectable* woman will stay!'

Mary was horrified by his outburst. Never had she heard such terrible things said about King Edward or King George but what he had said about Richard O'Neill had shocked her to the core.

'You're the one who's mad!' she cried. He must be. He must have escaped from a lunatic asylum somewhere. She looked quickly around. She had to get away from him.

'You take notice of what I say, girl, and get out from there with your childer!'

Mary began to struggle as he tried to push her backwards towards the castle.

He began to yell at her and she screamed for help: he was very strong and she was afraid he would push her into the canal.

'Leave her alone, you madman! Take your hands off her before I beat you to a pulp!'

Dinny Casey released her and turned, his attention diverted by the figure on horseback who seemed to have appeared from nowhere and who towered over them both.

Mary fell to her knees, crying with relief as Richard O'Neill, his face dark red with fury, raised his riding crop and brought it down hard on the older man's shoulder.

'That's right! Beat a poor old man! You filthy traitor! I've told her about you and that poor wife of yours! Beat me all you like but you'll not change my mind about *you*!' Casey yelled.

'By God, I'll kill you, you lying drunken sod!' O'Neill had dismounted and began laying into the older man with his fists.

Mary began to scream and the horse reared in fright.

'Mary, catch the horse! Catch him before he bolts!' O'Neill cried.

Somehow she managed to pull herself together and catch hold of the bridle and hang on to it until the animal had calmed down a little. Then she realised that another man had appeared.

'Let him go, O'Neill! In the name of God, don't you know what he's like when he's drink taken?' The new arrival had caught the older man by the shoulder and tried to shield him. 'What have you been saying, Da?'

'The truth! Only the truth! Leave me be, Peter!' Dinny Casey whined, rubbing his shoulder where the crop had made it sting.

'Get him out of here, Peter! I won't have him carrying on like this. Accosting and terrifying defenceless women with his drunken lies!'

'He's a lying blackguard of a traitor!' Dinny Casey shouted.

'For God's sake, Da, will you shut your mouth and get off home!' his son bawled.

'You should keep him away from the jar, Peter, or one day that tongue of his will be the end of us all!'

'I can't keep my eye on him every minute of the day, Richard, you know that. I do my best.'

'Just get him home and sober him up before he does any more harm!'

'Come on out of it, Da! You're a disgrace to everyone

carrying on like this.' Taking the old man's arm Peter Casey finally dragged his father away, casting a concerned backward glance at Richard and Mary.

O'Neill's anger had diminished; he was now full of concern. 'Mary, are you hurt?'

Mary shook her head, but she was shaking.

'Ignore him. He's mad with the drink. It always takes him like that.' He took the reins from her and mounted the horse. 'Here, give me your hand. You'll ride with me, you're too upset to walk.'

He swung her up into the saddle behind him and she was so filled with relief yet stunned with shock that she automatically put her arms around his waist and leaned her head against his shoulder as he urged the horse into a trot and then a canter.

Chapter Seventeen

———◦•×•◦———

WITHIN MINUTES THEY WERE clattering into the castle yard. She was still shaking when he lifted her down. She swayed unsteadily on her feet, and he put his arm around her. 'Mary, you're in a terrible state. Did he hurt you?'

'No! No, not really! I was just walking . . . It was such a nice day that I thought I'd meet the children from school and . . . Oh, my God! The children! What if he—?'

'Hush, there's no need to worry about them. Peter is with him now. He'll cause no more trouble. Come inside.' He spoke quietly and reassuringly but inwardly he was seething with anger. Why the hell couldn't Peter keep his eye on the old drunkard?

Mary held tightly to her employer, more upset at the ugly incident than she would admit. The sense of security and peace she had previously felt had been shattered.

241

'Glory be to God! What's happened? Is she hurt?' Mrs Moran cried as they came into the hall.

'No, just distressed. That old blackguard Dinny Casey was roaring drunk and has terrified the life out of her with his carryings on.'

Mrs Moran looked horrified. 'My God, what did he say to her?'

'The usual pack of lies! I'll take her into the drawing room; a drop of brandy will do her no harm.'

'I'll make up the fire. She's shivering,' Mrs Moran said, bustling away but with a quick glance of trepidation in the direction of Richard O'Neill. She fervently hoped the incident wouldn't make Mary pack her bags.

He eased her into the chair by the fire and then poured her a small glass of brandy. 'Drink it slowly, Mary,' he instructed.

She did as she was told but it burned her throat and she spluttered.

'Sip it.' He threw the remaining pieces of turf onto the fire and tried to stir up the embers with the toe of his boot.

'Did he hurt you?' he pressed. By God, if he had he'd not let the matter lie.

'No. Not really, you came before . . .'

'He wouldn't have beaten or killed you, Mary.'

'I . . . I wasn't to know that!' she retorted, feeling a little steadier. 'He . . . he said that you . . .'

'I know what he said! It's always the same thing. A tirade against the King and then against me.'

'It's not true then? What he said about you having a—'

'*None* of it is true!' he interrupted sharply. 'He's out of his wits when he has drink. He doesn't know what he's saying. One of these days he'll go too far with all that slander. He'll say it to the wrong person and then it will be jail or worse. I'm sorry, Mary. More sorry than I can say that you chanced to meet him and he in that state.'

She'd finished the brandy and felt much better. 'I was only being polite to him. He said he'd been to a funeral. He asked me who I was and where I lived and then . . . then he became abusive and started to say all those terrible things.'

'You'd be better to take care of where you walk, Mary,' Mrs Moran advised as she came in with more turf and tipped it into the basket beside the hearth.

'She shouldn't need to. It's a fine thing if a woman can't take a short walk outside her own door without being afraid of who she'll meet.'

'Then it's about time something was done about the likes of *him*!' the woman retorted. She sniffed in disapproval, then left.

'Maybe she's right.'

'No, please! I don't want to cause any trouble for you!'

He nodded slowly. 'If you're sure you're all right.'

She rose and handed him the glass. 'I'm fine now, thank

you, sir. Let's just put it all behind us. The children will be home any minute and I don't want them to be worried.'

'Then you won't be . . . leaving?'

'Leaving? Why should I do that?'

'Some have.'

'It's happened before?'

He nodded. 'Twice. I suppose I should have warned you but . . . I didn't want to alarm you or lose you.'

She smiled wanly. 'It will take more than that to make me leave. We have been very happy here – all of us.'

'And that's how I want it to continue, Mary. If ever there is anything, *anything* at all, that is troubling you, you will come to me?'

She nodded. 'I will, sir. I promise. Now, I'd better go back to the kitchen.'

'Where's Lizzie?' he asked.

'She went with Bridie to see the new lambs in the far paddock.'

'Good. At least she was far enough away from here not to see anything that might disturb her.'

When she'd gone he sat down and poured himself a brandy. It was something he rarely did. It was all too easy a habit to acquire, drinking during the day, but he often felt like it. He frowned. Dinny Casey was getting out of hand. The man had terrified Mary and if he hadn't been there God knows what would have happened, although he'd meant what he'd said to her. Dinny wouldn't intentionally set out to harm her. But she could have ended up in the canal and perhaps have drowned. He had a mental vision of her struggling in the cold treacherous water. Seeing her in such danger and so vulnerable and terrified had disturbed him greatly. He had such respect and admiration for her . . . but was it something more? The incident had shaken him and now forced him to look more closely at his feelings for her. Yes, he *was* fond of her. She had brought so much into his life, but was that all it was? You fool! he thought irritably. What else *could* there be? She was a married woman with three children. She was of a different class, background and religion. There could be nothing more and not just because of those reasons.

Julia Moran was very concerned about Mary as she fussed over her in the kitchen.

'Are you *sure* you're all right?' she pressed.

'Yes. Yes, I'm fine now.'

'You still look very pale.'

'Don't worry.'

'I don't want you to be thinking about packing your bags.'

'Mr O'Neill asked me the same thing. I'm not. Why should I leave here because of . . . that?'

'Well, I'm glad of that, Mary.'

Mary sipped her tea. 'Why did he say those things?'

'Ah, his brain is addled! The old eejit!'

'But why does he *hate* us so much?'

Julia sighed. 'I once told you this is a country with a troubled past but many look to the future too. I don't approve of violence but there're many who will resort to it. Oh, I'm not saying we don't have grievances, we do. We lack so many basic rights.' She looked reflective, choosing her words carefully. 'We're not even free, Mary. We can't govern ourselves, make our own laws, decide our own future. Every country has that right. We've never taken to English ways; we have our own. Our culture, religion and even language – though few now speak it. We can't own our own land; our wealth is taken from us; we can't hold high office. Yet we have a right to all those things. We have a right to *justice*, Mary. Can you understand that?'

Slowly Mary nodded. She was beginning to comprehend. It wasn't just a matter of land and money, it was far more.

'I never really grasped it. I don't suppose I ever needed to before. But what about everything . . . else that man said?'

'Put it out of your mind, Mary! Forget all about it! Now, we'd better get cleaned up before the children arrive home.'

Mary nodded, although she was still troubled. However, she could see by the set of the older woman's lips that there was to be no further discussion. The subject was closed. Julia had said all she was going to say.

* * *

Later that night, when Mary sat alone in her small sitting room, she watched the shadows of the flames from the fire making patterns on the wall. She'd drawn the curtains and pulled her chair close to the fire. It wasn't often she chose to sit in here alone. She usually preferred the warmth and the company in the kitchen. Tonight was different. Tonight she felt the need to be alone with her thoughts.

The events of the afternoon had deeply disturbed her. Not just Dinny's attack but his words, his accusations. She did understand more now, thanks to Julia Moran, but could she sympathise with or fully understand people who resented and even hated the monarchy? Never in her life had she questioned the monarch's right to rule her and the countries within his kingdom. But far worse were Dinny's accusations against Richard O'Neill. Were they true? Did he have a wife he kept locked up because she was mad? His instructions about never going to the upper storeys because of their dangerous state of repair came back to her. No, it couldn't be true! she told herself firmly. Mrs Moran and Sonny would surely have let something slip, nor could you keep anyone a prisoner in a house without some sign of it becoming apparent. She had never seen or heard anyone going up to the rooms beneath the five huge chimneys. And food would have to be taken up and she saw everything that was prepared in the kitchen *and* she cleared up. It was nothing more than the ravings of a man unhinged by a lifetime of heavy drinking. She'd seen it happen before in Liverpool. There had been too many old men staggering from the pubs, shouting abuse, in the neighbourhood she'd lived in.

She sighed and covered her face with her hands, trying to blot out the images, but failing. She'd never seen her employer so angry or act with such violence and it disturbed her. Yet when it was over he had shown such concern and gentleness that he couldn't be a *bad* man. Her cheeks flushed as she remembered how she'd clasped her arms tightly around his waist on the horse and then clung to him as he'd helped her across the yard and into the house.

She got up and leaned her head on the mantelshelf. Stop it! Stop it! she told herself firmly. There was no use tearing herself apart like this. She was still married to Frank and she *didn't* love Richard O'Neill! She should just be so thankful that she had a good job, a little money saved, a comfortable home and a good life for her children. She must control her feelings and her imagination. He was her employer. He was an educated man. He was of a station in life far above her own. He was a different religion. She must never, *never*, let stupid, irrational feelings rob her of all that good fortune had showered on her.

Life settled back into its normal routine and she put the incident to the back of her mind, but she noticed that Richard O'Neill seemed less talkative and somehow subdued towards her, and it made her feel uneasy and strangely hurt. It's your imagination, she told herself sternly, you're reading far too much into this relationship, which, when all's said and done, is only that of master and servant.

Easter came and went and the weather became warmer. The evenings drew out and she often sat on the river bank while Katie and Lizzie played nearby and Tommy fished. It was so peaceful with only the sound of the rushing water, the lowing of the cattle in the water meadows, the birds in the trees and hedgerows and occasionally the sound of church bells in the far distance.

Once or twice Richard O'Neill had walked past them and as always had stopped and spoken kindly to Tommy and Katie and bent to make the strange signs with his hands that he had taught Lizzie to use. He'd have made a good doctor, she thought once, seeing Lizzie smile as she'd had the strange 'conversation' with him. The children all looked so much more healthy. They had grown taller and sturdier and their cheeks were rosy. Tommy was a great help to Sonny; he was now quite competent at driving both the trap and the cart and was similarly proficient at fishing, which he delighted in. Katie often helped her and Mrs Moran and had developed a friendship with Bridie, who seemed to have no friends of her own. But it was Lizzie whose progress gave her the most satisfaction. She, too, had grown physically but it was the confidence the child now seemed to show that made Mary so thankful and grateful to Richard O'Neill, for the time and patience and interest he gave unstintingly to Lizzie. Lizzie in return offered him a devotion never before given to anyone other than Mary herself. The child had come on in leaps and bounds and was now capable of things Mary would never have dreamed possible when they'd left Dublin.

One morning in mid May, Sonny came bursting into the kitchen with the post. 'There's your usual one from herself in Liverpool, Mary,' he said, passing over Nellie's letter, 'but none from Dublin.' He took a keen interest in everything that was delivered; Mrs Moran had often remarked that if you didn't keep your eye on him he'd have the letters over the kettle to steam them open.

Mary wiped her hands on her apron, took it from him and sat down at the table to read Nellie's news.

Mrs Moran was plucking a chicken for the evening meal but she stopped and let the bird fall into the stone sink as Mary groaned and covered her face with her hands. The letter fluttered to the floor.

'Mary! Mary, what is it? Bad news?' she cried.

'The Lord save us!' Sonny exclaimed, crossing himself.

'Mary?' the cook pressed.

Mary looked up. 'Frank, my husband, has had an accident on the docks, where he works.'

'Oh, God have mercy on him! Is it bad?' Mrs Moran sat down opposite Mary.

'Yes. Nellie says he's lucky to be alive. They say he'll never walk again. He's broken something in his back.'

'Is he in the hospital?' Mrs Moran was very concerned.

'Yes, but when he comes out Nellie says he will need someone to look after him day and night and . . . Oh, I wish this had never happened!' she cried in anguish.

'Who has he?' Sonny demanded.

Mary shook her head, tears filling her eyes at the decision she must now make. 'No one.'

'Not a sister nor brother nor cousin?' Mrs Moran demanded.

'No. Just . . . me.' It was a whisper.

'Ah, Mary, no!' Julia Moran cried as the full implication of the situation dawned on her. 'Didn't he throw you all out? Didn't he make no attempt to stop you coming here? He's not written a single line to you in all this time! How does he know if you're alive or dead and the children too?'

'I know! Oh, Mrs Moran, I *know* all that, but . . . but it must be terrible for him and he is the children's father.'

'He's no right to expect you to leave everything and go to him, no *right* at all!'

'I'm his wife. "In sickness and in health . . ." Isn't that what Father McGrath will tell me?'

'He will and I've never gone against a priest of God in my life before, but, Mary, that man cut you out of his life and for no good reason. What right has he now to expect you to come running and wait on him hand and foot?'

Mary dropped her head in her hands. She agreed with every word the woman said. She didn't want to leave here. She *never* wanted to leave here and return to the tiny slum house in the narrow, crowded streets of Liverpool. Back to poverty and hardship and despair and with the memory of the life she had here always to torment her. But what choice did she have? Even if Frank didn't want her to go back – and Nellie hadn't said that he did or that he'd even asked for her – he had no one but her and she had stood by her wedding vows despite everything. Suddenly, the sunlight had disappeared; the day had become dark and so very depressing.

'Sonny, where's Himself?' Mrs Moran demanded of the handyman who was just staring at the two women in stunned disbelief.

'In the stables, I think.'

'Then I'm after going to see him. You put on the kettle and make some tea. Sure, she's had a terrible shock and is in need of a cup.'

Mary raised her head and cried out but she was too late, the cook was already out of the door and halfway along the passage.

Sonny made the tea and she sipped it slowly, waiting in some dread for Mrs Moran to return and praying her employer wouldn't be two paces behind. The last thing she wanted was to have to face him with both Sonny and Mrs Moran in attendance.

'He says will you go to him in the dining room in five minutes,' the woman announced on her return.

'What did you tell him? What did you say?'

'Exactly what I said to you! That that man has no *right* to expect your help now.'

'Oh, God!' Mary groaned.

'Off with you and get yourself changed and tidied up and, Mary, will you promise me something?'

'What?'

'Will you listen to what Himself has to say? Really *listen*?'

Mary nodded and went to change her dress and apron with a sense of dread hanging over her.

Heedless of the state of his boots Richard O'Neill strode across the hall and into the dining room. He threw his jacket across the table. Damn! Damn and blast the man to hell! Judging by the garbled tale Julia had told him, he certainly agreed that Mary owed this man no loyalty. And he didn't want to lose her. He didn't want her to take her children back to Liverpool. Yet he had to listen to Mary's side of it.

Oh, to hell with it! he swore to himself, pouring a large whiskey and downing it in one gulp. He'd tried to keep her at a distance. Tried to keep her out of his mind, out of his thoughts, but it hadn't been easy, especially through the long lonely hours of the night. But what could he say to her? He had no right to beg her to stay and definitely no right to tell her that he loved her.

'You . . . you asked to see me, sir?'

Mary's voice interrupted his thoughts. He'd forgotten to close the door and she was standing just inside it. The bright sunlight streaming in through the large window fell directly on her and he thought she'd never looked more beautiful, even though she was pale and her green eyes were haunted.

'Mary, is it true?'

She nodded. 'It is, sir. He . . . Frank will be a cripple and he has no one but me.'

'Is everything that Julia told me true? He threw you all out? Let you be handed around and kept by the neighbours? Didn't stop you coming to Ireland and has never made any attempt to contact you or provide for you or his children since? And all because of some imagined infidelity?'

'Yes, it's all true, sir, and believe me there was *no* infidelity! I did nothing wrong at all. I've never been unfaithful to him.'

'I believe you, Mary.'

'I don't want to go, sir! I'm so happy here, we all are, but . . .'

'Then don't go, Mary. Stay. You owe him nothing.'

'I can't, sir! My conscience won't let me!' she cried, stricken by his pleading tone.

'What about the children? What will happen to them back there, Mary? What will happen to Lizzie? She's doing so well! I understand her, I can help her, I *have* helped her.'

'Oh, you have indeed, sir! More than I could ever have done.' The tears were falling unheeded down her cheeks now and she looked so vulnerable.

He couldn't stop himself. He crossed to her side and took her hand. 'Mary, please reconsider. I *need* you here. You've made this place something it has never been for me – a home. Don't go, Mary, don't leave me. Don't take the children away from me too!'

She was totally confused. 'Sir . . . Sir, I . . .'

'Forget the bloody "sir"! Can't you call me "Richard"? Oh, Mary, there are very few times in my life when I have been reduced to begging but that's what I'm doing now. Don't go! Please, Mary, don't leave me.'

She couldn't speak. A wave of emotion engulfed her. What was he saying? Exactly what was he telling her? She felt suddenly faint and light-headed and yet there was a surge of elation too. Something she had never experienced before in her life.

'Richard . . . Oh, Richard . . .' she stammered.

He threw caution to the wind and took her in his arms and held her tightly. 'Mary, don't go,' he whispered into her hair. 'I can't live without you! I *won't* live without you!'

She clung to him. She could never deny it now. She loved him.

Without warning he suddenly released her and she looked up and saw the changed expression on his face.

'What is it? What's wrong?' she said, confused.

'What do you want, Bridie?' he snapped.

Mary turned, her cheeks burning, and saw the girl standing in the doorway with Lizzie clinging to her hand.

'Me da says Mary's had a letter from Liverpool and she's leaving! Is she?' Bridie demanded, upset, red-faced and very disconcerted by what she'd just seen.

'Ask Mary,' he replied curtly, turning away. Silently he cursed the girl. He'd been so preoccupied that he hadn't closed the door. A few more seconds, just a few more seconds and he knew Mary would never have left him. Now . . .

Suddenly Lizzie snatched her hand away from Bridie's grasp and ran to him, throwing her tiny arms around his knees and burying her face in the gabardine of his riding breeches. She had understood more than anyone realised and her little world was crashing around her.

Mary could stand no more. With a heartbroken cry she fled from the room, ran blinded by tears down the passage-way to her bedroom, slammed the door behind her and threw herself on the bed sobbing.

Chapter Eighteen

———◦◦◦———

I<small>T WAS MUCH LATER</small> in the day when Mary at last appeared in the kitchen, red-eyed but calm. Just before lunchtime, Mrs Moran had knocked and called through the door that there was no need for Mary to serve lunch or dinner, Mr O'Neill was going out and wouldn't be back until late that night.

She had cried and cried until there were no more tears left. How cruel was fate! Until this morning she had never been happier. She had everything one could wish for and on top of that had discovered that she loved him and that he loved her. Oh, he hadn't actually said it, but he'd begged her not to leave him or take the children away, and he'd held her in his arms and said he couldn't live without her: what further proof did she need? But with that came the realisation that she wasn't free to love him. She was married to Frank even though he didn't want her. She could have ignored her duty, her religion and the censure she would certainly face from even the likes of Mrs Moran, Sonny and Bridie, and stay here and live with Richard O'Neill as his mistress, but deep down she knew her conscience would never allow her to do that. And what kind of example would that be for her children? How could she teach them right from wrong, living in sin as she would be? That was the most powerful of the arguments she had with herself. But he's so fond of the children, part of her cried. Look at how he cares about Lizzie, *really* cares. Frank had never shown such affection or patience with the child. And what were they returning to? A house that held no love, no happiness. Where food would be scarce, comforts few. The dark, dirty streets would be their playground not the fields and woods and rivers. And how would she cope? Oh, the neighbours would all rally round and help, as they always did, but she would have to work, slave more like, to keep a roof over their heads and with nothing, *nothing* to look forward to. Why? Oh, why had this had to happen now? But if she stayed would it really be any better? Even though she loved him, she could never have him. Could she live like that?

'Oh, Richard! Richard! I love you! I love you so much!' she had sobbed into the pillow.

The hours had slipped by as she struggled to come to terms with it all. The worst thing that she had to face now was telling the children they must leave all this when she already had the heart-rending memory of Lizzie's behaviour that morning burned in her memory.

At last she had come to her decision. She *had* to go back. She got up and washed her face in the bowl on the washstand. Splashing the cold water onto her eyes might help the swelling. Then she changed her dress. She would have to face them all sometime.

'Will you have something to eat?' Mrs Moran asked, full of sympathy, when Mary appeared. At least she was calm. Lizzie had been inconsolable. Bridie had had to drag her back to the kitchen and just after that he had stormed in, informed them he was going out, then slammed the door behind him. They'd heard him ride out of the yard and watched through the window as he'd galloped across the fields, putting the horse to every fence and ditch as he went.

'No, thank you, I couldn't eat a thing. Where's Lizzie?'

'She's with Bridie and isn't the poor little mite destroyed altogether. I didn't think she understood but she did and Bridie said—'

'What *did* Bridie say?' Mary interrupted.

'She said she had to drag her off Himself and . . . and you . . .'

'She saw us,' Mary said flatly, not caring now if they knew.

'She did. Oh, Mary, I'm so sorry but it could never be.'

'I know. Oh, I *know*, but . . .'

The older woman came and put her arms around her and the gesture opened the floodgates again.

'You love him, don't you?'

'More than I ever loved anyone, including Frank.'

'And knowing him, he loves you, but . . .'

'Oh, please, it's so hard!' Mary wept.

'We've all grown fond of you, Mary. We're all desperately upset that this has happened and when I look at the little one, it breaks my heart. She'll miss him so, Mary.'

'We all will, Mrs Moran. We'll miss *all* of you!'

'Ah, Mary, can't you call me Julia?'

Mary managed to smile through her tears. 'It doesn't seem respectful.'

'Ah, to hell with respect! You've shown me more of that than anyone else ever did and if I'd had a daughter I would have wished her to be just like you, Mary. You're a good girl. A good mother and a good wife and I hope he appreciates what you've all given up for him.'

'I doubt it but I have to go.'

'When will you tell the other two? They'll be home soon.'

Mary made a huge effort to pull herself together. 'As soon as possible. It's best they try to get used to it. I'll write to Nellie tonight.'

'And when will you tell Himself?'

Mary was stricken. She couldn't face him. She might lose control of herself if he once again begged her to stay. If he touched her, she knew all her strength would desert her.

'I can't face him, Julia! I *can't*! Will you tell him, please?' she begged.

'I will so. It's better that way, for both of you. Now, let's have some tea. We're both in need of it.'

Both children were devastated.

'Why, Mam? I don't want to go back! I want to stay here!' Tommy shouted, trying to keep the tears from his eyes.

'I've told you, luv. Your da's very bad. He won't ever be able to walk again and he has no one to look after him.'

'But he didn't want us, Mam! He told us to go. How will Sonny manage without me?' the lad demanded.

'He managed before, Tommy.'

'I *hate* Da! And Lizzie hates him too, Mam!' Katie wailed, tears streaming down her cheeks. She loved it here, especially school. Miss Collins was the best teacher she'd ever had and she had friends, even though she never saw them out of school, except at Mass on Sundays. She had nice clothes too and plenty to eat, and this lovely big house to live in and Mrs Moran and Bridie to spoil her. She didn't want to go back to St Anthony's School and Millie Price always having more of everything. And if Da couldn't walk he'd always be in a bad temper and there would be rows and shouting and she *hated* that.

'Oh, Katie, that's a terrible thing to say! Ask God to forgive you this instant!' Mary exclaimed, shaken by the force of her normally quiet and placid daughter's reaction.

'I won't! It's God's fault this has happened to Da!'

'Stop that this minute, Katie McGann! I won't have it!'

'Ah, she doesn't mean it, Mary. She's upset,' Mrs Moran interrupted.

Katie gave a choking little cry and rushed from the room.

'She's right, Mam, and what about Lizzie? You know our Lizzie loves it here and she loves Mr O'Neill too!' Tommy cried, desperate to find something that might make his mother change her mind.

'Tommy, stop it! Don't you think I know she's broken-hearted to be leaving Richard? She already knows. She . . . knew this morning.' In her distraction she unconsciously called him by his Christian name alone.

The lad looked at her. 'You like him too, Mam, don't you?'

With horror Mary realised what she'd said.

'Of course she does. They get along famously and he's very upset that she's going, that you're *all* going,' Julia Moran interjected quickly. 'Now, you'd better go and help Sonny,' she instructed.

'Thank you, Julia. I . . . forgot. I didn't realise,' Mary said quietly.

Tommy stared hard at them both before he turned away. Something very strange was going on. Mam had called Mr

O'Neill 'Richard' and Mrs Moran 'Julia' and that had never happened before.

Lizzie was very subdued when she returned to the house with Bridie. She refused either to eat or to have anything to do with Mary, which twisted the knife in Mary's heart. She went constantly to the window, even after the daylight had faded and darkness had fallen, looking for Richard O'Neill's return. He 'talked' to her the way no one else could and he'd taught her so much, shown her so much. How could she leave him? And Bridie too. Mam was taking her away, back to Liverpool where everyone ignored her. She didn't understand why they had to go. Her da was the worst for ignoring her and she could see no happiness ahead of her.

'Oh, Julia, what am I going to do with her if she carries on like this?' Mary fretted after Bridie had finally got the child to bed.

'She'll get over it, Mary, in time.'

'She blames me. I can't bear to see the way she looks at me.'

'It's a terrible wrench for her, but she's very young, she *will* get over it, Mary.'

'Oh, I hope you're right.'

'I am. Now, you'd better write that letter. I'm going to leave a cold supper in the dining room for him and no matter how late it is when he gets back, I promise I'll see him and tell him. You have an early night, you must be worn out, child.'

Mary nodded. She was exhausted but she knew she would get little sleep tonight or in the hundreds of lonely, miserable nights that lay ahead of her.

Chapter Nineteen

S HE LEFT BALLYCOWAN FIVE days later and they had been nightmare days. The children were all miserable, surly and disobedient. In the long nights when sleep eluded her she heard both Katie's and Lizzie's muffled sobs. Bridie too was red-eyed and snuffled constantly until Julia, whose own nerves were stretched, shouted that if she couldn't stop her damned whining then she could get out from her sight and the girl had fled in floods of tears. The outburst had startled and saddened Mary but it was nothing compared to the torture she endured every time she heard his voice or saw him riding out of the yard.

With Julia Moran's help she had written him a letter, begging to be excused her duties of serving and clearing meals, asking that the cook should undertake these tasks. It was something Julia herself had suggested knowing Mary's state of mind. The note also informed him of the day of her departure. She had finished by saying that he must know how miserable she was to be leaving, that the children were heart-broken but that none of them would ever forget him. She had signed it, 'With love, Mary.'

'Do you think that's wise?' Julia had asked gently.

'It's all I can say! I *do* love him, I always will, you know that!'

The older woman had nodded sadly, taken it and placed it on his desk.

'Will there be a reply?' she'd asked that night after supper, knowing by his expression and the plate of half-eaten food that he'd read it.

'No. There is nothing I can say to change her mind, is there?'

She'd hesitated and then she had placed a hand on his shoulder. She'd never seen him look so totally miserable in all the years she'd known him, and they were many.

'You *know* there can be no future for you and Mary, Richard. She is tied to him and then . . . then there's Herself.'

'I wish to God there wasn't! Why the hell didn't my father put a stop to *that* the way he did everything else?' he cried vehemently, slamming his fist down on the table.

'He couldn't, you were of age and you insisted! The Lord alone knows he tried! Will you . . . will you say goodbye to her?'

He shook his head. 'I *can't!*'

'No more can she to you. Ah, well, time is a great healer but we'll miss them all.'

'I'll be away for the day – the whole day.'

'No one can blame you for that, it will be a hard day to get through,' she'd answered sadly.

It seemed to make it far worse that the sun was shining and everything looked so beautiful, Mary thought the morning Sonny brought the trap around to the front door for the last time. She'd heard Richard ride away and knew that she would never see him again but there had been little enough time to dwell on it. That would come later. Tommy had silently helped Sonny to load their bags and had been promised he could take the reins all the way to the station, the furthest he'd ever been allowed to drive.

'I'll *never* get to drive anything ever again. No one I know back there owns anything *to* drive!' he muttered rebelliously.

'But at least you're able to do it. It will help when you're a grown feller,' Sonny tried to console him.

Katie was sniffing loudly and Lizzie had buried her head in Bridie's skirt. The girl looked helplessly at Julia Moran.

'What's I'se to do?' she asked.

'Lift her up into the trap, Bridie. She'll go for you.'

'But not me!' Mary whispered to herself as Bridie deposited the little girl beside her sister on the narrow seat.

Katie put her arm around Lizzie and Tommy blinked hard, fighting back tears himself, although he'd promised Sonny he'd 'act like a big feller'.

Mary pulled herself together. 'They'll all be fine once we're on the ship.'

'They will so. It's a good decision to go straight to the docks and not go calling on your aunt. She'll understand,' Julia Moran said firmly.

'Goodbye, Julia! I'll never forget you – *any* of you!' As she hugged the older woman Mary was fighting hard to keep the tears at bay.

'God bless you, Mary! You're the best thing that ever happened to us and I bless the day you came here and always will – despite everything!' Julia choked. 'Now, get off with you or you'll miss that train.'

Try though she might Mary couldn't help looking back as Tommy drove the trap onto the towpath and towards the bridge. The walls of the castle rose high into the clear blue sky, its windows sparkling in the sunlight. The branches of the trees rustled in the light breeze and the air was filled with birdsong. The lush green meadows were dotted with cattle and in the distance she caught a glimpse of the Tullamore River as it meandered through the fields. Oh, how could she leave it all? It was so beautiful. It was where her heart would always remain for she knew that from somewhere, somewhere out in that dear, tranquil, verdant countryside, *he* was watching her go.

* * *

The journey was long, tiring and depressing. The children slept fitfully for some of the time but although Mary was emotionally and physically exhausted sleep wouldn't come. It was a calm crossing compared to their outward journey but there were times when she wished that the ferry would disappear beneath the waves, taking them all with it and ending their misery. She tried so hard not to think of everything she'd left behind and of what faced her when they finally docked. She even tried to make some plans. There would be so much to do but she had no heart for it, nor was she looking forward to seeing either her old home or Frank. How could she not hate him? How could she cope with the life that now awaited her?

She was so thankful to see Nellie and Maggie waiting for her on the Landing Stage when the ferry docked and she struggled down the gangway carrying Lizzie and one of the bags.

'Mary, luv, you look wore out! Here, give me that bag!' Nellie demanded, looking concerned. Mary's letter had upset her deeply. The girl obviously hadn't wanted to come back and she for one didn't blame her.

'Thanks, Nellie. I've hardly slept and Lizzie's at the end of her strength, poor little mite. She doesn't understand this at all.'

'Haven't you all grown!' Maggie said cheerfully, trying

to lighten the mood. Both Tommy and Katie looked as tired and miserable as their sister.

'It's all that good food and fresh air, Maggie. Come on now, let's get out of this crush. We'll get the tram home. Won't that be a treat?' Nellie smiled encouragingly.

Both women kept up a steady chatter all the way and as she looked out at the familiar streets and buildings Mary began to feel a little better. At least she could count on her neighbours.

'You're all coming home with me for a cup of tea and something to eat, first,' Nellie announced firmly as they got off the tram on Scotland Road.

'He's still in the Royal Infirmary so you've time to settle back in, like,' Maggie said. 'I've done a bit of tidying up but I have to say the place is not like it was when you were there, girl.'

Mary managed a smile. 'Thanks, Maggie. Well, hard work is what I'm used to – always have been.'

Her spirits continued to rise as they walked down Newsham Street and women called out greetings from their doorsteps.

'I just hope Queenie's got the kettle on, like I told her to have,' Nellie said as she pushed open her front door.

'She's 'ere! She's 'ere, Queenie!' Bella shouted from the parlour where she'd been keeping watch. 'Welcome 'ome, Mary, luv!' she beamed, hugging a bemused Mary.

'Is this a reception committee?' Mary asked as she

walked into the tiny kitchen and saw Queenie, Eileen Quinn and Hetty Price all waiting for her.

'It is indeed. Welcome 'ome, luv!' Queenie beamed.

'We've all missed yer,' Eileen added.

'It's just such a pity that it's under such terrible circumstances,' Hetty added sympathetically.

'Trust her to put the mockers on it!' Nellie muttered, glaring at Hetty who had a knack of putting her foot in everything, in Nellie's opinion.

'Would yer look at the size of 'em all!' Bella cried, giving each of the children a hug.

Mary looked around the crowded kitchen and suddenly felt ashamed. How good they were. Even though they had so little there was ham and bread and even slices of currant cake on the table.

'Oh, look at all this! You're so *good*! We couldn't have had a better welcome.'

'You deserve it, Mary. It can't be easy coming back here after what you've been used to,' Hetty said.

'For God's sake, Hetty, are yer determined ter turn this inter a flamin' wake?' Bella cried.

'It's all right. I know what she means and it *isn't* going to be easy, Hetty, but I've made my decision and I'll stick by it, come what may. Now, let's all have a cup of tea. I know the kids must be starving.' Mary smiled bravely and sat down at the table.

* * *

An hour later when they'd all gone and she'd helped Nellie and Maggie to clear up Mary knew she could no longer put off going back to the house she'd once called home. The children had reluctantly gone back with Hetty who had promised them a little surprise each, a sort of coming home gift.

'Oh, it's nothing much really, Mary. Just a few sweets and some coloured chalks for Katie and Lizzie and a bit of a catapult for Tommy. Our Georgie's got one and I'd hate the lad to feel left out,' she'd whispered.

'It's very good of you, Hetty. It's going to be hard for them, settling in again,' Mary had replied but thinking that a catapult was the most disastrous thing Hetty could ever have bought for both Tommy and Georgie. She dreaded to think of the damage they could do.

'Well, luv, you're going to have to face it,' Maggie said.

'I know. Come on, let's get it over with.'

'If you need any help, luv, you know where to come,' Nellie reminded her.

Mary nodded her thanks and followed Maggie back to their house.

It was worse than she had expected, she thought, her heart sinking as she looked around the kitchen. It was so small and dingy and everything looked dull and dirty. In some ways it reminded her of the way Ballycowan had been on the day she'd first seen it.

'Oh, Maggie, I wish . . .'

'I know, luv, and I wish you had never had to come back to this. It all sounded so great over there. Nellie used to read your letters to us all. No one else is much good at reading, you know that. And you sounded so happy. Really *happy*.'

'You'll never know just how much, Maggie. Well, standing here crying over spilt milk isn't going to help. I've a lot of work to do.'

'Will you go and see *him*?' Maggie asked tentatively.

'I suppose I'll have to. Do you know when visiting is?'

'Half past seven to eight and they're terrible strict about it too. Only one visitor at a time, not that there's been many who want to go and see him. He hardly spoke to a soul around here. He'd fallen out with just about everyone, the bad-tempered get!'

Mary sighed. 'How did it happen, Maggie? Nellie just said he fell.' It was the first time she had even been able to bring herself to think about it in any depth.

'Some fool left a hatch cover half open and he tripped. Fell the whole way down into an empty hold. He's lucky to be alive.'

'He won't think so, knowing Frank.'

'Well, the doctors won't take kindly to an attitude like that! Not after all their hard work. Now, I'd better get on with the laundry, I'm a bit behind this morning and, as usual, I need the money.'

'When I'm organised I'll give you a hand again, Maggie.

I'm going to need money too. I've a bit saved but it won't last for ever and then I'll have to find some kind of work to keep us.'

'There's nothing much, Mary, you know that.'

She nodded. 'I'll have to take what I can. I've worked in a flour mill so I suppose I can say I've a bit of experience of factory work, and I can go out scrubbing floors.'

'We've all had plenty of experience of that!' Maggie said flatly.

Mary took off her jacket. She had better make a start and then tonight she would have to go and see Frank, no matter how much she hated the thought. After all, he was the reason she'd come back.

Chapter Twenty

M ARY HAD LEFT THE children with Nellie and had caught a tram to the grim red-brick hospital in Pembroke Place. She had tried to prepare herself for seeing Frank again after so long. She wouldn't be bitter or hostile, she would try to be pleasant and sympathetic and practical; she would also try to see someone who could tell her exactly what his injuries were and the type of care he would need when he came out of hospital.

The ward was long and narrow and tiled from floor to ceiling. Tall, barred windows were set high up in the wall which lent the place a depressing air and reminded her forcefully that it had once been a Workhouse. The beds, covered with white cotton counterpanes, were set in two long rows down each side and a nursing sister sat at a table in the middle of the room. She was a thin-faced, officious-looking woman whose heavily starched cap and apron made her appear even more stiff and unbending.

'I've come to see Mr Frank McGann, please.'

'And you are?' the woman demanded.

'Mrs Mary McGann. I . . . I've just returned from Ireland. I haven't seen my husband since he had the accident.'

'So you've turned up at last then!' The sister's voice was heavy with disapproval.

'I came as soon as I could,' Mary replied sharply. How dare she speak to her like that? She knew nothing of how Frank had treated her.

'He will need constant care when he goes home. His injuries are very serious. He is paralysed from the waist down. I presume you *do* understand exactly what that means?'

With a sense of horror Mary suddenly realised *exactly* what that meant. He had no movement at all and therefore no control over his bladder or his bowels. She managed to nod.

'He's in the next-to-end bed on the right-hand side. Please don't over-excite him,' the sister instructed, turning back to her notes.

His eyes were closed. Mary walked on towards him, her footsteps faltering as she made out his appearance. He looked older, much, much older, and thinner. His hair seemed to have receded and his skin looked taut and waxy.

'Frank. Frank, it's me. Mary,' she said quietly, sitting on the hard upright wooden chair beside the bed.

He opened his eyes and turned his head towards her.

'What do you want? I never sent for you.' His voice was cold and a little rasping.

It wasn't what she had expected. 'I've come to see how you are.'

'You can see that! I'm a cripple! A bloody cripple! I suppose you've come to gloat!'

She stared at him, shocked. 'No! I came back because I thought you needed me, to look after you when you come out.'

'I wish to God I didn't! The last thing I need is your pity! In fact I wish to God I were dead!'

'Frank, don't say that. Not after the doctors have worked so hard. You're alive, you should be thankful.'

He turned his head away.

She tried again. 'Are you in any pain?'

'I've just told you I'm bloody paralysed!' he snapped. 'Don't you understand?'

'I do. I just thought . . .' She had to try to move the subject away from himself. 'Don't you want to know how the children are?'

'How are they?' he asked, expressionlessly.

'They've grown. Tommy isn't half the hooligan he used to be. He's become very useful around the place and he can drive both a trap and a cart. Katie's quite the little housewife and Lizzie, well, Lizzie's come on in leaps and bounds.' Oh, how it hurt her to think of how miserable they all were but she tried to keep her voice cheerful.

'Then they won't be very pleased about having to come back, will they?' He sounded very bitter.

'They'll settle down when you're . . . back.' She couldn't bring herself to call the house in Newsham Street 'home'.

'You'd better get back to them, Mary.' He closed his eyes.

She could find nothing else to say. She got up. 'I'll be in again tomorrow night. Is there anything you want?'

'I *want* to be a whole man again but seeing as you can't do anything about that, you don't have to bother coming.'

She bit down the retort that sprang to her lips. Whatever she had expected of him it wasn't to be treated like this. 'I'll be back tomorrow. Perhaps by then I'll know when they are going to let you out.'

His eyes snapped open. They were full of venom. ' "Let me out" just about sums it up. I'm like a bloody prisoner and always will be now and with you as my jailor!'

She walked away, tears stinging her eyes. Why had she come back? Why had she left everyone and everything she loved to come back to him? But she knew the answer. With a heavy heart she made her way along Scotland Road towards Nellie's. She was just turning a corner when she almost collided with a man.

'My God! Mary McGann!'

'Richie Seddon!'

He grinned at her and she immediately thought that he hadn't changed.

'You've come back. I heard you might. So, how was life in the Emerald Isle?'

'Much better than it is here. How are you? Married yet?'

He laughed. 'Mary, you should know better than that!'

'Don't you dare say you're waiting for me!'

He looked startled. She was smiling but there had been a hard edge to her voice. 'Mary, you know how sorry I am about all *that*,' he said quietly. He dearly meant it.

'I know, Richie, and in a strange way it wasn't *all* bad, me leaving Liverpool.'

He looked at her closely. She still looked beautiful. She was well dressed but there was something else. 'You found someone else, didn't you?'

She was too heart-sore to deny it. She nodded.

'And yet you came back to *him*?'

'I've been asking myself why all night. He wasn't very pleased to see me.'

'Then go back and leave him alone, Mary. He doesn't deserve you; he never did. Nellie always said he'd get his come-uppance and he has.'

'He didn't deserve this and I made a promise, Richie, to God.'

He shook his head sadly. 'I'd never be put in a position like that, Mary. It's one of the reasons I'll never get married. I look around me and think: What the hell is it all for, is it worth it?'

She smiled at him. 'With the right person it is, Richie, and one day you'll find her, believe me, and then I'll come and dance at your wedding. Now I'd best be getting to Nellie's to pick up the children.'

'I'll see you around then, Mary, and if there's anything I can do to help . . .'

'Oh, Richie, I wish there was!' she said sadly before walking away.

The following morning she went with Nellie and Maggie to see the doctor at the hospital. She'd sent the children to school, although Lizzie had cried and dragged her feet and Katie had almost had to pull her out of the door. Katie hadn't wanted to go herself.

'You'll have to make an appointment, this is most irregular,' the sister at the desk said, looking annoyed at this deputation.

'Then we'll make one now,' Mary replied.

The woman opened a large book and flicked through the pages. 'There might be something next week.'

Nellie was outraged. 'Next week! She's come all the way back from Ireland, left a good position and everything, and you say *next week*! We'll stay here until you find something sooner than that! What's she supposed to be thinking and worrying about until then?'

The woman glared at her.

'Please, my friend didn't mean to be disrespectful, but I

have left a very good position as housekeeper at Ballycowan Castle in King's County to come back to nurse my husband. I would be very grateful if an early appointment could be found,' Mary said.

Her quiet tone and deferential yet confident manner impressed the woman.

'Very well, if you would care to take a seat I will make some enquiries. It might mean a long wait. Hours even.'

'Thank you, I don't mind at all. I'm sure you will understand that I want to know exactly how things are, when he will be discharged and so on.'

The sister indicated a row of wooden benches and the three women went and sat down.

'The flaming nerve! A week!' Nellie grumbled.

Maggie glanced at Mary. She'd changed in the short time she'd been away. She looked better, more sure of herself. She looked as though she was used to better things now. How would she cope with the life that lay ahead? It wasn't going to be easy.

They waited for nearly four hours before finally the sister beckoned Mary to the desk.

'Mr Copeland will see you now. Nurse will take you to his office. He can spare you ten minutes.'

'Thank you, sister. I'm very grateful,' Mary replied and then followed the nurse down a long corridor to a small office.

Mr Copeland was a tall, grey-haired man in his fifties with a pair of spectacles perched on the bridge of his long, thin nose.

'Thank you for seeing me so soon, sir.'

'Please sit down. Sister informs me that you have just returned from Ireland and have no knowledge of your husband's medical condition.'

'That's correct, sir. All I know is that he had a bad accident and that he's paralysed. How bad is he and how soon will he be able to leave here?'

'There's no use me blinding you with medical terms, Mrs McGann. In simple language he's broken his back. He will need help with almost everything and I cannot give you any assurances that there will be no more medical problems. He may or may not live to middle age. As for being discharged from here, it will be some time yet.'

'Weeks or months, sir?'

'If all goes well I would think in about three to four weeks. You have work, Mrs McGann? Is there anyone in the family who can help out financially?' he asked with some concern. There would be no compensation for the man from his employers. The family would have to live as best they could without his wage.

'Not here, sir. I was employed as a housekeeper in Ireland but I will be needed in my own house now. I have a little money saved but I will find work of some sort when I have to.'

'You have children?'

'Three, sir. They are too young to work.'

He shook his head. Life was very hard for so many of the people he treated. He admired her courage. 'Then I wish you luck, Mrs McGann.'

Mary stood up. 'Thank you, sir, you have been very kind and considerate.'

'Well, what did he say?' Nellie asked as they left.

'Only what we already knew but he won't be out for another four weeks. At least that gives me time to get the place looking decent again.'

'You're going to need extra stuff, luv,' Nellie said.

'I know. Bedding, towels.'

'There'll be plenty of washing too, but at least I can help with that,' Maggie added.

'I know, but I can't ask you to do his washing, it will be very . . . messy. Still, I managed to save a bit of money. It will tide us over.'

'Go and see Uncle, he'll have sheets and towels and he'll let you have them cheap. Don't go buying new stuff,' Nellie advised.

'I will.' She suddenly thought about her wedding ring. Did Mr Dalgleish still have it? Did she want to buy it back?

'Well, come on home and we'll have a cup of tea, I'm spitting feathers we've been in that place for so long!' Nellie offered. 'And the rest of them will want to know how you got on.'

*   *   *

That afternoon she made a start on the neglected house. It would take her a couple of days to get it into shape, she thought, trying not to think of the large and well-furnished rooms she'd grown used to. All through the hours she had similarly been attempting to push from her memory what Mr Copeland had said about Frank maybe not living to middle age. It was wrong, it was *wicked* even to harbour a hope that she would one day find her release. It was her duty to do everything to ensure that he lived for as long as possible. How could she ever hope for any luck in life if she harboured terrible thoughts like that?

By the time the children came home Mary had given the kitchen a thorough clean and had a pie baking in the oven. Queenie had done some shopping for her that morning while she'd been at the hospital and she'd been very grateful.

'I'm just going to Uncle's. Stay out of mischief until I get back. I'll take Lizzie with me. He'll be glad to see her,' she announced. She didn't need to go so soon but she thought she'd better get it over with. She'd realised that it wouldn't be deemed respectable for her to be living with Frank again without his ring on her finger.

'Mary, I heard you were back! It's good to see you again,' Mr Dalgleish said warmly. 'How is he?'

'As well as can be expected, I suppose. He . . . he's finding it very hard to accept it.'

'I can understand that. And hasn't she grown!' he exclaimed, leaning over the counter and smiling down at Lizzie. He offered her the bag of sweets.

Lizzie smiled, took one and then made some rapid movements with her little hands.

He looked puzzled.

'It's her way of saying thank you. Mr O'Neill, my recent employer, was very good with her. He taught her a lot of things. She can write now.' She tried to keep her voice steady. It was the first time she had mentioned Richard since she got back.

'He must have been a very gifted and patient man.'

'He was and very kind and understanding.'

'I still have your ring, Mary. Is that why you've come?'

She nodded slowly. 'I'm still married to him.'

He thought he detected a note of regret in her voice but said nothing. He turned and opened a small black safe and took out a box. 'Here you are, safe and sound like I promised.'

She passed over the two guineas and slipped it on her finger. She hated it. It was a symbol of her misery but she was married, and no decent wife went without one.

'Will I be seeing you regularly? He won't have much need of his good suit now.'

'He won't, though if the rest of his things are anything to go by it won't be in a reasonable state.'

'I can still give you a few shillings for it. Will he be needing his boots?'

'I don't know.'

'Maybe later on some of his mates will carry him outside to sit for a bit so he can see what's going on in the street. Chat to people who are passing.'

'I can't see him doing that. You know Frank, he'd be bound to feel humiliated.'

'Well, then you'd better bring the boots. If he changed his mind you could always tuck a blanket around his legs and feet.'

'I will need other things. Bedding, towels. I do have some savings.'

'You'll need them, Mary. I'll see what I've got and make a bundle up for you and we can come to some arrangement over them and the things you won't need.'

'You're always so kind. Thank you.'

'I wouldn't do it for everyone, you know that, and you also know that I for one wouldn't have blamed you if you hadn't come back. He doesn't deserve such loyalty – he gave you none.'

'How could I do otherwise?' she said simply.

'Knowing you, Mary, you couldn't.'

She had to turn away so he wouldn't see the tears.

Chapter Twenty-One

L IFE SETTLED ONCE MORE into the dull routine of drudgery: cleaning, cooking, washing, ironing, shopping in the markets for the cheapest of foods. She'd heard all the local news, including the fact that Violet was expecting a baby in a few months. She'd been surprised and startled, however, when young Nora Phelps had sidled into the kitchen a couple of days after she'd got back. Nora had looked very shamefaced and had picked nervously at the frayed edge of her blouse cuff.

'What is it, Nora?' Mary had asked quietly, remembering the part the girl had played in the disasters that had overtaken her.

'I . . . I just came ter say sorry, like. I never meant ter cause so much trouble, honest, Mary, I didn't!'

'But you *did*, Nora, and you knew I'd done nothing wrong.'

'I know all that, Mary, and me mam belted me somethin''

shockin' and I've never even spoken ter that Richie Seddon since! I '*ate* him! I'm really sorry, Mary! I was just so jealous and *stupid*!' She drew her sleeve across her eyes, wiping away the tears of remorse and humiliation.

'Don't cry, Nora. It's all over now, let's forget it. You've grown up a bit and learned a hard lesson.'

'I 'ave indeed. I . . . I'm courting properly now.'

'Really?' Mary had asked but without much interest.

Nora had brightened up. 'A lad I met at work. Billy 'Ardcastle, 'e lives in Sylvester Street and me mam likes 'im.'

'I'm glad, Nora. Now, I'll have to get on with my work.'

Thankful that the dreaded interview was over, Nora had flashed her a smile and nearly run from the room.

Mary had stared after her. What did it all matter now, she'd thought miserably? What would have been the point of screaming at the girl? She had enough to worry about: the behaviour of the children and the hospital visiting for a start, and she didn't know which she was more concerned and depressed about.

She had known there would be trouble over that damned catapult and it had come in a variety of forms. Tommy seemed to have lost all the sense of responsibility he'd acquired over the last months, and reverted to his former wild ways. The last escapade – using the local constable's helmet as a target, a heinous crime – had resulted in a visit by the police. When she'd tackled him, he'd been defiant and as usual had blamed the whole idea on Georgie Price. At her wits' end, she'd dragged him forcibly to Bert and Hetty Price.

'Hetty, I know you meant well but those damned catapults have got to go! I've had the police on the doorstep threatening the reformatory and I'm inclined to let them take him there! He's blaming Georgie but I think it's six of one and half a dozen of the other.'

Bert was fuming. 'I bloody told you, Hetty! I said it was the stupidest thing you'd ever done!'

'Oh, that's right, blame me! You never take an interest in the lad, you're too busy with the Brewery and your flaming betting! More interested in the horses than your own son. Well, that's the end of me having Winkie Owens forever hanging around the back door waiting to be "running" with your flaming bets!'

'Talk like that, Hetty, will have *me* carted off in front of the bloody Stipendiary Magistrate and then where will you be?' Bert had roared, furious at both his wife's blatant indiscretion and her outright censure.

'Oh, stop it both of you! What are we going to do about these two? Meladdo here is out and out insolent,' Mary had cried, losing patience.

'Give me the bloody catapult and, Hetty, go and get both our Georgie and his catapult.' Bert had held out his hand to Tommy.

Sullenly the lad passed it over.

'Now you listen to me, Tommy McGann, your da is in a bad way and your mam has enough on her plate. If there's any more of this behaviour I'll take my belt off to both you and our Georgie! Do you hear me? You're getting off light this time, but it's only for your mam's sake. Put a foot wrong again and by God you'll regret it!'

'I didn't want to come back here! It's all *her* fault! I hate it here!' Tommy had cried unrepentantly.

'Well, you're here and there's nothing to be done about it, so bloody well behave!' Bert had roared. That had shut Tommy up, but her son's behaviour had both shaken and upset Mary.

When she thought of Katie, she sighed. The child seemed to have withdrawn into herself. She was unhappy but she wasn't defiant, just silently reproachful. Mary often caught her looking at her with an expression of mute misery on her face. Oh, she knew how Katie felt. Her own existence was utterly miserable too, and that's all it was – an existence.

But it was Lizzie who worried her most. The child had gone backwards. Mary tried hard to keep communicating with Lizzie in the way Richard had taught her to but she had very little time to spare and the child was uncooperative. None of the neighbours or the other children in the street understood Lizzie's strange way of 'speaking' and some of the kids even mocked and jeered at her. That broke Mary's heart and at the same time filled her with fury at their cruelty, but apart from soundly boxing their ears whenever she caught them tormenting Lizzie, there was very little she could do. The effect on Lizzie had been devastating. She had stopped making an effort at anything. She refused to go to school. There had been too many mornings when Katie had dragged her from the house and then brought her back and in the end Mary had given in and let her stay at home. It hadn't helped much. Lizzie refused to do even the simplest things, like dressing herself or fastening up her boots.

'Ah, leave her, Mary, she'll sort herself out. It's even harder for her, she doesn't understand *anything*,' Nellie had advised, but it all added to Mary's constant worries.

And then there was Frank. Dutifully she went to the hospital every night and every night it was the same. He would refuse to speak to her, and then when he did it was with such bitterness, such vicious words that it was very hard to take and she frequently left in tears and cried herself to sleep.

Those early days were almost impossible to get through, but the nights were far, far worse. In the long hours of darkness even though she was exhausted sleep eluded her and there were times when she was so close to despair, so close to forgetting the vows she'd made that she was ready to pack up and return to Ireland and to Richard. But when dawn came she always pulled herself together and faced whatever the day brought.

Four weeks later the day came when she was informed that Frank would be discharged at the end of the week. Alfie Phelps, Bert Price and Fred Jones moved the bed she'd bought into the downstairs front room that Maggie had used. Maggie would now share one of the upstairs bedrooms with Lizzie while she and Katie would have the other. She'd also bought a narrow pallet bed for Tommy and this was to be made up in the room where his father would spend most of his days. If Mary was needed in the night, Tommy would go up for her. It was not an arrangement that met with her son's approval and there had been another argument, but she couldn't bring herself to sleep in the same room as Frank, she told Maggie vehemently. She would do anything that needed to be done, except that.

'He hates me, Maggie! He really does and I won't humiliate myself by lying in the same room as him.'

Maggie had nodded her agreement. She, more than anyone, realised just how Mary was suffering. She watched her day in and day out.

Mary had bought a pile of sheets and towels from Uncle's and had taken Frank's good suit, his boots and his overcoat to the pawnbroker's.

'He'll have no use for them now, Maggie,' she'd explained after Maggie had queried what she was doing.

They were bringing him back in an ambulance and she'd given the house a clean, made some thick pea and ham soup and had made up the bed. She looked around the room with some satisfaction. Fred Jones had whitewashed the walls and she'd made it as neat as possible. The cotton lace curtain at the window was pristine and there was a pair of blue draw curtains that Hetty had given her, along with some new oilcloth for the floor and a clean rag rug to the right of the bed. On the small chest beside the bed was a small jug and a glass for water. There were pillows so he could be propped up if he felt like it and a clean if rather faded patchwork quilt covered the sheets. She'd bought a picture for the wall and a couple of second-hand books. She *was* trying to make him comfortable.

The children had all been instructed to be clean and tidy and to wait in the kitchen to welcome him.

'What are we supposed to say to him, Mam?' Katie asked tearfully.

'Tell him you're glad to see him,' Mary replied with false cheerfulness, her heart sinking at the sight of their faces and the apprehensive look Katie shot at her brother.

'I don't think Lizzie understands, Mam,' Katie added hesitantly.

Mary sighed. 'I think she *does*. I want no tantrums,' she said firmly, thinking of Lizzie's recent displays of temper, which had included the child throwing the nearest thing to her hand either on the floor or against the wall. She had been reduced to slapping her, but it had had little effect on Lizzie.

'The ambulance has just turned into the street, Mary, luv!' Maggie cried from the front step where she'd been keeping watch.

Mary patted her hair to make sure it was tidy and smoothed down her clean apron. Whatever else he might say, he could not accuse her of not having the place decent for him.

'Here he is, missus, safely home. Where do you want him?' one of the ambulance men asked cheerfully as Frank was carried in on a stretcher.

'In here please. The front room.'

'It's the parlour for you, no less, mate!' the man joked.

Frank made no comment.

'Wait. Please, could you wait a minute? The children would like to see him. It's been such a long time since they have,' Mary asked and Maggie ushered them out from the kitchen.

They squeezed into the narrow lobby beside the stretcher.

'Hello, Da,' Tommy said, rather ungraciously.

Katie bravely bent to kiss her father's cheek but he turned his head away from her.

'Don't worry, luv. It's all a bit much for him. Tiring, like. Bring them in when we've got him settled,' the other man said quietly, seeing the look of pain in Mary's face and the hurt mirrored in Katie's.

Maggie shepherded them back into the kitchen.

Mary fussed around as they lifted him from the stretcher and into the bed.

'Isn't this great? Very nice and cosy and you've everything here you need. I bet it's good to be home at last.'

Mary smiled. They were trying so hard to raise Frank's spirits but she caught the pitying glances that passed between them as he said nothing and closed his eyes.

'Let him sleep for a bit, luv.'

'I will. Thank you, you've been very kind. We'll be . . . fine now.'

'All part of the service, luv. Well, we'll be off now. Good luck to you, you're going to need it.'

'I know,' she answered sadly.

They had their meal and twice Mary went in to check that he was all right. Both times he was asleep, or at least he gave the appearance of being so.

'I wouldn't bother sending the kids in, Mary. Not tonight,' Maggie advised as they washed the dishes. 'Give them a chance to get used to it.'

'Tommy will have to go in later to sleep.'

'Aye, he will, but Frank might be in a better mood by then.'

Mary nodded. He might – but would Tommy?

Later on some of the men and their wives came in to see him.

'I've brought him a couple of bottles of stout. It's supposed to be a good tonic,' Bert Price said, deliberately forgetting that he'd barred Frank McGann from his pub on many occasions.

'I wouldn't mind a bit of a tonic like that!' Alfie Phelps joked.

'*You* wouldn't mind anythin' that comes out of a bottle! Tonic or not!' Queenie said scathingly to her husband.

'And I thank God I'm not in such a state to need that kind of a tonic,' Fred Jones added. 'Right, go in and tell him he's got visitors and see he's decent, Mary!' he added.

Frank opened his eyes as she came into the room. She *had* made an effort, he grudgingly admitted. He had far more comforts than he'd previously had but the knowledge didn't make him any happier. He was still going to be totally dependent on her and it was a bitter thought.

'Frank, you're awake. Fred and Alfie and Bert have come to see you. Shall I prop you up on the pillows?'

'What the hell do they want?'

'Frank, they *care* about you! It's very good of them,' she answered, trying to keep the annoyance out of her voice. Regardless of his agreement or not she heaved him up in the bed and arranged the pillows. 'There, that's better. I'm sure you'll feel better for a bit of company and Bert's brought you a couple of bottles of stout.'

'Has he now? He's changed his tune. The last time I saw him he showed me the door!'

Mary said nothing. She was determined that there would be no angry words between them tonight.

'Well, it's great ter see yer home, Frank!' Alfie Phelps said jovially, although he was shocked by Frank's appearance.

'I've brought you a couple of bottles of stout, mate, it's supposed to be a good tonic,' Bert Price said, placing the bottles on the chest.

'Thanks.' Frank's tone was barely civil.

'So, how are you feeling now?' Fred asked.

'How do you think I'm bloody well feeling? How would you feel if you were me?'

The men exchanged glances.

'Jesus! Frank, there's no need to bite me head off!'

'We're just concerned, like,' Bert intervened. This wasn't going to be easy.

'How's a man supposed to feel when he knows he can't walk, can't do a bloody thing for himself without the help of his bloody wife? Can't work and support his family? Where's his pride and self-respect, you tell me that?'

' 'E's bloody bitter!' Alfie muttered to Fred.

'I'm not effing well deaf as well, Alfie! I *heard* that!'

'Oh, Jesus Christ! Yer can't say a bloody thing right!' Alfie was losing his patience.

Fred tried to calm the situation. 'You know, Frank, it needn't be *all* bad. There was a feller that worked with me a few years ago – you remember him, Bert? Harry Nicholson, lives down the end of Burlington Street. He was crippled in an accident with a bolting horse. He's sort of come to terms with it. Thinks the world of his wife, says it's brought them closer together and his kids love the bones of him, will do anything for him.'

'I remember him. He sits outside all day in the good weather, laughing and chatting to everyone. Even the kids chuck him the ball now and then when they're playing in the street. You see, Frank, you *can* sort of get over it,' Bert urged.

'GET OVER IT! GET OVER IT! I'd sooner be dead than like . . . this! And don't think anyone's going to sit me in a chair and stick me out in the street all day to be pointed at and sniggered about!'

Bert lost his temper. 'Well, if that's the attitude you're going to take don't expect people to come visiting you! You'd do well to stop wallowing in bloody self-pity and think about poor Mary and what she's going to have to put up with and what she's given up!'

Frank turned his head away from them. 'I don't want to hear about *poor* Mary! It's *poor* bloody me!'

Bert shrugged. It was useless trying to talk to Frank McGann.

'So, luv, 'ow is 'e really?' Queenie asked when the men had all trooped into the front room and the women had seated themselves, making the tiny kitchen look crowded.

Mary put the kettle on but shook her head. 'Bad-tempered and ungrateful.'

'Turned his head away when Katie tried to kiss him, I ask you!' Maggie muttered.

Queenie tutted.

'It'll take time, Mary, fer 'im ter get used ter it,' Bella added.

'If he ever does,' Nellie said darkly.

When they'd all left with much shaking of heads by the men and a few muttered comments about how you wouldn't wish it on your worst enemy, Mary cleared up the kitchen, sending Maggie to bed ahead of her.

'You go on up, I'll have to go in and see to him. Tommy, luv, get yourself ready for bed and I'll call you when I've got your da settled for the night.'

The lad made no reply. Life was very bleak these days and looked as if it was going to get worse.

To her dismay and embarrassment she had to change both Frank and the bed, tasks that were completed in utter silence on both their parts. After she'd put the soiled linen into buckets of cold water to soak she went back to him. 'Have you everything you need for the night?'

He looked at the other unoccupied bed and then at her. 'You're leaving me here on my own for the night?'

'No. Tommy is going to sleep in here with you. If you need me, wake him and he'll come up for me,' she answered, putting the glass she'd half filled with water within his reach on the top of the chest.

'So, you can't stand to sleep in the same room as me?'

She took a deep breath. She was still resolved not to have an argument, not tonight. 'Frank, I have my pride. I will do everything else, but I won't share a bedroom with you,' she said quietly.

'I suppose I'm so disgusting that it offends your new polite notions! Or is it because with me just a few feet away you won't be able to dream in peace about all the fancy fellers you've had since you left?'

Her patience snapped and she rounded on him. 'Since I *left*! I *left*! You threw me out! You threw us all out! How *dare* you accuse me of having "fancy fellers"! I've never been unfaithful to you and I'm not likely to be now either. I worked to keep us all and I had a good job, as well you know, and if I've got "polite notions" it's because I worked for a "polite" man. A good, kind, sympathetic, caring man, which is something you never were and never will be! I'll send Tommy in. Goodnight.'

She tried not to slam the door behind her. Once outside, she leaned her back against it and closed her eyes. She'd not meant to shout at him like that on his first night back but he knew nothing, *nothing* of just what she'd given up for him and he didn't care either. He was obviously intent on continuing to make her suffer.

The weeks passed but Frank's temper didn't improve; he became more and more steeped in self-pity. Thanks to Mary's care he became physically stronger but it didn't seem to make him the slightest bit more optimistic about the future.

She always tried to keep her temper with him but there were times when she just had to walk out and leave him or she felt she would explode. Things were bad enough without there being continuous screaming rows which would only upset the children even more, to say nothing of herself.

One Saturday, after she'd slept very badly, she awoke with a dull throbbing over her right temple, which she prayed wouldn't develop into a splitting headache.

'Did you have a good night?' she asked, drawing back the curtains, when she finally went in to see to Frank.

'What do you think?' he muttered sullenly. 'And you took your time, I've been awake for hours.'

'I've had a bad night myself and the beginnings of a headache, so please don't start complaining already, Frank.'

'I suppose you couldn't sleep thinking of everything and *everyone* you left over there!'

'I try *not* to think about it,' she said wearily, pulling back the bedclothes.

'Liar! It's *him* you think about! I know there's more to it than meets the eye!'

She bit back the words that sprang to her lips but then cried out as he tried to lash out at her.

'Don't you dare raise your hand to me, Frank McGann! If you think you're going to start hitting me you've certainly picked the wrong time to do it. Start that and you'll get no help from me at all. I mean it. Can't you understand that you *need* me, even if you hate me, though God knows what I've done to deserve *that*.' She was shaking with temper. It was a threat that deep down she knew she would never carry out, but she wasn't prepared to be treated like that.

'You bitch! You hard-hearted little bitch!' he yelled, beside himself with fury and frustration.

'I'll come back when you've calmed down. I can't . . . *won't* stay here to be screamed at!'

He picked up the small jug of water from the bedside chest and hurled it at her. It missed her by inches and smashed against the wall, showering her with water and shards of glass.

She wrenched open the door and slammed it hard behind her. Oh, God, how was she going to bear it?

Chapter Twenty-Two

◆━◆═◆

S HE HAD BORNE IT for three years. Three long, heart breaking, wretched years. She now went four or five times a week to the washhouse with the washing she'd soaked in the big tub in the yard. It had become too much of a chore and a disruption to do in their small house. Her savings had long gone so in addition to her own washing she and Maggie had begun to take in more and more of other people's, and in the evenings, after an exhausting day, she went out scrubbing offices in the business sector of the city. There was no money for tram fares so she walked everywhere and it was often nearly midnight when she returned to Newsham Street.

'Is there anything you need before I take the washing to the bag wash?' she asked, poking her head around the door.

Frank looked up. 'No, but I suppose you'll be out all morning.'

'You know it takes time, Frank. I'm as quick as I can be.'

'I'm sure!' He laughed mirthlessly. 'I know you talk about me to the other women, moaning and whinging and looking for sympathy.'

'I do no such thing! People ask about you; they even care.'

'Like hell they do!' he snapped.

She refused to be baited. 'I'll be off then. See you later.'

He stared bleakly at the door she had just closed. It was a gesture that seemed to sum up his entire existence. He was shut in, closed off from the world and all the *normal* people in it. This was his world, his prison, and as each day passed he was finding it more and more unbearable. Oh, what was the use in trying to make any sense of it? What had he ever done to deserve to end up like this? He'd always worked hard, tried to do what was right – until she'd gone off the rails. She was the one who was at fault, not him.

But a small voice nagged at him. *Had* she betrayed him? Did he *really* believe that? Had all that business with Richie Seddon been nothing more than a flirtation he'd blown up out of all proportion, with the aid of that nasty little madam, Nora Phelps? He didn't want to admit it, but she had done her duty by him. She had come back and she looked after him well and she must be exhausted, yet she never complained.

Tears of despair welled up in his eyes and fell slowly

down his cheeks. When had things gone so wrong between them? It was useless now to try to tell her he was sorry, not after the way he'd accused her of being little better than a whore and called her all those atrocious names. He would never be able to find the words. And what if she laughed at him? Sneered at him and flung his apologies and offers of peace back in his face? No, he could never admit that he had been wrong. Never ask her to forgive him for throwing her out, driving her from her home and friends or for making her leave a good job and a comfortable home for *this*! He'd even said he hadn't wanted her to come back, but in his heart of hearts he'd known she would.

He turned his head and buried his face in the pillow. She'd been so beautiful then – she still was, despite her desperately hard life, but he knew he would never hold her again, kiss her or be able to make love to her. And then there were the kids. Oh, he'd never really spent much time with them, but he wished he had. He wanted to be able to laugh and joke with Tommy, even kick a ball around the street with him. The lad was growing up, he needed a father, but what kind of a father did he have? A useless cripple. And Katie, she was afraid of him. He saw it in her eyes. He wanted to be able to communicate with Lizzie the way Mary did, but he couldn't. Mary had always had such patience with the poor little mite; he never had. Now he admitted to himself that he had blamed Mary for the way Lizzie was. He'd felt it was some kind of a slur on him that the child was not perfect. Oh, God, what was the point of it all? His life was just that – pointless. There was no meaning to it at all. No future . . . nothing! Deep sobs of remorse and despair racked him and he beat the damp pillow with clenched fists.

'It's a good dryin' day, luv,' Nellie called to Mary as she came back down the street, pushing the old pram Tommy had found and which she used to transport the damp bundles from house to washhouse and back. Nellie was on her hands and knees scrubbing her front steps.

'Thank God. At least now the weather's fine I won't have to have it draped all over the kitchen. It makes the whole place feel damp and Frank complains.'

'Aye, it's easier all round when the weather's good. Have you time for a cup of tea? I've just finished here and I'm parched.'

'I should peg this lot out and he'll be wanting a drink and something to eat.'

'Ah, to hell with him! Come on in, you look worn out.'

Mary smiled tiredly. 'Oh, I suppose a few more minutes won't make much difference. I get the height of abuse no matter what I do.'

Nellie shook her head as she carried the bucket and scrubbing brush inside. Frank McGann was the devil himself these days. Mary was a saint to put up with him; many women wouldn't.

Mary put the washing in Nellie's scullery, sat down at the kitchen table and tucked some stray wisps of hair behind her ears. Glancing up she caught sight of herself in the mirror on Nellie's wall and really looked at herself closely for the first time in months. She was pale and there were dark shadows beneath her eyes and she was so thin that her collar bones stood out. Her hair seemed to have lost its colour and lustre and the drab, washed-out, almost thread-bare blue print blouse hung on her. Oh, how she'd aged! Tears pricked her eyes as she thought of the lovely cream pin-tucked blouse and russet-brown skirt she'd had for best when she'd first come back. And the smart brown cord jacket and small, jaunty brown and cream hat. They'd long since gone to Uncle's and had never been redeemed. Rags were all she had now and the serviceable but unfashionable shawl. The uniform of the poor. All her money went on keeping a roof over their heads, food on the table and coal for the fire, although there had been times when there had been very little food and she'd been reduced to sending the children out to scavenge in the gutters for rubbish that could be burnt. By comparison to her own, Nellie's kitchen was well furnished. Fred had regular work these days and most of her neighbours' older children had work too.

'Here we are, luv, good and strong and plenty of sugar.' Nellie set the mugs down on the table.

'Oh, Nellie, I just caught sight of myself in the mirror and I look so *old*!'

'You're wore out, girl, that's what's the matter with you and no wonder! I only said to Bella the other day, "That girl is killing herself." '

'What else can I do?'

'It might get easier when Katie and Tommy are old enough to leave school and get work.'

'That's not for another two years in Katie's case and three for Tommy and you know Tommy does what he can selling papers and chips after school.' He went out in all weathers selling the *Echo* and the small bundles of wood used to light the fires which were known locally as 'chips'. She had once hoped that he would get a good job, maybe even some kind of trade so he wouldn't become just another common labourer with an insecure future, but all hopes of that had gone. He would have to leave school at fourteen. There could never be any hope of him going to the Mechanics Institute, even after work.

'Aye, he does what he can but he's still not happy, is he?'

Mary shook her head. 'No. He's tried to get something driving horses but they say he's too young, he's no experience, and no one will believe him when he says he can drive. Sometimes even I think he's forgotten everything Sonny taught him.'

'It's been three years, Mary, and you have to admit that he has settled down and so has Katie.'

'Oh, they have. I don't know what I'd do without Katie,

she's such a help. She never complains. If only Lizzie had accepted it, though.'

Nellie nodded sadly. Lizzie was nine now and she went to school but seemed to learn very little. She was a withdrawn child who never smiled or laughed or even attempted to play with the other children. She just sat and watched them, lost in a world of her own that only Mary seemed able to penetrate with the strange hand signs that she herself was unable to fathom out. She knew Mary longed to do more for the child, to try to alleviate her unhappiness, but poor Mary had so little time for anything these days. She was exhausted.

'Oh, Nellie! It . . . it seems a lifetime ago, another world.'

Nellie looked at her closely. Mary seldom complained, and only very rarely spoke about the life she'd left behind. 'Do you still think of *him*, Mary?'

'Every day. Every single day.'

'I'm sorry, luv, I shouldn't have asked.'

'It's all right, I know you mean well.'

Nellie didn't want to probe further or open old wounds. 'So, how is Frank today?'

'Just the same. Bad-tempered, bitter, full of spite and hatred and accusations.' Practically every day now there was a row when he shouted abuse at her, not caring who heard his vile accusations. She tried not to shout back but sometimes the things he said, the things he accused her of were too much for her to stand and her patience and her

309

nerves snapped. But never once had she mentioned Richard's name, never once had she betrayed her feelings for the man whose memory still haunted her day and night. Sometimes she had almost screamed that she wished she had done the things he condemned her for, that maybe she'd be happier if she had *some* memories to comfort her, but she always bit back the words. She'd lost count of the number of times he'd shouted and railed against God and wished he was dead and out of the hell he lived in and, Lord help her, she'd tried not to echo his sentiments.

'Take no notice of him, girl.'

'I try not to but there are times when it really gets me down, when I feel I can't stand it another minute. I'm almost glad when it's time for me to go out to work and I can take out my temper on scrubbing floors.'

'God, Mary, I don't know how you find the energy!'

'Neither do I and sometimes . . . Oh, sometimes when I'm walking back I'm so tired and depressed that every step that brings me closer is harder and harder to take. I don't want to come back *ever*, I just want to lie down and sleep and never wake up again. Oh, Nellie, I know it's wrong, it's a terrible sin to think like that but I can't help it!'

Nellie got up and put her arms around the thin shoulders. 'Oh, luv, I wish there was something I could do.'

'You listen to me and it helps, it really does.'

'It's not much, Mary.'

'It *is*!' She struggled to regain control of herself.

Breaking down in hopeless tears wouldn't resolve anything. She knew that from bitter past experience. 'Well, I'd better get back. This isn't getting anything done. Thanks for the tea and the shoulder to cry on.'

'This door is always open to you, Mary, you know that.'

She smiled resignedly, took the mug into the scullery and gathered up the washing.

The house was silent when she let herself in. Maggie had gone to do some shopping in Great Homer Street and wasn't back yet. She'd better get the washing pegged out in the yard before she heated up what was left of the soup and then went and faced Frank and his complaints, she thought wearily.

Fifteen minutes later she carried the breadboard, which served as a tray, on which was a bowl of soup and a mug of tea, into the front room. She frowned. He was asleep. Now she would have to wake him or the soup and tea would be cold and he would complain. But he'd moan about being woken too.

She placed the board down at the foot of the bed below his wasted legs and shook him gently by the shoulder.

'Frank! Frank, it's dinnertime. I've brought you some soup. Eat it while it's hot.'

He didn't move and she bent over him. He was breathing deeply. She shook him harder but he still didn't wake. Her gaze was drawn to the small dark green glass bottle on the chest beside the bed. He had trouble sleeping these days and because she didn't want Tommy to be disturbed too much she'd gone to the Dispensary doctor and paid for a bottle of laudanum. A couple of drops in some warm milk helped. She snatched up the bottle and was horrified to find it was empty.

She shook him harder, half dragging him up in the bed.

'Frank! Frank! For God's sake, what have you done!' she cried frantically. Oh, how long had she been out? Four, maybe five hours? Had it been too long? She tried to think calmly. What should she do? Should she keep trying to wake him or should she go for help? She shook him again and then turned and ran.

She fell into Nellie's kitchen. 'Nellie! Oh, God, Nellie, come quickly!'

'Mary, what's wrong?' Nellie was startled and instantly anxious. 'What's happened?'

'I can't wake him! He . . . he's taken all the laudanum! He must have done it when I went out!'

'Oh, Holy Mother of God!' Nellie pushed her out of the room ahead of her and the two women ran back to Mary's house.

Frantically they both tried to rouse him but it was useless.

'I'll have to go for a doctor or an ambulance,' Mary cried, half distracted.

'Go for a doctor. Go to the Dispensary. Don't call the ambulance.'

'Why not? Wouldn't it be better? The Dispensary doctor might be out.'

'Mary, they'll have to inform the police! It's a crime to try to take your own life! A crime before God and man! Go for the doctor!' Nellie cried.

Mary's eyes widened in horror. She'd forgotten that.

She was out of breath and could hardly speak by the time she reached the Dispensary.

'Please, where . . . where's the doctor? I need him to . . . come . . . my husband . . .'

The nurse looked concerned. 'I'm afraid he's out, Mrs McGann.'

'Oh, God, no! Where's he gone? Please, please, I *have* to find him! He's got to come *quickly*!'

The woman grabbed a sheet of paper from the desk. 'His second call was number seven Athol Street; he should be there now. Is there anything I can do?'

Mary shook her head vehemently and left.

She ran all the way to Athol Street, pushing and elbowing people out of her way along Scotland Road, and it was with heartfelt relief that she saw his bicycle propped up outside the house. She burst in without even knocking.

The little group in the kitchen looked up in shock.

'Doctor, I'm sorry but I had to come and find you. It's . . . it's Frank, my husband . . .'

The man knew her well enough. He'd been called out to see Frank McGann on a number of occasions, and she often came to the Dispensary for advice and medicine, but he'd never seen her so distressed before.

'What's happened, Mrs McGann? What's the matter?'

Even in her distress she remembered Nellie's words. 'Can I . . . can I speak to you . . . privately, please?' she begged.

'Excuse me, Mrs Hepworth, I'll be back to see to your mother-in-law as soon as I can. I fear this is an emergency,' he excused himself.

'Now, what's the matter?' he asked when they were both out in the street.

'He . . . I came back from the washhouse and I couldn't wake him, then I noticed that he . . . Oh, doctor, he's taken all the laudanum!'

'God Almighty! The fool! The bloody fool! How long ago?'

'About five hours I think!'

'You should have called the ambulance.'

'I . . . I couldn't. It's . . . you *know* it's a crime!'

'You go back, I'll cycle to the Dispensary. I need a stomach pump. I'll be as quick as I can but I can't promise anything.'

She broke into a trot as he cycled furiously up the street.

'Where is he?' Nellie demanded. She had been joined in the front room by both Maggie who had returned and Queenie who missed nothing that went on and who had seen Mary tearing up the street.

'He's on his way. He was out on a call in Athol Street but he's had to go to the Dispensary before coming here.'

'Jesus, Mary and Joseph! What possessed him ter do it?' Queenie asked, full of concern for Mary.

'I don't know! He . . . he was always saying he wished he were dead but I never thought . . .' Mary sank down on the edge of the bed and covered her face with her hands, praying the doctor would arrive soon.

He came rushing in the door ten minutes later but it had seemed much longer to the three women.

'Would you put the kettle on, please? She's had a shock, she could do with a cup of strong sweet tea,' he asked of Maggie and Nellie and Queenie. He wanted them all out of the room. It was too crowded. Then he bent and examined Frank, took his pulse and listened to his heart.

'Mrs McGann, I don't think there is anything I can do. He needs to go to hospital, they have the equipment and the experience and the staff.'

'No! Oh, please, no!' she cried.

'I can't just leave him. It's my duty. I took an oath to save life and apart from that I could be struck off and prosecuted myself and that would help no one! I'm sorry.'

'If he goes and they . . . save him, what will happen?'

'It is a crime, Mrs McGann, but I doubt they'll send him to prison, not in his condition. That *would* kill him. I'd inform them of that fact and my colleagues would back me up. I have to call an ambulance.'

Slowly she nodded. He was right and she took some comfort from his words. He was a good man.

He ushered her into the kitchen where the other women looked anxiously from Mary to himself. He left them and went to find the nearest Emergency Police telephone, a very new invention.

'Where's he gone? What's he doing?' Nellie asked.

'He's gone for an ambulance. He had to. It's his duty.'

'Blast 'im an' 'is bloody duty!' Queenie said. 'They'll 'ave Frank in Walton Jail.'

'Iffen he survives,' Maggie muttered, glaring at Queenie.

'He said he won't let them send Frank to prison,' Mary said flatly, taking the tea from Nellie and sitting down.

'An' what notice does 'e think they'll take of 'im?' Queenie demanded.

'For God's sake, Queenie, will you shut up!' Nellie yelled, losing her patience.

'I believe him. He said other doctors would agree with him and speak up too,' Mary said.

'You see!' Maggie said triumphantly. Queenie was never much help in situations like this. Always looking on the black side when things were black enough already. But in her opinion it would be a blessing in disguise if Frank McGann succeeded in his attempt, although she wouldn't say so.

'Mary, you'd better get your things together, you'll have

to go with him,' Nellie advised. 'Maggie and me will see to the kids when they get home.'

'But drink yer tea first, luv,' a subdued Queenie added.

She was ready and waiting when the ambulance with its bell clanging loudly came down the street and Frank was quickly heaved onto a stretcher and carried out. She was a little alarmed by the presence of a policeman who took down a few details as they were driven to the hospital, then she was told to wait in a large, tiled room that smelled of Jeyes Fluid and ether, which made her feel slightly sick.

After a little while the parish priest arrived. Before he went to Frank he came to see Mary.

'Nellie Jones came for me. Mary, what possessed him?'

'Oh, Father Heggarty, I don't know! I just wish I'd been there. That I'd stayed in the house this morning or that I'd not dawdled on my way back. They're trying to save him.'

'I know, child. You sit here and pray to Our Lady that they succeed and that he can ask forgiveness for his sin and obtain absolution. I'd better go through now. The sister has told me which ward he's on.'

It seemed like hours. She did try to pray but she couldn't concentrate and she was thankful when Maggie poked her head apprehensively around the door.

'Any news?' She crept over to her.

'No. Nothing. I've been trying to pray but, Maggie, I just don't seem to be able to. Oh, it's my fault! I should have taken more notice of him. He said often enough he wished he were dead. I should have stayed in with him more often. I shouldn't have gone and had a cup of tea with Nellie!'

'Mary, luv, how were you to know? How were you to know he'd actually do it? You couldn't have watched him every minute of the day and night. It's not your fault, luv! You've done everything you possibly could for him. You had to go out. You had to work.'

But Mary wouldn't be consoled and Maggie fell into a silent reverie.

Half an hour later a doctor, accompanied by the priest, walked towards them; with a strangled cry at the expressions on their faces, Mary knew he was dead.

'Mrs McGann, we tried very hard but there was nothing we could do.'

Mary nodded slowly. Well, at least now he'd had his wish.

'There are some formalities . . . you do understand?'

'Yes. I know. He committed a crime,' she replied quietly.

'Mary, I'm so sorry and I'm even more sorry that I won't be able to give you the comfort of a Requiem Mass. Nor can he be buried in consecrated ground.'

She looked at the priest with horror. Every word he said was true and she would have to bear the terrible shame of it. Even in death he had humiliated and hurt her. Every detail would be talked about, and she would be held responsible by the women of the parish who in the main didn't know all the circumstances. Not the things that really mattered.

'Mary, luv, come on home. It's times like this that you need your friends,' Maggie urged, her heart heavy for Mary's suffering.

'Oh, Maggie, will I have any friends now?'

Maggie looked at the priest but he said nothing. She took Mary by the arm to lead her out. 'Of course you will!' she insisted. 'We know it wasn't your fault even if some won't say so!'

Chapter Twenty-Three

❖❖❖

MARY TRIED TO EXPLAIN to the children as best she could. She knew she had to be truthful because there wouldn't be the customary burial, which was something they'd all witnessed on a not too infrequent basis. In this slum neighbourhood disease took a terrible toll and death was no respecter of age.

'You know your da wasn't a happy man. He hated having to live the way he did. Well, it became too much for him to stand any longer and so instead of God deciding when he was going to die, he decided for himself. He didn't feel any pain. He just took all his medicine at once this morning and went to sleep and . . . died.' She looked at the white, tense faces of Katie and Tommy and the uncomprehending expression on Lizzie's features but soldiered on.

'But I'm afraid that it's not going to be so easy for us.'

'Why, Mam?' Tommy asked. He'd almost grown used to the bitter, moody stranger he'd shared a bedroom with but he had no feelings of love for him. His pity had been for his mam, something that had grown over the last three years as he'd realised how hard she worked, how much she had to put up with and how unhappy she was.

'Because what he did was a sin and, in the eyes of the law, a crime. There won't be the usual funeral. No Mass, no burial in the graveyard. Just us and a couple of the neighbours in a bit of land at the back of the graveyard wall.'

'Do we have to go, Mam?' Katie asked. There was a note of shame in her mam's voice that she had been quick to notice.

'Yes, luv, you do. It's the least we can do. Try to give him a bit of respect. It was one of the things he missed so much after the accident and now . . . well, no matter what he did or what people will say, we *have* to go.'

'What will we do now, Mam?' Tommy asked, his eyes becoming brighter as a long-buried hope began to surface.

'Do?' She was confused.

'Can we go back to Ballycowan?'

She was taken aback. She honestly hadn't considered that. She'd not thought further ahead than the next couple of hours.

'Mr O'Neill will have another housekeeper by now. He won't need Mam,' Katie said, but there was disappointment in her voice.

Her words sent a knife-like pain through Mary's heart.

He won't need you! He won't want you! The words seemed to hammer into her brain. He might even have forgotten about her; that was a thought that had haunted her and one she had tried so hard to banish from her mind and her heart.

'We could try? We could write and ask?' Tommy wasn't going to give up any chance he had of returning to that life.

Mary looked at the eager expression on her son's face.

'I might, Tommy. Oh, I'm not promising anything. I'll have to think about it. Now, you'd better get on with your chores.'

Tommy nodded: he had papers to sell and they needed the money. At least she had said she'd think about it.

Mary tried. She made three attempts before discarding them. It had been three years and a great deal could change in that time. Look at how much she had changed. She needed no reminder of how she looked now. Hard work and grinding poverty had brought her to this state. Let him remember her the way she had looked the last time he'd seen her, if he remembered her at all. Life should be easier now that Frank had . . . gone. She pushed the thought away, filled with guilt. It was a terrible thing to think and if she was capable of that thought, did she really deserve happiness? She pushed the half-finished letter away from her. He would have forgotten her by now; there might even be someone else in his life. She dropped her head into her hands. The events of this week had been too much. Deep racking sobs began to shake her.

Frank McGann's burial was an almost hole-in-the-corner affair. There were no prayers except those Mary herself said. Just an Our Father, a Hail Mary and a prayer that God would somehow understand and forgive Frank. Only the immediate neighbours and Bert and Hetty Price attended, but Hetty was so distressed at Mary's plight that she asked them all back to the pub for something to eat and a drink, to 'stiffen them up'.

No one, not even the usually tactless Queenie, had asked Mary if she had any plans for the future and she was grateful for it. She really didn't know what she was going to do.

The days became much warmer. Summer had truly arrived, she thought as she wedged open the back door to try to get some movement of air into the house. She had tried to make some plans but she found it hard to concentrate. She had to admit that things were simpler without Frank, but how was she going to make a better life for them all? She needed to get some kind of job that paid better than cleaning, but what?

After the burial she had scrubbed the house and re-arranged what little furniture she had. Got rid of the bed Frank had slept in. She couldn't sell it, although Mr Dalgleish had urged her to try. No one wanted a bed like that in their home. She had tried to eradicate Frank's presence and to an extent she had succeeded, but she would never get rid of the feelings she experienced whenever she went into the front room. The children simply refused to go in there.

During the last few weeks, after she had given the children their tea and before she had gone to work, she had taken to wandering down to the waterfront where the late afternoon breeze coming in from the estuary seemed to clear her head. She *had* to try to look to the future, for the children's sake. They couldn't go on like this indefinitely.

The waterfront was busy as usual and she watched the ferry plying its way across the flat grey water, wishing she had the money to take a trip across to Birkenhead and back. It would be cool on the open upper deck. Her gaze moved unseeingly across the people who were going about their business and then she gave a cry and her hand went to her throat. It was *him*! It was Richard O'Neill! Her eyes were riveted on his tall figure. He hadn't changed at all. Her heart was hammering against her ribs and it was all she could do to stop herself from crying out his name and beginning to run towards him. Her hand went automatically to her untidy, damp hair and then she looked down at her dress. It was old, faded, creased and grubby. Oh, God! What would he think if he saw her looking like this? Would he even recognise her? In that minute she knew she could never, never let him see her again. Despair made her feel dizzy and she clutched at a gas streetlight to steady herself. It's *over*! she told herself, but she couldn't take her eyes off him. What if he did see her and recognise her? She shrank back, afraid he would catch sight of her, but her gaze never left him. He was talking earnestly to someone, a man. And a man she vaguely recognised. Then it came to her. It was Peter Casey, of all people. What were they both doing here? Why were they in Liverpool?

She couldn't tear her eyes away. Eventually the two men parted company and, despite herself, she began to follow Richard as he walked away towards the three magnificent new buildings on the waterfront: the Cunard Building, the offices of the Mersey Docks and Harbour Board and the recently completed and greatly admired Royal Liver Building with its two tall towers on each of which was perched a statue of the mythical Liver Bird, one looking out over the river, the other facing over the city.

Making sure she kept far enough behind him so that if he turned he wouldn't see her, she followed him into the city, wondering where he was going. A wild, mad thought came hurtling into her mind. Had he come to look for her? She banished it. Why should he? And he had no idea even where to start searching for her. But still she followed until she realised that he was heading for Rodney Street. It was in a quiet and very affluent part of the city and many doctors and specialists had their offices there. Was he ill? The thought made her feel faint again. There couldn't be anything wrong with him, there couldn't! He had been so fit and healthy and he was only a young man. She stopped on a corner as she watched him go up the steps and ring the bell of one of the imposing houses. The door was opened and he disappeared inside.

She waited a few seconds and then she walked slowly towards the house and stopped outside. There was a highly polished brass plaque on the wall. She moved closer in order to read it. There were three names on it, all doctors, but what kind of doctors were they? There must be something wrong with him, and something bad if he had come all this way to see a doctor. They had important doctors in Dublin too, surely. She hung around in an agony of indecision. She should go home: what if he came out and saw her? But she wanted to see him again, if only from a distance. Passers-by looked at her askance and at last she realised that this wasn't the type of neighbourhood where she could linger for long. Soon, someone was bound to come and move her on, thinking she was a beggar or worse. She had to go back. She had to go to work. 'Back to scrubbing floors, which is all you're fit for, Mary McGann,' she told herself, casting a last, longing glance up the quiet street.

Richard stepped out of the doorway and looked down the street. It hadn't been a successful visit. In fact it had been yet another waste of time. He could have saved himself the time, effort, money and emotional upheaval. The sun was slipping below the rooftops and as he stepped forward he caught a glimpse of red-gold hair as a young woman disappeared around the corner. His heart leaped. Mary! He was certain it was Mary! He took two paces forward before he realised he had called her name aloud and that a dour, middle-aged woman was looking at him very oddly. He tipped his hat respectfully to her and began to walk away. What kind of a fool was he to think that in a city of this size he would find her with such ease? He'd tried hard enough in Dublin and Liverpool was twice as big and twice as crowded. He'd seen a glimpse of a woman with auburn hair. How many of them were there in a place like this?

When he turned the corner there were more people on the street; his gaze scanned them all, hopefully. There was no sign of her. He thrust his hands deep into the pockets of his trousers and walked on towards St Luke's Church. He hadn't come looking for her, he had told himself it was pointless. Well, he might as well make his way towards the Landing Stage for the ferry, stopping for something to eat and a drink on the way. He felt dispirited and depressed, despite the pleasantness of the summer evening.

He had reached the top of Lord Street and was debating whether to try one of the steak houses in Castle Street when at the top, just in front of the Town Hall, he once again caught a glimpse of auburn hair. Surely . . . surely it just *might* be? He hurried his steps, frantically thinking what he could say if it was indeed her. The traffic was heavy and when he reached the corner of Dale Street he thought he'd lost her but his gaze seemed drawn to a shadow that disappeared into the doorway of an office building. Now what? Should he follow? If it was her, why was she going into offices and at this time, when all the office staff were leaving? He must have been mistaken. Should he wait? What if he hung around here and it wasn't her? Oh, what else did he have to do?

After half an hour his optimism was fading. There were few people on the street and a strolling constable had eyed him curiously. He had wanted to see her so much that he had become obsessive. He might even have mistaken it all. It might just have been a shadow. Wearily he went into a pub. He needed a drink.

He had tried to read the evening paper but hadn't been able to concentrate. There were too many worries pressing on his mind. Too many questions unanswered; too many problems that seemed to have no solutions. The landlord had provided a scratch meal and at last he looked at his pocket watch and decided he would have to make his way to the ferry. The whole journey had been pointless.

He paid the landlord but hesitated before leaving.

'Something wrong?' the man asked.

'Those offices over there?'

'What about them?'

'Do . . . do people go there late on?'

'Only the cleaners. The women go in when the clerks 'ave gone 'ome.'

'The cleaners,' he repeated slowly.

'You lookin' fer someone?'

He nodded slowly. If she needed work would she . . . ? Was that it? 'What time do they finish?'

The man shrugged. 'Usually about ten.'

Richard looked again at his watch. It was nearly a quarter to ten, but the ferry sailed at half past. Could he wait? Could he risk missing the ferry? If it wasn't her, then what? 'Thanks!' he muttered, making his way to the door. He had to try. He had to see if it was her. Quickly he crossed the road, walked to the building and stood in the shadows beneath the arched stone doorway. He'd wait. If it wasn't her then . . . then he'd try and make a dash for the ferry.

Mary was tired, but at least these days she didn't have more work waiting at home for her. There was no bed to change, no washing to soak, no dishes to wash. In the mornings she didn't have to go to the washhouse at all. After she'd cleaned up when the children had gone to school the house stayed tidy.

As she came slowly down the stairs her mind went back to the late afternoon. If she hadn't gone down to the river she would never have seen him. Never have experienced the pain she had felt ever since, and the worry. Was he ill?

Yet what did it matter, she thought in despair. She would never see him again. He had gone out of her life three years ago.

No, she had to be truthful. She had walked out of his life. She had left him. He had begged her to stay, but she had come back to Frank. Had it been worth it? Three years of hell they'd been and not wholly because of Frank. All the memories had tormented her. Forget him! Forget him! she whispered to herself. Oh, she was so weary and miserable. Could she afford to get a tram home, she wondered? No. Lizzie needed a new dress, she was growing so fast.

She had reached the bottom of the steps. She stopped and pushed a few strands of damp hair away from her forehead, then she jumped, startled, as a figure moved in the shadows.

'What do you want? I've got no money. I'm just a cleaner.'

Richard couldn't speak. It *was* her! He would know her voice anywhere.

'What do you want? I'll call the police!' Mary was beginning to feel afraid.

'Mary! Mary, my God, it's really you! Don't be afraid, Mary!'

Her hand went to her throat. '*Richard!*'

He stepped forward, reaching out for her.

She backed away. He couldn't see her looking like this!

'Mary! Oh, Mary, I never thought I'd see you again,

then this afternoon I . . .' Ignoring her protests he took her in his arms and she clung to him. 'I waited for you, Mary! I was sure it was you. I never forgot you.'

She buried her face against his shoulder. 'I never forgot you, Richard. I . . . I've missed you so much.'

He raised her head and kissed her and she never wanted the moment to end.

At last he held her away from him and looked at her closely, realising for the first time how thin and worn out she was. 'Oh, Mary! Mary, what's happened to you?'

Tears pricked her eyes. 'Richard, I never wanted you to see me like this! When I saw you this afternoon I was so ashamed!'

'You saw me? Why didn't you come to me?' He was confused. Had she followed him? Why hadn't she approached him?

'I . . . I couldn't. I just *couldn't*. I felt so . . . humiliated.'

'What happened? Is he responsible for this?' He stroked her thin, grimy cheek.

'He's dead. He killed himself,' she said flatly, not caring that he knew.

Hope surged through him. She was free. 'Mary, I'm not letting you go again. Where do you live? Is it far?'

Appalled, Mary thought of the tiny, poorly furnished house in the slum street. 'No! No, Richard, please! Let me go back alone tonight,' she begged, her cheeks burning. 'I'll meet you tomorrow, I promise.'

'Mary, I don't care where you live! I can't – won't let you go!'

'Please, please?'

He looked hurt. 'Mary, does it matter so much?'

'It does to me, Richard. I promise I'll meet you. You . . . arc staying?'

He nodded. 'I was due to go back but I'll find a hotel. Let me find you a hackney at least?'

She nodded with some relief and he held her tightly again.

'Mary, you won't disappear again?'

She kissed him gently on the cheek. 'No, I'll never do that again.'

He held her close as they walked to the main road to look for a cab. He couldn't understand her reluctance to let him take her home but he had to respect her wishes. He didn't want to lose her again.

As she sat in the unaccustomed luxury of the hackney she could hardly believe it. After three long, desolate years he'd come back into her life and he *hadn't* forgotten her. He *hadn't* recoiled from her in disbelief and disgust, he had wanted to take her back to Newsham Street. She had promised to meet him tomorrow morning in a private room in the Acropolis Club. She would have had time to think and to tidy herself up; he would have had time to make some plans. How was she to sleep tonight? Would she tell

Maggie and the children? A wave of happiness washed over her. No, she would have this one night to keep her secret to herself, to savour it. Every minute of it.

She slept little and was up early and if Maggie noticed anything different about her she didn't comment. After the children had gone Mary went and asked Hetty Price if she could borrow a dress and a hat, telling her she had an important meeting in town, for a job. Hetty was curious but didn't press her too much. Poor Mary had had a terrible time lately, she thought. At least she deserved some kind of luck, even if it was only a better job than cleaning.

Mary felt much better when she left the house and walked towards the tram stop. The dress was a bit big but at least it was clean and fresh and stylish and Hetty's wide-brimmed straw hat with the pale green ribbons made her look less washed out.

She felt nervous as she walked up the wide steps and into the open doorway beneath the stone portico of the Acropolis Club. It was cool and dark inside but as she walked across the hall towards the porter's desk she saw him striding over and her heart leaped.

'My guest has arrived, Rodgers,' Richard informed the man, taking her hand.

'Right, sir. Will I lead the way?'

'No, that's all right, thank you.' Richard smiled, took her arm and led her down a narrow corridor.

Once inside the small heavily furnished room, he took her in his arms.

'Oh, Mary! I've hardly slept a wink.'

'Neither have I! Sometimes I wondered if I was dreaming.'

'Did you tell the children?'

She shook her head. 'I wanted to see you again first.'

'It's been very hard for you, Mary, hasn't it?'

She nodded. 'Yes. Oh, I've worked so hard. I *had* to, to try to make ends meet. Taking in washing and cleaning offices was the only work I could do and still look after . . . him.'

'When did he die?'

'Nearly five weeks ago and even then he humiliated me. There was no decent burial. Suicide is a crime in the eyes of the Church and the law. But it was a release for both him and me. Oh, he was so bitter! He hated me. He hated it that he had to rely totally on me.'

Richard couldn't begin to imagine what she'd gone through these last three years. 'I wish you'd written, Mary. I could have helped and I would have.'

'I couldn't have done that, Richard.'

'I tried to find you, Mary. I went to Dublin. I went to see your relatives to ask if they had an address.'

'You saw Molly?' She was surprised. She'd had two letters from her aunt but she'd never mentioned his visit.

'No. Your cousin's husband. A surly man who had no high opinion of you and said neither he nor your aunt had any idea where you were, and nor did he care.'

She nodded slowly. That sounded like Davy.

'I didn't know where to look, Mary. I did put three notices in the *Liverpool Daily Post*, but there was no response. But it's all over now, Mary. I'm taking you home.'

'Oh, Richard, for me Ballycowan will always be home. I was so happy there.'

'We will be again, Mary, I promise. And the children?'

'They hated coming back too. Katie and Tommy have tried to settle and I think that recently they did but Lizzie . . .'

'What about Lizzie?'

'She never forgave me. She missed you so much. She still misses you. She's so withdrawn and unhappy that it breaks my heart, it really does. She has temper tantrums and I can't do a thing with her. No one can.'

'I can. When can I see her? When can we tell them?'

Mary hesitated, still ashamed of their poverty-stricken home.

'Mary, it doesn't matter where you live. The house in Dublin wasn't a palace and I wouldn't have cared if only I'd found you there. I wouldn't have cared if I'd found you barefoot and in rags.'

She managed a wry smile. 'You very nearly did.'

'Then let me take you back? Let me see the children?'

'Tonight, when I've had chance to speak to them.'

He nodded slowly, a little disappointed, then he smiled. 'Today, we're going to enjoy ourselves. We're going to spend the whole day together. You deserve a treat and we have so much to catch up on.'

'Three years, Richard. It's a long time.'

'It's been a lifetime, Mary,' he answered with sadness.

They had spent the day wandering in the cool shade of the city parks and she'd told him of the terrible three years she'd endured. Her words tore at his heart and he'd been full of remorse that he'd not tried harder to find her, even just to have provided her with food and clothes and decent furniture and the means to ensure that she had not had to endure such backbreaking work. He'd told her of how miserable life had been at Ballycowan after she'd gone. Of his drinking and lunatic riding that had been the despair of Julia and Sonny. But all day the memory of his visit to Rodney Street plagued her until at last she took his hand and drew him to a seat in a small arbour.

'Richard, are you ill?'

He looked puzzled. 'No.'

'Then why did you go to Rodney Street? You went to see a doctor.'

He remembered his own circumstances and looked away from her. There were so many things that stood between them still: her strong moral beliefs, her religion and, not least, his own position. 'Mary, I'm not ill, I promise you.'

'Then why did you go to Rodney Street?'

'It . . . it's personal but it makes no difference, Mary. I'm going to take you home, all of you. I love you, you know that.'

'I know, but . . .'

'Mary, do you love me?'

'Oh, you know I do!'

'Then let me take you home?'

'And we'll get married?'

He buried his face in her hair. Oh, God! What was he going to tell her?

She sensed his hesitation. 'Richard?'

He drew away from her. 'Mary, I have to be honest with you. I love you more than life itself but . . . but I can't marry you.'

The light that had shone from her eyes began to fade. 'Why? If you love me and I love you and Frank is dead . . .'

'Mary, I can't tell you! I *can't*! You have to believe me when I say I love you and I want you for always! I know it's a terribly hard thing to ask, for you to believe blindly. To trust me implicitly with your life and those of the children, but I'm begging you, Mary! Come back to Ballycowan with me and I'll never leave you!'

She stared at him, confused. What was he saying? That

she should go and live with him as his wife and yet not . . . ?
'Is it because of my religion?'

'No! It has nothing to do with that! That would be the least of my problems. I would change for you, Mary.'

'Then why?'

'I can't tell you, my love! I will always take care of you, you have to believe that. We'll both be happy. We *deserve* to be happy. I've never loved anyone the way I love you and I know you love me. Trust me, Mary, please?'

All the joy she'd felt began to drain away. He was asking her to live with him as his mistress, not his wife. 'I . . . I can't!' Her voice broke in a sob.

'Mary, please, trust me? Don't throw away this chance for us to be happy. We've both suffered too much by being apart,' he begged. He couldn't lose her again. He couldn't. He *wouldn't*. 'If you'll come home I'll find a place for you and the children. You don't have to live at the castle. Mary, I can't lose you again!'

She got to her feet, the tears falling unchecked down her cheeks. 'I couldn't live like that, Richard! I . . . I'm going.'

He reached out but she pulled away from him.

'Mary! Where are you going? Don't leave me again!'

'Back to Newsham Street!' she cried, hitching up her skirt and breaking into a run.

He watched her go. Was anything worth this? Was anything worth losing her again for? He hesitated for a few minutes and then began to follow her. Newsham Street she'd said.

Her tears fell silently all the way back in the cab she'd hailed outside the park gates. Oh, why was fate so cruel? To bring him back into her life and then . . . She was so glad now she hadn't told the children. She loved him to distraction and always would but what was standing in the way? Was he married? Was he ill? Was there something else? Why wouldn't he tell her? Could she trust him? Did she believe him when he promised to look after them always? Was it worth losing him? What would her life be like now, without him? The questions hammered inside her brain until she was confused and shaking and the cabbie had to help her down when they finally reached Newsham Street.

'You all right, girl?' he asked, worried.

She could only nod and hold out her fare.

'Where've you been?' Katie asked, getting up from the step where she'd been sitting waiting for her mother.

'Just . . . just into town.'

'Mam, what's wrong?'

Mary shook her head. She couldn't even try to answer.

'Will I make you a cup of tea?' the child asked, fearfully. Mam was obviously very upset.

Mary nodded. She went indoors to the empty kitchen and sank down beside the table, burying her face in her hands.

Katie went quietly about her preparations, wondering

what was so very wrong. She put the pot on the table and went for the mugs but turned as Tommy came hurtling through the door, his face flushed.

'Mam! Mam, a cab's just pulled up and guess who . . .'

Mary uttered a cry and stood up. No! Oh, no! He'd followed her!

'It's Mr O'Neill, Katie!' Tommy cried.

Katie dropped the mugs and stood and stared wide-eyed as Richard came into the doorway.

Before any of them could speak a small bundle burst into the room from the scullery and hurled itself into Richard's arms.

'Lizzie! Lizzie!' Mary cried. He had lifted her up and the child was clinging to him and strange sounds were coming from her. Mary realised she was crying.

Richard stroked the tangled curls and his eyes met Mary's. 'Mary, for God's sake, for *her* sake, come home?' he begged.

She swallowed hard. Even after three years Lizzie had recognised him. What right had she to destroy Lizzie's life again? Lizzie loved him. She'd never got over having to leave him. It would kill her to have to be parted from him again and what about herself? Was she right to turn her back again on the man she loved?

'Oh, Mam! Mam! Can we go home?' Tommy begged.

There was silence. Four pairs of pleading eyes stared at her.

'I . . . we'll come home with you, Richard. But I can't . . . won't live with you, not as you want me to. It's for Lizzie's sake. For all their sakes. I can't take you away from them again, I'd never forgive myself.'

Chapter Twenty-Four

———◆———

IT HAD BEEN VERY late when he'd left. Lizzie had 'talked' to him for hours. It was as though everything she had held inside for three years now came pouring out. He was so patient with her, Mary thought, as she watched them. Oh, if only he would tell her why he couldn't marry her. It wouldn't matter. She wouldn't care what it was or what he'd done. She still suspected that it had something to do with his visit to Rodney Street.

In the end it had been he who had told Lizzie she must go to bed but that he would be back tomorrow. When Mary had carried her up the stairs the child had hugged her and kissed her cheek. It was something she'd not done for so long that it tore at Mary's heart.

When she'd returned to the kitchen he'd taken her in his arms.

'I'll find you a place, Mary, even if it's just a cottage, and you'll never want for anything ever again, I promise.'

She'd leaned her head on his shoulder. 'You do understand that I can't live with you as your wife, but it will be enough for me just to see you every day and maybe sometimes in the evenings? Will it be enough for you?'

It was hard, so very hard, but it was better than losing her completely. In time, maybe things would change?

'It will have to be, Mary. I can't lose you.'

'And I'll be your housekeeper? Do you have one?'

He'd smiled at her. 'There have been a succession. It won't be hard to get rid of the present one. She's a slut and Julia detests her. She'll be gone when you arrive. I'll send for you, Mary, as soon as I can.'

'Well, I don't have much to pack,' she'd said quietly.

'You won't regret your decision, my love, I promise.'

After he'd gone she went upstairs and sat on the bed. Who knew just what the future would bring? But it had to be better than everything she had endured here.

She heard Maggie come in and sighed. Maggie had been on an errand of mercy, sitting with Bella's old mother who she was sure wouldn't last the week. Mary was aware that the children were not asleep, too excited and happy at the prospect of going back to Ballycowan, although both Katie and Tommy had said they would regret leaving their friends behind. Still, it would be a far better life for them – all of them – she told herself firmly. She couldn't deny them a chance of a decent future and even if . . . things didn't work out between herself and Richard (although she pushed the thought firmly from her mind), she'd find other work; she'd make another home for them. She was no longer a stranger there. Life *had* to be better. She'd better explain it all to Maggie now.

'How is she?' she asked, sitting down opposite Maggie in the kitchen.

'Not good. It would be a blessing if God took her sooner rather than later. Poor Bella's worn out.'

'Maggie, I've got something to tell you.'

The older woman looked at her closely. 'What have you been up to, Mary? All this flitting off and not telling anyone where to?'

'I . . . I met someone.'

'Who?' Maggie demanded. Mary looked a little feverish in her opinion.

'Richard O'Neill.'

'My God!'

'I . . . I'm going back with him, Maggie.'

Maggie got to her feet. 'I think I'd better go for Nellie.'

'At this time of night?'

'She won't mind. I can see this won't keep until morning.'

Mary didn't argue. It was better this way. She got the mugs and put on the kettle.

Maggie returned with both Nellie and Queenie.

'What's all this about you leaving?' Nellie demanded.

'Sit down.'

'When did you meet him? Where?' Queenie asked.

'I saw him yesterday afternoon and followed him to Rodney Street. I didn't think he'd seen me but he had. He followed me to work, waited for me. I . . . I wouldn't bring him here, so I met him in town today at a gentlemen's club. I borrowed some clothes from Hetty. He . . . he still wants me . . . and the children. He wants us all to go back.'

'Oh, luv! I'm so 'appy fer yer! 'E knows that Frank's dead an' that yer can get married now?' Queenie cried, her face wreathed in smiles.

'Yes, he knows about Frank but . . .'

Nellie looked concerned. 'But what?'

'He can't marry me.'

'Why not?' Maggie demanded.

Mary twisted her hands together. 'I don't know.'

Queenie looked pointedly at Nellie. 'Is 'e already married?'

'No. At least I don't think so.'

'Mary, what kind of an answer is that? Was there ever a sign of a wife or even another woman?'

'No, Nellie, there wasn't. Surely Julia Moran would have said *something*? Surely Julia would have said it was all for the best when I was coming back here, that we could never be together because he couldn't marry me, he already had a wife? He begged me to trust him. He said he *couldn't* tell me.'

Queenie shook her head. It all sounded very strange to her. 'I don't like the sound of that, Mary. What other reason could there be?'

'I . . . I think he might be ill.'

'Why?' Nellie asked quietly. She could understand Mary's desire to believe him.

'Because he went to see a doctor in Rodney Street.'

'And if 'e is? Is it fair ter ask yer ter go back there an' probably look after 'im? Yer've already nursed one man.' Queenie was indignant.

'Oh, Queenie! I would *want* to. It wouldn't be a chore!'

'I can't see why 'is bein' ill should be such a big secret.'

'Oh, I don't know! I *do* know that I love him and that I have to trust him and that I can't turn him down out of hand because . . . because of the children and their future. Particularly Lizzie. Oh, you don't know how much she loves him. How good he is with her. I couldn't take her away from him again.'

'Mary, is that enough? It's a huge leap of faith he's asking of you.' Nellie was serious.

'It will have to be, Nellie. I've told him I won't go and live with him and he's promised to find us a house somewhere.'

'Yer're still leavin' yerself open ter temptation, Mary,' Queenie warned. 'An' people will talk.'

Seeing the tears in Mary's eyes, Nellie tutted. 'Queenie, you're not being helpful!'

'I'm just pointin' things out. She's a respectable woman, a good Catholic woman, an' if yer ask me 'e's bein' very dog in the manger. She could meet someone else who *could* marry 'er.'

'I don't want to meet anyone else! I will only ever love *him*! I thought my life was over and now . . . now I have to trust him. I *want* to trust him. I love him! And how can I deny the children a better future?'

'Mary, we understand, luv. We're just concerned for you,' Nellie soothed. While she could understand the girl, she still had her reservations. 'You'll be to all intents and purposes just his housekeeper?'

Mary nodded, relieved to have Nellie's support at least.

'Then we'll make sure that people around here understand that. We want no gossip that will upset the kids. Do you hear that, Queenie?'

'What are yer 'avin' a go at me fer? I think it's all a bit . . . odd, but, well, if she's 'appy and the kids are 'appy, all I can do is pray that whatever is stopping 'im will get itself sorted out an' soon.'

'Aye, maybe he'll come to his senses and tell you what's wrong and you can work it out between you. You deserve to be happy, Mary. God knows you've suffered so much these last years and I don't mean just Frank's accident. It started long before that,' Maggie said firmly. Like Nellie she sympathised with Mary's desire to go but like Nellie she was a little worried that Mary might not be able to help herself where Richard O'Neill and the future were concerned.

'I *have* to go. You *do* understand?' Mary begged.

Silently, all three women nodded.

It was three weeks before the letter arrived with their tickets. He'd written to her before that, twice a week, telling her that he had found a cottage a little further down the canal line in the townland of Kilbride and it was speedily being renovated and refurnished. It wasn't very big, just a large kitchen cum sitting room and two bedrooms but if she wanted it a separate sitting room could be built on, as could the luxury of a small bathroom. His present house-keeper had been dispatched in high dudgeon on her part but to great delight and relief on the part of everyone else. He'd sent money for her to buy clothes and anything else she and the children needed and begged her not to skimp. She'd had a lifetime of that. And in each letter he told her how much he loved her and missed her and he couldn't wait until she was once again back where she belonged. In his arms, his heart and his home.

They had been busy weeks for her. She had rigged them all out with underwear and nightclothes, dresses, jackets, stockings and shoes, hair ribbons for Katie and Lizzie and shirts, trousers, socks and boots, a Norfolk suit for best and two fine caps for Tommy. She'd bought good food and had put on a supper for the neighbours who had supported her through so much of her harsh and recently joyless life.

All the children were in a constant state of excitement and for once in her life Katie was the envy of Millie Price.

'All those new clothes *and* fields to play in, rivers to fish in!' Millie had exclaimed resentfully when Katie had proudly shown her her new wardrobe.

'*I* don't fish,' Katie had replied.

'But you can if you want to,' had been Millie's retort. 'Mam says it must be heaven to look out of your window or door at fields instead of dirty cobbled streets and houses black with soot.'

Mary had overheard her and smiled. It was, she thought. Oh, it was indeed and she'd never envisaged a day when Hetty Price would be jealous of herself.

At long last the day had come. Mary watched their bags being loaded into the hackney carriage, then looked around her for the last time. The neighbours were all going to see them off and they'd already gone by tram. Maggie would stay here, the rent paid by herself, with enough money for her to live on. It would come out of the salary Richard had insisted on paying her.

'You are still doing a job, Mary. I won't have you as an unpaid skivvy,' he'd written.

'I'd willingly slave for you without a penny,' she'd replied and had gone on to ask him if he minded that some of the money would go to keeping Maggie who had no one else in the world and who had taken them into her home.

'Your generosity and compassion continue to amaze me, my love. Do whatever you think fit with the money. It's yours,' had been the answer.

There were very few good memories here, except the births of her three children and the early days of her marriage to Frank. No, she wasn't sorry to be leaving this house. It was depressing. This belonged to the old Mary. The worn-out, downtrodden, humiliated and poverty-stricken girl. She patted her new tapestry carpet bag. All his letters were in there and she would keep them for ever.

She turned and caught sight of herself in the new hallstand she'd bought Maggie from Uncle's. Maggie had admired it so much that in a fit of extravagance she'd purchased it as a farewell gift. She looked so much better now. There was colour in her cheeks again. Her hair was shiny. She raised a white-cotton-gloved hand to the new hat. It was pale blue and white and matched the light linen dress and jacket, which had broad insets of blue ribbon around the hem of the skirt and the edge of the short jacket. It looked fine enough for a wedding dress. It was much more fashionable and expensive than the dress she *had* worn to her wedding thirteen years ago. Suddenly she wished it *was* a wedding dress. That she was wearing it to go to her husband. Richard O'Neill. 'Stop it! Stop it! You have more than you ever dreamed of!' she told herself firmly. It was time to leave.

* * *

The trip in the hackney seemed to Tommy a fitting start to a new life. Even Georgie Price had been impressed. But he hadn't boasted or gloated about it and everything that awaited him in Ireland. That would have been childish, he'd told himself, and he wasn't a child any more. He was growing up and was very thankful not to have to continue selling newspapers and firewood in all weathers. He would work hard, learn everything and be Mr O'Neill's right-hand man when he was old enough.

It was a beautiful summer evening. The rays of the setting sun tinged the turgid waters of the Mersey red-gold and bathed the new buildings on the waterfront in a mellow light. The breeze that gently lifted the sails of the few old-fashioned sailing ships anchored in the river was tangy with salt.

The neighbours were all waiting for them. Alfie helped unload Mary's bags and he and Fred carried them along the Landing Stage towards the *Leinster*. The women all clustered around her.

'It's a much better evening than the one when you went away last time, Mary,' Hetty Price said with a smile.

Mary smiled back. 'And this time we have cabins.' No expense had been spared. The journey would be very comfortable this time.

Nellie took her hands. 'It *is* the right thing to do, Mary. You *will* be happy and I'll pray that you can sort it all out.'

'Oh, I'll miss you all! I don't know how I would have got through everything without you!'

'Will yer ever come back, do yer think, Mary?' Queenie asked.

'Why would she ever want to come back *here*?' Hetty asked, mystified. Mary McGann's life had changed beyond all recognition. You only had to look at the way she was dressed now to see that, and she was going to live in a castle in the country. Was Queenie mad?

'Maybe for a visit sometime. I was born here. It will always be my city,' Mary replied. 'But I will write, I promise, and Nellie can tell you all the news of how we're getting on.'

'Well, I wish you luck, Mary. No one deserves it more,' Fred said gruffly. He had been told an edited version of Mary's decision and circumstances by his wife.

They all jumped and then laughed as the three long blasts of the Cunard liner *Lusitania*'s steam whistle shattered the evening air.

'Last call fer the crew still knockin' back the ale in the *Stylehouse!* Lucky beggars!' Alfie laughed. It was common practice among the captains of departing merchant ships to summon the stragglers amongst their crews from the pubs on the waterfront in this manner.

'And you'd better get on board yourselves,' Nellie pressed.

'You've been like a daughter to me, Mary, and I'll miss you,' Maggie said as she hugged Mary.

'Oh, Maggie! I'm just so thankful that I know you're going to be secure and comfortable.'

'God bless you, girl!' The old woman's eyes were full of tears. She would never have to face her worst nightmare now: the fear of ending up in the Workhouse.

The others hugged Mary in turn and then the children, something Tommy suffered in stoic silence.

Lizzie caught her mother's hand and began to pull her away.

Mary laughed. 'Look at her! She can't wait.'

'Come on, Mam!' Tommy urged.

'Goodbye, luv, take care and God bless you!' Nellie called as she watched the little group ascend the gangway, brushing away a tear. She would pray and pray hard every night that whatever it was that was standing between the marriage of Mary McGann and Richard O'Neill would soon disappear.

They all stood on the open upper deck and waved as the *Leinster* pulled away from the Landing Stage and moved out into mid-river and the figures on the shore grew smaller. Then Mary ushered them down to their cabins: small, neat and very well-appointed little spaces, with narrow bunk beds made up with sheets and green and white bedspreads tucked tightly in. There was even a small hand basin with soap and towels and, wonder of wonders, a tiny curtained cubicle with a commode, Mary marvelled.

She settled Tommy and Katie into one cabin and then Lizzie and herself into the other. She knew Lizzie was so excited that she would have trouble sleeping but as Mary lay in the bunk with the crisp white sheets she thought the same applied to herself. At last she was going home. To Ballycowan. And to Richard.

Chapter Twenty-Five

H E WAS WAITING AT the station for her and came towards them smiling broadly. 'Mary, you've arrived at last!' He made no attempt to touch her or kiss her, but it didn't upset her. People were watching.

'You look beautiful, Mary. Even more beautiful than when you were here last.'

'Thank you. I'm so happy, that's why.'

'Are you glad to be back?' he asked of Katie and Tommy. Lizzie was already clinging to his hand.

Katie simply nodded but Tommy grinned. 'It's *great*!' the lad enthused. 'Where's Sonny? Isn't he driving?'

'There wouldn't have been enough room for us all and the luggage. But if you can still remember all he taught you, you can drive us home.'

'I think I can! Oh, thanks, sir!' Tommy rushed towards the station yard, his progress slowed a little by the bags he was carrying.

'Do you think that's wise?' Mary asked.

Richard laughed. 'If he gets into difficulties I'm on hand and anyway that animal knows its own way home.'

'Oh, I'd forgotten how beautiful it all is!' Mary exclaimed as they drove out past Charleville Castle. It was high summer now and everything looked so green and fertile. In the fields crops were slowly ripening in the warm sun and cows and horses stood in the shade of the trees that overhung the hedgerows and lazily flicked away the flies with their tails. As they passed people came out of their homes to stare and occasionally to raise a hand in greeting.

'Word gets around fast,' he commented, amused. 'You see you haven't forgotten. It's something you never really do forget. Like riding a bicycle,' he added to Tommy who was managing the reins expertly, delighted with himself.

'Where are we going first?' Mary asked.

'Home. Julia would kill me if I took you down to the cottage first.'

'And she's happy with the . . . arrangements?'

He nodded. 'She's overjoyed you've come home and so is Sonny, even though he'll have to go back to cleaning up the yard. It's something that seems to have slipped his mind since you've been away.'

She laughed. 'I still won't have him traipsing in through the front door.'

And then they were on the towpath and the tall sandstone chimneys could be seen above the treetops.

'Oh, Mam! I'd forgotten how big it is!' Katie cried and Lizzie stood up to get a better view.

It was heart-breakingly beautiful, Mary thought, tears pricking her eyes. But they were tears of happiness.

Sonny was waiting at the gates and gave a roar of delight and approval as Tommy swung the pony into the yard. The lad was bursting with pride and happiness.

'Yerra! Would you look at the size of him now! A fine, tall, strong lad!' Sonny cried, taking the pony's head.

Julia and Bridie came hurrying from the front hall, their faces wreathed in smiles.

'You've come back to us, Mary! Thank the Lord! The procession of women I've had to put up with would make the Archangel Gabriel weep, so it would! And it's been a fierce black mood Himself's been in all this time, I can tell you.'

Mary hugged her tightly. 'I'm so glad to be back!'

Katie and Bridie were hugging each other too and exclaiming over each other and Lizzie clung to Richard's hand, still not quite able to believe it all.

Julia urged them towards the house. 'Come on inside with you all. You must be desperate for a cup of tea and I've been baking all morning.'

Richard kept hold of Lizzie's hand but with the other he guided Mary towards the house she thought she would never see again.

She looked around the hall. She'd forgotten how big

everything was, but it looked neglected. 'I see there's plenty of work to do.'

'But not today! Today is a holiday. Julia, bring the tea into my study, if you would. There'll be plenty of time for you both to gossip.'

'Sure that's one thing neither of us can be accused of and well you know it!' Julia retorted but she was smiling. She was overjoyed to see Mary back, yet a small doubt nagged at her mind. She wouldn't be around all the time to act as a chaperone. Would Mary be strong enough to resist temptation? Still, it was very early days yet.

Mary looked at the papers strewn over his desk and then ran a finger along the edge of the bureau. 'You've been badly neglected,' she said, looking at the dirty marks on the finger of her glove.

'I'd let no one in here but myself,' he replied, taking her in his arms. 'Oh, Mary, it's been so long and I lived with the constant fear that you'd change your mind. That I'd get a letter telling me you couldn't come home.'

'Oh, you *knew* I wouldn't change my mind! I've lived for so long without you.'

'And now I'll see you every day. I'm going to buy you a horse and teach you to ride. I won't have you walking everywhere.'

'A horse! Me *ride*! I couldn't! Richard, I couldn't! I'd fall and break my neck!'

'You won't. It's not hard and I'd be very careful in

choosing the right animal. A good steady schoolmaster that will take you everywhere safely.'

'Couldn't I just learn to drive the trap?' she asked, still full of trepidation.

He laughed. 'Mary McGann, you amaze me with such lack of confidence in me. But you delight me too,' he added, kissing her forehead.

Further conversation was curtailed by the appearance of Julia with a huge tray. Mary rushed to take it from her.

'Would you be so good as to try to clear a space on that desk?' Julia asked him, casting her eyes to the ceiling at the clutter.

He did so and Mary poured the tea.

Julia sat down with the air of someone it would be hard to dislodge.

Richard just smiled at her, well aware that she would protect Mary's virtue from all-comers to the last. Himself included.

'What are the children doing?' Mary asked, amused at the odd situation and wondering just how much he'd told Julia Moran.

'Out running all over the place with Bridie and Sonny. Tommy's already pulled his rod out of the outhouse and fired everything in there into a heap! You'll not get them away from here for hours yet.'

Mary laughed. 'I don't suppose I will.'

'Then when you've had your tea we'll be after taking

you down to the cottage and you can get unpacked. It's nothing grand, mind.'

'It will be wonderful compared to what I've just left,' Mary replied. She wanted to see it but she was disappointed that there could not be more time alone with him for now.

Julia had been right about the children, at least about Katie and Tommy. They had set up such cries of dismay when she had gone to look for them that she had no option but to leave them to their own devices. There was no leaving Lizzie behind, however. She clambered up into the trap ahead of them all and bounced up and down on the seat.

'Will you tell that child she'll have us all thrown out on the road if she carries on like that,' Julia demanded and Richard had to settle her down.

The cottage was just beyond the graveyard beside the little church, up a narrow track or bohreen. Mary's eyes lit up when she saw it.

'I never even knew it was here. You can't see it from the towpath.'

'It was in a shocking state. There's been some fierce hard work done on it, I can tell you, and I've given Matty Donelley the lash of my tongue when he's been up complaining about just how long it would take him to get it set to rights. If ever there's a man who's work-shy it's him!'

'Still, he did manage to get it done,' said Richard soothingly.

'But it was only the promise of the extra pounds from you that did it,' Julia shot back.

It was small but it was bright and comfortable. Obviously it had been furnished with things brought from the house, Mary thought as she looked around. Some of the things were far too grand for just a simple cottage.

'I wanted you to have every comfort here, Mary,' he said, watching her as she ran her hand lightly over the nice brocade fireside chair.

'And she has. There's plenty of everything,' Julia commented, opening the doors of the dresser for her to inspect the table linen and the food and condiments stored there. The top of the dresser was filled with blue and white delftware.

The bedroom for Tommy was tiny. There was just enough room for a single bed and a chest of drawers but Mary knew he wouldn't mind. The other room was larger and contained a double bed and a single bed, all neatly made up. There was a wardrobe, a chest and a washstand with a rose-patterned china bowl and water jug. On the broad stone window sill was a jug of wildflowers. Mary touched them gently.

'That was Bridie's idea. Sometimes she does be having some strange notions.' Julia shook her head at the vagaries of Bridie's mind.

'It's beautiful, it really is.'

'You do know that if you get tired of it or you feel cramped, your rooms are waiting for you above at the house,' he said quietly.

She nodded. But she knew she couldn't sleep under the same roof as him, she couldn't trust herself.

Julia shot him a guarded look. 'Why don't you take the child for a drive while we unpack? Sure, what use would you be here?'

He was reluctant to leave Mary. 'I could carry the heavy things.'

'And what heavy things would that be? 'Tis only a few bags.'

'I can see you can't wait to be rid of me. Come on, Lizzie.' He took the child's hand and went out, she skipping along beside him.

'Oh, she missed him terribly. I had such a time with her. It was so worrying.'

'Didn't you have enough things to be worrying about? Was it very bad, Mary?'

'It was. I don't know how I got through it. He hated me.'

'Ah, don't think about it now. It's all behind you. You're back where you belong. I was never so glad as when he came back and told me he'd seen you and that you were going to come home.'

Mary looked at her steadily. 'Just what did he tell you, Julia?'

The woman sat down in the armchair and Mary pulled a little three-legged stool out and sat facing her.

'That your man was dead. That he killed himself, the Lord have mercy on him! That you were living like beggars.'

Mary nodded. 'We were. There was only the money I could earn and it wasn't much.'

'He said you were out of a night scrubbing floors.'

'It was all I could get.'

'Ah, God love you, child!'

'What else did he say?'

Julia pretended to inspect her hands. She couldn't tell Mary of the fierce argument there'd been between them or that only she, because she'd known him for so long, could have said the things she had done.

'That he loved you, which I already knew. In the days and weeks after you left I thought he'd go mad. He was drinking from morning to night and barely eating enough to keep a bird alive. And when he wasn't too drunk he was riding the fields all day and driving poor Sonny witless. We were afraid he'd come off that animal's back and break his neck, but he never did. Thank God. And then he seemed to pull himself together but he was not himself at all. He missed you, Mary.'

'I missed him. I never thought I'd see him again.'

'Then he comes home and informs me he's met you and that you're coming back as his housekeeper but that you won't live at the castle.'

'I can't! He says he can't marry me but won't tell me why. Do you know why, Julia?'

'I know well enough, Mary, but it's not my place to tell you. I swore to him I wouldn't.' Her mouth closed like a trap and her eyes were downcast and Mary knew she would get little more from her.

'Just tell me one thing, please? I saw him visit a doctor. Is he ill?'

The woman looked surprised. 'Holy Mother of God, he never ailed a day in his life.'

Mary nodded. She would have to be satisfied with that. 'Surely you see why I can't live with him, even though I love him so much. I wasn't going to come at all.'

'What changed your mind?'

'Lizzie. He's the only person in her entire life who brings her any joy.'

'But she loves you, Mary, doesn't she?'

'In her way, but she never behaves with me the way she does with him. Oh, the other two couldn't wait to come back. They hated living with Frank. They missed the fields and the river, although they did have friends and I suppose they'll miss them. But it was different for Lizzie. She was utterly miserable all the time.'

'Ah, well, you'll all be happier now. If anyone in this country can be happy. Anyone in the world with all this talk of war. Sure, we've seen enough of war and rebellion here. It brings nothing but misery.'

Mary had heard the talk and the rumours but had had too many other things on her mind to worry about it.

'Do you really think there will be a war?'

'Himself thinks there will be, but it might all blow over, please God. Now let's get started or there'll be no meal on the table this evening.'

Mary stood up. 'I'll be up to set the table and to serve and then tomorrow Bridie and I and Katie have plenty of work to do.'

'Sure, the last one was a lazy slattern. I wasn't sorry to see the back of her. And insolent with it too. Didn't want to soil her hands. Wouldn't get down on her knees and scrub, oh, no! Poor Bridie had to do most of it.'

Mary suddenly remembered something. 'I saw him in Liverpool, before he saw me. He was down at the Landing Stage and he was talking to Peter Casey. What was *he* doing there?'

Julia looked startled but hastily recovered her composure. 'Peter Casey? Sure, I have no idea. He might have relatives there he was visiting. He might even be taking himself off to America. Now I think on it, perhaps I did hear he was talking about taking the emigrant ship. Don't you worry your head about it.'

'What about his father?'

'He's dead these past twelve months, God have mercy on his soul!' She crossed herself devoutly.

'What happened to him? Was it the drink?'

'In a way it was. Wasn't he mad with it and coming home along the towpath and didn't he take it into his head that he'd cross by the little bit of a plank that runs beside the lock gates? He fell into the lock itself and they found him in the morning. He'd drowned. Even if he'd been able to swim it's ten feet down and there's not a hope of climbing out and the lock-keeper as deaf as a post.'

'I'm sorry.'

''Twas his own fool fault. I wouldn't blame Peter for up and leaving. What is there to keep him here?'

Mary walked up to the house at half past five to help Julia and Bridie with the evening meal and found all three of her children sitting at the kitchen table, ruddy-cheeked from the sun and fresh air and decidedly grubby from their exploits. Even Lizzie looked untidy and she'd spent most of the afternoon with Richard.

'Would you look at the state of you three! I wonder Mrs Moran let you in here.'

'They've washed their hands and it's good to see them running about and laughing. There's two fine brown trout gutted and ready for the oven.'

Mary smiled at them. 'I hope you've made the most of today. Tomorrow it's down to work for all of us.'

'Set two places in the dining room, Mary,' Julia instructed.

Mary raised her eyebrows.

'Himself says he wants you to eat with him. He won't have you taking your meal in the kitchen.'

'But . . . ?'

''Tis what he said and I wasn't arguing. *You* take it up with him later, if you've a mind to.'

Mary was a little disconcerted. It didn't look *right*, the housekeeper dining with her employer. And in the eyes of the local people that's what she was. She had even changed into her new black dress and white apron and cap.

He was startled by her appearance when she took in the soup.

'Mary, why are you dressed like that? There's no need.'

'There is. And I don't think it's a good idea for me to dine with you. People will talk.'

'What people? There's only Julia, Sonny and Bridie and they'll say nothing.'

'What about the children? They think I've come back just to work.'

'I'll explain.'

'You'll explain *what*?'

'That now you've come home you will help Julia but that because you're my good *friend* you'll take your meals with me and wear normal clothes.'

She shook her head. 'I don't think they will understand and what if they pass some remark at school?'

'You'll have to tell them not to. They never used to

discuss anything here with others. I won't have you sitting in the kitchen.'

'Richard, I don't want to upset you but I think it would be best if I did eat in the kitchen with them. I have always had my meals with them, at least I've always tried to. I could spend the time after supper with you – and after lunch, if you like?'

'I don't want to separate you from the children. Could we all eat together?'

She shook her head. 'No, that would set tongues wagging and it would confuse the children.'

He smiled. 'You win. But will you sit with me just for tonight?'

She nodded and took off her cap and apron.

When the meal was finished she took the dishes back to the kitchen and began to stack them in the sink.

'What are you doing, Mary?' Julia demanded.

'Washing up, like I always used to do.'

'No. His instructions are that Bridie has to do it now. After dinner at least. You're to sit with him. You need time to talk.'

She went back to the dining room but found it empty. She went in search of him and found him standing in the small reception room at the side of the house, looking out at the fields and hedgerows behind which the sun was starting to slip down, throwing purple and red shadows over the land. She went and stood beside him.

'It's beautiful, isn't it? I always loved summer sunsets in Liverpool but they were never like this.'

He put his arm around her waist. 'Nothing was beautiful after you left me, Mary. I hated this place.'

'I heard. Julia said you were . . .'

'Inconsolable and drunk for days on end.'

'I'm so sorry I caused you so much pain.'

'I should have thought of what you were going through, not wallowed in self-pity and degradation.'

'It doesn't matter, though Julia said there were times when they feared for your safety.'

'Oh, Mary, there were times when I *wanted* to die! I put Juno to the most dangerous and impossible walls and banks. Thank God she carried me safely over them all or I wouldn't have been here to rescue you from that appalling life.'

'I thank God she did too,' she said with sincerity.

'But we're together now, that's all that matters.'

She kissed his cheek. 'From the first time I set foot in this house I felt I was at home, even before . . .'

'Before you fell in love with me?'

She nodded.

'I'll never leave you, Mary.'

Suddenly she remembered her conversation with Julia earlier. 'Do you think there will be a war?'

'What made you think of that?'

'It seems as though everyone is talking about it.'

'Things in the Balkans are looking grim and if Germany supports Austria against Serbia, and Russia and France go to Serbia's aid, then Britain will have no choice but to side with her allies and go to war.'

'But what about Ireland?'

He smiled at her naivety. 'Mary, Ireland is part of the British Empire. We will have no choice.'

She thought there was a note of bitterness in his tone but she was more worried about the implications of his words. 'So you would have to go? You would have to leave me?'

'Don't talk of leaving, Mary. I've only just found you again!'

'Then I will pray to God that war doesn't come. I don't think I could stand it.'

Chapter Twenty-Six

THE LONG HOT GOLDEN days of July passed slowly and Mary was almost blissfully happy. The house was looking much better thanks to the care she lavished on it, for now she thought of it as her own and of the things it contained as theirs. The former orderly routine was quickly re-established with a few minor changes and the children were once more content, none more so than Lizzie.

For the past couple of weeks little Maureen Slattery from Kilbride had come every afternoon to play with her. Mary had been surprised when the child had arrived at the back door and had shyly asked for Lizzie.

'Mammy said I was to ask you first,' the girl had added.

'That's all right, Maureen. She's down beside the barn with Katie. I didn't know you and Lizzie were friends?'

'Oh, we are so, Mrs McGann! Lizzie is my best friend.'

Mary had smiled. 'Then off you go.'

'Was that the young Slattery one?' Julia had asked, glancing out of the window.

'It was. She says she and Lizzie are friends and I think she's right,' Mary had replied, smiling as she caught sight of Lizzie coming around the corner. When she'd seen Maureen, Lizzie's face had broken into a smile and she had run towards the child.

'How do they get on? I mean how do they "talk" to each other?'

'Look,' Mary had instructed, feeling a sense of relief and joy surge through her. Maureen was slowly and hesitantly copying Lizzie's sign language, with interruptions and corrections from Lizzie herself. Lizzie was teaching her friend how to 'talk' to her and Maureen was sufficiently interested and fond of Lizzie to try and learn. Lizzie's world was expanding beyond the confines of family and it filled Mary with infinite pleasure. Oh, she had so much to thank Richard for.

'Well, I'll be blessed! Isn't that a great thing altogether and doesn't it do your heart good to see it!' Julia had exclaimed.

And yet two things disturbed Mary as she sat in the little kitchen in the cottage each night, after she'd returned from the house. She'd fallen into the habit of sitting by the open window once she had checked that the children were asleep – which they invariably were, worn out by the exertions of the day, much of which was spent in the open air, for harvesting would soon be upon them. The stillness of the summer night was something she derived much pleasure from. The sky was a vast expanse of indigo velvet scattered with stars that looked like diamonds. The rustling of the breeze in the trees was like a soft melody and the scents and sounds of the night came wafting in. It was all so very different from the stifling, stinking, noisy nights of the past three summers. But it was a time when worries also came to disturb her.

The talk of war was becoming increasingly difficult to ignore, although she tried hard to do so. The newspaper was full of it and she prayed hard every morning and night that it wouldn't come and that Richard wouldn't have to leave her. She realised that many young men would be lost and that it was selfish of her just to fret about the one man she loved, but she could not bear to think of him being wounded or worse. Far, far worse. If she were to dwell on that she would go mad. Oh, how she loved him. She told herself she was content with the way things were but at heart she knew she wasn't. She had been married; she wasn't a young girl in love for the first time; she wanted him. All of him. That was her other worry. They sat together every evening and talked and then would come the moment she loved and loathed at the same time: when he would take her in his arms and kiss and fondle her, which was all she would allow. But the longing and passion that rose and swamped her was becoming more unbearable with each day. She knew she had crossed the line the priest would consider unbreachable. She knew what she was doing was considered a sin but she prayed that God would forgive her. In her heart she believed that He would. He knew she truly loved Richard. It wasn't just wanton lust. He would understand, providing she didn't go beyond the point of no return. These last few nights she had had to tear herself away from him before all her resolve and willpower deserted her and she gave in to the overwhelming desire that was blotting out everything else. She had fled from the room, with just a strangled 'goodnight', and run all the way back to the cottage.

She knew it was taking its toll on him too. There were times when he was short-tempered and sharp, not with her, but with Julia and Sonny, and that made her feel worse. It wasn't their fault, it was hers. There were long nights when she tossed and turned in her bed, when she ached for him and asked herself over and over again: was she just being a fool? Was it really worth denying herself? What if he had to go away to war and didn't come back and she had denied both herself and him the ultimate expression of their love? Round and round in her mind the questions would circle and torment her until she fell into a restless sleep. In the morning everything would once again seem clearer; right and wrong would be white and black with no room for grey areas.

She stood up: it was time for bed. If she started to think

like this she would get no sleep tonight either and she was so tired.

She had been asleep for some time before something woke her. It was warm and stuffy and both Katie and Lizzie had kicked off the single sheet that covered them, for they slept together in the double bed. She got up, opened the window wider, and bent to cover them again. Then she heard it. Muffled voices and the almost inaudible sound of cartwheels and hooves. Noise carried for long distances in the still night air. Who on earth was around at this time?

She pulled a cotton wrap over her nightdress and slipped on a pair of soft leather shoes that had become too scuffed and worn for day wear and which she used as slippers.

The warm air, perfumed with night-flowering blossoms, seemed heavy and oppressive. As she walked down the bohreen the sounds came closer. At the bottom of the pathway she stopped and drew back into the deep shadow of the wild fuchsia bushes, for the moon was bright. There *was* a cart and its wheels and the hooves of the horse that was pulling it were bound in sacking. With an intake of breath she recognised it. It was theirs. She also recognised the two men beside it. One was Richard and the other was Peter Casey! What were they doing? What was loaded on the cart hidden beneath sacks and why were they moving it in the dead of night with the wheels muffled? She didn't move. Some instinct told her not to call out, not to move out onto the towpath.

She watched them until they passed the side of the lock and disappeared and then she turned and slowly and silently walked back up the bohreen. The last time she'd seen Peter Casey he'd been in Liverpool and Julia had said she'd heard he was emigrating. But he'd been talking to Richard then. Should she confront Richard in the morning? If he had wanted you to know about this he would have told you, she thought. The whole episode had shaken and disturbed her.

It had troubled her so much that she had slept little and when she went up to the house early that morning she looked and felt tired and a little depressed.

'Mary, you look worn out. Did you not sleep? It was very warm although the walls are so thick in this place that it stays cool,' Julia commented.

'I didn't get much sleep but it wasn't just the heat.' She decided to confide in Julia. 'I was woken by noises.'

'Noises? And what kind of noises would they be?'

Bridie was raking out the kitchen fire and Mary motioned the older woman towards the open back door.

'I got up and I saw them,' she whispered.

'Who?'

'Peter Casey and Richard and they had the cart. They were coming along the towpath from the direction of town. They had something on the cart and they'd put sacking around the wheels and the horse's hooves to deaden the sound.'

'Merciful Mother of God! Are you *sure*, Mary, that it was them?'

'I'm certain. I don't know what to do. Should I tell him?'

'NO!' Julia hissed fiercely.

Mary was startled by her vehemence. 'Why not?'

'Tell no one. Not even Sonny or the young one in there. Forget about it, Mary. You saw *nothing*! *Nothing* at all! There are things that it's best to leave alone. They don't concern you – or us. Believe me, it's best not to know and he won't thank you to mention it. He'll be angry and annoyed that you were snooping.'

'I wasn't snooping! Julia, what's going on? Is it something to do with why he says he can't marry me? If it is don't you think I have a right to know?'

'Mary, forget it! Let sleeping dogs lie. The last thing he wants is to put you or any of us in danger.'

'In danger? I don't understand?'

'One day you will, but not now, Mary. For the love of God, *forget it*!'

She moved away, back towards Bridie and the range, leaving Mary staring at her in confusion.

There wasn't time even to mention it to Richard for half an hour later he came into the kitchen with a letter in his hand, looking distracted.

'Mary, I've to go to Dublin at once and I don't know how long I'll be away. Could you put some things into a bag for me, please? Julia, could you put me up something to eat? If I hurry I might catch the milk train, though God knows it will take me hours on that, it's so slow!'

'Is there anything wrong?' Mary asked, still thinking about the events of the night. Did this have something to do with Peter Casey too?

'Don't worry, I'll be back as soon as I possibly can. A day or two at the most.'

Julia nodded and pursed her lips. When had that letter come? Last night? It was too early for the day's post, which didn't arrive until lunchtime. Had it been brought by hand this morning? 'Is it the same as last time?' she asked.

He nodded curtly.

'Then I'll pack up some ham and soda bread and you make sure you eat when you're above in Dublin,' she said with a scolding note in her voice.

'I'll have to find Sonny and get him to saddle up Juno. The trap is too slow. He and Tommy can come in in the trap later to collect Juno, I'll leave her in the care of Jim Hartigan at the station,' he informed them and then he was gone, striding out into the yard to look for Sonny.

'What's the matter?' Mary demanded of Julia.

'Urgent business up there, to do with the estate. It happens sometimes. It's nothing for you to worry about. Now, you'd better go and pack for him. He has twenty minutes to catch the milk train but sure to God he'll have a brasting headache by the time he gets there the way they roll those milk churns around. It sounds like the end of the world and the Devil coming to collect his own, so it does!'

To Mary's bewilderment and the dismay and disappointment of Lizzie, he left ten minutes later after a flurry of frantic activity. He had kissed Mary quickly but passionately to the astonishment of all three children and Bridie, who stared with open mouth and wide dark eyes at such a display of affection never before witnessed in this house.

'Mam, why did Mr O'Neill kiss you like that?' Katie voiced their collective thoughts.

'Never you mind, miss! Have you seen the three little brass monkeys in the study?' Julia said sharply.

Katie wondered what the little ornaments had to do with this but simply nodded.

'They represent "See no evil, hear no evil and speak no evil". You take note of that and do likewise, and the same goes for you too, Bridie!'

Katie was still confused but said nothing.

Julia shook her head and shot Mary a warning glance. 'Little jugs have big ears! Sometimes I do think that man has no sense!'

Mary agreed and decided the best thing to do was set them all to work, herself included. But as the hours passed she began to worry more and more about what was going on. If anything terrible happened to Richard, what would she do? What would happen to the children? She couldn't bear to contemplate the fact that once more she'd be left alone to provide for them. She could hardly bear to face the thought of life without Richard. She couldn't just wait here, saying nothing, asking nothing. She had to do something. Ask someone.

Tommy and Sonny had returned later that morning with his horse tied to the back of the trap. It was one of Tommy's dearest wishes to be able to ride the big chestnut hunter but so far all hints had been ignored. He hoped one day to have a horse of his own. One just like Juno. His mam had so far managed to delay the purchase of a horse for herself and the riding lessons she so dreaded, but he wished she would relent. He was certain Mr O'Neill would let him learn on any old slowcoach of a horse he bought for Mam.

With her work finished, Mary got washed and changed into a light sprigged muslin dress. She put on her wide-brimmed straw hat with the pale blue ribbons and asked Tommy to drive herself and the two girls into town. Sonny didn't often accompany them now. There was no need. She spoke only to the shopkeepers she dealt with and who knew her and treated her deferentially but without probing questions. Katie just smiled at them and they were aware of Lizzie's afflictions.

'Mary, will you pick up some butter muslin for me from Dolan's? What I have is little better than useless for straining anything, it has so many holes in it,' Julia called.

'I will so,' Mary called back from the recesses of the dining room where she was tying the ribbons of her hat under her chin.

She was descending the steps into the yard when a man came running in through the gate. It was Peter Casey and he was red-faced and sweating.

'Where's Himself?' he demanded.

'He's not here.'

'Where's he gone? For the love of God, woman, it's *important*!'

A dart of fear went through her. 'He's gone to Dublin. He went early this morning on the milk train and I don't know when he'll be back. A day or two, he said. That's all I know.'

He seemed relieved and wiped his damp brow with the sleeve of his shirt. 'Good. When he gets back, tell him . . . well, tell him I've gone.'

'Gone where?'

'To America, but I'll keep in touch. He knows how.' He turned away.

'Wait!'

He turned back.

'What is going on? I . . . I saw you both last night, on the towpath,' she blurted out.

His eyes narrowed. 'It would have been better if you hadn't! Forget it! If anyone asks, it never happened!'

'Why? Why can't you tell me what's wrong? Is Richard in any trouble?'

'It's none of your business!'

'It *is* my business if anything happens to him!' She

reached out and caught his arm tightly. 'I . . . care about him!'

'I know that well enough and that he cares about you!'

'Then tell me!'

'And put us all at more risk? If you really care about him then say nothing! He got away. He won't put you or your children in danger if he can help it. He's a careful man and trustworthy. That will have to be enough for you! Say nothing and no one will come to any harm. Now, I have to go. Trust him, Mary, and for the love of God keep your mouth shut!'

He turned and ran from the yard before she could say another word, leaving her staring after him, full of foreboding.

They had all had their evening meal in the kitchen and Mary had decided that she would walk with Katie and Lizzie along the river bank while Tommy fished. It was another beautiful evening yet she was unable to put the day's events to the back of her mind. In town there had been nothing but talk of war but it was August Bank Holiday in a week's time and she was hoping to persuade Richard to take them all on an outing to Banagher on the River Shannon where there was a small marina. He was sure to be back from Dublin by then.

They'd walked for a long time, following the course of the river until it joined the Rahan River, then they'd turned back for Lizzie had started to lag behind, a sure sign she was tired.

'I wonder how many fish Tommy has caught by now?' Katie mused.

'It's a wonder there's anything left in that river by now, but Julia will put it in the cold press in the pantry.'

'Mam, why do you call Mrs Moran "Julia" now? You never used to,' the child queried.

'Because now she's more of a friend than she used to be. Ballycowan's become our home and I suppose Julia and Sonny and Bridie are our family, sort of.'

'And is Mr O'Neill a friend too? Is he family?'

Oh, how she longed to say, 'He is. He's your stepfather.' Instead she looked at both girls sternly; she knew Lizzie could lip-read now. 'Yes, he is a friend. He's been very good to us, but it's nothing more. You heard what Julia said this morning about the little monkeys. Now I want to hear no more about it.'

Katie said nothing. It looked to her as if he was more than just a friend to her mam. She was growing up and she'd heard some of the things that were whispered about when they came out of Mass, but it was best to say nothing.

They'd reached the wooden stile when they saw Bridie running towards them, her feet bare, her long dark hair flying. 'Oh, Mary! Ma'am! Come quick!' she screamed.

Mary started to run towards her, catching sight of both Tommy and Julia who were attempting to catch Bridie up.

My God! Oh, Jesus! Please don't let anything have happened to Richard! she prayed, her heart hammering against her ribs.

'Bridie! Bridie, what's wrong?' she cried as the girl flung herself into her arms.

'It's the polis! The polis have come for him!' the girl gasped between frightened sobs.

'For who?' Despite the warmth of the evening she felt icy cold.

'For me da and Himself!'

Julia and Tommy had caught up. Julia was panting heavily.

'Why have the police come for Sonny and Richard?' Mary cried, clutching Julia's arm.

'To arrest them! Oh, Jesus, Mary and Holy St Joseph! And they're after Peter Casey too. Haven't they locked up half the men of the parish?'

Mary was horrified. What was going on? Was this something to do with Peter Casey's visit? She pushed a terrified Katie and Lizzie towards Tommy. 'Take care of them. Take them back to the cottage. Go across the fields; don't speak to anyone. I'll come down as soon as I can – don't let *anyone* except me or Julia in! Go!' She gave him a little push towards the stile.

'Go back to the gatehouse, girl, and lock yourself in! Your da will be fine. Take heed of Mary, don't open the door to anyone but myself or Mary!' Julia instructed Bridie.

'But, ma'am, what if the polis come? What if they break down the door?' Bridie cried.

'Then you can't stop them and it's no use trying but they won't. They have nothing but the word of turncoats and informers!'

The girl ran like a frightened rabbit.

'Oh, Julia! Why have they come looking for Richard? And Peter Casey was here early this afternoon!'

'The Lord save us! What did he want?'

'He was looking for Richard. I told him he'd gone to Dublin on the milk train and he seemed glad. He said he was leaving, going to America, but that he'd keep in touch.'

'Well, that's one mercy. I pray he's on the mail boat by now and will be halfway across the water to Liverpool before the police in Dublin come to hear of it.'

'Hear of what? Will you tell me what's going on, please, and what it's got to do with Richard?'

'Mary, you must never, *never* breathe a word of this to *anyone*! Promise me?'

'I promise. What is it?'

'Richard O'Neill loves his country as well as the next man, despite him being a landlord's agent and people around here despising him for it. Though not everyone does. A few really *know* him. There are plans . . . plans to make Ireland a free country.'

Mary's eyes widened as the full implication dawned on her. 'You mean a . . . rebellion? And Richard . . . ?'

'With all this talk of war' – Julia smiled crookedly – 'well, there's a saying: "England's difficulty is Ireland's opportunity." '

'That's what they were doing last night? What were they moving?'

'Arms. A shipment came into Waterford by boat last week. They've been moved up through the country. Richard was to be responsible for getting them safely through this county and into Westmeath and Kildare. Then they'd be distributed amongst the new brigades in Dublin. But now the police have heard about it and are looking for the arms and for him! From what little he told me, nothing was supposed to happen for two years, nineteen sixteen, at Easter time. They have new men now in Dublin who plan carefully and will tolerate no informers, though it seems we have one down here who will take traitor's gold! May he burn in hell!'

Mary was trying hard to take it all in. 'And Richard is part of this?'

Julia nodded grimly. 'He can go up to Dublin without too many questions being asked.'

'And to Liverpool. Was that why he was there with Peter Casey, the day I saw them?'

'Most likely.'

'Is this why he can't marry me? Is *this* what he meant? Oh, Julia, I would have married him anyway! I love him, no matter what he's done!'

Julia shook her head. 'No, Mary. It's bad enough but it's not that.' She uttered a cry. 'Oh, God! They've come looking for us! Say nothing, Mary! You know nothing and neither do I!'

They stood clutching each other's hands as four burly members of the Royal Irish Constabulary marched grimly towards them.

Chapter Twenty-Seven

T HEY WERE ESCORTED BACK to the house, refusing on the way to answer any questions about Richard O'Neill or Sonny or Peter Casey. To her horror Mary saw that there were police everywhere: in the yard, in the barn, in the stables and – from the clearly audible squealing of the sow and her litter – in the sty as well.

The house was in uproar. Men in dark green uniforms seemed to be everywhere. Furniture was overturned and rugs flung haphazardly over it; ornaments smashed; drawers pulled out; Richard's papers scattered across the hall floor.

'How dare you! How *dare* you!' she screamed, anger chasing away fear.

'Oh, so you can speak!' the inspector who was in charge roared at her.

She held her ground. 'This is a disgrace! Is there any need for this wanton destruction of a gentleman's home?' Her green eyes were blazing.

'And where is this *gentleman*?'

'I don't know. I'm merely his housekeeper! All he told me is that he had to go away on business. It's all he ever tells me. I need to know nothing else. It's not my position.'

'From what I hear your *position* is something more than that of housekeeper.'

She drew herself up and stared icily at him. 'How dare you! I am a respectable widow with three young children. I do not sleep in this house; none of us do. You will apologise for your disgusting and slanderous remarks or your superiors will hear of this from Mr O'Neill, who, I might remind you, is an agent.'

He was a little taken aback. He hadn't expected this. There were very few people around here who were not afraid of him. But he soon recovered himself.

'Apologise my arse! Where do you think the warrant came from? And as for Mr O'Neill, agent or not, he's involved in all the treachery that's been going on around here. They all are!'

'We know nothing of any treachery, as you call it. We are decent, law-abiding, hard-working people.'

'And I suppose you've never heard of Peter Casey?' he sneered.

'I've heard of him but I don't know him.'

'Nor his old sot of a father? A man who had a very loose and slanderous tongue.'

'He's dead and well you know it.'

'Well, seeing as Mr O'Neill isn't here, we'll take you along and see if you change your mind.'

'No! I've done nothing!' she cried.

'You leave her be, you bullying misbegotten son of Satan!' Julia Moran yelled. She too was terrified but Mary's courage had stiffened her resolve. She had never admired Mary more than at this moment.

'You watch your mouth, old woman, or you'll be coming along too!'

'What about the girl, sir, the young one we saw running like a rabbit for a bolt-hole?' a sergeant asked.

'Bridie knows nothing. She just lives in the gatehouse,' Julia said, glaring at the man.

'Sonny's her da.'

'She's little more than a child,' Mary protested, thinking frantically about her own children, alone and terrified, not knowing what was happening.

'Leave her for now. Take Sonny and this one here,' the inspector said.

The sergeant made to take Mary's arms but she angrily flung off his grip. 'Don't you touch me! I can walk quite well.' She turned to Julia, her face white with shock and anger. 'Julia, see to the children, please? Tell them – tell them I won't be long.'

'I wouldn't count on that!' the inspector snapped.

Two sweating constables came into the hall.

'Well, did you find anything?'

'Nothing. They're either well hidden or there's nothing here.'

'That bastard who gave us the information might have been wrong,' the sergeant whispered to his superior.

'I'll break his bloody neck if he is! Now get them out of here and get back to town!'

Mary had never been more afraid in her life. She hadn't realised that things like this could happen, not to people like herself, and although she didn't understand the politics she swore to herself she would say nothing that would incriminate Richard.

They questioned her long into the night. Over and over they asked her the same questions. At one point she asked for a drink of water but it was denied and the interrogation started up again. She had no knowledge of the law and therefore no idea of how long they could keep her here.

Time and again she told them she was just Richard O'Neill's housekeeper. That she knew nothing of his business or the reason for his visits to Dublin. She told them she knew and cared nothing for plots and rebellions. She was from Liverpool. She was a loyal subject of the King and always had been.

Eventually, when she was almost dropping with fatigue, she was taken and locked in a cell, empty but for a narrow wooden bunk covered with one dirty, greasy grey blanket. She sank down onto it, buried her head in her hands and broke down. Oh, Richard! Richard! she sobbed. What would they do to both of them and poor Sonny? She feared their treatment of him would be far harsher than that meted out to herself – and what if he talked? Did he know anything? She didn't know. She just didn't *know*. She prayed that Peter Casey had escaped, but had the Dublin City Police been informed? Were they even now searching for Richard? And what would happen to him if they did find him? Oh, there was no end to her terrors and worries!

Utterly exhausted, she at last lay down on the bunk and tried to ignore the scurrying sounds all around her and the terrible smell. The place was alive with vermin and reeked of sweat, of terror and despair.

At last – she had no idea how long she had been lying there – the streaks of a golden dawn crept through the barred window and fell on the dirty flagged floor.

She got up and tried to tidy her hair. Her dress was grubby and creased and it was sticking to her with the sweat that had seemed to ooze from every pore in her body during that terrible night. She still didn't know what time it really was and as the hours crept by the warmth of the sun only increased her thirst. She was too afraid to feel hungry. She wondered about the children. What had Julia told them? Oh, they would be so frightened. Tommy would try not to show it but he'd been as terrified as the two girls. She'd seen it in his face.

Hours dragged by and eventually a constable brought

her a mug of water and a slice of thick bread spread with mutton fat. She had gulped the water greedily but the smell of the fat turned her stomach. Surely they had to let her go soon? They couldn't keep her here for ever. She'd done nothing wrong. She'd broken no law. There was nothing for them to prove. She knew they would have to take her before a magistrate or a judge at some time; surely then someone would believe her? She knew that even if they arrested Richard he would tell them that she knew nothing. He didn't know she'd seen him. There had been no time to tell him. She was thankful now that she'd heeded Julia's warning. But what would happen to him?

By what she judged must be late afternoon they came and brought her out and as she stumbled along the dank passageway her hand went to her throat and her eyes widened then filled with tears of pure relief. She could hear his voice! He was *here*!

'My God, Mary!' he cried as she was ushered none too gently into the room. She'd never seen him so furious as he turned on the inspector. 'By God, you'll answer for this, Mulrooney! Not only do you invade my house and property and vandalise it, terrorise my servants and accuse me of treason, you drag an innocent, defenceless woman to this hell-hole and keep her here for nearly twenty-four hours! You've come perilously close to breaking the law of habeas corpus and I could have *you* in one of your own bloody cells!' he shouted, almost beside himself with anger.

The man's face turned blood-red. 'Don't you threaten me, O'Neill!' he blustered, furious that O'Neill had an alibi as strong as the Rock of Cashel for when he was supposed to be moving arms around the countryside. He had been up in Dublin having dinner with a prominent Dublin magistrate *and* the District Inspector for South Dublin City. There would be hell to pay and he knew it. He was still stinging from O'Neill's tirade complaining about his temerity in accusing a loyal subject of the Crown and the Agent of the greatly respected Augustus Coates of being involved in some nonsensical plot against that very Crown.

'Do you think I'm a fool?' O'Neill had bawled for the whole barracks to hear. 'Do you think a man of my standing would get involved in the petty machinations of a collection of half-educated peasants?' he'd gone on. 'You'll be lucky to come out of this a sergeant! Now where is she?' had been the final furious demand.

Richard O'Neill had never been angrier in his life. The whole trip had been bad enough. Almost too late he'd learned there was an informer. He thanked God he had had the sense not to hide the stuff on his own property but in a much safer location, known only to half a dozen men, but he was worried sick about them all. So much depended on their silence and their alibis. Thank God his own had been not only fortuitous but cast iron. But Mary! His poor, innocent, gentle Mary to be treated like this. My God, what must she have gone through? And he'd rushed back so happy, so overjoyed at the news he had to tell her. He'd been horrified by the state he'd found both the house and Julia, Bridie and the children in. He'd half killed his poor horse the way he'd ridden it here to the barracks and, now, to see Mary like this!

'Mary, I'm taking you home now! This will never happen again, I promise! Heads will roll, believe me, and the first will be that of District Inspector James Mulrooney!'

Ignoring all the policemen he put his arm around her waist and helped her out into the evening sunlight.

She was so filled with relief that she felt faint and dizzy and she clung to him, repeating his name over and over.

He lifted her into the saddle of the still sweating and heaving hunter, whose mouth and nostrils were flecked with foam, and swung himself up behind her. With his features carved as though from granite he ignored the small and curious group of people who had crowded together outside. News travelled fast, he thought bitterly as he pushed Juno forward, scattering the gawpers.

All the way home the only thing that filled her mind was that he was safe. They were *both* safe. Shock set in and she sobbed quietly for the rest of the journey.

Julia and Bridie, followed by three white-faced, anxious children, came rushing down the steps as they rode into the yard.

'Mam! Oh, Mam! Are you all right?' Katie cried.

Tommy took the horse's bridle as Richard lifted her down. Despite all the traumas Mary managed a smile and gathered her children to her. They too must have been out of their minds with fear and anxiety. 'Yes, yes. I'm fine now that I'm home. You've nothing more to worry about. No one will hurt you or me. Now, go inside with Bridie. I'm very . . . tired.' She swayed and Julia rushed forward to steady her.

'Mary! Oh, Mary, what have those devils done to you?'

'Let's get her inside, Julia, she's half hysterical. I'll have Mulrooney's hide for this, by God I will!'

Julia took her into the small drawing room – which had been only half tidied after the police raid – and eased her down in a fireside chair. 'I'll make some tea and I think there's something to calm you, if I can find it.'

'She's going to be fine. There's nothing more to worry about. No one is ever going to hurt or frighten any of you ever again, I promise!' Richard said gently to the three silent and shocked children. They'd never seen their mother in such a state before, nor had they gone through anything as petrifying as the last twenty-four hours. 'Go along now with Julia, your mother needs rest,' he urged.

Julia turned at the door. 'What about Sonny?'

'They'll release him. I've demanded that someone see him home and it had better be done. I don't think he'll be long now.'

'Thanks be to God! Poor Bridie is destroyed altogether.'

Julia closed the door behind her, and Richard bent down and took Mary's hands.

'Oh, Mary, I'm so sorry!'

She managed a smile. 'It's all over now and you're safe. Oh, I prayed you would be!'

'I should never have put you in this position. Any of you.'

'I knew, Richard. I knew about it all. I saw you and Julia told me. You and Peter Casey, with the cart on the towpath the other night. And Peter came here, to warn you I think. He's gone to America.'

'Oh, Christ! Mary, if I'd known that I would never have left you! And you said nothing?'

'No. They questioned me and questioned me but I never told them and I wouldn't have told them even if they'd sent me to jail. It doesn't matter what you did or what you do, I love you and I always will!'

He took her in his arms. 'Oh, Mary! My darling, sweet, brave and loyal Mary! I've been such a fool!'

'No! You did what you believed was right. You *believed* you were doing the right thing.'

'Thank you for understanding, Mary! I love you and I want to make you mine – for ever. I didn't want to tell you like this, but I want to marry you.'

She looked up at him in disbelief. 'But you can't? You said you—'

'I can now, Mary. I couldn't before because I wasn't free

to do so. I did have a wife. A very beautiful wife, called Isabelle. I met her when I was a student at Trinity. I was captivated by her. I was too young to know that it was only infatuation and to my father's outrage – and against all his demands – I held out and I married her. I was twenty-one; he couldn't stop me. It wasn't long before I found out that she was mentally unstable. She got worse until in the end I had no choice but to have her committed to an asylum, a good one, in Dublin. She was demented, Mary. Mad. She had become unmanageable. She had to be restrained to stop her from hurting herself. I kept on trying to help her. That's why I was in Liverpool, seeing yet another specialist who couldn't help.'

Her eyes were fixed on his face and the terrible pain that was so evident on it. 'So . . . so Dinny Casey was half right.'

'Yes. I don't know how news of it got out here. Oh, Julia knew, and Sonny, but they would never have breathed a word. I've known them both from childhood and they're devoted to me. But I never kept her in this house. She never came here. Father wouldn't allow it. He'd heard rumours about there being mental instability in her family, that's why he was so against it. Oh, there have been so many times when I wished to God I'd listened to him – for once!'

She reached up and stroked his cheek. 'And now?'

'She . . . she died, Mary. That's why I had to go to Dublin. They sent for me. She was dead by the time I got there. It was a release for her and a blessed one for me. I had dinner with two of her uncles. That was my alibi. That's why they could pin nothing on me; they had no proof.' He drew her to him. 'Will you marry me, Mary?'

Her heart felt as though it was going to burst with happiness. 'Oh, you know I will, Richard! You *know* I will!' she cried, tears falling down her cheeks. Tears of pure joy.

Chapter Twenty-Eight

THEY WERE MARRIED FIVE days later by special licence. It wasn't a decision that pleased the parish priest one bit but Mary told him firmly that she had had enough of abiding by the rules, and she had more than done her duty. That she loved Richard O'Neill and after what they had both been through she was certain God would want them to be happy and to provide a secure and loving home for the children, and if that meant she was to be excommunicated then so be it. She would become a member of the Church of Ireland, as Richard was.

This had been met with outright horror and angry condemnation. 'Think of your immortal soul, woman! You will be destined to burn in the fires of hell for eternity!'

'Father, I've had my hell here on earth and I can't believe that God is so unforgiving, so narrow-minded, so vengeful that He excludes everyone who is not of the Catholic faith from entering heaven. Nor do I care what people will think of me. I never mix, as well you know.'

'You will never cross the threshold of this church again, Mary McGann, and neither will your children. Nor will they be educated in the local school.'

'I can't believe you would be so bitter as to do that! But no matter, they will be educated in a far better school. Possibly in Dublin or England.'

'I am not bitter! I am deeply saddened and I am obeying the teachings of the Church.'

'Then it is a Church I have no wish to belong to. God knows the state of my soul and my heart, I will always love Him and His Christian religion, and I will try to live my life by His commandments, but not by those of a Church so restrictive in its laws. Good day to you!'

'I expected as much, Mary. You know himself is a stickler,' Julia said after Mary had informed her of her argument with the priest.

'But can't he even try to understand? After everything that's happened? The police, my arrest, Richard's wife's death, don't we deserve to be happy? Aren't we getting married? I'm not living in sin with him!'

'You will be in himself's eyes.'

'As I told him, God knows the state of my heart and soul.'

'And the children? Don't you worry about them, Mary?'

'I don't believe God would punish them. They've done nothing wrong.'

Julia shook her head a little sadly. Mary had to do what she thought best. They were her children.

'Are you very upset, Mary? If you are I will convert,' Richard had said when she'd told him.

'No, and you will not convert. I will attend your church and so will the children. Isn't the world in a terrible enough state without all this?' she'd replied firmly.

The children had all been astonished when they'd called them in that evening after he'd brought her home from the barracks and told them the news.

She'd been so touched at the way he'd told Lizzie. He'd taken her on his knee and had signed it to her and Mary had watched the little face still streaked with tears from the day's ordeal break into a dazzling smile. It had struck her for the first time that Lizzie was going to be a beauty.

Lizzie had thrown her arms around Richard's neck and hugged him tightly. She'd been so frightened when they'd taken her mam away but then he'd come home and gone and brought Mam back to them and now . . . now he would be her da. She'd never be frightened in her life again.

Katie had started to cry, seeing the tears on her mother's cheeks, and Richard had asked her was she not pleased that they were going to be a family?

'Yes! I never want to leave here again! I'm crying because, like Mam, I'm happy!' she'd sobbed and Mary had hugged her and wiped away her tears.

Tommy had struggled to find the right thing to say.

Mam was going to marry Mr O'Neill! They'd never be poor again and he knew that life now had far more in store for him. He could look forward to a bright future.

'No words of congratulation, Tommy?' Richard had asked.

'Yes. Oh, yes!'

'You're a good lad and we'll make sure you're set up in life. Anything you want to do I'll support you in.'

'I want to learn to ride Juno!' he blurted out.

Richard had laughed. 'I was thinking a little more ahead than that, but I'll buy you a horse of your own. A gentleman should have a decent horse and be a reliable judge of horseflesh as well as a good rider!'

'Oh, thank you, sir! Will I . . . will I be a gentleman?'

'You will if I have anything to do with it. I'm not having you grow up wild and uneducated. But I won't stand any nonsense, lad, better to get that straight now.'

'There'll be none, I swear it, sir!' Tommy, even in his wildest dreams, could never have envisaged such prospects. What would Georgie Price say to all this? he thought, but somehow it didn't seem to matter.

Julia had been delighted too. 'Oh, he deserves to be happy and he's not been for so long.'

'Why didn't you tell me about her? I would have understood. I wouldn't have been breaking my heart.'

'I couldn't. I swore to him on a stack of Bibles. And if I had, would you have come back, Mary, when he found you and asked you to?'

'I don't know, Julia. I don't think I really could have stood it, had I known definitely that he was married.'

'It may have been sinful of me, but I prayed that that poor demented creature would die and put all of you out of your misery – herself included.'

'God obviously heard your prayers, Julia.'

'He did and I praise Him for it and I'll come to your wedding even if I'm denounced from the pulpit for doing so!' she'd finished grimly. Then she smiled. 'Well, you'd better write and tell your aunty Molly and – Rita, is it? – your news.'

Mary smiled back. 'I'm so glad I got in touch again, despite Davy. Molly and Rita were always kind to me.'

'They'll be pleased for you, Mary. Just as we all are.'

There was to be no honeymoon; the outing to Banagher would be enough, Mary insisted. And then they would all move into the castle. But the outing was postponed when the news came through that Britain had declared war on Germany.

They stood together looking out over the peaceful green countryside bathed in the light of the August sun.

'I've prayed so hard that it wouldn't come to this,' Mary said quietly.

He put his arm around her. 'So had I. So had all right-thinking people, but it has.'

'What will you do? Will you go?' It was painful even to

say the words. Such a short time to be married. Such a short time of complete happiness.

'If I have to.'

'And what about . . . Ireland?'

'Men will go from here too, Mary, in their thousands. Perhaps our day hasn't come yet but I pray to God that one day it will. That we'll be a country able to rule ourselves. Make our own decisions. But I won't go as a soldier. I didn't finish my medical studies – perhaps I can do so now. If not, I'll go as an orderly, not a combatant. We'll be needed.'

'And what will happen to us?'

'You'll stay here and keep the home going for when it's all over and I come back. And I *will* come back, Mary! And whatever happens, I'll make sure there's a safe and happy home for all of us.'

The Liverpool Matchgirl

by

Lyn Andrews

Liverpool, 1901. The Tempest family is all but destitute,
barely able to put food on the table. When Florrie falls ill
with pneumonia and Arthur is imprisoned after a drunken
fight, their thirteen-year-old daughter Lizzie finds
herself parentless, desperate and alone.

Despite her young age, Lizzie has spirit and determination.
In a stroke of luck, she gets a job in the match factory,
and foreman George Rutherford takes her under his wing.
A new home with the Rutherfords promises a safe haven,
but the years ahead will be far from trouble-free. And when
Lizzie gives her heart, how can she be sure she has chosen
a better man than her own father?

Available soon from

HEADLINE

Lyn Andrews

'An outstanding storyteller' *Woman's Weekly*

Now you can buy any of these books from your bookshop
or direct from Lyn's publisher.

To order simply call this number: **01235 827 702**
Or visit our website: **www.headline.co.uk**